The
BORDERLANDS

BY
C. L. CRAIG

Library of Congress Cataloging-in-Publication Data

Craig, Carol, 2025
The Borderlands / Carol Craig.
p. Cm. -- Mainstream Fiction
ISBN 978-1-73622227-9-9

Cover design by Darrin Brenner: D. Brenner Art & Design.
Formatting by Sienna Arts

To all those who feel as though they don't fit in.
This book is for you.
May you never forget how special you are.

On the Gallows Tree

Farewell my love, Farewell to Thee
Farewell my bonnie lad,
O'er yon we go, to the other side,
My Jamie boy and me.

We danced to the fiddle,
We danced to the song,
We danced to the hero's tune.

But now 'tis time to lay to rest,
On the Gallows Tree.

Will ye think of me, on the other side?
Wait to hold my hand?
Comfort me, as I do ye, until the end of time?

Farewell my love, Farewell to Thee
Farewell my bonnie lad,
We've loved and lost on the Borderland,
On the Gallows Tree.

Writte by Esme Stalwart
1703 Scotland

Contents

Chapter 1
Destiny Jacqueline Kismet-2025

The moss-covered stone shifted under my foot, and with a gasp, I flailed for a branch that wasn't there. For a terrifying second, I was a tumble of limbs, my world a flurry of green and brown. A second later, I landed with a thud, my body a chorus of complaints. With a hefty sigh, I heaved myself down onto a fallen log, my blistered feet sore from miles of hiking through Douglas fir and incense cedar, stopping only to nibble on a sour salmonberry or the occasional huckleberry with my daughter.

Where is it?

My honey-brown hair fell into my eyes as I undid my shoelaces and tore at my boots, then socks, now wet with sweat that stuck to my feet. I winced with equal parts pain and relief as I peeled my socks back slowly to avoid sloughing away the translucent skin on my heels or the red and bubbling skin between my toes.

"Ooh, that doesn't look good, Ma," my daughter said, as she rushed to reach me, her face a mask of worry.

Cassidy, twenty-five going on fifty, was an old soul even as a child. She'd cradled the cares of the world on her sturdy shoulders from the time she could walk, and she had no plans to give in to worry now. And indeed, she tucked her blonde hair behind her ears as she bent over me, moleskin in hand, ready to do battle with my foot-weary soles.

"I knew we shouldn't have gone this far," she growled. "You're not an experienced hiker. Besides, you should have worked up to this."

I moaned at the incessant pain. She was right, of course. But I'd jumped in, with both feet. What would my family think of me now, Destiny Jacqueline Kismet, a grown woman, lost in the Coast Range, with a map, a GPS that currently held no signal, and a dead phone?

"You really know how to come prepared, Ma."

When Cassidy saw the dead phone, she raised a single brow that reminded me of her father and grazed me with an all-knowing eye that held a hint of mirth and a reprimand as if to remind me of all the things I was...or *wasn't*. I wasn't organized enough, though at 45 I was getting better at it. At five feet six inches tall, with a few extra pounds around the middle and the slightly narrowed features of my Celtic ancestry, I wasn't quite pretty enough for the world at large, though for my age, I wasn't a total slob. Lastly, I wasn't focused enough because I was a "Creative", the new millennial term to describe an artsy person. But I liked the new word better. The word "artsy" came with too much baggage. *Stuck up. Full of herself. Someone with her head in the clouds.* Much better to be a Creative.

"Well, where's *your* phone?" I countered.

"*Touché!*"

Cassidy laughed. She had an easy way about her. After working with kids and later with wayward adults, she'd learned that humor was her friend and used it often.

"Right here," she said, lifting it from her jacket pocket. "But I have no reception."

"Okay then, Missy, you're one to talk."

She placed the moleskin around my toe, and though it may have been my imagination, she seemed to pull it extra tight. I let out a brief gasp. There went the eye again.

"So, we're both lost," I said, trying to make light of our current predicament.

When she was finished fixing up my heels and toes, I pulled the map out of my backpack, willing myself to see a landmark that would reveal our location. I turned the map first one way, then the other. Overhead, I heard a screech, and both our eyes widened.

"Don't worry, Ma. It's probably just the turkey vultures circling their future meal."

"Thanks a lot," I said.

"No prob."

She plopped down beside me on the log and immediately set to work picking at the lichen that had covered one side of the fallen log. She'd managed a nice little pile at her feet when suddenly she lifted her chin and used it to point at the forest.

"You know moss and lichen grow on the north side of trees."

I held my map out and compared it with the trees. Seeing that the map was facing south, I flipped the map over so north was the same direction as the moss.

"There!" I said, proud of myself.

The first real twinges of fear settled in my stomach as the sky darkened slightly. How many times had I read a newspaper article about people who had become lost in the wilderness, only to be found months later, their frozen or decaying bodies the sole reminder they'd once lived?

Cassidy seemed to sense my mood because she said, "Don't worry, Ma. We'll get out of this. Somehow."

My face warmed at the memories because, truth is, she'd rescued me more than once. Like the time I had fallen overboard when kayaking, and she'd brought the boat around and held a paddle out to me. With one oar, she'd managed to paddle me to shore. Or the time I'd nearly slipped on some rubble on the coast and fallen into a pit of water called The Devil's Churn, another location that had given newscasters their lead story on more than one occasion.

"So, got any ideas?" I asked.

"Let me look at the map."

She leaned in, her eyes narrowing as she inspected it. Cassidy was one of those natural beauties. The kind they used for tanning commercials in the 80s. Blonde hair, blue eyes. A perennial tan. But most of all, a smile that lit up her entire face, courtesy of an orthodontist and $4000, a huge sum for us in those days. But seeing her now, it was well worth every penny, and I felt lucky to have such a smart and enterprising young daughter. I just hoped today her rescue skills were up to the challenge.

Squinting, she peered up at the mountains as though she could divine the way out through sheer will and determination.

"Okay, see here. We're in a valley of the coast range."

"Tell me something I don't know," I said, to which she gave me the stink eye.

"Let's read what the directions for the geocache say. If we can find that, we can find our way back, because then we'll know where we are. I think we got lost"—she poured over the map—"there!" She pointed in the direction from which we'd come. "See the river?" She read the directions. "We should have turned back there. The geocache site's not far off the trail, from the look of it. So let's circle back. Then we just retrace our steps. Okay?"

She made it sound so easy. "Okay." I handed her a ham sandwich from out of my pack and got to my feet. "Let's go."

Too bad my body wasn't in alignment with my suggestion because I hobbled like an old lady.

An hour later, we found the trail and headed east. Sure enough, Cassidy was right. There, in the center of a clearing, stood an old Douglas fir stump, feathers and baubles giving it away as the treasure for which we'd risked our lives. I stood on a gnarl at the base of the tree and peered in.

"What's up there?" Cassidy asked, squinting into the cloudy sky.

"Someone placed coins here to make a wish, I guess." Did wishes in tree stumps come true? I shrugged, unsure.

"What else?" She scrunched her nose like she did when she was thinking.

"A plastic container the size of a large lunchmeat box."

"Pull it down!"

She lifted her arms, her blue eyes peering up at me. I handed it to her. It was heavier than I'd expected. After all the blood, sweat, and tears...*literally*...my arms ached. Still, we had landed the prize at long last.

"Open it!" I said, eager to see what was inside.

We both leaned in as she peeled back the lid. To my surprise, a missive rested inside atop something heavy wrapped in linen. The letters were stylized, the Fs looking like Ss and a line through the capital Ts.

Cassidy got out her reading glasses. "I can't make it out. Can you?"

I picked the vellum up and turned it toward the sun. I stumbled over the words but made out enough that I could translate.

My name is Esme Stalwart, and I was born on the Scottish Borderlands in 1677 in the year of our Lord. It's here, amid the ever-raging war for territory, I met my true love, Jamie MacPherson, son of a Scottish laird and a Traveller... a Gypsy.

Jamie rescued me from the Borderlands. Now, it is my turn to rescue him from the gallows. But first, I need yer help. It is yer Destiny to help him ... to change the course of history. Come. I am waiting.

Yer ancestor, Esme Stalwart

A finger of apprehension clawed down my spine. What did she mean it was my destiny to change the course of history, and who was this woman? An ancestor, as she claimed, or was this some elaborate hoax? And how had she known my name, as surely the note was meant for me because she had capitalized the word Destiny? I turned to my logical child, the one so like her father in that regard.

"What do you think?"

She peered up at the sky again, which had suddenly turned dark. A squall would make landfall soon.

"I think we'd better get packing. Grab whatever's in the box, sign the logbook and add our code, then replace it with this."

She pulled our cache from her backpack, a purple and white geode. Until now, I'd thought it quite the treasure, but after reading the letter, I wondered whether maybe I'd been too hasty.

"Shouldn't we see what's inside the linen?" I asked.

But before she could answer, the storm cloud released its fury, pelting us with sharp droplets filled with small pellets of frigid hail. We dove for cover, where we donned our rain jackets and bid a hasty retreat, my glasses dripping water along with my raincoat.

"Run!" Cassidy nearly dragged me down the mud-strewn path.

Several times I slipped in the goo and muck, only to pick myself up and continue running. No way did I want to be caught out in this mess after dark.

Every muscle in my body ached by the time we reached the trailhead back at camp and my daughter's waiting car. We didn't look at the linen-wrapped geocache until we'd reached the main road back to Eugene.

"Open it." The windshield wipers slapped in time as Cassidy pointed to our prize.

It was soaked, almost as soaked as the pair of us, and lay heavy in my hand. I stripped the discolored linen from the object beneath.

"What is it?" she asked, taking her eyes off the road for only a moment.

"It's a Celtic Cross."

"That's odd. What does it have to do with us?"

She chewed on a piece of jerky she'd left on the dash and handed me one, too. I bit into it, glad for anything to quiet my rumbling stomach, which had decided to protest loudly now that we were safe and on our way home.

"I don't know, but this is strange."

"What's that?" she said, absentmindedly.

"It's got a carving of two people with two children nestled between them."

I had the oddest sensation that the one child was meant to be my daughter, and I was one of the two adults standing beside her, but if that was the case, who was the second child or the other adult? My husband? And why did I get the distinct feeling we were protecting the girl in the middle? Though truth be told, I would protect my daughter with my life, cross or no cross. I was letting my imagination run away wild...probably due to lack of food and rest. And because we'd been tramping through the forest for hours, lost.

As if on cue, my feet began aching, and I peeled off my shoes, still wet from all the rain. My toes and heels were already missing skin. Lots of it.

"So when are we going?" Cassidy asked.

"Going? Going where?" I asked, confused.

"To the Borderlands of Scotland, of course."

Cassidy was probably the least spontaneous person I knew. But one thing I did know about her, she prized family above all else. Apparently, even a three-hundred-year-old family.

I laughed until I realized she was serious.

"I've always wanted to go to Scotland," she said, more subdued now.

"You have?" Actually, I had to admit the Isles held an allure with their castles and history. "But what about Dad?"

"What about Dad? You said so yourself; he's going to be away for three weeks. Why not go now?"

"Now?"

My logical, organized daughter wanted to do something spontaneous? I shook my head, droplets of water cascading over me. Something else had to be behind the snap decision, but what? I read that *something* in her eyes, yet I also knew now was not the time to ask. Until she was ready to divulge what was eating at her, wild horses wouldn't pull it out of her. She'd been like that her entire life.

She drummed her thumbs on the steering wheel. That, too, was like her father when he was worried. Suddenly, her face lit up. "I can have us on a plane by tomorrow."

My mouth formed a wide "O". Something about this definitely didn't read right. "Why don't you spend the night at our house? Think about it. Then, if you want to go to Scotland, we'll go to Scotland."

Her lips curved into a watery smile. "Okay. We'll rest up, and then we'll go change history."

Chapter 2
Esme Stalwart-1698

They were coming. I sensed it in my very bones. I pulled the shawl tightly around my shoulders as I ducked low and ran for my cottage, which seemed impossibly far away. The cold chill had settled into the hillside along the Borderland, that area of No Man's Land between Scotland and Wales. I traveled between the two countries freely.

For him.

The rain pelted me with its sharp, stinging nettles, bits of frozen pellets inside them. A warning, I felt. A presentiment. As if to let me know my world was about to change. It had always been like that. See, I had what my mother, and her mother before her called the second sight, but what others from my country called witchcraft. Yet, I was no more a witch than any other woman. No. That's why I sent the cross, so all would know my true calling. For I was a healer, or soon would be.

The rain became a downpour, the cold sinking into my bones and chilling me to the marrow. There, within sight, was my front door...slightly ajar.

It's him!

I raced forward, slipping in the mud and muck so I looked a right mess by the time I flung open the door and cried out, "Jamie!"

But I halted, my heart beating a staccato as a hand thrust out at me from a man in uniform, his fingers clawing at my arm.

"Looking for someone, are ye?"

I tore at him, but still he held fast. A growl escaped my lips, so low and ominous that at last the man let go, but I heard the click of his flintlock pistol and knew to be wary.

"What do ye want? Why have ye invaded my home?" The volley of words flew from my mouth like a series of gunshots.

"Where is he?" the man demanded, a glorified slave patroller, if ye ask me.

"I dinna know what yer talkin' about, man."

He backhanded me across the face, the slap a starburst of pain to my cheek, where it immediately began to swell and turn red, rattling my teeth. I licked the inside of my mouth and tasted blood, but I would never give James MacPherson away. Never!

"If ye're hidin' him, lass, ye *will* be punished."

My heart heaved in my chest, but I stood erect, a deer in the forest hoping for cover in my silent stillness. For what seemed forever, we stood there, and as I looked at him; he looked at me.

Finally, he broke the silence, his voice rumbling with undisguised hatred and threat. "My name is William Duff, of Braco. Lord Braco to you. By authority of Nicholas Dunbar, Sheriff of Banffshire, I command you to turn James MacPherson over to me if you are harboring the criminal."

"Criminal, you say?" I laughed at him, despite the trembling that jostled my bones. "The way I hear it, he steals from the rich to give to the poor. Those greedy—" Yet, I never finished my sentence, as he lifted his hand once again. But I couldn't keep the curl from my lips nor the snarl from my tongue as he pummeled me with a meaty fist.

"You best be careful, lass, aye?"

My throat felt parched, my tongue thick. All I could do was pray he would leave. As if my prayer had been answered, he took one last look at me through narrowed eyes, then stomped past me and flung the door open to the rain and wind, not even bothering to close it behind him. The rotter.

For a time, I stood shaking, then finally, I sank to the floor, giving in to the tears I had refused to shed so long as that brigand dared to invade my privacy. The day had turned to dusk by the time I heaved myself up to close the door and ready the evening meal. But before I could get the kettle on the stove, the door once again flew open. I released a small scream until I saw who it was. *Jamie!* I raced to him and threw my arms around him.

"He was here, Jamie," I cried, but he shushed me with a smile and a laugh.

"Not to worry, Esme, wee lass. Your Jamie is here now, and my men have fanned out in the woods. He'll not be troublin' ye."

"Oh, Jamie!" I buried my face in his neck, the warmth of him leaving me slack with relief and fatigue.

"I brought ye a gift," he said, pulling a small burlap bag from his pocket.

I opened the bag and peered down at the…"Buttons!" I squealed. Celtic horses graced the front of them. I'd never seen anything more lovely, and I told him so, then launched myself at him once more, relieved to have him home.

"Now, where's dinner?" he asked, prying me away so he could get a good look at me.

With his thumb, he tenderly touched the spot on my right cheekbone that was swelling even now, but I quickly set my hands to the task of preparing his meal to hide the pain and the raw emotion that tugged at my heart. Soon, he had gathered his stool and began playing the fiddle while I jigged to the tune, the worries of the past few hours gone. But for how long, and at what price?

"Hurry!" I whispered to the two women, my future heirs, who I had summoned through will alone. "I need you. *Jamie* needs you."

"What are you carrying on about?" Jamie asked, never slowing his bow that danced across the string as though the two were inseparable…just as Jamie and I had been all these years.

But I feared if the two women didn't arrive soon, our time would come to an end. I had seen the women's names written in the air, as though backlit, the twin images floating as if by magic. Destiny and Cassidy, mother and daughter. And although they may not know it yet, the girl whose name I had read as Cassidy was to be the reincarnation of me, her destiny intertwined with mine.

Chapter 3
Destiny Jacqueline Kismet

The next morning, every ounce of my body ached as I sat at the kitchen table, downing my coffee as though it were my last drink aboard the Titanic before it struck ice and sank. I had yet to put my feet into anything other than a loose pair of slippers. The idea of placing them inside sneakers had me feeling queasy with fear of the pain that would follow.

Outside, the tulips had finally decided to bloom, their bright yellow and red heads mocking me. *Come outside*, they called, and yet the last thing I wanted to do after yesterday's ordeal was to go anywhere near nature, though normally I loved it. No, today was for resting up in pajamas, feet elevated, and watching old movies. In my head, I scrolled through the variety of shows I might watch. Cassidy and I would sit on opposite couches and take turns crying and laughing. I sighed with pleasure as I envisioned my day.

Just then, I heard the bedroom door open, and Cassidy tottered down the hallway in bare feet. When she entered the kitchen, she was scrolling through her phone and barely looked up as she marched over to the coffee station and poured herself a cup, adding in the usual creamer.

"I've been up all night checking into Ancestors.com, and it turns out we *do* have a distant relative named Esme Stalwart," she said, her eyes alight with excitement.

"Really?" I held the steaming cup of coffee, enjoying the warmth.

"Yes, really, so guess what?"

"What?" I said with a shrug.

"I got them," she said as she pulled up a chair beside me.

"Got what?" I asked, absentmindedly, my thoughts still on my vision for the day.

"The tickets."

"Tickets?" I looked up, not understanding.

"To the Borderland."

"Borderland? In Scotland?"

We'd talked about it yesterday, after we'd read Esme Stalwart's letter again, but that was a pipe dream, like those bucket list items my husband and I had always talked about doing before our time ran out. Surely, she was kidding. *Haha, Ma, fooled ya!* But her face was dead serious.

"We deserve a mother-daughter trip."

Her voice sounded strained, as if I might contradict her. But Scotland? Tickets?

"When?"

"We leave tonight."

I had just taken a sip from my mug when the words tore at my throat, and I began to cough until, finally, she rushed over and began patting me on the back as I choked on my coffee.

Moments passed before I could speak. "What will your dad say?"

"We'll be back before he returns from the Mideast."

Michael's position at his IT company had taken him all around the world. Until Covid, we had sometimes traveled together, but with the latest unrest, caused mostly by the current climate in our country, Michael had decided it best I stay behind so we'd risk only one life. The memory of that conversation had never fully settled in my mind. He would be furious if, after all our discussions about the current dangers involved in traveling, his daughter and wife went gallivanting around the globe. And yet, I had a feeling this trip was of vital importance to Cassidy for some unnamed reason I had yet to learn. Also, that this was a test of some sort. Of mother and daughter bonding. The way I saw it, I had two choices. Stay and play it safe, but risk losing my daughter forever, or go and hope she'd finally confide in me the reason for this sudden need to escape.

"Okay," I said, my voice betraying my lack of conviction. "What time?"

"We leave at four."

Why hadn't I seen it before? The paleness around those beautiful blue eyes? The laughter that covered a hint of sadness. What had happened over the course of the past few weeks that had created a change so profound she would alter her entire life in a matter of moments to escape what had her by the tail?

I glanced at the clock. On its face was a picture of a ship that had set sail, like we were about to, although we would be crossing the ocean by plane.

"That leaves us six hours to shower, pack, and drive to the airport," she said.

"Do you think we can do it?"

She peered over her poised mug so only her eyes were visible, but I read in them a question. A plea. *We'll never know unless we try.*

I stood to my feet and groaned. My eyes went to the couch—to the television set with a list of streaming movies awaiting me. Did I really want to give up all that for a romp across a country I knew little about? As I stood there, trying to make a decision that would make sense, the phone rang. I peered down at it.

Michael.

Cassidy and I stared at it. We both knew if I picked it up, we'd never go. He, like his daughter—at least before today—would make the logical choice. The sensible one. We'd stay home, order pizza, and livestream some romance movie that would make us both cry. We looked at each other.

"What are you going to do, Ma?"

Maybe Michael could come join us in Scotland. He'd always wanted to visit, but his work had never taken him that direction. This new game plan ameliorated my worries somewhat. It would be a family trip. We hadn't been on one in years.

The phone finally stopped ringing, and we both let out a sigh of relief.

"I'll call him when we get there. I'll have him come join us. What do you say?"

Cassidy smiled for the first time since we'd found the geocache and had learned we had a relative on the Borderland, many times removed. But did we? Or was this all some big hoax at our expense? Either way, we'd taken the bait. And like it or not, we were headed for Scotland.

Chapter 4
Esme Stalwart

"Where are you off to, James Macpherson?" I said as he pulled on his breeches.

He stuck his foot inside his boot before answering, his dark, lank hair falling over one eye. "I've got work to do, woman."

"What kind of work?"

Normally, I knew not to ask. He would never tell me the truth anyway. It was an unspoken agreement we'd come to early on. He would show up when he could, bringing with him something to ease my days, as he did everyone else's, then go.

He ignored my question, so I said, "I'll get the kettle on. Ye'll not be leaving here without a hot cup 'o coffee and a meal in your belly."

I eased out of the bed in my nightgown, but before I could climb down the ladder of the loft, he took my hand and kissed it, the love in his eyes glowing with an aura that always gave me butterflies. The man—whom I loved like the first rays of sunshine, like the droplets on the rooftop when it rained—held me in his warm gaze.

The thought that he was mine but would be leaving soon filled me with equal parts peace and dread.

Return soon, my mind whispered even as I saw William Duff's evil gaze warning me he would be back, and if he found Jamie, he would put him in prison, or worse.

We kissed long and hard, knowing this might be our last, each day precious because we never knew if there would be another before he...

No, I refused to think it. He would be safe. I had to believe that, or how could I go on? Our eyes lingered on each other for some time, until at last the spell was broken and I made my way down the ladder to the kitchen, where I began the arduous task of preparing a simple breakfast.

Not long afterward, I heard his boots clomping down the ladder as I worked over the cast-iron skillet, frying several eggs laid by *Bakie*s, a black speckled breed of hens native to our area. He came up behind me and wrapped his arms around my waist, the scent of him making me want to set the eggs aside and head back up to our bed, still warm from a full night's slumber. But I knew he would want to be on his way soon.

I peered out the window. From this distance, I could see trails of smoke rise up from the forest where his men, outlaws, caterans all, prepared the morning meal for their upcoming departure. It wasn't safe for Jamie...for any of them...to stay in one place for any length of time.

The light through the window, which moments ago had filled me with peace, drifted behind a cloud as if it foreshadowed a change in fortunes. Soon, Jamie would be off to who knew where, and I would once again be alone in my little cottage, waiting for his return. With him would go my heart. Until then, it would stop beating, and my life would once again dim under the shadow of fear.

"They're lookin' for you, Jamie." I set his eggs out onto a plate and dragged the wooden chair out from under the table to sit.

"They're always lookin' for me," he said, not the least bit perturbed as he tucked into his breakfast.

"Yes, but this time I fear they'll find ye. I cannot bear it."

He slowed his chewing to really look at me. "You're frightened, aye?"

"Aye." I peered down at my fingers, which I threaded back and forth in worry.

He placed a hand on my shoulder and, with his other hand, lifted my chin. "Ye must ha' faith, woman. What I'm doin' is important. If not for me and my men stealin' from the rich buggers, we'd ha' naught to eat. Nor anyone else in these parts. We keep our clan alive, you and I. And my men."

Hot tears formed in my eyes. I could feel something arriving on the traitorous winds. Feel the noose tightening. How could I tell him all this without him thinking me daft...or touched. Still, my heart refused to listen to what my head was tellin' me. No, this was foolishness, pure and simple. I knew the truth. He hadn't long before this Lord Braco or what's-his-name Duff, returned with a posse that would take him from me forever.

"Jamie," I said, my eyes boring into him. "Promise you'll lay low for a while. Just promise me."

"You know I can't." He tucked a stray strand of hair from my eyes, his touch both tender and loving, as only a husband's could be. "If not for the cattle we brought these people, many wouldna live. Ye wouldn't want that on your hands, now would ye?"

I fought down the pain in my throat, the hollowness in my chest. "No, I suppose not."

"There, then," he said, as though it was settled. "Let's not speak of it again."

He swallowed down a gulp of fresh milk—milk I had available due to his generosity. His thievery. But it had done much to keep me fed, as had the chickens he'd stolen from some manor or other.

When he was done, he jumped to his feet and used the linen napkin to wipe his mouth clean. Then he gave me a perfunctory kiss.

"I hafta go. I'll be back in a month's time, if not before. But first, take this."

He handed me a pistol, one of two he kept at his waist. I quickly tucked it away in a drawer, then followed him to the door, a heavy weight settling in my chest. He shoveled his arm into his coat and afterward set his hat upon his head. Then, with a smile that melted me like a heated candle, he kissed me one last time and headed across the glen, where I knew his horse and his men would be waiting.

I raced after him in silence as a breeze tugged at my skirts, a presentiment I felt certain.

Oh, Jamie, why must ye go?

For several minutes, I watched through the thickets, eager to get a final glimpse of him. Then I ran to my cottage because I knew what I had to do. Though I couldn't save him in this century, I could protect his future.

For Cassidy. For me.

Chapter 5
Destiny Jacqueline Kismet

The silence on the airplane ride to Scotland left me feeling hollow inside. Now, as we rested before tackling the new day in a new city, tucked neatly inside a 1600s inn, I wondered where my cheerful, funny girl had gone. I looked over at Cassidy, who unpacked her clothes and placed them in a drawer. I figured we were due for a rest after our 13-hour flight. Yet I had scarcely closed my eyes when, through my closed lids, I saw a shadow standing over me. My eyes fluttered open.

"I texted a cab. It should be here in..." She glanced at her watch. "Exactly fifteen minutes."

"A cab? For what? We just got here."

"Well, if we're going to find out who this Esme is, we're going to need to get hopping."

I sat up, still road-weary from the flight over. "When do you have to be back at work?"

Her face paled, and her eyes flitted about, as though searching for a story upon which to land. But in the end, her eyes betrayed her because they soon filled with tears that spilled out onto her cheeks.

"Oh, honey, what happened?" I said, leaping from the bed and snatching her up in my arms.

For a moment, she said nothing, merely allowed the sobs to release whatever weight she'd been carrying. I rocked her in my arms, cooing. "There, there. It'll be okay." But even as I said it, I couldn't be sure. Not until I knew what "it" was.

"I lost my job," she said in sobbing gasps. "They fired me."

"Who fired you?"

My daughter had always been hardworking, and always well liked wherever she went. As a result, she had quickly moved up the ladder—had received calls from other social agencies asking for her to come work for them. How could someone with her reputation be fired?

"I don't understand."

"No one does," she said, her lip quivering. "It was part of the mass government firings to cut the budget."

"But why fire you? Why not just lay you off?" That's the way it was normally done when the government decided to cut back. It gave those laid off time to land on their feet. To collect unemployment. But then it dawned on me. If they were fired, there would be no unemployment. No money going out. Just a devastated worker in desperate need of a job.

"This will go on my record, Mom. Plus I can't draw unemployment."

"We can help," I offered.

She shook her head fiercely. For Cassidy's entire life she'd been independent, strong. I admired her for that. Her dad and I both did, and it was precisely because I knew she'd never ask for help that I wanted to help now, but I also knew she'd never accept it.

"What will you do?"

"I don't know."

She shrugged, but I could see for the first time in her life she had no Plan B. Esme was her Plan B, for now. Yet every penny she spent here would be one less cent she had to survive.

"Well, you know you always have a place with us."

For a moment, I saw the old spark in her eyes. It said "fat chance," which lifted my spirits because it meant she was ready to fight again, to try to put her life back together despite the current chaos burning through not only our country, but the world.

Just then, I heard her phone buzz.

She glanced down at her cell. "The taxi's here."

I grabbed my jacket off the back of a chair. "So, where are we going?"

"Where do you think we're going?" she said, her smile returning. "To the library."

Chapter 6
Cobra

Frank Abernathy leaned back in his chair and stretched, recalling the day he'd been given the code name Cobra. It had been his handle as part of a particularly brutal investigation that ended with four men dead. But they'd busted up an international ring that day, and he still felt a twinge of pride to know he had been partly responsible.

He yawned and blinked rapidly to get his blood stirring after so long at the computer screen. For hours he'd pored through the material coming to him from Scotland Yard. Ever since the London bombings, the FBI had facilitated a Legal Attaché program to fight terrorism and cybercrime. He rubbed his tired eyes, then he drank down the last of the bitter coffee he'd rewarmed. One way or the other, he was going to catch the men behind what presumably was a cyber plot in the making, and when he did...

He licked his lips, his eyes drifting out the 4th floor window of FBI headquarters on Pennsylvania Avenue in Washington, D .C. The square, concrete structure reminded him of the old Soviet-style buildings. Utilitarian. He checked his watch. 3:30. He had one more appointment, then he could head down that long corridor toward his home in Bethesda, Maryland, a Dutch Colonial-style home in the heart of the Chevy Chase community. He and his wife had bought it back in the day, before prices had skyrocketed. His wife, Mia, had since remodeled the home to showcase all the treasures she'd collected on their travels over the years.

He was just about to close out his screen when it suddenly went wild, spots lighting up to mark locations all over the world.

"What the...?"

But just as quickly as the bright dots appeared, they vanished. He could almost believe he'd imagined it, but his heart was still pounding, and he felt certain this had something to do with his investigation, but what? Had he accidentally tapped into an illegal network? He began typing furiously, searching his browser history for answers, but no matter which avenue he took, he came up empty. He ran his meaty fingers through his salt-and-pepper hair. With a growl, he turned off the screen.

"I'll get Jeremy to look into it," he muttered, used to talking to himself. To thinking out loud. Sometimes, no matter how hard he tried to come up with an answer, it wasn't until he began speaking aloud that something clicked inside him, and the problem would come to him unbidden. "Young kids these days...." He shook his head. Computers were like pablum to them. They'd been raised on them.

He picked up his phone and began speaking into it. "Note to self—call Scotland Yard and see if they've experienced anything similar." If the anomaly had come up on his computer, it might have come up on theirs as well. It was a long shot, but he'd caught more than one perp that way.

He stood, then reached behind his chair and picked up his suit jacket. He slung it over his shoulder, feeling a headache coming on. They'd been arriving more frequently with this case. Probably the pressure. It was tough getting enough sleep when his mind was spooling through hours of records, searching for that one missing piece of the puzzle that might get him the breakthrough he needed.

As he walked toward the door, the pressure mounted and dizziness swept over him in a tidal wave that nearly knocked him to his knees. It had been happening more often these days, and when it did, he heard voices—his and another man's in this case, only it had an odd burr to it. Probably just muscle memory after his days working with Scotland Yard.

Just as he reached the door and started to open it, a round of nausea cascaded through him, and he let out a moan.

One of his colleagues who had been passing by stopped and grabbed his arm. "You okay, man?"

Frank nodded, sweat dripping off his brow. "I must have eaten something that disagreed with me." But he hadn't eaten anything. Maybe that was the problem.

"Looks to me like you might have an ulcer. Better check into that before it gets worse."

Cobra forced a smile. "I'll do that."

But as he said it, his vision blurred in and out, and he could swear he was somewhere else—in another time, before computers and airplanes and all things mechanical. But how?

Thankfully, Frank's colleague moved on. Time to get to the elevator. Maybe call it an early day. He'd have to reschedule his next appointment. He just hoped to God he wasn't going crazy.

Chapter 7
Esme Stalwart

Though I'd watched out the window for days, hoping to see Jamie return, his damning silence frightened me. I needed him now, more than ever. Something was stirring inside of me. A hand. A foot. A baby. *Our* baby. But then again, perhaps it was just my second sight, foretelling of a child in my future.

So where is he?

Try as I might, I couldn't get Lord Braco's face out of my head. It haunted my dreams, filled my waking days with fear. Had the man found Jamie? Captured him? And what would the villagers do if they had? Jamie was a good man who had kept many alive, me included.

The waiting acted like an anvil on my chest until, finally, I could stand it no more. If he didn't come here, I would go looking for him. Surely, someone would know what had become of him. I packed a few things, being sure to bring the gun Jamie had given me, then went to the barn, where I saddled my horse. Afterwards, I filled the saddlebags with supplies. It took me most of the morning to prepare, but what else did I have to do, save to tend to the chickens and the garden? Fortunately, neighbors lived just up the road and happily helped me whenever I needed to go to town to purchase goods, as did I whenever *they* needed to be away, so I stopped there first.

Once I had their assurance that my land would be well looked after, I set my sights on Edinburgh. It was surrounded by the Flodden and Telfer walls to protect the people within from any possible British invasion. If I kept a steady pace, I could be in Edinburgh by nightfall. That's *if* I wasn't robbed along the way. I kept the pistol Jamie had given me hidden beneath my skirts just in case.

I was nearly to the outskirts of town when, in fact, a man came riding toward me at such a great speed I had no time to grab my gun. But as he neared, I could see it was one of Jamie's men.

"Oh, mercy. Thank the good Lord it's you, William. Ye gave my heart a start, ye did."

"Sorry to frighten ye, ma'am, but I have news for ye."

William was a scallywag, a man born to mischief. Yet today, his face appeared pale against a shock of black hair, and he seemed truly sorry, though sorry for what, I had yet to fathom.

"Spit it out, man, before you give me a right *fleg*, aye?"

For some reason, the poor man was tongue-tied, and yet it was not his wont to be so. If anything, he was quite often glib, always playing practical jokes on those around him, but I feared this was no joke.

"Good god, man, ye're scarin' me."

My horse seemed to sense my worry and stamped his feet and bobbed his head as if in alignment with what I was feeling.

"I don't know how to say it, except to speak it true. Jamie has been captured and taken to the gaol to be tried."

I gasped. "The gaol?"

My worst fears had been realized. I dug my fist onto the saddle horn, wishing my horse into action. I would race down there and demand he be released. But how could I? To the courts, a woman was no better than a pesky fly to be swatted or ignored. No, I could do nothing.

Or could I?

After all, Jamie had been born into a lairdship. Surely he had family, friends, someone who could help him. It was only later, after his *faither* had died that he had gone to live among his mother's kin. The Travellers. The gypsies. For centuries they had been treated as little more than thieves and scoundrels who'd learned to steal to survive. And yet, Jamie had turned his hand at horse breeding and had done a fine job of it. But he'd seen the other side, too. Of Travellers who could not find work, with few opportunities, the only thing available...

My throat suddenly felt dry. I quickly thanked William for the news and was about to spur my horse to action when a thought occurred to me. "What will ye do? The lot of yers?"

"What can we do? We'll try to bust him out of prison, but we havna much time, aye? We'll send word if anything changes. 'Tis best if you stay put, Miss Esme."

I knew he was right, but as long as James was in prison, how could I? No, I would be a sorry sight for a wife if I stood silently by and did nothing.

"I understand yer concern, William. But Jamie is my man, and I will fight to my last breath to be certain he is alive, ye hear me?"

It's then I saw a bit of the old scallywag return, because he held a knowing glint in his eye, as if I were one of the gang and he respected me for it. My horse gave a single flip of its tail, then I snapped the reins and was off at a gallop. Without a backward glance, I headed for Edinburgh. For the one man who could save my Jamie.

Chapter 8
Destiny Jacqueline Kismet

The National Library of Scotland in Edinburgh was a large blocked structure made of granite, ashlar, and rusticated stone. The austere building was done in the Interwar Classical Modern style. It appeared particularly imposing on this wet and dreary day.

"Not all that warm and inviting," I said, as we pushed up our umbrellas and stepped out of the cab.

Cassidy seemed not to notice my trepidation as, for one brief moment, I thought of turning around and getting back in the cab. Maybe go for some scones and tea instead, on this rainy March day. Back at the hotel, I had read about some quaint tea shops.

"I've made an appointment with a curator in the historical portion of the library. He should be able to help us with any questions we have."

"We have questions?" I squeaked. When exactly did *we* put these questions together?

"Right here." Cassidy pointed to a notebook page on her cell phone where, indeed, while I'd been sleeping on the flight over, she'd put together a rather extensive list of questions.

"Why doesn't that surprise me?" I said with wry humor.

From the time she was little, she'd been organized, planning her itinerary out carefully. Researching everything beforehand. When it came time to leave home, she'd already purchased a car and all of the belongings she'd need to fill up an apartment: a sofa, a bed, a kitchen table, and chairs. She'd even collected the wall decor.

"So, what is this curator's name?" I asked as we shook off our wet clothes after a spring rain.

"Benjamin Campbell."

For some reason I was expecting an older man with a gray sweater and wellies. Instead, the man who greeted us at the information desk was a young man full of vibrancy, his curly hair hinting at a bit of red, his jacket patched at the elbows. His green eyes danced as he spoke, but Cassidy surprised me with her silence, clearly dumbstruck by his appearance. Indeed, her expression had softened, and the tension behind her eyes had become more relaxed as if she were meeting someone she'd known for a lifetime, someone special who she clearly adored.

Why the reaction?

I tilted my head, studying her until, finally, she took notice and snapped out of it.

"Uh, hello, Benjamin. This is my mother, Destiny, and I—"

"You're Cassidy," he finished for her.

He clasped her hand as if to shake it, his eyes taking her in, as though he, too, felt a spark of recognition. For a moment, they stood there, each taking in the other until I could stand it no more and said, "Ahem!"

"Oh, yes." Benjamin shook her hand and then quickly dropped it to her side. "So, you were looking for a woman named Esme Stalwart. Right this way."

We followed him past a succession of statues beneath a high vaulted ceiling, then through a series of warrens and into the historical section, where he stopped in front of some rather ancient-looking tomes.

"Let's see." He placed his index finger on the spine of the books, scanning them as he hummed a melody.

"What is that you're humming?" Cassidy asked. "It sounds familiar."

"Tis *The Parting Glass.* Twas said to be a farewell song to a woman before her love was hanged, in this case Thomas Armstrong."

"I swear I could hear words to it," Cassidy said, her voice suddenly filled with mystery.

"Aye, the song goes something like this. 'This night is my departing night for here nae langer must I stay; There's neither friend nor foe o' mine, what wishes me away. What I have done thro' lack of wit, I never, never, can recall. I hope ye're a' my friend as yet; Goodnight and joy be with you all.'"

I bit my lip, surprised to see how taken Cassidy was with the lyrics, perhaps because she'd just lost her job. And yet it felt more personal, as though the song had been written just for her.

"I added a lyric of my own to the woman I once loved and whom I love still."

His words felt intimate as he continued to scan the spines of each book. So intimate, that I felt like a third wheel, and yet I was drawn into the drama playing out between my daughter and this man as if their magnetic pull reeled them closer together, nearly head-to-head as breathless, they read the titles.

"Aye, I wrote it myself. 'Twas once a lass, a pretty lass, what rode the briny sea. And there she waited o'er the years, she waited just for me. As I await the gallows still, the noose around my neck; I see her standing there, her eyes upon me yet. I see her standing there again, my babe inside her arms. I see her standing there again, the woman of my dreams. Farewell thee Esme, love of mine. Farewell thee Cassidy, too. For I have loved and lost. Goodnight and joy to you."

My throat burned, so parched I could scarcely get the words out. "Did you say Esme?"

"And Cassidy?" Cassidy pointed at her chest.

"Aye, I did," he said with a hearty laugh. "And here's the book ye'd be lookin' for."

He pulled it down off the shelf. It smelled of must and age, its faded red binding cracked and torn.

"Let's go take a seat."

He donned white gloves as they found a table and set it out for all to see. I sat on one side of him, Cassidy on the other, her expression intent, as though she might divine the very words from the closed book itself. She leaned in, their shoulders touching. I hadn't seen her this relaxed since before the firing. It was as if the shame and anger that had haunted her past few days had sloughed away, leaving the old Cassidy. And yet, I detected something different in her, too. It was as if a shadow hung over her of another person—this Esme character, whoever she might be. As though the idea of her had somehow taken root, invading the body of my daughter. I shook away the odd musings. It was jet lag, nothing more.

"Ah, right-o, here it is." Benjamin pointed to words that were hard to read, their shapes foreign to my untrained eyes.

"What does it say?" I asked.

"It says, 'My love is headed for the gallows, and I must leave before they come for me.'" He pulled off his spectacles and looked first at me, then at Cassidy. "Esme Stalwart was in love with James Macpherson, a cateran."

"Cateran?" both Cassidy and I said in unison.

"A gang, if you will. They're also called Reivers. They robbed from the rich to give to the poor and also earned a living as hired mercenaries. James Macpherson was an expert swordsman and fiddler. He was the illegitimate son of a Highland laird and a tinker woman."

"What is a tinker woman?" Too late I realized I had spoken too loudly and received an angry "shush" for my efforts.

"It's a woman who travels from town to town repairing pots and pans."

Cassidy and I glanced at each other, her raised brow reflecting my thoughts exactly. What was a laird doing with a tinker woman?

"At first, the laird accepted Jamie as his own and brought him up near Kincraig at the Invereshie House. Later, the laird was killed by caterans, and Jamie went to live with his mother's family in Aberdeenshire."

"So he went from wealth to—" Cassidy seemed deeply moved.

"—to an outcast overnight," Benjamin concluded.

For a moment, no one spoke, each of us deep in thought. When I had come to this foreign land, I had expected to learn only of Esme. Instead, we were learning of a man whose life was one of privilege and poverty. Joy and sorrow. I sat back in my wooden chair, but a question nagged at me.

"I don't know how much Cassidy told you—"

"I told him about the geocache site, Ma. About the message Esme wrote saying she was a relative and she needed our help."

I leaned in and whispered, "Do you suppose we could go to the Invereshie House?"

"I can take you there," Benjamin offered. "I'm off tomorrow. Would you like to go?"

We both nodded in agreement. "You're sure it wouldn't be too much of an inconvenience?"

But I needn't have asked because I saw the way he looked at Cassidy, and she at him.

"Alright then. Tomorrow it is!"

Chapter 9
Cobra

"Did you read what came across your desk?" Charles popped his head in the office doorway and tilted his chin toward the stack of papers Frank's secretary had brought in.

Charles Jacobson had been named the agency head of the FBI due to the recent turnover of administrations. Frank didn't much care for him, but he kept his nose clean and his head down, just as he always did when a newbie became top dog. No use getting into office politics. It had saved him when others had fallen.

Frank shuffled his papers until he came to one that piqued his interest. "This one?"

Charles nodded.

Frank lifted it up and scanned it quickly, his eyes narrowing at the last line. Some looney was claiming this so-called world-wide resistance was part of a Robin Hood scheme to change the world order by taking away power from the big boys. Big boys who had formed a network of protection that scanned the globe.

"What do you think of it?" Charles asked once he was finished reading.

"What do I think of it?" Frank shrugged. "We get these conspiracy theories all the time." Whether from the left or the right, each one had their wild hare ideas. Frank had his own, but he wasn't about to tell his boss that.

"Think it's worth investigating?"

Frank scratched the back of his neck and grimaced. "I think we should round file it."

Abernathy laughed and slapped the door several times with his hand. "Your call, pal." Then he was gone.

Frank pulled out the trash can, a satisfied smile tugging at his lips as he dropped it in with a loud thunk. No use adding more work to his day if he didn't need to. Now, back to the real work.

An hour later, he was rubbing his temples at the oncoming headache when a call came through. His wife. He picked it up and slid the button.

"Hey there, Mia, what's up?"

She responded with a shrill screech, her words coming at him so fast he couldn't decipher any of it.

"Hold on, sweetie. Slow down. I can't get what you're saying."

Mia struggled for breath as the words came tumbling out. "It's Juanita! They have her."

"Who has her?" Frank sat up straighter and bent into the phone, as if that might help him understand why his wife was so upset.

"ICE. They picked her up this morning. They said they're sending her back to Guatemala."

Frank read the panic in her voice. Juanita had been with them for years, had helped raise their two sons, and when they were grown, she'd stayed on to clean house and cook.

"There's nothing to worry about, Mia. Juanita is documented. Her papers are all in good working order, or we never would have hired her. You're getting worked up for nothing."

A couple of sobs rang through the phone line. Frank rubbed his forehead, the pain intensifying. For several seconds, he saw a man swinging from the gallows, then the image was gone. He'd read a case study once, where some guy had migraines that came with hallucinatory images, only usually they were auditory or olfactory, rarely if ever visual, other than zigzag lines or the occasional aura. His had gone well beyond that. Frank needed to see a doctor, but he could never find the time. He sighed into the phone.

"Listen, Babe, Juanita's going to be fine."

"Fine? *Fine*? Can't you *do* something, *call* someone? Surely you've got connections."

He rubbed his chin, surprised to find newly forming stubble. Agents were meticulous. It was part of their standards as an agent to be cleancut, shoes polished. It's one of the things that had drawn him to the agency—the order after such a chaotic upbringing.

"Okay, give me an hour. I'll call around and see if we can locate her. I'm sure it's all some misunderstanding."

"Thanks, Frank." She sounded less frantic now.

"Of course. I'll take care of it. Love you," he said, then hung up.

That's what he did—take care of things. As the oldest son of a Scottish father, two generations removed, he'd been the one to pick up the pieces of their lives when anything went wrong. He'd been the stoic one, the strong one. It made his life messy at times, but it also taught him self-control. So, the FBI had been a perfect fit. He didn't question right from wrong, just facts, figures. If the law had been broken, he would get his man, even if the law didn't see nuance. Didn't take into account the kid who had been passed from foster home to foster home and then pushed out on his own at age 18 with no skills, no support system. Who'd then turned to violent crime, robbed a bank as a means of survival. Or the single mom with children to feed and a low-paying job, making her ripe for embezzlement. The law was black and white, just like his suit and dress shirt. It made life simple to think in those terms, but lately he'd had trouble compartmentalizing.

He stood and peered out the tinted window of the building at the street below. The only people allowed near this building were people like him...agents. Suddenly, the air conditioner banked on, and a sweep of air stole up his back, chilling him to the bone. He turned, but as he did, he caught an image in the window. It was of him, only bigger, wearing a blue jacket, vest, and kilt with knee-high socks. He sported a beard, his hair swept back. But what stopped him from moving were the twin bits of coal for eyes, their glint hard. As if the man were judge, jury, and executioner, all rolled into one.

He backed away, bumping into the desk, his stomach roiling so that he thought he might be sick. Something was going on. He needed to get to a doctor, yet he needed to solve this case first. Then he'd go. He clutched his stomach, willing it to calm. But first he had to find Juanita. He'd get his secretary right on it.

Chapter 10
Esme Stalwart

I found Jamie's cousin, Donald, sittin' inside the Rose Tavern with a pint in one hand, his sword in the other, waving it to anyone who dared listen as he told them of the evil deed done to poor Jamie. Peter Brown drank at his side, his dark eyes rheumy from the ale. Donald was a rather large man with reddish hair and a ruddy complexion, no doubt accentuated by the drink, while Peter sported the darker features of the Romani from Jamie's Gypsy clan on his mother's side. Together, they made a sketch of contrasts as they sat in the dimly lit pub, whiling away their hours. Men surrounded them, feet up on chairs, bent over, a cheer erupting every now and then, while the women sat in a corner designated especially for them. Though I knew better than to interrupt men in their folly, these were extraordinary circumstances. So, I lifted my skirts and plowed forward, the men stepping aside and the room suddenly silent as I approached.

"Donald MacPherson?"

He sat up, the smell of liquor heavy on his breath, his eyes gauging me, judging me.

"Who's askin?" he demanded, to the men's scattered laughter.

It was clear he wouldn't make this easy for me, but I was a Stalwart, and I lived and died by the name. I pounded a fist on the table, the laughter abruptly halting.

"What are ya' doin' here drinkin' while my man is in the gaol, eh?"

He sat up straighter, no longer so insolent.

"Ye're going to let yer men here watch you do naught as my man hangs on the gallows? Is that what yer tellin' me? And what about you, Johnny? Would ye be laughin' if it were you swingin' from the rope? Or you, Beety Dick?"

The men chuckled nervously at the insult, but I was not to be stopped, now that I had my feet under me. "Ye'll not sit here as my man rots, I tell you that. Get up, you miserable sots, and go help him."

Donald peered nervously at Peter, who pushed his pint away, embarrassment burnishing his cheeks. It was then I realized Peter had Jamie's sword, a beauty at that. Like his fiddle, he went nowhere without it.

"Where'd you get Jamie's sword, Peter, hmm?"

A swath of chestnut hair fell in front of one eye. "Jamie asked me to keep it for him."

"He did, did he? And this is the way you repay him?" I grabbed him by the shoulder of his waistcoat and lifted him to his feet. "Sittin' here drinkin' the pint and tellin' stories?"

By now the room had silenced, and all eyes were upon me, even those of the women who had been quietly listening in the corner.

Finally, one enterprising young woman, Flannery, if I wasn't mistaken, shouted out, "Yeah, Donald. Ye talk a big game, but why aren't you out there helpin' that poor boy? Ye should be ashamed of yerself."

The women, who normally spoke quietly amongst themselves, all murmured their agreement, and one even stood, as if to make a point. Soon, they were all on their feet and moving our way.

"All right! All right! I'm going." Donald threw up his hands in surrender.

One young man stepped forward. "I know someone who works at the gaol. For a shilling or two, he can take us in through a back entrance."

"There ye go," I said, as if it were a done deal.

Donald pulled at his tight collar. "C'mon, Peter," he growled. "We best get on with it before there's a mutiny."

"Aye," Peter concurred.

A half hour later, as the town square filled with those who'd heard the rumors of Jamie's imminent release, I watched, when out popped Jamie. He wore a wide smile and waved his sword to the eruptions of cheers from the growing crowd. When he spotted me, he swept my way and caught me up in his arms, twirling me to the excited cries of those around us.

He lifted his sword once more and shouted, "To freedom!"

"To freedom!" the crowd roared.

Then he jumped onto the back of my horse, and together we made haste to the forest. An hour later, in a wooded glen southeast of the gaol, we were welcomed into his band of Reivers with a cheer. And by nightfall, by the light of the moon, as sparks floated from a bonfire into the night sky, Jamie played his fiddle. We danced and sang into the wee hours of the morning, stopping only to catch our breaths. But I knew it wouldn't last. Happiness never did.

Chapter 11
Destiny Jacqueline Kismet

"So this is Invereshie House." I looked up at the large granite structure. At this time of day, it had almost a pinkish tinge to it.

"It's ashlar granite and sandstone," Benjamin said. "The MacPhersons were not only lairds, but also fierce fighters." He smiled as though recalling some long-fought battle of the MacPhersons. "Jamie was the illegitimate son of Laird MacPherson and my *maither*—I mean, *his* mother." He flushed a deep crimson. "The tinker woman."

"Isn't that unusual?"

"Unusual, how?" he asked, his head tilted to one side.

"For a laird to, well, you know...with a Gypsy."

He could see where I was headed and paused, but his face flushed again; only this time I worried I had offended him somehow.

"It was more common than you can imagine." He coughed as if wishing to change the subject. "Besides, his father took him in, raised him as his own…until the laird's untimely death."

To my surprise, I saw not only sorrow written into the lines of his face at the laird's death centuries past, but I also noticed Cassidy's hand on his arm as though consoling him for a death that had nothing to do with him.

I caught Cassidy's eye and gestured to her with hands raised. She registered my meaning and gave me a look that said I knew nothing at all. Well, she was right there. I *did* know nothing. In fact, I was completely in the dark. This whole excursion grew more and more odd. From the time we'd met Benjamin, it was as if he and Cassidy had known each other their entire lives. They even finished each other's sentences. Throughout the car ride over, they had talked and laughed, while I had felt like a cog in the machinery, an unwelcome one at that. Before I could stick my foot in my mouth any further, the phone rang. I put up a finger and then pointed toward a copse of trees. It was Michael.

"Your dad," I whispered to Cassidy, then nodded my apologies as I excused myself.

I waited until I was near the trees to answer the phone. I plopped down beneath a Scots pine before swiping the button.

"Hello, Des, you there?"

Michael had called me Des from the first time we'd started dating, back in the Stone Age. "Yes, it's me."

"Where are you? I've been trying to call you for the last two days, but you didn't answer my phone calls. I was starting to get worried."

I peered up at the unreliable sky, where storm clouds gathered as we spoke, May one of those fickle months when it came to weather. I pictured Michael, dark hair fanning his brow. It dawned on me then how much Benjamin reminded me of my husband despite the difference in their hair color or the fact that Michael's hair was straight, whereas Benjamin's held a slight curl. Is that why Cassidy had taken to him so readily...because he looked like her dad?

"Where are you, Des?" Michael repeated, only now his words were laced with urgency. "Are you home?"

"No, I'm..." How to tell him without getting a lecture. "I'm..."

"Talk to me, Des. This isn't like you."

And it was true. I was nothing if not dependable. Perhaps *too* dependable. "I...I'm in Scotland," I blurted. "With Cassidy," I added to soften the blow.

Michael released a stream of air followed by a sound I couldn't make out, but just like the sky, I felt a storm brewing.

"What are you doing in Scotland?"

I knew I'd get the lecture about planes crashing, the world in turmoil, terrorists around every corner, but I decided to press my advantage while I had it, so I explained the whole geocaching thing. The note. The summons, really. Cassidy losing her job, or rather being canned for doing a good job by people at the top who knew nothing of her hard work or the people she helped.

"Wow! I need to sit down. I was calling to tell you I was going to get a flight out in two days."

His job was such that he often couldn't tell me where he was going or what he was doing, and especially not over the phone, so I decided to wait until I saw him to ask, though I knew I'd get only a half-truth, if even that.

"Why don't you come to Scotland?" I asked.

Silence.

"We could make this a family vacation. When was the last time you got to spend real time with your daughter?"

I knew that would be the clencher, because he and Cassidy had always been tight. The pair were like two peas in a pod, whereas I was just the pod that had birthed the pea.

"Yeah, okay. Where should I meet you?"

"I'll pick you up at the Edinburgh Airport. Just text me the time once you book your flight."

"Okay, but Des...?

Here it comes. The lecture. The what-ifs.

But to my surprise, he said only, "I love you."

"I love you, too, Michael."

Then the phone went dead.

Chapter 12
Cobra

"What do you mean she's on a plane? A plane to where?" Frank ran his hands through his thick salt-and-pepper hair. He'd been one of the lucky ones. He still had his hair at fifty-six. Most men his age already started balding.

"I called around," Shannon said, tapping her stylus on her cubicle countertop. "I finally spoke with a…"

She peered down at the words she'd written on her memo pad. To Frank, the words appeared like gibberish.

"Detective Lang. I had to go through a lengthy process, but Juanita's being sent back to her home country in Guatemala."

His ginger-haired secretary with light orange freckles had been with him for the past eight years. Though normally, they meshed well together, between his raging headache, his wife's pleas, and his frustration over Jeremy's inability to locate the trail of the lighted map he'd seen online, he pounded a fist on her table. Shannon pulled back in surprise.

"I'm sorry, Shannon. It's just been a bad past few days. The house is going to crap with Juanita missing, and my wife is expecting me to fix this problem with ICE."

Shannon peered around before speaking up. "I think we're all on pins and needles with the talks about cutbacks and layoffs. A friend of mine on the third floor just got her notice."

"Notice?" He rubbed his temples.

"Haven't you heard?" She leaned in and whispered. "Along with some minor staff, all six senior FBI officials are being escorted off the property as we speak."

"What?" he shouted, then turned down the volume when he noticed his colleagues staring. "How do you know?"

"I'm a secretary. Leave it at that." She lowered her head.

"What else?" He sat on her desk as he had a thousand times before, one knee up.

"They're going after multiple targets at the field offices as well. It could be any of us next."

Frank heard the panic in her voice. She was a single mom with two daughters to feed and a house with a mortgage. This job had provided her stability, just as it had him. He blew out a breath of air. He'd heard the administration planned to take away tens of thousands of federal jobs, but the sheer breadth of what was happening spiked Frank's blood pressure.

"I'll look into it. Now, what airline is Juanita on?" Frank asked. "Maybe I can intercept it."

Shannon dropped her stylus on the desk, where it rolled, coming to an abrupt stop at the base of her computer.

"Here's the thing. The plane left two days ago. She's already in Guatemala."

"What the—" He'd taken to shouting again, then leaned forward. "What do you mean she left two days ago? That didn't give her any time to plead her case."

"They're not giving them any time. They're calling it 'shock and awe.'"

"But that's illegal," he hissed.

"It's all illegal," she whispered. "They've thrown the constitution out the window."

Until now, Frank thought he had heard it all, but this...*this* was different. It smacked of dictatorship, and in a dictatorship, there was no rule of law. A chill froze him to the core. What would he tell Mia? Or his children? Juanita had become a fixture around the house. They loved her like a family member.

Just then, his phone rang. He peered down at it. *His wife.*

"Aren't you going to answer it?" Shannon asked.

"Right. I'll just take it in my office."

She gave him a wan smile. He started to walk away but then turned back.

"Oh, and Shannon..."

"Yeah?" She turned soulful eyes on him.

"Thanks!" He splayed his hands to encompass everything she'd told him and done for him in finding Juanita.

She nodded, then turned back to her work. Frank peered at the phone as he entered his office, relieved when it finally stopped ringing.

Chapter 13
Esme Stalwart

We couldn't go home after Jamie's escape from the gaol. Instead, we kept on the move, driftin' from one safehouse to the next in our underground network of friends, for that's what they had become...friends. Yet, despite their kindness, I grew weary of havin' to wake up day after day, pull on trews I'd borrowed from one of the men, and hitch up my horse for another quick getaway.

The sun was high in the sky on an exceptionally cloudless day, and weary as I was, I couldn't help but revel in the beauty of it. As if the birds all felt the same, they chirped and warbled, calling to their mates as I called to mine. In that moment, as I breathed in the sunshine, a glorious happiness settled over me. But like a sunny day, clouds were never far behind, so it came as no surprise when I heard Jamie call out to me.

"Hey, Esme, darlin'." He clucked at me as one would at one's horse, his mare's head dipping in the burbling stream to lap up water with relish. "Me and the boys, here, ha' been talkin'."

Jamie, bless him, never failed to smile with delight, but the nervous banter of his men died as I neared. He was up to somethin', that much was clear.

"Aye, ye have, ha' ye?" I lifted a brow to the men, who all peered down at their boots as if they'd found somethin' interestin' there.

Jamie scratched at the beard he'd grown ever since leaving the gaol. He'd worn it in defiance of his right to choose how he looked, how he talked, what he did. But more likely to hide a new scar gleaned during his most recent capture.

"Aye, we're running low on supplies, we are. As are the villagers. We need to do a bit of scavenging. We'll leave one of the men with ye, for safekeeping."

I knew eventually I would come face-to-face with the unsavory side of his occupation, but still it put a knot in my stomach that left me gasping for air. Every time he went out on a "foraging expedition," I feared it would be his last.

"So, ye'll be leavin' me behind, eh, Jamie...*boys*?" I used that last word on purpose, certain it would grate at them, but I'd become little more than a cook and a trail hand. And despite their bravado, several of them *were* still boys.

I had to hand it to Jamie. He kept his good-natured smile, though he knew I wished he'd go clean, start a new life. Raise and sell horses, a trade he had learned from his father.

"What if I did go clean?" he'd said last night as I lay next to him in the hayloft. "What then?"

"What do ya mean, what then, Jamie MacPherson? We could start a family, a life."

His eyes held such sorrow for me to speak to him so. He entwined his fingers with mine, love etched into his blue eyes, love and loss woven into their fabric.

"And what of the villagers, eh? Who will feed them? You would ha' me see them starve? The barons care not a whit about their lives, their happiness. They only care about the toil of their labor, every ounce they can get for naught, if they could. It's men like me and the other Reivers who keep the villagers from drownin' in sorrow. Who pays for their food? Their funerals, eh? Not the robber barons."

The cords on his neck stood out, and for the first time in a long time, I saw him cry as he thought back to all those people he had helped...or had buried. They loved him for it, almost as much as the barons hated him for stealing their wealth, though it was naught but a pittance in comparison to what they owned and what they owed.

"I love ye, Jamie MacPherson," I said as I took him into my arms and kissed him.

For a time, we lay there, each with our own thoughts. He was right, of course. Even if he'd wanted to go clean, it could never be. Too many William Duffs wanted him dead, hung in the nearest tree or on the gallows in the town square. I knew the end of this story, even as I knew I would fight with every ounce of courage to prevent it.

As I faced him now, with his men at his side ready to follow him into any battle, I recognized the truth. Like other days, he would ride off, and I would pray he'd return unharmed. Because, God spare me, I loved the man. Loved him like the earth and the sky and the rivers. And so, I did the only thing I could. I moved my horse closer to lean in and kiss him with such tenderness that the men all stirred.

"You remember that when you're out 'foragin'."

His eyes lingered on me, strumming me with a look that set my heart on fire. Then, with a smile, he dug his heels into his horse, and the last I saw of him was his horse's hooves stirring up dust as the lot of them flew down the lane and into the forest providing the cover they would need to keep them safe.

One lone man stayed behind. A man they all called "Coot." A wiry man with bushy blond hair and an even bushier beard.

"Ma'am," he said as he donned his cap, "we best find shelter until they return."

"How will they know where to find us?" I asked. But then I saw it in the man's one lazy eye. They'd already planned their meeting place. The only one who'd been left uninformed was me.

I laughed. So, this is how it would be, then. Fine!

"C'mon, Coot. It appears you and I have a date with destiny."

He tilted his head. "Ma'am?"

"Never mind. Merely a private jest."

He smiled uncertainly. Then I clucked and dug in my heels, my horse racing through the glade with the wind at my back. Two could play at this game, because I had a plan of my own. What would Jamie think of me then, eh? I laughed again as I rode off into the afternoon sun, while Coot desperately clung to his hat as he spurred his horse on.

Chapter 14
Destiny Jacqueline Kismet

For the entire rest of the day, as we perused the MacPherson home and then the museum where Jamie's fiddle and sword were kept, I couldn't help feeling that Michael was keeping something from me. Not just as a result of his job either. It was as if he knew something was brewing...something that might sweep us off the map, but what?

I saw a newspaper on the gift shop counter and looked around to see if anyone was watching. Fortunately, I had gone ahead while Benjamin pored over artifacts he treated like loving mementos. When he'd arrived at the fiddle that had been bashed in a fit of rage because no one would play a tune the outlaw James MacPherson had written before his hanging, a tear sprang up in Benjamin's eye. And, for some strange reason, he appeared betrayed that no one had played the tune for the dying man. I tapped a fingernail on the counter and frowned.

Who was Benjamin, *really*, and what did we know of him or his near obsession with James MacPherson? I shuddered to think. This entire episode began with Esme pleading for us to rescue the man she called Jamie, and now this. I blew out a sigh.

The curator had gone with Cassidy and Benjamin to offer pointers about the history, so once again, I glanced around before fingering the newspaper. My heart skipped a beat when I saw the latest article. Every day, a new disaster awaited the American people. First, laws were broken, then mass firings, and now...this. Zelensky's forced departure from the White House. *The Scotsman* was touting it as a victory of sorts, claiming the US president's strategy was to outwit the Kremlin. I had my doubts. The whole episode left me feeling sick, as though a disease had run through the American psyche. A disease that had yet to be cured. At least in Scotland, I could breathe fresh air, put politics behind me and remember what it was to live without oppression. And yet, here I found oppression of a different sort. The feeling that history was repeating itself and that Esme and Jamie—and now Cassidy and Benjamin—were part of it.

I heard Benjamin's sudden laugh, along with that of the curator, as the group headed my way. When they entered the gift shop, my eyes fell to Cassidy's arm entwined with Benjamin's. Without hesitation, I pushed the paper away, so it didn't appear as if I'd been snooping. Then I forced a smile, but my stomach strained with tension.

"What did you think of the museum?" Benjamin asked.

"Very interesting!" I said. But my mind was busy replaying Michael's words on the telephone yesterday, searching for a hint of something that might help me parse his words. Yet the only clue that stood out was the fact that he hadn't chided me for coming to Scotland. Instead, he'd seemed resigned.

Resigned.

That's when it struck me—if Cassidy could be fired, so could...*Michael? Oh, dear God, no!*

"Mom? Are you okay?"

Cassidy rushed to me just as my legs gave way and I slid to the floor. If my guess was correct, we were a family without a country, just as thousands upon thousands of hard-working Americans not on the right side of the political divide had been forced out of jobs, out of homes, out of lives. What had happened to the country I had known and loved? Home of the Free. Land of the Brave. We had fought and died for the very rights that were now under attack. Tears rushed to my eyes.

"What is it, Mom? What's happened?"

How could I possibly lay such a burden on her when I didn't yet know if it was true? But deep in my heart, I recognized the truth. Just like in the McCarthy era, we had been blacklisted. A tingle of fear raced through me, making me feel as though I might be sick. Suddenly, I understood both Jamie MacPherson and Esme Stalwart. He had been half-Romani, half a human in the eyes of the Scots due to his Gypsy heritage. Just as we were now considered outsiders, despite the fact that both of us had lived our lives for our countries and had been on the right side of the law. For the first time I understood what could happen when everything was taken away from a family...from a people. You did what you must to survive.

When I looked into my daughter's eyes, we both blinked back tears. Without a word, she seemed to understand I finally knew...really *knew* what she was going through. She reached down to give me a hug. For several moments, we stayed like that, until finally, the curator cleared her voice.

"Can I get you water, ma'am?"

I swiped at my tears. "Yes, thanks. It's probably just jet lag." I smiled wanly. But I was fooling no one, least of all myself.

Chapter 15
Esme Stalwart

Ne'er before had I stolen from anyone, yet as I crept up on a manor house I'd seen from a hillside overlooking it, my heart pounded a rhythm in my chest, and I felt faint.

And the most alive I'd ever felt.

I hitched my horse to a tree a half mile down, then bent low and hurried to the tall beech hedges that lined the manor. With one eye, I watched through a narrow opening. Unlike Jamie and the others, I wasn't looking for horses or other booty to sell. I had my eye set on the gardens—ripe courgettes, eggplant, and beans—but what I prized most were the *tatties* that could be stored and eaten long after they'd been unearthed. I knew I must be quick. I leaned forward and pressed myself between the hedges, their sharp edges prickling me and leaving welts that would itch for days to come. From where I stood, I saw the vegetables lined in neat rows, ready to be picked. My eyes went to the case windows. I pictured a harried mother starin' out at her patch o' vegetables.

"God be with me," I whispered beneath my breath.

Oh, I knew it to be blasphemous, askin' the Lord to help me steal. But the hunger that gnawed at my ribs told a different story. Surely, the Lord wouldn't want me to starve. And hadn't I done everything right my entire life? Except that I loved Jamie.

My mind whirred to his unfortunate past. A dead father. His life uprooted. Going from the son of the laird to the child of gypsies. The jeers and curse words painting him as less than, unworthy. His change in fortunes had been so abrupt he hadn't had time to process it. But what he had learned in those intervening years is that poverty and racial hatred made a person do things they might not, in other circumstances. To stay alive. With a whoosh of air, I cleared my mind and counted down from ten. When I got to one, I peeled off on the toe of my foot and ran as fast as I could, my sack extended so I could pluck the succulent vegetables from their vines and drop them into the bag.

For the next ten minutes, I moved as fast as possible, the smell of fresh-stirred soil filling my senses. I grabbed the courgettes first, then pulled entire vines of ripe tomatoes into my sack. Next, I wasted no time turning my attention to the tatties and yams. With my bare hands I clawed at the earth, satisfied when I came up with an oblong brown or orange-skinned tuber.

I had just begun with the onions and peppers when I heard the back door open and saw a woman wearing an apron and house bonnet. She let out a cry of fright. Then, as if it, too, had heard her, a sparrowhawk shrieked overhead. That's all it took for me to jump to my feet. I ran like I had never run before.

The man of the manor must have heard his wife's cry because he came out just as I thrust my body through the beech hedge, not caring that it tore at my sleeves and left scratch marks up and down my arms. Why, oh why, had I tied my horse to a tree? A mistake I would be wont to make twice.

I heard the pistol go off behind me, but it was too far away to be but a warning. Finally, my horse was in sight. That's when I heard the sound of hounds baying in the distance. They'd been released. My heart felt as though it might burst out of my chest by the time I reached my horse and ripped the reins from the branch, a twig still attached as I leaped onto her back and kicked at her sides. The dogs, which had been in the distance only seconds ago, now licked at my horse's heels, so she kicked at them as she galloped away. Fortunately, her speed soon outpaced them, and I made my way into the hillside where Coot waited for me.

"What ha' you done?" Coot squeaked, his voice just starting to change to that of a man.

"Later!" I shouted. "Run!"

It didn't take any more urging. Soon, the two of us raced through the countryside. We didn't slow until our horses' sides were white with lather. It would have taken the laird of the manor time to gather his men and his horses to come after us. If we'd taken more than just food, I knew there would be no stopping them. But vegetables grow back, my one saving grace. Hours later, we made it to our final destination. The place where we would meet Jamie and the others. I just hoped I hadn't put them all in danger with my antics. But my worries were soon replaced by new worries, because at our next safehouse, I noticed a trail of blood leading to the house. And I saw Jamie's horse tied up outside.

"Dear God!" I cried.

I hadn't come to a complete halt before I leaped down, trusting that Coot would deliver my horse to the stables. Despite my embarrassment for my poor manners, I burst into the house in time to see Jamie laid out by the fire, his chest wrapped in white linen.

I skidded to my knees in front of him.

"Jamie, my love. What happened?"

The woman of the house put a hand on my shoulder. "Ye'd better sit a spell. He'll ha' time for the tellin' later. *If* we can keep him alive."

The breath stilled in my chest. *If?*

Chapter 16
Cobra

Frank heard the gun go off and popped up in bed, drenched in sweat. The sights and sounds were coming faster now, in his waking hours and his sleep. His breathing came in short bursts, his hands shaking.

"What is it?" Mia cried, sitting up in bed.

But he had no words to convey his growing terror.

"You can't keep doing this. You're sleep deprived as it is."

Mia was a dark-haired beauty. For years, he'd wondered why she'd picked him, the son of an information security analyst, but he was thankful for it. For her. At first, he'd thought it was because of his family's wealth, but as the years passed, he'd come to discover she loved him. He had no doubt she'd be just as happy living in a hovel with him as in this luxury home. Sometimes he wondered if she wouldn't prefer it.

Frank shook his head as he forced his breathing to slow. Deep breaths. Isn't that what his therapist had told him? But it didn't stop the night terrors. His dreams had seemed so...so *real*. The fight, the shot that rang out, his hand on the gun. He peered down and swore it was still there. Even the smell of sulfur and smoke lingered in the air. Then it was gone.

"Something's bothering you." Mia laid her head on his shoulder. "And I know it's not all about Juanita. Are you worried about your job?"

He'd told her all the gory details, or at least the ones he was allowed to share. The rest he kept to himself, as he always had. Still, this was different. It didn't have to do with the firings, and it didn't feel like normal PTSD. Plus, he wasn't sure what had set it off. He couldn't get over the sense he was being called to Scotland, but why? Although he wanted to talk to his friends at Scotland Yard about his current assignment, it felt like more than that. He couldn't shake the visions of a woman, an unsettling apparition of child-bearing age, fear written in her hazel-green eyes. An unsettling thought followed, whispering that he was the cause for her anger, but again, why? When he'd gone online and typed in the words "pictures or drawings of Scottish women," he'd kept going back in time until he'd found drawings of women from the early 1700s. That's when he had seen one particular drawing of a woman in old-fashioned clothing. It set his heart racing.

Who is she, and why is she haunting my dreams?

He shook himself, hoping to dispel the image. The woman clearly thought he was responsible for something, but what? The noxious odor of sulfur returned. Had he shot her or someone she loved? He punched his pillow. This was crazy. The woman lived a few hundred years ago, if at all.

The stress was getting to him.

He threw himself onto the pillow, but sleep wouldn't come. Finally, in the wee hours of the morning, he gave up trying. He snuck out of bed once Mia had finally gone back to sleep. After grabbing a mug of hot milk, in case he did have an ulcer, he went to his study and turned on his computer. To his surprise, the computer screen came up with an article on The Borderlands.

"Why does that sound so familiar?" he whispered, his gaze glued to the screen.

He rubbed his sleep-weary eyes, then yawned as he sat down and placed his mug next to the keyboard. He began to read. As he scrolled down, he realized the article was about Scotland.

"That's odd."

He put on his reading glasses. According to the article, the Borderland was a disputed area, fought over for centuries.

"Armed groups of men called the Border Reivers plundered the region, stealing livestock and source material," he read. "The Marcher Law allowed for retaliatory action from those on the borders, creating a sense of lawlessness, thus making this area dangerous to the extreme."

As he read the article, he saw those same wild, untamed green eyes staring back at him. Had this woman—whoever she was—lived on the border? And if so, what was his connection to her? To any of this? And did any of it fit in with his investigation? He often got unusual sensations when he was closing in on his prey, but this was downright weird. Normally, he'd make connections in real time, not with some woman from three centuries past.

He finished reading the article, then turned off his computer screen. Although he knew Mia wouldn't like it, not with her birthday coming up soon, he needed to get to Scotland Yard and then to Scotland, to try to figure out what his intuition was telling him. But that was for another day. For now, he needed to get a few hours of shut-eye. He stood and stretched, then tottered off to bed, the alarm clock winking at him like a threat.

Chapter 17
Destiny Jacqueline Kismet

The next two days inched by. The morning after our trip to the museum, Benjamin offered to drive us to see the Borderlands, specifically Esme's house. He picked us up at the motel in a compact black British saloon car, a jaunty smile on a face filled with sunshine. Despite my worries, I found myself smiling to see Cassidy so happy as she flounced into the passenger seat beside him. The pair talked nonstop all the way there as I soaked up the breathtaking scenery from the cocoon of our car. Outside, spring seemed to have taken hold overnight, the Scottish bluebells popping up in bouquets of color, while daphne scented the air.

The hills rolled by in a panoply of greens with the occasional hedge to break up the landscape. I was about to ask Benjamin about a tower I'd seen near St. Mary's Loch when I saw a movement out of the corner of my eye that had me gasping for air. Benjamin had reached over and entwined his fingers with Cassidy's, his expression one of utter longing. And though her face flushed, she returned the look. I scrolled back through my memory banks searching for the moment that had led to this. Yes, they talked like an old married couple while laughing like young lovers. But this...this was more serious. It was a *next step*.

Then it dawned on me, and I covered my mouth to keep from shouting the "aha!" that lay buried there. Last night, she'd sat inside the bathroom talking at length, and though I'd heard her muffled voice and laughter, I'd assumed she was talking to a friend in the US. Now I realized she'd been talking to Benjamin. They'd talked for hours until, finally, she'd been forced to plug the phone in to keep the battery from dying.

"So, Mrs. Kismet, how long will you be staying in Scotland?" Benjamin asked as if he had just realized I was in the car.

"For a week or two at the most," I said, "right, Cassidy?"

Truth is, I hadn't asked her the return date, and if they'd been talking as much as I suspected, she must have already told him the date.

"Uh...right," Cassidy said.

The pair shared a glance that revealed he was all too aware of the date, so why had he asked? Furthermore, why the uncertainty in Cassidy's gaze, as though she had no intention of...

...returning.

I fell back in the seat, blinking rapidly as I grappled for something sturdy to grab onto. First, the news that Cassidy had lost her job. Then, Michael's evasiveness about his arrival. And now this. What other bombshell might be dropped on me before I returned home? But I had only to turn on the television set to know that bombshell after bombshell had landed at home, from massive firings, to the wholesale dumping of Federal government agencies, as if to suggest the Justice Department was up for grabs, as there was no longer a need for justice in a dictatorship.

For once, I was grateful to be far from home so I wouldn't have to witness the destruction of our democracy. I bit my lip, holding back the sob that had lodged itself in my throat and was clawing its way out.

"Are you okay, Ma?" Cassidy asked, peering at me in the rearview mirror.

All I could do was nod, but try as I might, I couldn't hold it in.

"Oh, Ma! Pull over, Ben."

"But the house is just there," he protested.

Benjamin pointed toward a small whitewashed stone house that appeared lonely against the stark contrast of the mountains and the few trees that bordered it.

He drove down the drive and parked the car while I spilled tears over his leather seat covers. Without hesitation, he reached inside his glove box and handed me a handkerchief, the old-fashioned kind. I wiped my tears on it and blew my nose. As I pulled it away, I saw it was vintage linen with the initials JMP.

JMP.

But his name started with B for Benjamin. For a moment, I sat mesmerized by the hand-threaded embroidery, but then it came to me with a clarity of vision. *James MacPherson!* Had he stolen it from the museum? True, I hadn't seen a handkerchief like the one I was holding, but that didn't mean he hadn't discovered it before I'd entered the room. Still, that would be theft, and Benjamin seemed the least likely person to steal, and yet what did I know about him? What did *either* of us know about him?

Just then, the door to the cottage opened, and a young woman peered out on tiptoe as if to see us better.

"I suppose we best introduce ourselves," Benjamin said. "Would ye like to come, Mrs. Kismet?"

I pulled myself together, but I could see I had worried Cassidy, and that was the last thing she needed now, with an uncertain future ahead of her. I offered a silly smile.

"I must still be tired from our hike."

"Hike?" Benjamin puzzled his brows.

"Geocaching, remember? Ma and I hiked out in the wilderness. That's where we first heard about Esme—the note about us being family."

"Oh, right-o," he said. But his words lacked conviction.

Together, we exited the car. The woman at the door had a far-away look, and for one brief moment, I could swear she faded in and out, like a photo that had warped over time. I shook my head. *I really need to get a grip.* Yet, as I walked toward her, I felt as though I knew the woman with the curly auburn hair. That I had seen her somewhere before. Then I saw Cassidy turn toward Benjamin with the same faraway look, and I knew where I'd seen that face. But how? How could the two women look so similar and yet so totally different? I blinked rapidly, wondering if my eyes played tricks on me. With each step, I felt like I was going back in time. By the time I reached the door, I knew I'd turned a corner.

Into another century.

Chapter 18
Esme Stalwart

I held Jamie's hand as I rocked back on my heels, moaning.

"He canna stay here," the woman of the house said. "If we're found harborin' a murderer, well...we'll be swingin' from the gallows along with him. I'm sorry."

Her husband stood in the background, but I noticed a glance pass between them, a thanks for her sayin' what he could not. I peered up at Coot and two of the other Reivers, who hovered around, while others stood guard outside.

"How bad is it, Peter?" I asked.

"If we can get him somewhere safe and find him a healer, we should be able to keep him alive."

The only place available for a man in his condition was our home on the Borderland, but Duff's men would be staking it out. If only we could create a diversion, something to buy us time.

"Peter, can yer boys help create diversions all across the county?"

Peter looked to Jamie's cousin, who shrugged. "I suppose so."

"Fine, then I will need a dozen men to come with me. The rest are to spread out and cause as much havoc as possible."

I listed the men to accompany me, then turned back to the woman and her husband.

"I need a carriage and a stretcher. We'll return it as soon as possible."

The husband looked at his wife for only a moment, then nodded.

"Right, then, we leave in an hour. Coot, go out and get the carriage ready. Call for me when yer done, aye?"

Coot shot to his feet and sped out the door, Peter right behind him.

"I ha' a drying rack we could use as a bed," the missus said, her eyes moving to the rustic ceiling where it hung suspended.

The husband sprang into action. He unwound the rope from a peg on the wall and lowered it to the ground.

"Could I borrow some bedding to cushion the movements of the carriage?"

Though the wife of the house sighed, she did as asked. Once we'd prepared the bedding on the rack, I reached down to Jamie, who, in his delirium, muttered incoherent words, my name thrown into the mix. My heart warmed to hear that, even in his present state, he thought of me.

"I'll need yer help to move him."

The husband took one side of the linen sheet, while the wife and I took the other. On the count of three, we heaved him onto the pallet we had made. A sound, similar to a growl, escaped his lips, continuing until the throbbing pain subsided. Moments later, the door burst open.

"We're ready, Ma'am," Coot said.

I looked up, stunned, because Coot was no longer a young man. Instead, *he* was a *she*, an older she at that. He wore a gingham dress and a bonnet that hung low over his eyes.

"What on earth are ya doin', man?" I blurted. "What's this all about?"

"Sorry to say, ma'am, but they'll be lookin' for a young woman and a man on the run, not two sisters." He smiled, revealing a gap between his two front teeth.

I had to say, he made a lovely woman. I smiled, despite myself. "Well, then, what shall I call ye?"

"Elspeth, after me granny."

The three of us stood there, unable to speak, then suddenly, the two burst out laughing, all except me, still too worried about Jamie to laugh. When we were finally able to control ourselves, I said, "Aye, well, Elspeth, we best get Jamie on the road."

Soon, my group of ragtag warriors followed at a distance so no one seeing us would realize we were together. For hours, we skirted towns, following any vegetation we could use for cover, which was scarce in this part of the world. The carriage wheels clattered along the rock-hewn roads—what there were of them.

Once, nearly an hour from home, my heart stopped to see a group of watchmen ride toward us on horses weary from travel. As they neared, they tipped their hats, and I could almost swear one of them flirted with Coot, never noticing the tent we'd formed to hide Jamie from view was not hay, as was visible from the two ends, but a wanted man who would hang on the gallows if we didn't find safe harbor soon.

We didn't respond until the men rode off into the hills. Then we sighed in relief, a well of emotions roiling in my stomach as I checked to make sure Jamie was okay as he lay moaning in the cart beneath us.

The next half hour was the longest of my life, and I didn't breathe until we had him next to the fire, warming him and tending to his wounds. Later, as I prepared a meal of potatoes, onions, and peppers and the bit of remaining meat the men had found, I prayed for Jamie. Prayed he would find solace in the meal. Prayed he would heal and the law wouldn't find him. But most of all, I prayed he would live. Without that, nothing else mattered.

Chapter 19
Destiny Jacqueline Kismet

My heart wouldn't stop pumping in my chest as I breathed in the room. It felt...*familiar* in some way. The room was mostly dark. The only light streamed in through the window sashes and left gashes of sunshine on the bare wooden table perched next to the hearth, where most of the cooking was done. A wooden chair sat in front of a spinning wheel. In a basket beside it was yarn made from sheep's wool, no doubt from the sheep I'd seen as we'd neared the home. Across from it sat another chair, empty and forlorn. Above us, clothes hung from the wooden rafters left to dry next to the fire.

"Let me introduce myself," the woman said.

She was young, pretty, with burnished copper hair that hung in loose swirls, framing dark circles beneath her eyes, as if she hadn't slept for a month of Sundays.

"My name is Esme Stalwart. I've been expecting you. I had hoped ye'd come."

I was so shocked I took a step back and tripped over her black cat, which screeched and ran off into a corner. It was then I saw a man in the shadows, his brow dripping with sweat and his face sallow, a linen tourniquet wrapped around his midsection. At the sound of the cat, he moaned softly.

"And that's me husband, Jamie...Jamie MacPherson."

My entire body stilled as though paralyzed. I stood like that for a moment. Then my nerves kicked in, and I began to shake uncontrollably. Before I could turn to Benjamin and Cassidy to have them help me make sense of what I'd heard, Cassidy changed form...faded in and out, then walked over to Esme and into her body, the two becoming one.

My lips quivered, and I bowed slightly at the sight. I turned to Benjamin. "What's happening?"

My voice faltered, fear written into the words, yet no one seemed to notice but me. As I reached out to Benjamin, he began to flicker as well. He stepped over to James MacPherson and sat down, then lay beside him, and the two men melded into each other.

I grabbed the one empty chair in the room and sat, placing my bag at my feet, the back of my throat choked with tears. Was I having a mental breakdown, or had I really gone back in time and had my daughter become Esme and Benjamin become Jamie?

"Can I get you some water, Ma?" this blended version of Cassidy and Esme asked me.

I merely nodded, too frightened to speak. She dipped a ladle into a large clay jug and placed it into a mug she handed to me. Then she sliced a piece of bread and slathered it in butter.

"Why did you call me here?" I demanded, my breathing coming in wispy gasps.

"I need yer help." She bent down next to me, her eyes imploring me to do what I could to help her man. "My Jamie is slated to die. I know that now. Not today, of course, but someday soon. It's only a matter of time."

I knew the history from the books Benjamin had shown us, and she was right. He would be hanged, his fiddle broken in frustration when no one would play the dirge he'd written, too frightened of what the law might do should anyone aid him in any way. I swallowed down the liquid she'd poured me, wishing it was something stronger than water. Though not given to drink, except on rare occasions, I could have used one now.

"How can I possibly help? I'm not even from your time."

"Aye, I know. But ye're from theirs, Benjamin and Cassidy's. They're our reincarnations, the pair. That's why they get on so easily."

And it was true. I saw the way they looked at each other, the way they talked as though they'd known each other their entire lives. Now, I realized why. They *had* known each other—only their lives belonged to a different century.

The tears I had kept hidden began to fall unbidden down my cheeks. Esme stood and reached down to hug me as Cassidy had countless times throughout her life.

"There, there," Esme said. "I know it's a hard shell to swallow, but it's the truth. Ye ha' only to look at the pair to know 'tis true, aye?"

"Yes," I said, though I wanted to say otherwise. To go running out the door and climb into the car and never look back on an impossible truth. Instead, I said, "So, again, how can I help?"

Esme took a seat again and grabbed my hand, entwining her fingers with mine. So many of her actions reminded me of my daughter that I had to work to keep from letting out a squeal of surprise.

"I need ye to keep Cassidy and Benjamin safe."

"Safe from what?" I shook my head, not understanding.

Esme shot a glance at Jamie, who lay curled in the corner, his breathing ragged. "Benjamin...he's involved in somethin'...somethin' that could land him in the gaol if caught."

Benjamin? The librarian from Edinburgh? How much damage could a librarian do, after all? It wasn't like he was living on the edge.

Esme flashed me a harried look. "Ye dinna understand, and our time is running short. Ye must leave soon."

I looked for a clock, as though that might explain the urgency, but there was none. And when I checked in my bag, I saw my phone had disappeared.

Because it wasn't invented in 1700.

"Jamie's a good man."

Esme sounded on the edge of hysteria as the time drew near for me to depart.

"But he has this sense of justice, he does, and sometimes it gets him into trouble." She stood and began pacing. "He canna see women and children starve while the gentry class amass huge amounts of wealth off 'a their labor."

"Well, of course not. I feel the same way," I said, without understanding what it was she said.

"Yes, but you do nothing to help."

Her condemnation pierced me. Made me cringe. What did she mean by that? She hardly knew me, but then I thought of Cassidy, who resided within her. Cassidy knew me. Is this how she viewed me? As weak and ineffective in the face of injustice?

I fell back in my seat, shocked at her assessment. "So, explain to me. Exactly how does Benjamin *help*?"

Esme paused and licked her lips, as though determining how much to tell me. Finally, she said, "In this time, Jamie robs and gives to the poor by going house to house in search of goods."

"And Benjamin? What does *he* do?"

Her face paled, and for a moment, I thought she might not say anything, might reveal only a half-truth, if any at all. But at last she said, "He robs from the rich, too. Distributes it to the most needy, he does. The bawbees just go poof!"

From her words I could almost see a puff of smoke carry away millions of dollars from the billionaires who had paid little or no taxes for decades, if not longer. But what frightened me most is instead of being shocked, as I should have been, I felt a sense of camaraderie with Benjamin that I hadn't felt before. I peered over to the man who lay injured on the hard cot in the dark corner of the crofter's hut, a new sense of admiration growing for the young man. And yet, how could I? His actions were illegal. But was it really, when the rich stole from the workers all of their lives, never caring whether they could feed their families or not, whether they would live to see tomorrow given the danger of many of those jobs? No, I shouldn't feel this way, but I did. I threw my head back in confusion and growled.

Suddenly, as if the hands of a clock had turned, Benjamin awoke from his slumber, and his ghost-like form stood up, his image becoming solid. When I turned back to Esme, I saw Cassidy's image shift, and she stepped outside of Esme's body, once again the child I had raised and loved.

"We best get going, Mrs. Kismet," Benjamin said. "Thank you for your hospitality, Mrs. Stalwart."

Esme turned to me before we left. "You remember what I said. It's up to you."

But how could *I* do anything? How could I change the course of history? And yet, I knew if Cassidy were involved, I'd do whatever it took to change their fates. To watch them grow into an old couple in a world much more humane than the one we currently lived in. Until then, I had work to do.

Esme put her hand on my shoulder. "Thank you for coming."

"I wouldn't have missed it for the world," I said with a weary smile.

When we were outside the hut, Cassidy leaned into me and said, "What was all that about?"

I breathed a sigh. "Wait and see." Then I took her hand in mine, grateful for this day where she was safe, for a time. Now I had to make sure she stayed that way...for the rest of her life.

Chapter 20
Esme Stalwart

They came, Jamie!

I watched the trio as they drove out of sight, breathing only after I coul' no longer see their carriage. Then I broke down. It was as if the future and the past had come together for a few startling moments, the future and the present, one. My hand trembled as I released the curtain from my balled fist and tumbled to my knees, tears cascadin' down my cheeks. For a time, I rocked back and forth, attemptin' to make no noise that might awaken Jamie, but at last, I let out a short wail to be so close to the woman who held the future in the balance, both Jamie's and mine.

"Wha' is it, lass?" Jamie peered at me through gritted teeth, his voice weak and raspy, his head dewy with fever.

I gathered my skirts and rose to my feet. "Nothin' to worry about, Jamie. Go to sleep."

He held his hand out to me. "Come here, Esme."

Seeing him so, I marched over and knelt down beside him. Despite his problems, Jamie brushed the hair from my eyes and held me close. "There, there, it canna be tha' bad, now can it?"

I shook my head and sniffed. "I suppose not."

He lifted his chin toward the door. "Who were those people, and what was that noise I heard? I've not heard anythin' like it before."

How to explain? They're the reincarnation of you and me, Jamie, and the woman who will save us all. And that noise you heard? 'Tis a carriage from the future that moves faster than a horse.

Surely, he would think me daft if I said all that, but I must if I had any hope of his understanding. So, I chose my words carefully. "Jamie, you know how I believe we go on after we die? That out there, somewhere, we will meet again?"

"Aye!" he said with a laugh and then coughed. "What are ya' tryin' to tell me, woman? That the young couple is—"

"Us," I finished for him. "Did ya not feel a draft, a presence?"

His face, which had been pale to begin with, grew ashen. "Surely, ye're not suggesting..."

I nodded.

"And the sound?"

I threw my head back and sighed. For a moment, I closed my eyes, then opened them, ready to face him head-on. "Some sort of carriage, Jamie, only much faster than anything we have. It's not like here. It's...different. Made of metal."

"Metal?" He tried to sit up, but I pushed him back down, his head hitting the pillow with a groan. "Ye're makin' no sense, woman."

"Just tell me you didn't *feel* it...feel Benjamin."

He could see by my conviction I was serious, deathly so. He placed a hand over his eyes, as though afraid to look me in the eye.

"I did feel it...feel *him*." He shook his head, then peered at me from beneath his now open hand. "More than that, I saw him. Thought I was hallucinatin', I did. The young man sat right down on the bed and it was as if he—"

"Became you?"

"How did you know?" His expression turned pained.

"Because it happened to me, too."

Jamie reached out a feeble hand and held mine in his, as if checking to see if it was solid. Reassured that it was, he entwined his cold fingers around mine. I wrapped my other hand around his frigid fingers, hoping to keep them warm.

"Do you know why they were here?"

He shrugged, but I knew he wouldn't be awake much longer. His strength seemed to ooze out of his fingertips along with the heat.

"I asked them to come."

His eyes, which had been slowly fluttering closed, blinked open. "But why? Why bring them here?"

"Jamie, my love, it's only a matter of time before the authorities catch up with ye, and then it will all be over. I want you to live on. That's why I called them here, to warn them that the future Benjamin—your new name—will follow in your footsteps, only this time I want him to be saved. To live on, to have children, to grow old...with me."

Jamie breathed in, then exhaled slowly. "And who are you...in this future you speak of?"

"My name will be Cassidy, and this time ye'll no die on me, Jamie. This time we'll grow old together, if I ha' any say about it, ye hear?"

An odd smile curved his lips, even as his eyes closed and he drifted to sleep. For the next few minutes, I watched the curvature of his spine, the slow inhale and exhale of his breathing, and the flutter of his dark eyelashes. My heart ached to be near him, to keep him safe, but how could I? Not in this lifetime, but maybe I could in the next.

I had been so absorbed in my thoughts, it took me a moment to realize a tap had sounded at the door. Another one followed. I froze, praying it was not Duff, returnin' to take his bounty. To take my Jamie. Should I answer it? But what choice did I have? All one had to do was kick open the door, and there we'd be because I had no way to move Jamie. I stood on shaky feet and toddled over to the door, then I took a deep breath and opened it.

Chapter 21
Cobra

Each day Frank entered the office, he felt eyes on him, as he did now, as if gauging his status. Would he be one of those who stayed, or would he be given his notice? He fought his uneasiness by pouring himself into his work. And indeed, the next few days had been a blur of activity with daily meetings to go over each of his findings. Then he'd made calls to foreign agencies for more insight, and lastly, he'd received constant calls from Mia asking if he'd heard any more about Juanita. He hadn't.

He ran his hands through his hair as he swiveled his chair to stare blankly at the DC skyline, these past few days a nightmare. It went on like this for a couple more days.

But then all that stopped as a heavy blanket of fear settled over the agency. It was as if a death had taken place inside these halls, everyone afraid to speak for fear of waking the dead. But they did speak, in hushed whispers that died the moment a new person entered the room. The rumor mill in the agency was awash with speculation about who might be next. Who would be uprooted and sent packing? The whole thing made his shoulders ache, and he rubbed at his neck, desperate to get the kink out, but it seemed to have settled in for good.

By Friday, he needed to walk off the tension. Frank grabbed his suit jacket and slung it over his shoulder. The day was one of those typical days in early May where the sun would poke out from time to time to remind him that summer was around the corner but also to remind him that winter hadn't yet given up the ghost. He felt it now in the chill that rushed in off the East Coast, nearly an hour away.

But instead of the lunch break he'd planned, he found himself back at his black Chevy Suburban. Before he knew what he was doing, he headed toward home, his head throbbing with the constant stress of these past few days. Halfway there, he got on his Bluetooth and told Sandra to cancel his afternoon appointments.

"I'm not feeling well," he said truthfully.

Sandra, who was more like a mother to him than a secretary, told him to rest up, she'd handle everything. At least he had that to be thankful for. Maybe if he got out of Dodge and went to Scotland Yard to see what they could tell him about the IT ring, things would die down and the powers-that-be would overlook him. At this stage of his life, he didn't find the idea of having to search for a new job appealing in the least. Especially not with so many other government officials losing their jobs under the draconian leadership of the new administration.

But he no sooner entered his driveway than he saw the front door left wide open. "What the heck?"

He quickly parked and replaced his sunglasses with his non-glare glasses. As he stepped from his Suburban, their Belgian Malinois came bounding up to him. He'd purchased him for protection for the family. The dogs were popular in law enforcement and military assignments because of their protective instincts and their intelligence.

"What are you doing out here, boy?"

Frank reached down to pet the dog, fear settling in his chest. Early on, he'd learned to listen to his instincts. They'd kept him alive more than a handful of times, and in this line of work, you needed that.

He hurried into the house, the dog at his heels. "Mia?" he called. "Mia, where are you?"

"In here," she called, her voice weak.

He rushed into the library, where she lay on the carpet, the book ladder and a pile of books at her side.

"What happened?" he said, helping her to her feet.

She looked pale. He knew she hadn't been eating well lately, with Juanita gone, but he'd attributed it to her mourning her lost friend.

"I was just bringing in groceries when I went to pull a cookbook down from the shelf, and I don't know what came over me. One minute I was on the ladder, the next I was on the floor." She swept her dark hair out of her face with the back of her hand and giggled. "I bet it was a surprise finding me on the floor."

"You can say that again."

For a second, she looked blankly at him, then said, "What are you doing home early on a Friday?"

Frank didn't want to add to her worries by telling her about the chaos back at the agency, so he simply said, "I missed my favorite girl."

"Really?" she said, leaning against him to steady herself. "Have you had lunch?"

"Not yet."

"Then maybe you can finish bringing in the groceries, and we can have lunch together." She sounded pleased, a slow smile lighting up her narrow face.

"I would love that," he said.

He held her hand as she limped along next to him. Just as he was hiding something from her, he couldn't help but think she was hiding something from him, but what? That was the million-dollar question.

Chapter 22
Destiny Jacqueline Kismet

No matter how Cassidy tried to pry it out of me, I couldn't explain the pallor that made me appear ghost-like in the rearview mirror of the car. Instead, I rested my head against the window, relieved to feel the coolness on my burning skin. Had I had a mental breakdown? Is that what had happened? I watched the countryside slide by, the rolling landscape somehow familiar...achingly so. Had I been here once, and if so, who was I? According to Esme, Cassidy and Benjamin were the reincarnation of her and Jamie, but then who was I? I yearned for blessed sleep, but despite my obvious attempt to forget what I'd just witnessed, Benjamin seemed naively optimistic.

"There's something I want you to see," he told Cassidy, who kept glancing back at me.

"Oh?" She bit her lip, a clear sign she was worried about me...about taking any more detours.

"Aye, but it's a few hours' drive. We could be there by mid-afternoon and return in the morning, in time to pick up yer husband." He peered at me through the rearview mirror, his eyes a question mark.

Cassidy spoke on my behalf. "Where did you want to go?"

"To the William Duff house, in Banff. That's close to where I...I mean, *Jamie*, was hung. Duff sat in the House of Commons. He hated Jamie for stealin' from his rich friends. Said he would get Jamie, and he did...twice."

"Twice?" I sat up, despite the headache that had formed around my temples.

"Aye, once in Aberdeen, and the final time in Banff. Just wait 'til ye see his home, if you can call it tha'. More like an estate. Did ya know tha' it was illegal to be born a Gypsy, as if a person has any control over how they were born? Duff hated the Gypsies and wanted them gone, setting out to rid Banff of any such Travellers, or Romanis—as they were referred to then."

I had heard of the Romanis and had watched a program on them once. They'd been described as a dark-skinned, charismatic people known for their fiddle playing and dance, though I'd also read somewhere that Scottish Travellers were often more fair-skinned, many of them blond. But both groups had a penchant for theft, namely pickpocketing, according to what the travel shows led people to believe.

"They carried a stigma, they did. The only work available was that of a tinker, so they had to turn to theft to stay alive. Once upon a time, they were thought to be wizards because of their predictions of the future." He laughed at the absurdity of it.

But as I thought back, I recalled a sobering statistic. Nearly a half million Romani had been killed, along with the Jews, in Nazi concentration camps. A chill coursed through me. If it was true—that James MacPherson was half Romani—then it put him in grave danger, and yet that was in a past lifetime. In this lifetime, his skin was nearly as light as mine. But soon another chill fingered my spine because Esme had assured me that Benjamin, like his counterpart, robbed from the rich to give to the poor. What if his ruse was discovered? Would we be considered accomplices? My headache raged on, and I leaned back, feeling as though I might be sick.

"Ma? Are you okay?" Cassidy turned in her seat and reached out a hand to me, which I took gratefully.

"I could use some aspirin and water."

We'd been driving for nearly an hour and a half, and we were finally closer to civilization. Up ahead, Cassidy saw a small market and pointed it out to Benjamin, who pulled the black sedan over, then raced in for aspirin and a drink to wash it down.

Once he was gone, Cassidy leaned in and said, "I know you, Ma. You haven't been the same since we were at the crofter's house. What happened back there?"

"Don't you remember anything?" I asked.

She tilted her head, as if she were thinking. "The odd thing is, I recall walking in and leaving, but I don't remember anything in between."

"Nothing?"

She shook her head, clearly confused.

"That's because you were…"

"I was what?"

I shrugged, but I saw my opportunity slipping away to tell her as Benjamin exited the store. I couldn't hold off any longer.

"Cassidy, you and Benjamin…"

"Yeah?" When I paused, she added, "You're scaring me, Ma."

"You *became* them. You're Esme and Jame's reincarnation, you and Benjamin."

Cassidy let go of my hand and fell back in her seat. "That's not funny, Ma!"

Just then, the car door opened, and Benjamin handed me a bottle of chocolate milk and two aspirins, but by his expression, I could tell he knew something had come between me and Cassidy. How to make this right?

He put the car in gear, but the tension lingered in the small cab. I had twenty-four hours to turn things around, and then Michael would be here, and I'd have a whole new set of worries. Who knew what he would tell me? I just prayed the aspirin would kick in quickly, before I succumbed to an all-out migraine. For now, I closed my eyes. Later, I would try to smooth things over, if possible.

Three hours later, we were standing in front of the Duff House, a massive Georgian-style manor house with a horseshoe staircase leading up to the main entrance. According to Benjamin, it had been built by the architect, William Adam, and displayed fine furniture and artwork worth millions of dollars.

"Just wait 'till you get a load of what this sot collected," Benjamin said as we entered the grand foyer.

True to his word, each room was more amazing than the last. Gilded chairs, priceless paintings, tapestries, and herringbone floors garnished the space. The wealth in one room alone could have kept a family fed with a roof over their heads for years. A part of me quailed at the opulence in the face of such poverty. No wonder the Romanis had turned to theft. I viewed Benjamin through a new lens. Maybe Jamie *was* the Robin Hood the museum had proclaimed him. It was clear from everything I'd read he was as well loved by the poor as he was hated by the rich.

As Benjamin entered what I had come to call the "Blue Room" because of its gilded blue chairs lining the walls, huge paintings above them, he spun in a slow circle, his head raised to obtain the clearest view of the room. Then he did something that surprised both me and Cassidy. He began to dance a jig and sing, soon bringing me and Cassidy into the mix, until finally, Cassidy stopped him with a giggle.

"Shh!" she chided. "You'll have the curators kicking us out," she whispered.

But Benjamin only laughed and winked. If he was the reincarnation of James MacPherson, I could see why Esme loved him. Something about him drew people in. He had what the French called a "*joie de vivre.*" Despite everything he had experienced as a

Romani, he'd managed to keep his sense of humor, to laugh, and to sing. To enjoy life.

He caught me staring at him, head tilted. "How do you sing and dance–"

"When the world is burning?" he finished for me.

I nodded.

He paused, as if sizing me up and deciding I wasn't such a bad specimen of the human race after all.

"It's because I've seen such suffering. Such poverty. At some point, if ye dinna learn to laugh, ye'll cry and never stop, aye? So I choose to laugh."

He winked, as I'd seen him do with Cassidy moments ago. I couldn't help but smile as I watched the two turn and walk arm in arm, my Cassidy and Esme's Benjamin. It struck me then that Benjamin was a derivative of the name James or Jamie. But where did the name Cassidy fit in?

"Oh, my! Of course," I whispered, placing a hand over my mouth in shock. Her first name didn't hold the key. It was her middle name. Cassidy *Emma* Kismet.

Esme.

Chapter 23
Esme Stalwart

I peered around the room that had begun to feel like a prison. Where was Coot? He was supposed to have returned over an hour ago. He'd gone into the nearest town for supplies, which was well over fifty miles away. Knowing him, he'd probably located the nearest tavern and hadn't stepped foot out of it in hours. I knew we couldn't keep Jamie here much longer without drawing attention to ourselves, and yet where would we go? Jamie's *faither* was long since dead, and his *faither's* wife was dead as well. And although his real *mathair* lived among the Romani, his Reivers born among them, they were an easy target because of their color and their cultural differences. The only thing keeping them safe was that they were constantly on the move, makin' it hard to locate them at any given moment. How would I ever find them? I let out a low growl, causing Jamie to stir. He blinked, then his eyes narrowed from the light streaming in through the north-facing window.

"How long ha' I been asleep?"

"Hours," I said, glad for some company.

For the first time in days, he grappled to stand as I raced to his side and helped him onto unsteady feet.

"Take my arm," I urged as we made our way to the chair next to the table. "I'll get ye some *scran*."

Fortunately, I'd kept the fire burning ever since we'd arrived. It helped to stave off the cold that seemed to come from somewhere deep inside Jamie's bones and cause him to shiver despite the extra woolen blankets I'd placed over him. Perhaps the food would warm him from the inside out. Early this mornin', Coot had brought in a cache of fresh eggs that sat in a basket on the table. That, and fresh bacon from the larder should help to sustain Jamie, who could barely lift his head, but at least his fever had subsided, and sweat no longer dotted his upper lip and forehead.

We'd sent for one of the cunning folk, those odd people who brought with them a satchel filled with strange-smelling herbs like the antiseptic heather, Bettony, to heal wounds, and Carline thistle, a cure for any infection. To that, the woman healer had cast a spell and given Jamie a potion of some foul-smelling liquid that made him gasp and choke, but he'd managed to get it down, in the end. He'd been asleep ever since.

"How are ye feelin'?" I asked as I set about cracking eggs into the cast-iron skillet.

"Weak," he said.

"Well, we'll change all that," I said, offering a reassuring nod. "But first, we need to get some food into ye."

He rested his head on the table, but his eyes never left me. "Sing me a tune."

I thought I had heard wrong. "What?"

"A song, woman. Sing me a song. It brings me comfort."

The only one that sprung to mind was Loch Lomond, a sad song about a soldier bound to die, who comforted the other soldier freed from prison to meet his true love in the Highlands. As I sang it, Jamie joined in, his harmony bringing tears to my eyes because I knew which one of us would take the high road and which one would take the low road. He would hang from the gallows, and I would take the road to the Highlands. I would be the one set free to live out my days in peace. If I could have halted the drive toward his destiny, I would. But it was too late for that now. All I could do was to try to prevent the same fate from happening in the future. By the time the song ended, a tear fell from my eye and sizzled in the pan—Jamie's eggs mixed with my grief. Forever after, a part of me would live inside him. I just wished it could be something other than my sorrow.

Chapter 24
Destiny Jacqueline Kismet

The next morning, I peered out the window of the inn onto a rain-soaked village shrouded in clouds. *Banff.* Though the mood had changed since yesterday afternoon's jig in the Duff manor, at least Cassidy had softened toward me and seemed less angry. For Benjamin, I imagined the jig was like dancing on the grave of the man who had killed him...only in a previous life. Shivers fingered up my spine.

"Ready to go see your dad?" I asked Cassidy as I folded the last of my clothes into my carry-on luggage.

Silence.

"Cassidy?"

When I looked up, to my surprise, she burst out crying and flounced onto the bed, head curved.

I bent down to comfort her. "Don't you want to see your dad?"

"Of course!" She flung her arm out as if I knew nothing, which apparently I didn't, because I had no idea what had set her off. Then it dawned on me. "Oh! This is about your job."

She nodded, tears dripping down her cheeks.

"Are you worried you'll disappoint your dad?"

Again she nodded, swiping at the tears.

"Sweetie, he knows what's going on in the US. He reads the paper. Besides, thousands upon thousands of really dedicated people are losing their jobs right now. People with amazing records of service. Maybe you can see this as a fresh start, to do something different. To do what makes *you* happy."

She peered up. "Do you think?"

"Of course. Now let's go get your dad."

She smiled up at me through the haze of tears, and I glimpsed that spark before the "powers-that-be" had done what they could to extinguish it. From the time she was small, she'd been motivated and well-liked, always at the top of her class. But none of that mattered now. Not until the collective whole put a stop to this madness would we ever see normalcy of any kind. We were all at the mercy of the party now controlling the house and the government and its daily whims. I glanced over at the latest headlines—at the newest agencies under attack. All I could do was shake my head.

"C'mon. We'd better get going if we're to make it to Edinburgh on time."

Twenty minutes later, we were back on the road. Yet again, I had the eerie feeling I'd been here before, in the countryside. But how? If Cassidy was Esme, who was I, and did I have a doppelganger in the past like Cassidy and Benjamin? If so, was I from the same time period? I tried to look at things logically. If I'd been a village girl, how could I know so much about the countryside? Unless I was...*a Traveller*. My blood went cold, and I pulled my jacket tighter around me. Had I been Jamie's mother in a past life?

Then why am I here? To save Jamie? To bring them together, or both?

I huddled in silence, drinking in the landscape. It was like coming home. Like a piece of me had been missing my entire lifetime, and I was just now finding it. Why hadn't I seen it before? Suddenly, images began flashing through my head of me standing by a pond, but I was someone else. I watched the manor where the laird had taken Jamie, hoping to get a glimpse of him, but then I saw his nan, who yelled, "Go away, Isla. Ye're not wanted here." I felt the sting of her words, hurled at me like sharp flints. But then, when I peered down at my image in the water, I gasped, for I was another woman, this Isla whose name had been hurled like a curse.

"What is it, Ma?" Cassidy asked, turning toward me, her brows furrowed.

"Oh, it's just so beautiful."

She assumed I meant the countryside, but it was my image that had made me gasp because I *was* lovely, stunningly so. Wavy brown hair fell past my shoulders and I wore a linen dress covered in red roses. Where had I found such lovely material? But as I looked at the manor, I knew. Laird MacPherson, Jamie's father, had bought it for Isla. Had loved her for her beauty and for much more. Enough so that he'd kept Jamie, protected him from the vagaries of Gypsy life. But still, my heart ached to have Isla's son—*my* son taken from me, even though I knew it was for the best. My fingers bit the palm of my hand as I came to grips with what I was seeing, tears pooling in my eyes at the injustice of it.

But then I saw Cassidy and gratitude overwhelmed me. I'd been fortunate with her. She was one of the twin loves of my life, she and my husband, Michael.

And now, I had found my son in another lifetime. My entire family was back together. At last, I understood Esme's sense of urgency. She'd given me a wonderful gift, and I dare not squander it.

Chapter 25
Cobra

Over the course of the next few days, Frank had managed only smatterings of new information about the IT ring and their plans. All across the globe, he'd heard theories that this was an inside job, and he was beginning to believe it. And although the Resistance had made no move as yet, he could feel it in the pit of his stomach. It was coming. But what would they do, and how?

His secretary knocked on his door. "Come in," he said.

Today, she was dressed in a grey pantsuit and white blouse, her unruly blonde hair tucked behind her ears. "Someone's here to see you."

She stepped aside as the man entered. Frank couldn't shake the feeling that the man seemed vaguely familiar, but he couldn't place him, though he did have the look of law enforcement in his suit and tie. Yet it was the slight bump next to his waist from the holster that gave him away.

"What can I do for you?" Frank asked, giving the man his entire attention.

"My name's Nick...Nicholas Dunbar."

Again, the name sat just beyond Frank's reach, and yet he was certain he'd heard it before and knew the man well, but how was that possible since he was meeting him for the first time? Suddenly, the world spun, and his eyes blurred. He blinked several times in rapid succession, his eyes focusing in on what looked like a coat and waistcoat with an insignia just below the lapel where moments ago there'd been a normal three-piece suit. But what had him reeling was the sword at the man's side. His vision faded back to Nick as he swallowed down the rising panic. First the headaches, then Juanita being captured by ICE and sent packing, and now this. What next? He reached for two aspirin he kept in his desk drawer to quell the internal tremors. He swallowed them down with the water he kept on a tray beside his desk.

"Do I know you?" Frank asked once the bitter pills had gone down.

"FBI, part of the Counterterrorism Division." Nick flashed his badge.

As a member of the Cyber Crime Division, Frank often worked hand in hand with the Counterterrorism Unit. He scratched his head, trying to recall the man. Was Nick a new hire put in place by the recent administration? Since the transfer of power, the FBI had been a revolving door of people leaving and new people arriving. The chaos that ensued had left the staff demoralized, and their jobs had suffered as a result, his included.

"You're dealing with a cybercrime ring, yes?"

Frank wasn't sure how much to divulge to the untested man, yet he couldn't help but feel he'd worked hand in glove with him in the past. Had he? But when, and in what capacity? Lately, his stomach had soured, and he pulled out a roll of antacids, downing one. Nick looked at the package with one raised brow.

"Sorry, things have been a bit—"

"Stressful?" Nick finished for him.

"Yeah," Frank agreed, hoping his nervous laughter wouldn't give away too much. But then again, the FBI was trained in body language 101. It was part of their job to be able to tell when people were nervous. Or lying.

Fortunately, Nick left it at that. Instead, he pulled out his briefcase, landed it on the table, and clicked open the hasps. Then he reached inside and pulled out a sheet of paper with names of locations printed on it, the country of origin at each heading.

"These are the countries where we've received pings. They're not your usual hotspots for counterterrorism, which is what has us confused. Can you make sense of them?"

Frank inspected the list of countries and locations. "They could be using a GPS scrambler to hide their identity and location, but I'm sure you're aware of that."

"Not this time," Nick said, tapping the page with his finger. "They're not using any known spoofing app we have on file. And there's just something...*different* about them. Usually they hide them in places like Africa or India, but these are all from European countries. And though I hate to say it, our government has been pissing on our allies for a while now, especially with the tariffs."

"You think someone got fed up with what's going on?"

Nick splayed his hands out like he was laying his cards on the table. "What do you think?"

Truth is, the thought had occurred to Frank that maybe their allies had said enough's enough and were beginning to fight back, and he couldn't blame them. The US government had been throwing its weight around lately, and it'd made a heck of a lot of enemies. For all the times he'd talked the current administration up to Mia, he had to admit, even he was feeling the heat—wondering whether they were doing the right thing, but he'd never voice those opinions out loud, especially not in today's climate.

"It's possible," Frank agreed. "But then that would mean—"

"We're not fighting the enemy any more. We're fighting each other."

That thought sobered Frank. Any more of this and their government might crumble, and if it crumbled, they would be open to attack from places like...Russia.

Nicholas stood. He handed Frank his card. "I'd like us to keep in touch. If you hear any more, you can contact me any time, day or night. Agreed?"

"Agreed," Frank said with a heavy sigh.

But what Nick said next as he headed for the door had Frank's head spinning...again. "Don't worry. We'll hang them from the highest tree once we find them."

And with that, he left.

Chapter 26
Esme Stalwart

I loaded Jamie into the cart as I had the other day, Coot seated next to me in his women's garb. In the distance, I heard a bird call, but I recognized it, because it was sung by none other than one of the members of Jamie's gang who had stayed behind to protect Jamie and me. They used the call of the song thrush, its many sounds given varied meaning. The tattooed song was a warning. The lilt upward meant all was okay. I listened for this latest message and heard it on the hillside, but try as I might, I couldn't see a single member of Jamie's band of warriors. Either they had camouflaged themselves or were hidden, but where in this godforsaken land could they hide, I wondered as I scanned the horizon? Yet, I suppose if you'd been hunted your entire life, you'd learn concealment. Learn it well.

"Have you spoken to the men?" I asked as the wheels turned on the earthen road, clacking out a rhythm against the many stones that dotted the landscape.

"Aye, I have." Because Coot was young, his voice could be mistaken for a woman's, but I had no doubt that would change soon enough.

"Do they know how to find Jamie's *mathair*?"

"They're searchin' for his *mam* now. In the meantime, they say to head north toward a region where we're most likely to find her." Coot nodded toward "the cargo" in the back. "Is young Jamie up to travelin', do ye think?"

I soaked in a breath of fresh air, a hint of the sweet scent of yellow gorse floating in on the morning breeze. Though I hoped and prayed Jamie would be okay, I knew he was far from safe. And yet, I had seen improvements and knew Jamie to be a strong lad.

"He'll make it, so long as we find his *mam* soon."

I wondered how many days of this bone-shattering ride he could withstand, but I refused to voice my fears with Coot or anyone else. Up 'til now, I had done all I could to bring Jamie back to health, and though he had been walking in recent days, he still needed rest, lots of it.

As we wended upwards, I heard a new bird call that included a bit of a whistle. This one meant "follow me." If anyone had been listening, they would think nothing of it. But I knew somewhere, along the ridgeline, the men were urging us forward.

We had been traveling like this for close to an hour when suddenly I heard the tattooed warning I had come to dread. It meant danger was close at hand.

"Quick!" I hissed. "Over there."

Fortunately, we were near a rare copse of trees. Coot needed no further caution, having experienced firsthand where disobedience might lead. We'd barely entered the woods and driven the cart behind a thicket of brush when we heard the clatter of horses pounding out a rhythm behind us and heard the riders urging their mounts onward. I peered through the thicket in time to see my nemesis, and that of my husband's, a thick, surly man who believed it his duty to protect the rich at all costs—to keep the riff-raff down so they didn't bother the gentry class, even if all the riff-raff was doing was trying to survive. To eat. To keep a roof over their heads.

My heart didn't stop pounding a drum in my chest until the last of the dust had settled. I leaned back against the carriage seat and closed my eyes, then breathed out a huge sigh. Once they were gone, Coot and I laughed. I heard Jamie stir.

"Are you alright, husband?" I ventured, relieved to hear his voice, even if it was just a moan.

"Water!" he gasped.

"Hurry!" I told Coot.

I jumped down from the carriage and opened the keg of water we kept tied to the seat. Then I ladled out a large sip of the cool, refreshing liquid while Coot lifted back the tarp and helped Jamie to a sitting position.

"Are they gone?" he asked, his voice raspy.

"They are." I placed the ladle to his lips, and he sipped greedily, never stopping until every last drop was gone. His hair was wet from sweat and his face pale, but he was alive, thank God. Alive.

I dug through my stores and brought out the basket of food I had packed. No time like the present to replenish his spirits, not to mention his stomach.

As with the drink, he ate and ate until he could eat no more, a good sign, I felt certain. When he was done, he wiped his mouth with the back of his hand and smiled as only Jamie could. It was as though he'd been born under a twinkling star that shined down on him alone for all to see, especially me. My heart ached every time I looked at him to think that one day he might not be here. With me. How had it happened? That he'd captured me so fully? I was no less a captive than a prisoner in the gaol, as he may one day be. Had been, in fact, until days ago, when he'd been sprung by his men and me. Frightened by the memory, I kissed him on the mouth, needing to take in his warmth, to smell his sweet scent, to feel him next to me. He returned the kiss, and when he was through, a chuckle welled from deep inside his throat. And if it hadn't been for the circumstances, I believe he would have pulled out his fiddle and played a jig for me right then and there, but we weren't safe. Not yet. Not until we could find his *mathair* and the Romanis. The Gypsies. The people I had been taught my entire life to avoid.

Chapter 27
Destiny Jacqueline Kismet

I knew the moment I laid eyes on Michael something was wrong. His brow was furrowed, and he was pacing the airport lobby as he awaited his luggage from the carousel. When he looked up and saw us, he didn't light up like he ordinarily did. Instead, he made a beeline our way and headed straight for Benjamin.

"Thanks for looking after my girls." He shook Benjamin's hand, his lips pinched tight when he spoke.

In the short time he'd been gone, he'd aged. The first sprinkling of gray grew at his temples, and his eyes sagged, as if he hadn't slept well on the flight over. In the end, I chalked it up to jet lag, and yet I had my doubts.

Michael had worked in IT most of his adult life and managed systems worldwide. It had allowed us a good life, though a sometimes lonely one for me when he was on the road. Just then, the carousel dropped another set of luggage. Michael grabbed it and headed for the sliding door, the rest of us trying to keep pace.

Outside the air terminal, taxis rushed back and forth as they picked up passengers. We walked to the loading zone while Benjamin and Cassidy went to grab the car and bring it around for pickup. Now that we were alone, I turned to Michael.

"Okay, spill. What's going on?"

He wasted no time. "How do you know Benjamin?"

"What do you mean?" I asked, confused.

"I mean, I've been working with Benjamin for weeks now. How do you know him?"

I couldn't have been more stunned than if he'd said he had quit his job.

"How is that possible? Benjamin has been here with us. You've been...God knows where."

I knew he couldn't tell me where he'd been but was certain he hadn't been in Scotland this entire time. The wind swept up a breeze, lifting both my hair and my skirt. I wrapped my coat tighter around me, the spring chill brusque against my face and hands. Seeing that, he pulled me into his arms.

"I know, but the thing with IT is you can do it anywhere, with anyone."

Then why don't you do it from home? I wanted to say but thought better of it.

"So, how do you know you've been working with Benjamin then?" I patted my hands together for warmth.

"We have a tracking device on him."

"A tracking device?" I watched as Benjamin pulled into line. "You're scaring me, Michael. None of this is making sense. Is Benjamin under suspicion for anything?"

"Of course not." Michael sounded especially terse.

"Then why—"

"I'll explain it when we get to the hotel. I've booked a room for the two of us. Cassidy will be in the room next to ours."

"Do you think that's wise, putting her in a separate room?" I said, just as the car pulled up to the curb with the two of them in tow.

He paused and tilted his head, his hand on his luggage. "What does that mean?"

I could see we weren't getting off to a good start. I breathed a sigh and said, "Nothing. We can talk about it later."

He frowned, then ran around back to put his luggage inside the trunk Benjamin had opened. Cassidy smiled at me from the passenger seat. I knew that smile. She was falling in love, but who was Benjamin? A librarian, or someone working in IT? And what did Esme mean about protecting him in this lifetime? Protect him from what? The small bits of money he was supposedly moving from rich accounts to those in poverty—a few dollars here, a few dollars there? I was eager to get to the hotel so I could pick Michael's brain.

For the next half hour, we drove in silence, each of us lost in thought. Only Cassidy spoke from time to time as the early spring scenery shot by. It appeared more bleak now than I remembered it from yesterday and all the other days. It's as if a blanket of doubt had crept over it, creating a fog that made the moors feel eerie. Once again, I slipped back in time and felt as though I was looking at myself through the eyes of another, the woman I'd once been, the Gypsy. *Jamie's mother.* When I peered at myself in the rearview mirror, I saw not me, but her, Isla McPhee. Her shiny coat of reddish hair swirled past her shoulders, her skin the color of ripe walnuts, and her eyes the clearest blue. She wore both an impish smile that hinted at playfulness and a dress that fell from her shoulders.

I could see why the laird of the manor had fallen for her. She…no, *I* was so different from anyone he'd ever known. In the mirror, I saw a fun-loving woman who looked a man in the eye and wasn't afraid. Who, despite all odds, thought she was his equal. In 1700s Scotland, that would have been a bold thing—for a woman to believe herself a man's equal. Even now, in my own country, a woman still couldn't become president. In less than a hundred years, we'd gone from being deemed the property of a man in the 1800s to earning the right to vote in 1920 to owning our own property in the early 1900s. And finally, in the mid-70s, we'd even managed to be able to apply for our own Visa card and get it, though some credit card companies held off well into the 80s. Most young people couldn't fathom the changes that had taken place in my lifetime alone, much less my mother's and grandmother's.

I rolled down the window, needing air, but quickly rolled it back up when I saw Cassidy's hand on the knob as she attempted to increase the heat in the small cab. For one last time, I looked at the woman in the mirror. Did her son resent her for giving him to the man who would become his father?

In my thoughts I asked her, "How could you give your son away?" Because I knew in this lifetime I would rather die than give up Cassidy. How had it been so easy for Isla to give up *her* son?

Her reply?

"How could I not? I loved Jamie. Loved him like the air I breathed and the water I drank." Her eyes filled with tears. "I loved him too much to want the Gypsy life for him. So you see? We are all trapped in a web of our weaving. We can never truly escape our fate. Nor can you, *Destiny*."

I stifled a gasp because I had been called Destiny for a reason, I saw now. My destiny was to save my son in this lifetime, and my daughter from a future that would dog her if what I believed was true. But how? How did you save a person from themselves?

Chapter 28
Esme Stalwart

We had been combin' the countryside for days, and still we were no closer to finding Isla McPhee.

"Where are you, Isla?" I murmured beneath my breath as Coot silently slept.

He stirred when I spoke but quickly fell back to sleep. Just then I heard a bird call from the hillside. I'd heard them often enough over the course of the past few days to know what this one meant. "This way." It had an urgent ring to it, as though whoever made the call had found something of interest. Sure enough, as I breached the tall hill and gazed out over the valley, I saw smoke curling in the distance from a copse of woods where the Travellers were known to stay. With any luck, Jamie's *mathair* was among them. I spurred the horses on with a fierce tap to the reins. Sensing my urgency, the horses lurched forward, and we hurried down the dusty path leading to the Scottish Gypsies' resting place.

But to my disappointment, by the time we reached the camp, they had heard us and pulled up stakes, embers still burning around the campfire. However, I didn't have long to wait before

I heard a laugh and saw a man enter the clearing. Soon, others followed his lead until the clearing once again housed a menagerie of Travellers who welcomed us in.

Coot, who had been fast asleep, awoke to a crowd of men draggin' him from the carriage and heavin' him into the middle of the melee. Someone drew up a fiddle and bow and began to play, while others danced the sleepy Coot through the clearing.

Suddenly, the merriment halted as a woman entered the fray. Although I had heard Jamie's *mam* was a looker, I hadn't the words for what I saw now. Despite her age, an aura cloaked her that sent chilled fingers up my spine. She wore a white bohemian-style blouse with a tartan plaid skirt that swirled around her as she moved. All those around her gave her a wide berth. Her pale blue eyes, so in contrast with her olive skin made it hard to look away, such was her charisma.

"Where is my son?" she demanded, hands on hips.

I jumped down from the wagon and quickly pulled off the skin tarp. Though pale, Jamie was able to sit up. Isla rushed to him and ordered he be lifted out. Two young Gypsy men climbed up into the wagon and lowered him down. In my head, I'd always assumed Jamie's men must be unusual, as they were tall and thin with bright eyes and keen intellects, but I could see now this was true of all his clan.

"Where will ye be takin' him?" I asked, fearing his *mathair* would want nothin' more to do with me.

"To my wagon."

She nodded toward a caravan on the far side of the *outwith*. "And me?" I asked. "Where shall I stay?"

She appraised me with the eye of an eagle, then dropped her hands to her side. "I suppose ye'll be stayin' with Jamie. C'mon then."

With that, she turned on her heels and strode through the men and women who stepped aside to accommodate her. I trailed behind, stumbling as I went. At the edge of the caravan stood a red vardo, a Gypsy wagon, the design a throwback to the Romanichal. The framework was made of wood with an arched roof and elaborate scrollwork, in both the front and back, and four oversized wheels on which to travel through the rugged countryside. Although I had heard of such things, I had never seen one, Jamie's men preferring to sleep rough when on the road.

The men loaded Jamie in and settled him first, then bade me enter. I peered around, my eyes widening in surprise at the opulence of such a small carriage, for inside, at the far wall, stood a raised bed, its bedcovers made of the finest rich silk and brocade. Heavy red velvet curtains hung on either side to serve as a privacy screen when sleeping, and above it all, a wooden valance richly decorated in gold. To the left of the wagon was a cooking hearth, also dressed in reds and golds so the entire space appeared sumptuous. While to the right, a gold velvet sofa sat beneath an intricate cabinet filled with chinaware that could ha' rivaled the queen's.

Isla entered behind me and urged me to sit as she prepared me tea over the wood stove. Though I did as ordered, I felt out of place and shifted uncomfortably on the sofa, the heat stifling in the small wooden wagon. As I sat there, taking stock of the rich aubergine carpet, I wondered at the opulence. Had Jamie's looting supplied his *mam* with luxury befitting a queen, no matter how small the manse?

She nodded toward the fine furnishings. "Ye think Jamie gave me this, do ye?"

How to respond? At last, I shrugged in answer.

"It 'twas my...man...gave me this. Jamie's father, a laird. Did Jamie not tell ye?"

"Aye, he did." I fingered my dress, which I'd thought pretty before, but now it seemed poor fare indeed compared to the grandeur of the vardo. "I just hadn't known..." I allowed my words to die out, too embarrassed to go on.

"That he paid not only for Jamie but for me, as well?"

My face flushed hot. "I suppose so, *mam*." If there'd been more room, I would have stood and curtseyed, such was the presence of Jamie's mother, but the tight quarters allowed for little movement.

A moan pulled the pair of us out of our stalemate, and just as I shot to my feet, Isla turned and we collided. If I'd had any dignity before, it was gone now, as I fell back on the cushioned sofa. For not more than a hair's breadth, she paused to take stock of me, then she went to tend to her son.

"Esme," he murmured, having succumbed to the stress of the day's travel. "Esme!" He spoke more loudly this time and began thrashing.

Mathair or no, I rose to my feet and rushed to his side. "I am wit' ye, darlin'," I said, taking his hand and stroking it. I placed a hand to his forehead and pulled it away in shock, as he was burning up, a fire eating him from within.

"Get your healer," I hissed.

She paused.

"Now!" I commanded, but still she made no move. "Are ye deaf, woman?"

"I am a healer."

It was my turn to pause. "You?"

She let out a scornful laugh. "Is it so hard to believe I could be a healer, eh? Mistress of the great Laird of Aberdeen? Mother of the famous, or infamous, Jamie MacPherson, take yer pick?"

I shook my head clear of the cobwebs building there. "No, I suppose not."

"Then help me. Remove his shirt, and I'll get the compresses, aye?"

Then she turned to her hearth and began collecting herbs from a shelf above it, each herb creating a smell all its own, both earthy and biting. Not until she was done mixing and stirring and had steeped the brew for several minutes in hot water did we begin the torturous prospect of getting the drink down him, after which I could do nothing but pray.

Chapter 29
Cobra

Frank rubbed tiger balm onto his temples as he took the Metrorail downtown, the heat from the gold-colored ointment radiating blissfully into his skin. Now, if he could just get rid of these headaches.

Out the window of the Metrorail with its rhythmic clack-clack, he spotted the Capitol and its rounded dome. He headed to the Washington Hilton for a class on AI and cyber defense put on by the SANS Institute. AI had become a double-edged sword. It provided the authorities with revolutionary new ways to fight cybercrime, but it had at the same time provided criminals with new ways to prevent detection. So far, it had been a cat-and-mouse game that kept the ball moving forward just far enough out of reach to keep the FBI's Cyber Unit on its toes. Deepfakes and advanced impersonation had allowed criminals to blackmail unsuspecting targets, and phishing attacks were becoming much more sophisticated, so much so that even with systems in place that detected data breaches at lightning speed, they were often one step behind the criminals.

At the Dupont Circle Station, the Metrorail slowed and stopped, the brakes squealing and the door opening onto a state-of-the-art underground system that reminded him of a beehive. From there, he would have a four-block walk in the busy noonday traffic.

He gathered his briefcase and slid his sunglasses on as he disembarked from a full car with people coming and going. When he stepped onto the escalator, the green vegetation that encircled it reminded him of a cat's eye, the all-seeing lens of the tread bisecting it, while the oval glass facade acted as the sclera. It gleamed, as though studying his every move and giving him the impression that Big Brother was watching over each and every one of them. In response, he pulled his briefcase tighter to him.

The Hilton was a ten-minute walk from the station, and the weather was chilly. Still, it gave him blessed time outdoors in daylight. For weeks he'd been holed up in his stuffy office, and although he had a view out his window, it felt sterile. He missed wide open places, not that this was the fishing hole he and his father used to go to when he was a kid. If he'd known how little time he'd find for the great outdoors in this job, he might have viewed his time as more precious as a child. But he had assumed that's the way it would always be—the campouts, the picnics, the hikes. Now he realized those times were finite and most of one's adult life was spent working under fluorescent lighting or behind a lawnmower.

By the time he reached the crescent-shaped building and entered through its lobby, the weight that had settled on his chest lifted.

He walked up to the front counter and gave the woman his name. "I'm here for a cybersecurity meeting," he said.

"It's in the ballroom, sir," the woman said, handing him a nametag and pointing toward the concourse level.

Frank thanked her and headed in that direction. The event had been catered, and although he'd been here before, it never failed to impress with its luxuriant chandeliers and nearly 30,000 square feet of seating. Presidents and notables had spoken here over the years. And indeed, it looked presidential with its five screens and dozens of monitors running horizontally across the ceiling of the room.

He grabbed the literature from the staff manning the doors, then went to find his seat. Already, dozens upon dozens of people were taking their seats or standing in groups of three or more, talking to people they knew or were meeting for the first time. Tired from lack of sleep and eager to rest up a few moments before the main event began, he scooted down a row close to the rear. He was just about to take his seat when he heard a man call his name in a British accent. To his surprise, when he turned around, he saw Joe Henson from Scotland Yard.

"Hey, Joe, what are you doing here?" he asked, pleased to see the man. He had worked with him on a recent case eighteen months in the making, but they'd finally caught their man.

"I had to be in the states anyway for a case I'm workin' on and thought I'd learn a little more about AI. It's really taking the world by storm, aye?"

"It is at that," Frank agreed.

Joe paused, pensive. "I have a case that has me puzzled. I thought maybe we could help each other, aye?"

Just then the lights started to dim, and everyone rushed for their seats. Frank said, "Tell you what. Why don't we meet over lunch? You can tell me what you're working on, and I'll tell you a little about my project."

Joe quickly agreed, then returned to his seat as Frank settled into his. Before anyone spoke, the screen lit up with squares of people from all parts of the world speaking at once. All appearing to be real people. All AI generated.

Chapter 30
Destiny Jacqueline Kismet

The moment the door closed behind us and we were alone in our hotel room, I turned to my husband, whose blue eyes bore the strain of whatever weight he carried on his broad shoulders. Besides, I'd waited long enough to ask the question that had been eating at me the entire ride to the hotel.

"Okay, explain yourself."

"What's to explain?" he said, throwing his suitcase onto the luggage rack in the corner, then plopping down onto the bed. "I've been working with Benjamin for weeks now."

"On what?"

Michael ran his hands through his black hair. "You know I can't tell you that. But why don't *you* tell me how you came to be here? And why didn't you say anything before you decided to gallivant halfway around the world? I've been trying to call you for days."

I sat beside him on the bed, then laid my head on his shoulder as I always did. He bent his head to meet mine. We hadn't even kissed. We always kissed when he returned from his travels. As if he recognized that fact, he leaned in, his lips tender against mine. Only when we came up for air could I breathe again. I'd been waiting days for that, the need for him always lurking in the background.

He placed an arm around my shoulder. "Okay, start from the beginning."

I knew it was going to sound crazy—two grown women traveling thousands of miles on a whim. I decided to start slowly.

"See, Cassidy had heard about this geocaching thing and thought it would be a good mother-daughter bonding experience, since she loves to hike."

"And?" he prompted.

"So, we did it—traveled to the coast—only we got lost in the mountains."

Before I could explain any further, he stiffened. "What were you thinking, Des? That was dangerous. What if you hadn't found your way back? Do you know how many people have to be rescued from those mountains each year?"

"But the point is, we *did* make it back because you've raised a really resourceful daughter."

He chuckled and pulled me closer. "We both did."

I smiled because Cassidy had inherited the best parts of both of us—Michael's good looks and common sense, and my care of those less fortunate. Until she'd been summarily shoved out of her job, she had done great work that should have earned her a raise and a promotion but instead had kept her one step ahead of the bills. As her mother, to me she represented all that was good in the world.

"So what did geocaching have to do with your trip to Scotland?" He stood and walked over to unzip his case. He began to place his folded clothing into drawers, as if planning a lengthy stay.

"Well, we found this letter along with this cross in an old stump."

I rummaged through my purse and pulled out the letter along with the silver Celtic Cross. Michael whistled when he saw it.

"That looks like pure silver."

"It is pure silver," I told him.

"I know, but it looks like something that should be in a museum, not in your purse next to your handi-wipes."

I laughed at the incongruity of it all. Here I held a relic in my hand that was probably centuries old, and I had been carrying it around in a plain handbag. Michael's eyes scanned the vellum, and when he looked up, one eyebrow rose in question.

"You went on a wild goose chase because of this?"

I bit my lip, wondering how much to tell him. I knew I couldn't keep it to myself for long, so I told him the truth. "Cassidy needed a new start. She lost her job."

"What?" He spoke so loudly I feared people might hear him through the thin hotel walls.

"I know, right? She works so hard and pours her own money into every project, but then they turn around and can her."

"It's because of what's happening in the government, isn't it?" Michael's eyes danced with a rare fury. Once again, he plopped onto the bed, fire igniting his cheeks. "They can't do this...any of this. None of it's legal."

"I know, but who's going to stop them, Michael? They're bent on destroying the very institution they serve!"

"I agree." His words were more sullen now, the fire extinguished as quickly as it had inflamed. "Part of the reason I'm here is that I decided not to go back to the States."

"What do you mean?" I said, a hint of worry creeping into my voice. "You work for the government."

He crossed his arms and stared at the wall, refusing to look at me. I placed a hand on his arm. "Talk to me, Michael. What's going on?"

"It's not right what the new government is doing, Des. They're walking all over the constitution like it's a doormat. The vets, people from the Pentagon, teachers. And now they're talking about doing away with Social Security and going to war with China?"

I stood and marched over to the window, needing fresh air, but when I opened the sash, all I smelled were fumes from the city below. How? How had this happened? Sure, our country had its ups and downs, but this was something new. This tested the very limits of democracy. And the thing that frightened me most is that they were getting away with it. No one had risen to stop them.

"Des?"

The breeze swept past me, and I closed my eyes, grateful for a moment of respite before Michael's coming announcement blew us both out of the water.

"I quit my job."

And there it was. My heart sank, even as I knew it was the right thing to do. After all, how could Michael work for a government that put entire swaths of people out on the streets? They'd taken every safety net, including our own, apparently, and burned it to the ground. How would people survive? Many were already homeless, and now they would have trouble feeding their families, and for what? A man with a vendetta? A group of people who were so filled with hate, they couldn't see that without workers and the middle class, there would be no one to feed or fuel their businesses, no one to buy their products? They were cutting their own throats as surely as they were cutting ours, and we all knew it. The ones who cared enough to look, that is.

"What'll we do? How will we survive?" I asked, my voice choked.

He grasped my hand and walked me over to the open suitcase. I stood there, shaking my head in confusion.

"What?" I fought back the edge of hysteria that had taken root, my body trembling. "It's just a suitcase."

I was crying now. In a matter of days, our entire world had been upended, and it was happening over much of the country I had grown up loving. What sort of future could we possibly offer our children after this?

To my surprise, Michael lifted out his clothing and set them aside on the table. I saw nothing but an empty suitcase. But then he pressed a button that lifted the side panel of the luggage. I gasped. Because there, in the bottom of the case, were stacks of $100 bills.

Chapter 31
Esme Stalwart

Although I'd been with the Gypsies for only a week, their zest for life had failed to escape me as they danced around the fire, often scoopin' me up in their arms to the tune of the fiddle, the accordion, and the cauld wind pipes.

For Jamie's part, he healed just as his *mathair* had predicted, and though not yet ready for either fiddle or dance, he managed to clap along with the music while eyeing his brethren, to be sure none would sweep me off my feet as he had.

As the music wound down, I thanked my partner, who tilted his hat in acknowledgement, and then I went to sit beside Jamie around the fire. He held me tighter than usual, as if to remind me I was his. I squeezed his hand in reassurance amid the crackle of the fire. It soothed me, as it often did when troubled. And though I had danced for nearly an hour, I *was* troubled, because tomorrow we were to set sail for parts unknown in these Gypsy ships on wheels, as I had come to view them. As so often before, the Travellers had been shooed on, given an evening, no more, to move along.

"Why don't they let ye stay, Jamie?" I asked, my voice hushed so none would hear my lament.

"Because we're Travellers, don't ye know? That's what we do. Travel. It's our lot in life. That's what happens to an outlawed people."

I bent forward to see if he was serious, but he ne'er cracked a smile. "Outlawed? How can an entire group of people be outlawed?"

The firelight played across his face, outlining the deep cracks and crevices, making him appear older than his 24 years. He warmed his hands over the fire, his expression suddenly grave.

"If they catch us, we will hang from the gallows, just fer bein' born. How's that for a dilemma?"

I felt a catch in my throat. It was inhumane. "If that's the truth, Jamie MacPherson, then why'd they tell ye to leave instead of hang the lot of ye?"

Jamie shrugged. "'Tis their way. Meant mostly just to scare us off. But as you can see, it works. If we stayed, they *would* hang the lot of us."

One thing puzzled me. I lifted a stick and placed a piece of venison on the tip, then roasted it over the fire, relieved to hear the sizzle and pop as the fat hit the coal and embers below.

"Why did they not ask about yer whereabouts when the law came calling? Surely, they must know ye're here by now?"

Jamie laughed. "They do know I'm here."

I nearly dropped the meat into the fire. "W-what? I don't understand."

"Actually, there are quite a few good men in this town who don't want to see me hanged. Men who are just as much at the mercy of the landed gentry as you or I, Esme. They help me and my kin."

Shock settled in, the night cloaking me in darkness. I shivered, and Jamie rushed to place a cape around my shoulders for warmth, but 'twasn't warmth I needed as much as clarity. All these years, I had thought the situation black and white, dark and light. But it was more than that. Beneath the cruelty of the institutions lay a blanket of resistance, people who fought back in hidden ways, who pushed back on the rich who would outlaw a people. Hang them just for existing.

"They help us steal from the rich."

Jamie could see I was havin' trouble keeping my roasting spit from fallin' into the ashes, so he took it from me to give me time to recover.

"What do ye mean, help ye? How?" I eyed him suspiciously, waiting for the moment when he jumped to his feet and began to laugh at my naivete, but he never did.

"They inform us where and when to find things of value. And Esme, lest ye think me daft or foolhardy, I take only what is necessary for my people to survive. It's no more than a knick to their conscience and their pocketbook, aye? They still ha' enough money and riches for several lifetimes and then some."

I tried to wrap my head around this. How had I lived all these years and never known any of this? Why hadn't he told me? As I sat there, stewing, I felt my dander rise, and before I knew it, I was on my feet, my voice raised.

"Why are ye tellin' me this now? Why not when we first met, ye rotter?"

His kinsmen stared at me. He pulled me down, and I tripped, falling into his lap with a plop. An arm wrapped around me to secure me in place, and though I fought it, and despite him being ill, the man was strong from years of relentless work and sacrifice.

"Shh! Behave yerself, Esme Stalwart, or I'll bend ye over my knee."

I knew he'd never do it...not without a fight, at any rate. Finally, I gave in with a sigh.

"I didn't say anything because the fewer who know the truth behind our raids, the better...for all of us, ye included."

"Then why tell me now?" I pouted like a child and was acting like one, too, but we'd always been truthful with each other...until now. I didn't like secrets. Especially when they were kept from me.

"Because you need to know...in case something happens to me."

I wanted to feign ignorance, but I knew only too well the vice was closing in on him. Someday, he'd rub William Duff the wrong way, and the man would come after him again. This time he might succeed in seeing him swing on the gallows. The thought sent a chill racing through me like a herd of runaway horses, but I could no more stop it than protect Jamie against the danger that lay ahead.

"That way, you'll know who to call on should ye need it."

He leaned over and whispered the name of the man in my ear. To my surprise, it was none of the men close at hand, nor a man I was familiar with in the least. He gave me directions where to find him, and though I wanted to close my ears to any talk of Jamie's death, I knew I must be ready, should the day come. And yet I prayed it never would. But prayers often go unanswered. I, of all people, should know this, because I had a secret of my own, if my second sight was true. A secret I had yet to share. I hugged him tight, grateful for his warmth. No, I would keep it to myself a little bit longer. Then...maybe, if the time was right, I would tell him. But then again, when is the time ever right? An owl hooted overhead, owls the harbingers of hidden truths...or warnings. Which was it? I didn't know, but I feared the worst.

Chapter 32
Destiny Jacqueline Kismet

Eyes wide, I stood inside the hotel room gawking at the one hundred dollar bills stacked neatly inside the suitcase. When I looked up, my eyes met Michael's.

"What's this all about?" Had he robbed a bank? None of this computed in my now fuzzy brain.

Michael reached for my hand, but I pulled it away. "Des, listen to me. I didn't steal it. It's ours."

"What do you mean?" I demanded, panting from both fear and anger.

He ran his hands through his wavy black hair. "I could see what was coming down the pike, and I knew it would only get worse. There are no guardrails on this administration. Any of us could lose our job at any moment. What they want us to do is illegal."

"If it's illegal, then don't do it," I said, throwing up my hands.

"You still don't get it. No judge in the country is going to stand up to them. Have you heard how many of them have had their lives threatened? They may stand up to them for a short time, but they'll eventually capitulate. The administration is counting on it."

I turned away from him, needing time to think. I rubbed my hands over my eyes. They felt gritty suddenly, as if I hadn't slept in a week. I held my hands to my lips as though in prayer and took a deep cleansing breath before turning to face him.

"You're overreacting. Surely there are judges who will stand up to them, even at the cost of their own lives."

A short, bitter laugh escaped Michael's lips. "That's just it, Des. They may be willing to put their own lives on the line, but what about their family members? These people have wives, husbands, children, sisters and brothers, mothers and fathers."

"What are you saying? They would go after everyone?"

I had expected Michael to say, *of course not*, but he just stood there looking more tired than I'd seen him in a very long time. Were they really the monsters he was making them out to be? Michael pierced me with a look of such sorrow it sent my emotions careening down a slippery slope that came crashing to the bottom. I sat down on the bed, my throat raw with emotion. Things couldn't be this dire, could they?

He kneeled down in front of me, forcing me to look at him. When he finally had my attention, he clasped my hands in his. "Des, I pulled our money out of the bank before things get worse. I'm hoping we just have to outlast the chaos. We can do that here. Then if things get back to normal—"

"Don't you mean when?"

"*If* they ever go back to normal, we'll return, but we're not safe in the US right now. No one in the government is...except those loyal to the regime."

I clutched at my chest, feeling as if I couldn't breathe. Once upon a time, we had a safe, secure life. We had expected to retire with a nest egg. Now that nest egg was dwindling. Furthermore, the stock market had taken a precipitous drop.

"So, what do we do?" I asked once I could catch my breath.

"We ride it out."

I bit my lip. "Does Cassidy know any of this?"

"No," he assured me, and his expression made it clear she never would.

"Is that fair...not to tell her?"

He shrugged. "What's fair? I don't even know anymore."

His shoulders slumped as silence cradled the air between us. My thoughts turned to Benjamin. Michael had promised me an explanation about their connection once we arrived at the hotel.

"So how do you know Benjamin? What does he have to do with all of this?"

Michael sighed, his hair falling over one eye. "I was bored one night and turned to the internet. This guy wrote something that really stuck with me. See, there was this discussion about what's going on in the world, and he said he knew how to fix it."

"To fix it? Fix what?"

"The power imbalance."

I folded in on myself. "I'm listening."

"Apparently, he's not just a librarian. He's their IT guy. The guy's a genius."

I narrowed my eyes as I pictured Benjamin. He was witty and charming, but a genius? I had my doubts. Below, I heard the clanging of heavy machinery outside our window.

"And...?"

"He came up with an idea about how to even the playing field."

For the next half hour, Michael regaled me with everything he had learned over the course of the past two weeks, but that still didn't explain the huge coincidence that Cassidy and I had been called to Scotland at the same time Michael was being pulled in on the other side.

Then it dawned on me, and my blood froze. *Because it's not a coincidence, you ninny.* But if it wasn't a random event, then who was pulling the strings on this puppet show? Esme? Benjamin? Jamie? Or perhaps somebody else entirely.

I placed my forehead on Michael's, wishing I could somehow divine what it was he knew that would make him give up everything, as Cassidy and I had, to come halfway around the world to learn the truth. But learn it we would. Because my name wasn't Destiny for nothing. I sighed and stood.

"I better get some sleep," I told Michael, yawning, even as my head churned.

Because tomorrow I have a date with Destiny.

Chapter 33
Cobra

Frank entered the Sidecar Restaurant, packed with those from the conference who preferred a drink or snack before heading back to listen to the afternoon speaker. So far, he'd had all his worst fears confirmed. Just as the government agencies hired top cybercrime analysts to halt criminal activity on the internet, the criminals were far outstripping them. They had more money to hire the best of the best and knew how to either attract them into their fold, or use blackmail to get them there. Either way, the criminals were winning...for now. But that's why he'd entered the field, to make a name for himself. To make a difference.

He scanned the room once, twice, then he heard his name, and a raised arm lifted at the head of the room where a bar formed a wide arc. Joe stepped off his stool to greet Frank with a handshake.

"Glad I finally get a chance to talk to you, aye?" Joe said.

The guy was a company hack who didn't mind a pint now and then, from what Frank had gathered when he met him in England. He was already nursing a gin and tonic. So much for lunch.

"So," Joe said, launching right in, as Frank hailed down a waitress and asked her to bring him a BLT and some tomato juice. "We've got a really sophisticated operation taking place in Scotland, at least we think it's in Scotland. It could be anywhere, really. It's not ransomware or anything like that, at least not yet. It's like they're testing the waters, which makes me think something big might be in the offing."

"How can I help?" Frank thanked the waitress who brought him his tomato juice.

"We've been trying to trace them, and the funny thing is, we traced them to your office. Do you know why?"

Frank was just about to take a sip of his juice but stopped, stunned. He paused, peering at Joe over his small glass. "No, why?"

Joe took a quick gulp of his gin and tonic and tapped the bottom of his glass for a refill. Within moments, the bartender handed him one.

"Well, we have our suspicions."

"And?" Frank prompted.

"We think they reverse engineered their software to find out who was tracking *them*."

"So you think these are people *I'm* investigating."

Joe sucked on the lime from his gin and tonic and set it aside on his napkin. "Are you?" he asked, his eyes never leaving Frank's.

"Well, I am, b-but..." Frank frowned, his mind whirring. If they knew who he was, then they might know where he lived. "Look," he said, clenching his teeth together, "do I need to be worried?"

Joe put a piece of ice in his mouth and bit into it, unnerving Frank with his crunching.

"I don't know, you tell me. Do you?"

The waitress appeared with Frank's BLT, but he pushed it away, no longer hungry. "Thanks, I think I'll just take it to go," he told her.

She removed the plate and went to wrap it for him. As Frank peered around at the tables, he saw people he recognized on the daily news. Congressmen. Senators. Which ones of them, even now, were helping to dismantle the constitution? Their democracy? The thought chilled him almost as much as the realization he was being tracked. But by whom, and why? That question sent ice flowing through his veins at the implications, if it was true. And he had no doubt it was true. None at all.

Chapter 34
Esme Stalwart

As we traveled the hidden corridors of Scotland, careful to stay clear of "polite" society, I carried my secret with me like a money pouch, close to my heart.

Ahead, as before, the scouts' bird chirps guided us through the forest and into the clearings. Then silence. Everyone paused because they had heard it, too. Jamie, who was finally able to ride his horse for short bouts, held up his hand. As leader of his band, a troupe put together from the strongest and most able of his clan, he had the final say. Whether the horses had been trained to listen to even the smallest of details, or they had learned the men's sign language over the course of years, I couldn't say. I only knew they paused now, not a jingle from their bridles. It was uncanny and sent a shiver of fear coursing through me at the unknown.

"What is it?" I whispered, but Jamie shrugged me off with a sharp tilt of his head.

We waited, the silence threatening. Then a lone rider came racing into the clearing, lean, his dark eyes wild. "Turn back! The sheriff and his men are ridin' the woods. There's a place where ye'll be safe. Follow me."

I'd never seen this man before. Could we trust him? Jamie must have thought so, because he didn't hesitate to follow. Once the caravan was moving into the ravine, Jamie circled back to bring up the rear and to ensure every man, woman, and child made it to safety. Before, I had never known a person could smell danger, but it came with a metallic odor that seemed to breathe through the very pores of the Travellers' bodies. And mine.

Soon enough, I saw where the rider was takin' us—a ravine up ahead that led to a hollow. It sank into the earth itself as if it had swallowed us whole. From a distance, one would see only the bare horizon. At the base of the hollow was a depression where fresh spring water gave life to a weary people and their animals. And still we were silent. I had never lived among people who could be so loud, so boisterous one minute, and as silent as church mice the next. My skin prickled with anxiety. Where was Jamie? The last I'd seen of him, he was bringing up the herd of caravaners, but he had never arrived with the final vardo.

"Ha' ye seen Jamie?" I asked his *mam*.

By now I had seen past her beauty. And she had come to trust me with Jamie's life, and I her. Saving her son had brought us closer together, thank the Lord. I could see why Jamie loved her so. *And* the Travellers. Though they were thieves, the lot of them, they also worked hard and cared for each other. They laughed and danced and played the fiddle until the wee hours of the morn. Had they not been so reviled by society because of their strange, roving ways, would they have become brigands? I had no answer. I knew only that I had come to love these people in our short time together and trusted them with my life.

"Jamie does whatever he darn well pleases, and ye best get used to it, aye? I've spent my life tryin' to understand the ways of men, Esme, and there's no use in it. They're born different. They care more for each other's company than ours. We get small, treasured moments with 'em, if we're lucky. If we're not, then we live a separate life. It's just how it is with men."

Her cold calculation of men and their customs shoved a cold fist of anxiety in my stomach. Is this all I could hope for? A few stolen moments over time? And yet what had I had with Jamie up 'til now, aye? Those treasured moments of which she'd spoken. Slices of life, that's all. And yet, he was like the sun to me, light and warmth. Like an old apothecary chest, he filled the small drawers in my mind with memories. Cherished ones.

I chewed on Isla's words for some time when finally, near sundown, Jamie and his men came hooting and hollering into the clearing. With them, they brought three saddled horses. I shot Isla a nervous glance, and she lifted a single eyebrow as if to say, what did I tell ye? When the men were through congratulatin' Jamie and the others, I caught his attention. He walked my way, his swagger returned, though he was still pale.

"Where did ye get the horses, Jamie?" I demanded, fire burning in my belly.

"Relax, woman," he said. "Tis only the sheriff's horse...and his men's."

I threw up my hands in protest. "What on earth were you thinkin', Jamie MacPherson? They'll be after yer hide fer certain now."

"They'll ha' to find me first," he said with a grin. "I waited 'til they were far afield and restin' their horses before we stole 'em. Though we'd best not linger long." He peered over to the rest of the clan and shouted, "What say ye, men? Should we crack on?"

They cheered as one, but I knew it was just one more nail in Jamie's coffin. It left a festering anger in my chest to know he could be so cavalier about something that might have lasting consequences. For me, and for him.

Chapter 35
Destiny Jacqueline Kismet

We spent the next day at the National Library of Scotland, where Benjamin took us to a conference room so we could speak in private. The sounds of our feet echoed off of the tile as we each took a seat around a table where Benjamin had piled stacks of books, each of them earmarked with pages of information related to our search. But the search he had planned wasn't for Esme and Jamie, as I had suspected; it was information pertaining to our government and its current status.

Once we were all seated, Benjamin started by saying, "Your president is currently suing CBS, ABC, Meta, and is threatening to take PBS and NPR to court as well."

"Why?" Cassidy asked, her blonde hair weaved into a single braid down her back. Despite the chill, she wore a flowery dress this morning with slate-blue leggings and sandals.

"To cause fear of speakin' out against the regime. And conservative governments across the globe are watching how it all plays out, aye?"

"Why are you so interested in our politics?" I asked Benjamin.

To this, both Michael and Benjamin shared a nervous glance, but no one spoke. Cassidy was the first to break the silence.

"Benjamin told me about him and Dad—that they've been working on a project together to address what's going on back home."

I jerked my head up to Michael, who offered an apologetic shrug. "There's a lot to go over and not much time."

What did he mean by that? I fell back in my seat, a rush of wind escaping my lips. Once again, I was the clueless one. "So explain. What are we talking about?"

Michael placed a hand on my shoulder. "Why don't you wait and let Benjamin go over his findings?"

I crossed my arms and chewed on the peppermint gum I'd popped in my mouth upon entry into the cavernous room that felt more like an echo chamber.

"You've heard about all the other things your new government is doing, I assume. They're trying to eliminate the Department of Education, as well as rolling back protections for both wildlife and national parks. And they're abolishing any plan for inclusive hiring."

I had scoured the papers each morning and had gone online only to get the latest news on the mayhem taking place back home. So much for the constitution that, one short year ago, had been waved with the words "Read your constitution." What had happened to *that* rhetoric? It had gone out the window along with the rule of law and all those who fought for it. I rubbed a circle over my heart, wishing it all away. Wishing I might wake up and this all be a horrible nightmare.

"But what you may not know is that the owners of the top three businesses have accumulated more wealth than the bottom half of society, nearly 170 *million* people in total." Benjamin eyed me.

"I didn't know, but it doesn't surprise me," I said.

"According to USA Today, those three men earn a grand total of almost a trillion dollars between them."

Michael whistled.

"A two-adult household earns just $33,000 each, on average, in yearly income. Of that income, the average taxpayer pays 24.3% of his income toward taxes. That means a person earning $33,000 took home just $24,981 per year. And what of single parents when rent alone is over $1000 a month for an apartment?"

It was my turn to whistle. How did people survive? I'd been lucky because Michael worked for the government, until recently. Soon we would be living on that amount or less, unless Michael could find a job in the private sector. I looked over at Cassidy, who had paled at the numbers. She knew only too well what it was like to work at the poverty level, despite the fact she had graduated from a top college, earning a magna cum laude and a master's degree. Even with limited earnings, she'd managed to help those around her, taking them under her wing like a mother hen tending her chicks. As a result, she had been well loved. I took her hand and gave it a squeeze, her smile shy and self-deprecating.

"Nearly 38 million people live at or below the poverty level in America," Benjamin continued. "In fact, seventy percent of all those in poverty are women and children, whereas the top three earners in the US paid just 3.22% in taxes. What if that rate were 24.3%, like the average American? You'd have another 16 billion dollars to distribute to those at the poverty level, $42,000 to be exact. Imagine how much easier life would be for everybody."

Benjamin had clearly done his homework, bless him, but what rich man would ever pay his fair share of taxes if he didn't have to? None that I could think of. Plus, they had the politicians in their pockets. Somehow, people believed that the average American must pull themselves up by their bootstraps, and yet so many of the oligarchs were living off the dole in one way or another, whether it was through subsidies or tax deferments.

I looked at Benjamin, who clearly believed in what he was doing, and remembered what the curator had said about Jamie MacPherson. "He was a Robin Hood, always givin' to the poor."

I stifled a laugh. Despite the centuries that had passed, if Benjamin was indeed the reincarnation of Jamie, he hadn't changed a whit. He still cared for the poor and the downtrodden. After all, he'd seen it firsthand with his people, the Travellers.

Chapter 36
Esme Stalwart

"Don't be like that, Esme," Jamie said, takin' me by the hand as I tended the fire. "The sheriff can spare a horse for poor Travellers, he can."

I yanked my hand away, poking so fiercely at the fire that embers flew into the sky, lighting it with little sparks that reminded me of glowworms common to Wales. Tears blurred my vision, and I swiped at my eyes with the back of my arm, feeling like a child, and Jamie the parent, though some parent he was.

"Look, Esme," he said with a sigh. "Ye know how it is, aye? We're tinkers. Where d'ya think they got the phrase 'tinker's damn'? 'Cause no one gives a tinker's damn if we live or die, if we eat or starve. Yes, we can make money from time to time doin' an honest livin'. But most of the time, we aren't given the opportunity. You may not care that my people starve, but I care, Esme."

He came around and pulled the stick from my hand.

"Look at me, Esme." He held my gaze. "I once thought like you. I was raised in a manor with servants. My *faither* was wealthy... and kind. But he was the exception. I didn't know hunger until my *faither* died and I was sent to live with my *maithir's* clan. Do ye know what it's like for your belly to be so empty it swells like a ripe watermelon—sounds like one, too. Do ye?"

He shook me. I stared down at my feet. The truth of it is, I didn't know.

"Do ye know what it's like to go to bed hungry, not knowin' where your next meal will come from... if there will *be* a next meal?"

I heard the tremble in his voice and looked up. Tears laced his lashes, the memory of it turning his face red in anguish.

"I'll not ha' my *mam* or these children goin' hungry, Esme. Even if it means stealin' the sheriff's horse, do ye hear me? Do ye?"

Again, he shook my arm. That's when I heard a rustle and Isla's words, "Jamie, let her be."

Time seemed to stand still as we all looked at each other, caught in a web of our own making. Jamie returned from whatever torment he had been reliving, a tear running down his face as he turned on his heel and tore out of the clearing behind our hut that allowed us that small bit of privacy in a large caravan.

Isla came to stand beside me and ushered me to a log Jamie had rolled beside the fire so we could sit and watch the sun go down. She took a seat beside me, then clasped my hands in hers.

"I know this is hard for you to understand, Esme, but our people have had to beg, borrow, and steal our whole lives to survive. We're the scavengers of the human world because we aren't allowed entry into society. Our lifestyle doesn't fit with those of our neighbors.

We don't stay put for long. But that's because we have been driven out of every place we go. Persecuted."

For several minutes, neither of us spoke. I wanted to understand, but I had been raised to believe stealing is wrong. More than that, I loved Jamie and was afraid for him. The fire crackled and popped, the smell of wood smoke adrift on the night air. Isla spoke softly, as if fearing that if she spoke at a normal volume I might bolt.

"When Jamie first came here, he was like you."

I tilted my head, unsure what she meant.

"He was full of ideals about how people should behave. He believed in fairness, in equality. But then he saw how our people were treated. How we often went hungry because of our identity. He watched people spit on us, call us names, as though we were the lowliest of the low, and it changed something in him, Esme. Something inside him cracked." Isla smiled, albeit a sad smile, as she recalled that day.

"What happened?" I turned to her, sensing she would have preferred to keep this secret to herself.

"We hadn't eaten in two days. He kept beggin' me to feed him, but I had nothin', nor did any of the rest of us." She closed her eyes, as though wishing away the memory, and when she opened them, her eyes were filled with tears.

"And?" I said more forcefully, holding her hands in mine.

"He...he..." Her voice cracked. "He went stormin' out of the caravan, he did. I was terrified he'd never return. He was gone for a day and a night, but when he returned, aye...ye shoulda seen him. Ridin' in on a horse, he was. Said his *faither* taught him to ride, and he was a great horseman, that one." She laughed, some of the sorrow subsiding. "And he brought wit' him not just a horse. He brought *food*. He brought a band of other Travellers he picked up on the way who joined him in lootin' one of the rich manors. That McDuff, or whate'er his name is, who lives on the west coast. That's why he has a vendetta against Jamie. Stole the laird's own horse and food from the larder, too. Got a few chickens in the lot...and eggs. He even absconded with a cow, he did, and a bull. We been eatin' ever since. That's what my Jamie did. She wiped at her eyes with her skirt. "Kept my people alive."

She didn't add he'd done it "at his own risk", but it lay between us like a two-headed sheep. And yet I could see she was as proud of him as any mother would be. He'd been the savior of his people, just as he was the villain to the villagers, leastways the rich ones. Still, I recalled his words—that there were those in the village who helped him, who would help *me* should the time come.

I knew I owed Jamie an apology, but it was hard to let go of my way of thinkin'. Finally, Isla stood.

"Whether ye know it or not, Jamie's a good man. Half the people here wouldn't be alive if not for him. Ye're a smart woman, and these are hard truths. It takes time to wrap yer head around, aye? But someday ye'll see what it's like to be a Traveller. And if ye love us the way Jamie does, ye'll understand why we do what we do."

Just then a little girl of about six raced into the clearing giggling. I swallowed down my emotions. How would I feel if she'd had to starve the way Jamie had as a child? And I knew then, I would do whatever it took to keep her alive. To help her thrive. Because love made you do things you might never have imagined, in ordinary circumstances. But the Travellers' lives weren't ordinary, and as the wife of a Traveller, mine wasn't either.

Seeing the giggling child, I tried to conjure up an image of Jamie as a *faither*, but every time I saw him with our child and heard her laughter as he tossed her into the air, I saw just as clearly his image fade. As if, even now, he knew his time was short. I only prayed I was wrong.

Chapter 37
Cobra

Until today, Frank worked around the clock, but Mia had talked him into a day at the beach. She'd been looking pale lately, but every time he asked, she said she was just overworked. With Juanita gone and Mia working full time, he had no doubt it was true.

He looked out at the Chesapeake Bay from Sandy Point State Park. It was still too early in the season to go sunbathing or swimming, and in fact the wind and cold were brutal. He zipped up his parka as he and Mia pressed into the nearly gale-force wind. They spent no more than fifteen minutes on the beach before giving it up and racing to their SUV for the eighteen-minute trip to Annapolis with its red brick and blue buildings, which acted as a beacon for their windswept souls.

They found a quiet corner in a coffee shop where they ordered hot coffee and pastries. Once it arrived, Frank said, "Okay, tell me what's really going on. I'm worried about you."

"Worried about me?" she answered with a false laugh. "What about you? Your job? Your health? You've been so wrapped up in work lately that you haven't had time to breathe."

"I've got a big case at the moment," he said, not adding that work had become nearly impossible with all the firings and layoffs.

"How are you handling it?" Mia asked, taking his hand.

Frank had never been one for close contact. His father had been strict to the extreme, and his mother distant. He supposed that's why he'd picked Mia, because she was so different. So warm and caring. It kept him grounded whenever his work life began to spin out of control, as it was now.

"Like I always do, I just keep plugging away."

"I'm not talking about that," Mia said tenderly, her brown eyes looking right through him. "I'm talking about this mess—with all the firings and the government looking through files."

"Oh, you've heard about that, eh?" He stared at his coffee as though he'd find answers there. To top it all off, he hadn't found the courage to tell Mia he'd been tracked by the people whose case he was handling. With everything going on between the firings, Juanita's expulsion from the country, and his current workload, he'd kept as much as he could to himself.

"It's all over the news," she pressed. "Friends and family keep asking me if you still have a job."

Frank lifted his head, stunned. So everybody knew what was going on at FBI headquarters? He rubbed his face with his hands. He'd survived other politically motivated attacks in past years, but he had to say, this was the worst one since he'd been at the FBI.

Politics was such a dirty business and only getting dirtier by the day. Sometimes he wondered if he shouldn't have gone into the private sector instead.

Mia paused and ran a finger around her coffee mug rim. "I've been thinking."

"Oh?" He took a sip to quell his nerves.

"What if we sold the house, packed everything up—"

"Whoa!" Frank set his coffee down and put up his hands to stop her. "Where is this coming from?"

"We could make enough of a profit to go somewhere...I don't know. Far away. Somewhere cheaper to live. Maybe we could even take some time off for us...before looking for new jobs."

Frank ran his hand through his hair. "I'm in the middle of a big case, Mia. I can't just drop it now. I would lose everything. Besides, you love this house."

"I know, but sometimes...I think this job, this life, is just eating us alive. That we'll get to the end of our lives and wonder what it was all for. I mean, you catch these guys, but the real thieves are the ones selling our country down the tubes. Who live like kings while the Juanitas of the world are treated like cattle. I'm just so tired of it, Frank."

Frank clutched his chest. How had he slept beside this woman for nearly thirty years and not known she felt like this?

"But I'm one of the good guys, Mia."

"Are you, Frank?" she asked. He heard the cry in her voice. The uncertainty. "Are you really? Or are you just an arm of an institution that keeps the rich in power and the poor poorer?"

Frank's jaw tightened. How could she say that? Everything he'd worked for, *they'd* worked for, and she was accusing him of this? It was too much. He scooted his chair back.

"I'm done," he said. "Vacation's over. I've got work to do."

"Frank, listen, I didn't mean to—"

He didn't let her finish. He quickly paid the tab and waited for her in the car as she freshened up for the ride home. It gave him precious moments to cool down. To ask himself if any part of what she'd said was true. But, in the end, he couldn't go there. Life was tough enough without laying that on him. Then why did he feel like he'd just been gut punched? Or that maybe just a tiny part of what she'd said was true?

Chapter 38
Destiny Jacqueline Kismet

As we drove through the countryside, I churned over the facts and figures Benjamin had laid out in the library over an hour ago now. The distribution of wealth between the 99% and the 1% was staggering. Neither Benjamin nor Michael would explain the relevance of those figures and what they planned to do about it, which left me in a quandary. Did I stay, assuming the men would eventually tell me, or return home and try to pick up where I'd left off and hope Cassidy and Michael would return with me? In the end, I elected to see things through until tomorrow, then I would come to a decision whether to leave or stay.

Cassidy and Benjamin planned to meet up with us later that evening. In the meantime, Michael drove me out to the St. Giles Cathedral, presumably where J.K. Rowling had found her inspiration for the Harry Potter series. Benjamin had taken the week off and planned to drive us to Kingussie in the morning, home of the MacPherson clan.

"MacPherson means son of a parson," Benjamin had said earlier in the day, when I'd asked about Jamie's heritage. "The Celtic church used to allow their priests to marry."

How times had changed.

After exiting the car, I peered up at the St. Giles' grand Gothic edifice with its many spires. The towering columns loomed over me, as though God himself looked down on me and found me lacking in some major way. I wondered if this is how Jamie had felt all those years ago? If perhaps, as an ancestor to a priest, genetics had played a role that made him more empathetic toward the downtrodden. Or maybe Jamie had simply been guilted into action to help his people. But then again, when I thought of his mother, a Gypsy, and all the stereotypes that must entail, I understood the pain. I had watched my daughter struggle through jobs that paid little—had experienced prejudice firsthand myself. Had heard the whispered complaints against women. *They can't become president. They're too emotional. What if they had their hand on the nuclear button?* I wondered what people thought of us now. A woman would have been a far superior choice to a man without compassion.

Michael grasped my hand, and together we walked the path to the cathedral. Once inside, my eyes flew up to the blue vaulted ceiling, to the stained glass windows that allowed light to filter in through a prism of color, sending shafts of it streaming all around us in motes of crimson and gold. St. Giles, I'd been told, was the official chapel for the Knights of the Order of the Thistle, the helmets and coats of armor displayed in all their glory.

"Why did you bring me here?" I asked Michael.

"I don't know," he said.

But I could see something warring in his eyes. Had he come here to seek absolution? But absolution for what? I couldn't help but think this had something to do with his relationship with Benjamin. But what, exactly, did that entail? I knew no more than when Michael first arrived on Scottish soil. Normally, I had understood the nature of his work, but this felt different somehow. More personal.

"Michael, you have to tell me what's going on." I pulled him toward a pew and sat. He did likewise. "This isn't about your work, is it?"

Michael breathed in a sigh. "No," he finally admitted.

"Then why can't you talk to me?"

He clamped his jaw together as if to give himself time to think before speaking. A loud clatter from the back of the room made me turn to discover what had caused it. For one brief second, I could swear I had seen Esme, her dark eyes piercing me with an expression I couldn't quite read. My heart trembled to know she was watching our interchange, but I forced my attention back to Michael. I wanted...no I *needed* an explanation.

"Because," he said, peering down at his splayed hands, "I'm afraid you'll talk me out of it."

"Talk you out of what, Michael? You're making no sense."

His blue eyes flashed with pain. "You wouldn't understand."

"Understand what?"

"You always believe in right and wrong, but some wrongs are more right than the original wrong, don't you see?"

"No, I don't see," I growled, exasperated by this circular line of reasoning. We were getting nowhere.

"That's just it. If I tell you, you'll make me change my mind, and I can't. Too many lives are at stake. Too much happiness is at stake. Yours and mine," he said through gritted teeth, his eyes rimmed with tears...tears Michael would never shed.

He'd always been the strong one, the one with the broad shoulders, but I realized now I must be the one with the broad shoulders. I must be the rock.

"Look, Michael, if you've done something wrong, we can fix it."

"I haven't...yet."

"What do you mean, yet?" I hissed, frustration spreading like a wildfire.

"I have a plan. But neither you nor Cassidy can know about it. Promise me you'll trust me," he whispered.

Just then a group of people approached us, nodding as they passed. I plastered a smile on my face that quickly fell the moment they moved on.

"Listen," Michael said, placing a hand on my shoulder. "Benjamin and I...we know how to fix the problem."

"What problem?" I dug my fingernails into the palms of my hands, not caring that it hurt, rather relishing the fact I could feel something other than the pain of his words.

"The problem with this." He threw up his hands as if to encompass the world. "This fever that's taken hold."

"You mean in our country?"

I looked up at a carving of an angel playing bagpipes. But instead of bagpipes, I saw Jamie and his fiddle. Saw his sardonic smile in the face of the angel. Had he witnessed a similar fever, too, back then? In his time? Had it always been like this, where one man and his followers could turn a world on its axis for good *or* for evil? Where the rich lorded their wealth and status over the poor, and people accepted it, believing that somehow they would be exempt from the fervor? I tugged at my hair, wishing I understood what Michael was trying *not* to tell me. The footsteps of tourists echoed down the center aisle, a tribute to the thousands upon thousands who had gone before them and would soon follow.

Was Michael like Jamie... like Benjamin? A Don Quixote tilting at windmills? But with Don Quixote the enemy had been imaginary. These were no imaginary enemies. They were way too real. And I feared we'd all end up like Jamie, hanging from the gallows, whether metaphorically or for real.

I leaned in and hugged Michael, wishing I could stop the progression of events, but just as with Esme, life has a way of moving at its own pace, and I could no more stop our future than I could halt the progress of time. Life would go on, with or without me.

Chapter 39
Esme Stalwart

I found Jamie by the riverside, brushing down his horse. He murmured to her in gentle tones, telling her his woes. From inside the copse, I watched and listened, my heart aching to be the one he told his troubles to, but lately he had gone silent, worried I might chastise him for his actions.

I waited until he had tired of speaking so intimately to his horse before stepping out into the clearing. His horse greeted me with a nicker and a nod of her head. Jamie turned, his cheeks flushing at the sight of me.

"How long ha' ye been standin' there, aye?"

"Long enough," I said.

"So ye heard what I was sayin' then, eh, lass?"

"I did."

He'd asked the horse to understand what he did, he did for his people, for his family. For me. But unlike me, the horse had listened intently, had never interrupted, and had accepted him for who he was—the leader of his people, a husband who looked after his wife and family...and a thief. Why could I not get past that last part?

"I'm only stealin' from those who rob from us first, by takin' our labor and toil and given' us so little in return. That's a form of robbery, too, is it not?" he'd told the horse. The mare had nodded, as though even an animal could understand such a simple concept as this. "These self-proclaimed demi-gods take our land, our homes, the very food out of the mouths of our babes and care not a whit of our suffering."

My mind reeled back to what Isla had said. How the Travellers had been starving and displaced at the whims of their masters. I'd heard whispers among the Travellers about how many of them went unpaid for the work they did as tinkers. The laird would commission their work only to turn them in before they could be paid. It was a ploy used throughout the centuries to keep a few men wealthy and the others poor. Jamie was right. He'd been given no choice but to save his people from starvation.

Then why does it sit so poorly with me?

The inconsistency of the way I'd been raised versus the reality of life warred within me, and I couldn't seem to quiet my shattered soul by all I'd witnessed. The stream burbled, a balm to what ailed me. I walked over to Jamie and leaned against him, savoring the sweetness of his scent.

"What will we do?" I peered up at him and read the tenderness in his eyes.

"We do what we've always done, *mo chridhe.*"

My heart. I shivered at the term of endearment.

"We survive. It's what the underclass has always done. Some men hitch their wagon to the rich and think themselves better for it. But there's a price, in the end. There always is. Whether it's one's dignity, one's family, or what a person's forced to do in order to maintain their grip on the silk strand that attaches them to the purse."

He held me to him. Already, I could feel that same silken cord slipping from me...the one that kept me tied to Jamie. He leaned down to kiss me, his mouth moist and supple. I wanted him then, as I had wanted no other. He must have sensed it, too, because he pulled me into the grass clearing and nestled me into the womb of the natural enclosure, his kisses more passionate now, as if I were dinner and dessert, all in one. And I wanted it, too, this memory I knew must sustain me through dark times in the future. For us to be one, a single entity, so I would be forever his, and he forever mine. Our bodies wove a rhythm older than time. A tempo that spoke of love and lust and beauty. Of everything passing and fragile, the bloom of the flower, too soon gone.

For what seemed like an eternity, we tested each other's love with our lips, our bodies, and when we were through, we lay side by side, me nestled in the crook of his arm, staring up into the sky. Above us, a hawk screeched as if in warning. As if to remind us our moment of peace and ecstasy was over, that now it was time to ride on, as Travellers must, for we had no home, no welcome place to land, to test our feet. To run unbidden through the water with our toes bare. No, this land was not ours. It belonged to but a few lairds of the manor, of whom Jamie's *faither* had been one. But even they weren't immune to the vagaries of time and fate.

Destiny.

My mind came into focus at the memory of her name. In this life, she was Isla. "What does the name Isla mean?" I asked on a whim.

Jamie laughed and hugged me to him, his head against my chest. "Does your mind never stop whirrin', woman? We just made love."

"I know, but—"

"I know, but—" he mimicked in a falsetto to make me giggle. "I know, but what? You ask about my *mathair* now, of all times?"

It did sound odd when he put it that way.

He gave a deep, purposeful sigh as if to remind me what a challenge I was to raise, but because of his good nature, he said, "Her name means 'geography'."

I pulled my clothes to me and sat up as I dressed. "Geography? What an odd name for a woman."

He shrugged. "Not if you're a Traveller. After all, what are we, if not our geography?"

I had to laugh. He had me at that, for they were always on the move, never settling in one place as other Romanis might.

He stood up and slipped on his pants, his bare chest soaking up the afternoon sun. I ran my hands across it, reveling in the feel of his dark skin under my fingers.

"Sing me a song," I said, as we gathered our things and he loaded me onto the horse. Then he came to sit behind me. He flicked the reins, and as he did, it was as if he were the conductor and musician all in one.

In a tenor that matched the spirit of the water, he sang Flow Gently Sweet Afton, but when it came to the woman's name, he substituted Esme for Mary. I nestled in the cove of his love, as together we returned to yet more tumult, more flight, because although the river might flow gently, our lives did not. I had hitched my wagon to a people whose very right to exist was in question. And someday, my child and I would be among them.

Chapter 40
Destiny Jacqueline Kismet

After we left the cathedral, we drove northward to Arthur's Seat. As we gazed out at the rolling hills, my heart began to race, and my mind splashed to another time. It was as if I could see myself in a wagon, and when I looked down, I saw a Gypsy dress...*my* dress. *Isla's* dress. I let out a cry of fright, and Michael pulled the car to the side of the road as a truck whipped past us, unfurling a blanket of wind that shook our car.

"What is it? What's wrong?" he asked.

I looked into his eyes, yet I saw not Michael, but the man who had stolen my heart all those years ago, Laird MacPherson. Michael faded away as I stepped out of the car only to see my mirror image, Isla. The road fell away, too, replaced instead by the ruts of wagon wheels.

She took my hand. "I brought ye here. 'Tis time ye know the truth of it."

My skin prickled as I recognized my counterpart from the late 1600s. She was stunningly beautiful. Never before had I felt so dowdy and out of place, though she stood out among the other Travellers as well.

"I met Laird MacPherson at a dance, did ye know? A wedding it 'twas. He saw me, and that was the end of it...for me *and* for him. Nine months later as the midwife delivered my precious Jamie, the laird stood beside me, and took my wee bairn to live with him, though it wasn't custom at the time for him to do so."

My body trembled, because I *did* remember. Remembered Jamie's cry, the proud moment the laird saw his son. The moment when he cradled him in his arms, followed by a brief squeeze of my hand. Then he was gone, my bairn tucked inside the crook of his elbow.

I burst out crying at the memory. It was 1675, Banff, Scotland, in Aberdeenshire. I recalled the torment afterwards, the longing to have my child back. The empty years of Travelling, always wondering where my precious boy was now, what he was doing. On the rare occasion when we were in the area, I would go to Invereshie House and watch from a distance, prayin' the laird wouldn't see me and shoo me away. Once I had the chance to wave at wee Jamie, and he waved back, that sweet little boy with a thick head o' brown hair with red highlights. It melted my heart at the sight, but too soon the governess would spot me, and I would slink into the shadows, disappearing just as I had appeared, from thin air.

"He was a lovely boy, were he not?" Isla said, placing a protective arm around my shoulders as she walked me through her memories. *My* memories.

I could only nod, tears spilling onto my cheeks to see my boy but not be able to be there for him, to comfort him when he fell ill or was hurt. A nanny would take my place. The pain of it fluttered in my stomach even as my throat felt raw.

"Why? Why could I not keep him?" I searched her eyes but saw only her torment reflected back at me, for she, too, had suffered loss. I fell to the ground, the bitter emotion tearing from my throat as I cried out in supplication.

She knelt before me. "It's okay, *mo chridh*. He came back to us. Our Jamie came back to us."

I sobbed, wanting to believe her. Then I saw him—my child, only a young man now. And he was playing the fiddle...playing it just for me, his *maither*. The tears slowly subsided as I crouched on my knees, a smile replacing the earlier tears. He was back. *My Jamie is back!* I wanted to scream, to shout to the heavens the joy I felt to finally have that missing piece of me returned, whole and unharmed. But like everything good in life, it didn't last.

Isla leaned into me. "This is enough for now. 'Tis time you returned to your own family. But remember this," she said, peering up at the now fading image of Jamie, our son. "The end is near for him in our time. But in your time...you have a chance to save him, because you are both his *mathair*, and Esme's *mathair*...or at least the reincarnation of her, aye? Don't forget," she said, beginning to stand, her voice ebbing in and out even as her image grew faint.

"Only you can save them in this next life. We are counting on you...Jamie, Esme, and I."

I let out a cry. That's when I realized Michael was on his knees, shaking me, his troubled blue eyes meeting mine.

"What happened to you out here?" he demanded, bending down to take me into his arms.

I blinked rapidly, and although my mouth moved, no words came out.

Michael lifted me to my feet and helped me into the car, then got in on the other side. "Let's get you to the hotel," he urged. "Maybe you took in too much sun."

But as we drove south, the sun seemed tepid at best. This was no sunstroke. I had met myself in another time. I had met Isla, her message clear. I must save Benjamin and Cassidy. Myself and Michael, too, if my hunch was correct. But save them from what? As long as they kept me in the dark, I had no chance of saving anyone, least of all myself.

Chapter 41
Cobra

"Take a look at this," Trevor said, setting his laptop on Frank's desk.

Trevor was lean and clean-shaven, like most of those at the FBI. The only difference was he wore an earring and had a tattoo that was barely visible above his collar line.

"What am I looking at?" Frank asked.

But before Trevor could answer, Frank's eyes scrolled down from the original comment to the many responses that followed. He blew out a breath when he came to the end and cradled his neck with his entwined fingers to ease the dull ache caused by sitting in front of a computer screen for too long.

"Wow!"

He thought he'd seen it all, and maybe he had, but the vitriol shocked even him, more so because he had voted for this clown along with people just like this. He'd always voted for big business and conservative values, family values, but these weren't values he adhered to. The original comment had been from a woman who lamented the starving children in Gaza and the concentration-like camp, specifically to house immigrants, illegal or otherwise. To Frank's surprise, one young man boasted that this was exactly what he'd voted for. He'd followed it up with "if they want to eat, they should get sticks and hunt like the rest of their kind." And what followed only got worse. One poor woman was told to do unspeakable things that made even him blush. Racism and misogyny were running rampant now, endangering everyone.

Frank had seen the news—the baby's spine laid bare from lack of food. The infant died shortly after the picture had been taken. He saw his own kids in the eyes of young children whose ribcages engulfed a skeletal frame. Whose eyes told of torture and anguish. How could anyone witness that and not be moved? He would rather die than see any of his children put through that, and yet an entire group of people, young to old, had no sympathy for their plight. None. Instead, they made fun of the suffering. The loss. He'd been on edge for the past few days, ever since Mia had accused him of not caring. And now this. He slammed the laptop shut.

"I know, right?" Trevor said. "It gets worse by the day. It's hard to believe… Never mind." He didn't finish his sentence. Instead, he grabbed his laptop and tucked it under his arm. "Hang in there," he said as he was leaving.

But before the door could shut, his secretary, Shannon, entered with a memo. The report detailed changes taking place within the bureau, adjustments that could stifle their ability to investigate certain things properly, like the Epstein case, for one. Now twelve lawsuits had been filed by the young women involved, claiming the FBI hadn't acted on evidence of the man's abuse. It sent a chill through him to know that maybe Mia was right. The FBI were supposed to be the good guys. When had that changed? But he could mark the day.

Shannon was about to leave when he stopped her. "Shannon?"

"Yes?" she said with a deep sigh.

"I'm sorry if I've been such a grouch lately. It's just—"

"I understand," she said. "I go home every night and take a hot soak with a glass of wine, and I don't even drink." She let out a self-deprecating laugh.

"At any rate, I didn't mean to make things worse. We're all under a lot of pressure these days."

"Tell me about it." Then she was gone.

He sat back and turned his swivel chair to view the skyline. He'd been doing a lot of that these days, even though his view sucked. Still, it was better than facing all the mounting pressure from those in charge. Each day he returned to work, he looked to see whose desks had been cleared. For the most part, it was the new hires, men and women who had been given accolades for their job performance one month, only to be turned around and fired for poor job performance the next. It didn't add up. Nothing did.

At least give them unemployment while they search for other jobs, for God's sake.

Finally, he could stand it no more. He grabbed his jacket off the back of his chair and slung it over his shoulder. Though he couldn't yet admit to Mia she was right, he wasn't opposed to getting away for a while to have space to think.

He left his office and headed for the elevator. He entered, then pressed the down button just as one of the other agents squeezed in.

"I hear Joanna was fired today," she whispered to someone next to him.

"Joanna? But she's a single mom with three kids. What's she supposed to do with no income?"

"Beats me," the other woman said. But their faces said it all.

Yep, he definitely needed to get out of Dodge for a while. Maybe it was time to take that plane and pay a visit to Scotland Yard. He pressed the button for the next floor, relieved when it opened. He would take the stairs up to his office, then get Shannon on the phone with the airlines. He needed time away, and Scotland Yard would make for a nice diversion. Then, when he had his head on straight, he would talk to Mia. Maybe they could pull up stakes and move.

Or maybe not.

Chapter 42
Esme Stalwart

We fled into the wilderness, putting as much distance as possible between us and the sheriff. Until Jamie sold the animals he'd stolen, none of us would be safe. Fortunately, he had a buyer in the south, but that meant bypassing Banff and the sheriff and his ne'er-do-well companion, William Duff, who had it out for Jamie. As such, we'd been forced into the forests and copses or into hidden valleys that only Jamie and a few others knew. These locations had served them well, as they did now, and yet danger lurked like an aura around us, so much so that even the birds had gone silent. As if they knew we were being hunted.

Isla slid up beside me on the sheriff's horse she'd borrowed from Jamie. "I saw her."

"Saw who?" I asked, intrigued by the almost frightful expression in her wild brown eyes.

"The woman."

My blood curdled at the way she said it, as though she were a wraith, not a human. So who was this woman who had frightened her so? I rested my hand on the pommel of my saddle, awaiting her explanation, but when it wasn't forthcoming, I repeated, "What woman?"

She peered around her, even now, as though every tree held a watchful eye. I rubbed my chest of the pain that had settled there because I knew whatever she said in the next few moments would change my life.

"The one from the future. A *fetch*. The reincarnation of me."

I blew out a breath of air, my hands trembling because I'd known what she would say before she said it.

"Aye, and I have seen a *fetch*, as well—a reincarnation of me...and Benjamin."

Her eyes grew wide as saucers, and her chest swelled with fear. She reached out a hand, and a current of energy passed between us, shocking me with its strength.

"I canna save Jamie here and now," Isla said, "but I ha' asked my future self to save ye and Jamie."

So she knew—we were doomed, Jamie and I. "*Tapadh leat*, and I ha' done the same."

We rode on in silence, only the clop of our horses' hooves to break the monotony of our retreat into the wilderness and beyond. Jamie seemed to instinctively know when people were close at hand and would steer us away just in time. He possessed an animal-like instinct of danger that showed in his eyes and the perking of his ears. His eyes gazed in the distance, not at what lay before him, perhaps a gift of the second sight, that all-knowing third eye allowing him to see what the rest of us could not. As we continued on, he folded his hands around his pursed lips and made a bird call that signaled danger and another foretelling the direction we should take to avoid a nasty encounter with a people who believed we had no right to exist.

I opined on my cozy home set out along the hillside. It had been nearly a fortnight since I'd last seen it. Though I had asked my neighbors to keep an eye on it, I wondered how long they would continue to look after it before finding it too much of a chore. I longed for it now, the safety and security it represented. But had I ever truly been safe? Not as long as a man like William Duff stood ready to claim it, as he had so many others he saw fit to seize. He could say that as the wife of Jamie MacPherson, any debts owed due to Jamie's thievery were mine as well, and therefore, all I owned would be forfeited. My blood ran cold at the thought.

We traveled on in silence, but the quiet was stifling. Its oppressive weight pressed against my bones. Finally, I could no longer stand it. I dug my heels into the horse's side and galloped forward, but no sooner had I done so than Jamie fell back and grabbed my reins in passing, nearly upending me. He didn't speak, but the set of his mouth and the sharp glare said it all. I had done the unthinkable. I had put them all in danger by the noise I'd made. He released another bird call, and this time he led us into a narrow ravine, its geography either our salvation or our undoing, depending upon whether we'd managed to escape a trap or had fallen into one. We wouldn't know until we made it to the other side.

No one breathed until nearly a half hour later, when we rode up out of the ravine and everyone sighed with relief, and still we could not halt. Not until we'd put miles and miles between us and the sheriff and his men.

We didn't rest until well into nightfall. We ate our food cold that night, fearing a fire might give us away. Again, Isla came up beside me, a plate of food in her hands. The moon was riding high in the sky, and the night owls hooted a warning, but we were safe, for now.

"So," she began. "When are you going to tell Jamie?"

"Tell Jamie what?" I said, then tore at the cold chicken, my stomach so empty that hunger clawed at my ribs.

"That you are with child...Jamie's child."

My throat felt parched suddenly, so much so that I found it hard to swallow. "What do you mean?"

"Don't pretend you don't know." She laughed, a burbling sound that brought with it a rush of joy. "Aye, ye're more like us than you care to admit, Esme Stalwart. It's in our blood to know things."

I peered down at my dress and rested a hand on my stomach. It was true. I had been gifted with the second sight, but how could she possibly know I was with child? How could anyone know so early on? Yet, in my heart of hearts, I knew she had the second sight like me, and that inside me lay the seed that would one day germinate so no matter what happened to Jamie or I, there would always be one left behind, one who carried our name, our memory. Our love.

Chapter 43
Destiny Jacqueline Kismet

For the rest of that evening, and into the morning, Michael treated me as though I was fragile, and I suppose I was because I had experienced something no sane person should experience. Myself, in another lifetime.

I quickly showered and dressed, then Michael and I met Benjamin and Cassidy down at the restaurant on the first floor of the luxurious Scotsman Hotel. They were seated beside marble pillars, which rose to meet the vaulted ceilings, almost forcing one to look skyward.

Cassidy wore jeans and a green dress jacket, her cascading blonde hair in ringlets. Benjamin had his arm around her. For a moment, I couldn't breathe as I stared at them. Their faces flickered and sparked as the images of Jamie and Esme slid into place, two ghost-like wraiths inhabiting their bodies. The stunning realization they were indeed one and the same, set my stomach whirling.

"Do you want breakfast before we go to Kingussie?"

"I already had something back in my room," I lied, though a little white one because I did have coffee and a scone, if that counted for breakfast.

"Okay, then." Benjamin leaned over and gave Cassidy a brief kiss on the mouth.

That small, intimate gesture set my nerves tingling. Isla was right. I had only to look at the pair to know they were in love. Now, the only recourse left was to save them, but save them from what? I had the barest of ideas that it related to Benjamin's research on poverty in America and his theft of small amounts of money he gave to the poor. But why was he so keen on poverty there, since it wasn't his birthplace?

It's Cassidy's birthplace, you fool, a little voice in my head said.

But how had he known about Cassidy—that she was the reincarnation of Esme? Had Benjamin and Esme decided jointly to contact us through the geocaching site? Had he invested so much time and interest in Cassidy's well-being and the welfare of her people because he knew Cassidy was the reincarnation of Esme?

I could almost hear Isla say, "That's how Jamie were born, aye? To take care of his clan."

And now it was up to Benjamin.

For the next two hours and some, we drove the road north into the Scottish Highlands. Before I glimpsed it, I knew a castle sat atop the hill just south of where we were headed. It filled me with a presentiment that turned me to jelly. But when I saw it, something was wrong.

"What's the name of that castle?" I asked.

"It's actually Ruthven's Barracks, placed there by King George the First's government following the Jacobite uprising in 1715. But before that, it was the Inverlochy Castle built by the 'Red' Comyns, lords of Badenoch and Lochaber."

"Ah!"

That was the name I recalled, or should I say Isla recalled, but I didn't dare speak it aloud, or Michael would have me committed. And yet, if my estimation was correct, Michael was the reincarnation of the elder MacPherson, the one Isla had fallen in love with and lost both her child and heart to. Did he remember nothing? I gave him a sideways glance, and whether I was simply imagining it or not, he seemed edgy. Whenever Michael struggled with something, he pinched his fingers together and rubbed them back and forth, as if to soothe himself. He was doing it now.

I rolled down the window, the smell of the countryside taking me back to the time when the elder MacPherson had told me about Kingussie, his family homeland. I welcomed the breeze that flowed over me, stirring up memories.

"The founding member of Clan MacPherson was believed to be a priest named Muireach Cattenach. Mac Phearsain means son of a parson. Cluny Castle is the historic seat of the clan."

And though I heard Benjamin's words, another set of remarks mirrored them, that of Jamie's father. As Isla, I had cherished those moments together with the laird. How was I to know they were simply words meant to make me feel as though I mattered? As though Isla mattered. For a young Traveller, who had witnessed so much prejudice, he had made her feel like she belonged. If only I'd known then it was his way of setting the young Isla at ease.

I tasted the bitterness at the back of my throat even as tears stung my eyes, but I couldn't afford to shed them. Not without revealing too much to the man beside me. Michael. And I'd already revealed way too much when he'd seen me revert back in time. As if he shared my fears, Michael grabbed my hand and held it tight. Was he recalling what had happened earlier, when we'd stopped at a local store for drinks and snacks? The clerk had been watching a television set. On it were Americans out in force all over the country, determined to resist the changes taking place in what was quickly becoming a dictatorship. I'd stood, riveted, wondering where all this would lead and thankful we were miles away.

"These tariffs are somethin'," the clerk said, shaking his head. "Never thought I'd see the day. Your president has a business here, he does. Many of us old-timers used to like 'im. Some still do, but after this...no." He shook his head sadly.

I was glad to see that at least some people had awakened to the truth. As I watched, I felt guilty for not being there, for not resisting as many of my compatriots had, but when we returned to the car, Michael gave a cryptic response that had me wondering how much he knew about our shared past, the laird's and mine...Isla's.

"There are other ways to resist, Des. Ways that are more powerful than what they were doing by picketing the administration."

I asked for an explanation, but he merely shrugged and looked out the window. However, I saw Benjamin peer through his rearview mirror and witnessed a shared glance between the pair, a knowing one. The two were planning something. I could feel it in my bones. And whatever the game plan, it would have far-reaching implications. Consequences that would keep us all caught in a web of deceit that could either be our undoing or our salvation.

Chapter 44
Esme Stalwart

As the days wore on, I wondered if I would ever see my home again. We had traveled far north into the Highlands, further and further away from our home. The hills here bore little vegetation from which to hide should we need to, the isolation deafening. Even the birds were few and far between. As I listened to the lapping of the bay against the shore, I wished for a boat to take us to an island all our own where we could live in peace. But winters in the Highlands were bitterly cold. Crops wouldn't grow, and even sheep had little to eat. I knew we could never sustain such a primitive lifestyle and that Jamie and his band would soon turn to thievery in this barren outpost, but for now, we were safe and alone.

We spent the next few days repairing wheels and stitching up clothing that had ripped during the long journey. We washed our linen by the seashore, the kittiwakes circling above us and calling out in a high-pitched cree. The reprieve lent a brief cheerfulness to our group of Travellers, and, for the first time in weeks, we relaxed, but we knew the respite was only temporary. In a few days' time, we would head back to the southwest coast to avoid any run-in with those from Banff, where our nemesis lived.

I looked down at my dress as I had before and felt my belly. Though still not swollen, my monthly time had failed to arrive again, and it filled me with equal parts joy and dread. I had yet to tell Jamie, but I must before he left. And though I knew he would welcome a son or daughter, I also feared it might make him more daring in his attempt to provide for the child. I finished washing the clothing and then hung it on a line between two caravans, our neighbor doing likewise. That's when I spotted Jamie in the distance descending the hillside where he'd gone to scout out our next move. I met him halfway through the meadow, preferring to be alone with him. When I caught up with him, he scooped me into his arms.

"Where ha' ye been, true love 'o mine?"

How is it that Jamie could always make me feel wanted, loved? I threw my arm around his waist as he reached down to kiss me, his hands cupping my chin as though it were precious. As though *I* were precious. Like a Firecrest, my heart fluttered inside my chest. When I came up for air, he smiled down at me.

"Okay, what is it, lass? What ha' ye come to tell me?"

It was unnerving how he could read me, and not for the first time I wondered if his mother was right. If Isla's clan had the second sight, as I had.

"I ha' some news, Jamie," I said, feeling suddenly shy.

"Out wit' it then. Dinna leave me in suspense."

My face warmed, and I placed my hands on my cheeks to hide my embarrassment. "I am wit' child, Jamie...yours and mine."

We had continued walking when he paused, tilted his head, then his eyes lit up, and he let out a whoop of delight. He picked me up and whirled me so that my head grew muddled and my stomach took flight. When he saw how piqued I had become by the sudden movement, he fussed over me, apologizing again and again.

"No worries," I said, holding up a hand to give myself time to breathe and for my stomach to settle. "I'm just a bit nauseous these days."

"Aye, I'll be more careful in the future."

Then, as if the importance of the occasion had just dawned on him, he grasped my hand and nearly dragged me down the mountain. Many in the caravan had seen us coming, me stumbling and tripping most of the way down, until finally almost the entire group had come out to see what all the commotion was about.

"Gather 'round!" Jamie called, cupping the air with his hands. "We ha' good news."

"What is it?" Isla asked as she dried her hands on a nearby towel. But then she saw Jamie's grin, and she smiled over at me and winked.

"I'm to ha' a son!" Jamie cried.

I nudged him.

"I mean *we* are to ha' a son."

I nudged him again.

"Or a daughter," he amended, his face as red as the wild rowan berries.

Those of the caravan laughed, and finding any reason for celebration, the fiddles and accordions soon came out, along with a *clàrsach*, the Scottish harp. Soon we were dancing in circles, Jamie and I, and everyone joined in until finally, to the shouts and prods of the other members of his band, Jamie picked up the fiddle and rosined up the flax strings of the bow. Then he did a jig as his bowstring flew over the fiddle, lighting up the late afternoon air with a magic that went well into the evening. Finally, at midnight, as the moon rose high into the sky and the eerie wolf howls called across the meadow to unseen mates, one by one we wandered off to bed until only Jamie and I were left standing. Now, alone in the moonlight, he confessed his love for me and our baby.

"If anythin' should ever happen to me," he said, making my heart ache, "promise me ye'll tell her that her *faither* loved her, aye? Tha' he woulda been here if he could. Ye'll tell her tha', will ye?"

"I'll tell her," I said even as I choked on the words. Because my dear, sweet Jamie already had one foot out the door. I knew that now. Knew he, like his *mam*, had the gift of sight and that my baby would be a girl. And she would never see her *faither* grow old, just as I would never have him by my side to raise her.

I peered into his eyes, the moon a halo around his head. "I love ye, Jamie MacPherson."

"And I love ye, Esme Stalwart."

And with that, we held on tight, each awash in our pain, wishing we could stay together forever. But morning always comes. *Always.*

Chapter 45
Cobra

Although Frank still had yet to apologize or to tell Mia he was at least beginning to see her point, though he hated to admit it, they had formed an uneasy truce so that by Saturday morning, he broke the news to her. He found Mia lying on the reclining loveseat in the sunroom amid planted palms and a Norfolk Island Pine, where he'd found her reading a beach novel. He joined her on the cushions, where they had a view of the garden. The tulips were beginning to bloom in rich reds, yellows, and pinks. Above them was a fan that reminded him of a plane's propeller. All around him were Mia's special touches. She'd had a designer's instinct for color and style, and he had been the beneficiary, allowing him to feel calm on those rare days he got to spend at home.

He decided to broach the subject carefully. But first, he needed to know they were okay. Tenderly, he kissed the top of her head.

"Have you heard from the kids lately?" he asked.

Both of the twenty-somethings texted Mia on an almost daily basis, coming to him when they had a problem only he could handle, usually something to do with carpentry or plumbing.

"Jen's getting ready for her finals, and Jacob's applying for a summer job at a camp in upstate New York."

Frank hadn't seen the kids in weeks and suddenly felt homesick to have them all under one roof for a day. With everything going on lately, he wanted to keep them safe, hold them a little tighter.

"Why don't we plan a get-together?" he said, hoping that would lighten the load a little before he laid the news on her.

"When?" she asked.

"How about before I go to Scotland Yard?"

"Scotland Yard? In the UK?" she said, sitting up so she could get a better look at him.

Frank tensed, certain this wasn't the time, and yet he needed to delve deeper into his investigation, and before Joe left, he'd urged him to come to Scotland Yard.

"I'll only be gone a week, two at most."

To his surprise, she merely nodded. "But, Frank, while you're gone, think about what I said. I'm still considering quitting my job."

Frank's chest heaved. He hadn't even thought to ask her how things were going with her. She'd been teaching at the third-grade level for a dozen or more years now and had seen administrations come and go. Had seen funding cut. Had been forced to buy supplies the school district would no longer cover. When it came right down to it, by the time she paid taxes and supplies, she wasn't earning much. Plus the internal feuds between left and right had left most of the teachers reeling as administrators were forced out because they were either too liberal or too conservative, depending on the latest wave of politics. Anymore, almost everything was politicized.

"Are you okay, Mia?"

She pursed her lips. "We'll talk about it when you get back. When do you leave?"

"In three days," Frank said. "I have a lot to cover before I leave, but I'll try to take a day off before I go. Maybe we can see the kids then."

Mia stood. "Okay, I'll text the kids and see if we can't have a barbeque before you leave, but Frank."

"Yeah?"

"When you get back, there need to be changes, okay?"

He paused, uncertain what she meant. Was she talking about moving again? Because if she was, that wasn't going to happen. Not if he could help it. He loved this house.

"Okay," he said, unwilling to commit. "We'll talk then."

Chapter 46
Destiny Jacqueline Kismet

As we drove around Kingussie, Michael became more and more excited. "There!" he cried. "And there!"

Displayed in a shop window in the center of town was the MacPherson clan plaid, a bold red mixed with deep blue, black, and gold threads. A thin white pinstripe ran through it.

"Touch not the cat, but the glove," Michael said with a throaty laugh in a surprisingly good imitation of the Scottish brogue. Benjamin laughed with him.

"Where did you learn to talk like that, Dad?" Cassidy asked.

She'd worn just the barest of perfumes, and her face held the first bloom of love in the offing. When she wasn't looking, I saw Benjamin glance over at her, appraising her and liking what he saw.

"You pick up a thing or two when you travel," Michael said.

When has Michael ever traveled to Scotland?

But then again, what did I know of his travels? What did I know of him at all? I had always just accepted his work and need for secrecy. Now I wondered if I had taken too much for granted, accepted without question. Just as Isla had accepted what the laird had told her, believing he loved her and would buck the system to be with her. She was wrong, just as I had been wrong not to ask more questions.

"This entire area was believed to be founded by the Picts prior to the 9th Century," Benjamin said, pointing to what he described as the Kingussie Stone, a Celtic burial stone.

The Picts were covered in indigo woad and had come and gone without explanation, their genetics passed down to the modern-day Scot. Cassidy brushed back her hair to reveal a recent tattoo I had yet to see.

"Where did you get the design on your neck?" Even I heard the accusation in my voice, as if I had any say over my grown-up daughter or her body. I flushed at the realization.

"This?" She fingered the tattoo gently. "I got it after I was fired."

I lifted an eyebrow. "Oh?"

"Yeah, it's The Shield of Destiny. It protects against evil spirits...against danger."

"Particularly on battlefields, or around sick people," Benjamin added.

I couldn't very well complain. After all, it had my name in it, and, come to think of it, hadn't Isla asked me to protect Benjamin and Cassidy? To help get them through whatever danger they might face so they didn't end up on the...? I breathed a sigh of fear and frustration, knowing Benjamin's ancestor had ended up on the gallows. But what had become of Esme? Had she died an untimely death as well, or had she gone on to live a full life filled with love and laughter?

To relieve the overwhelming feeling of helplessness, I once again took in the city's monolithic buildings. We continued on into the countryside, where eventually we came to a large manor, the Balavir Estate, once owned by Allan MacPherson-Fletcher, according to Benjamin.

"It was sold in 2015 for the equivalent of 5.25 million US dollars."

Michael whistled, his fascination with everything MacPherson intriguing me.

"The home was designed by Robert Adam in the Edwardian-Adam revival style," Benjamin explained. "James Macpherson bought it after he made his money in the East India Company. It overlooks the Spey Valley and is said to have a resident ghost, a young woman named Sarah who was spurned by the butler and threw herself off a bridge into the Raitts Burn. But apparently she's a good ghost to have around because she folds clothing, starts a fire in the morning, and makes coffee for the home's inhabitants."

Michael laughed at the incongruity of it all, while I stared up at the gray and white mansion set in the middle of a forested glen.

"The series *Monarch of the Glen* was set here," Benjamin said.

We'd been so busy taking in the sights that I hadn't noticed a car pull up until suddenly I heard a dull roar from a black Austin Sheerline. It reminded me of one from a British horror film, *The Man in the Back Seat*, I'd seen on one of those off channels."

"Uh-oh!" Benjamin said.

Michael tensed behind me and hissed, "Put it in gear! Now!"

Benjamin didn't hesitate. He swiveled the car around with surprising ease and took off in the opposite direction, but my heart stalled in my chest as I saw a man with a gun pointed our way.

"Get down!" Michael yelled.

Before I could react, Michael shoved my head down and did likewise with Cassidy, but not before I heard the gun go off. Pop. Pop. Pop.

"Who are they?" I asked, but no one answered. Yet, I knew by Benjamin and Michael's responses that this was no game.

I heard the tires squeal as Benjamin took corner after corner, dodging this way and that. I had so many questions, but there was no time for that as my heart pressed against the cage of my chest, and the car took off at a surprisingly quick speed that in no way matched the style of the car.

The car has a racer's engine. Why?

They had planned for this, Michael and Benjamin. My mind reeled at the implications. We were being hunted, but why and by whom?

At last, the car flew up an incline and abruptly turned onto a dirt road. After several minutes of battling the washboard road, Michael finally said, "All clear. You can sit up now."

I turned to Michael, but before I could demand answers, Cassidy spoke up, her voice trembling. "What's going on here, Benjamin? Dad?"

Neither of the two men spoke.

"Well, someone had better speak up," I said, my voice just as strained as Cassidy's. "Why were those men chasing us...with guns?"

The two men looked at each other. "I think we need to explain, but not here," Michael said. "We can't go back to the hotel, either. We need somewhere else to stay."

"I know just the place," Benjamin said, "but we'll have to take the back roads."

After everything that had happened, I was all for taking back roads, and I knew Cassidy was as well. I reached for her hand and gave it a squeeze, but to my surprise, she didn't release it. I was her lifeline, and she was mine. Whatever was going on, both she and I had been dragged into this morass, unwillingly. Only now, it had turned to quicksand, and we were all going down together. I just prayed Michael and Benjamin had a plan of some sort. A good one.

Chapter 47
Esme Stalwart

It was no longer just me and Jamie I had to worry about, I realized as we cut stakes and began moving southwest toward Scotland's western shore, and none too soon. The foul weather was startin' to set in along with the rain. Soon, the rain would turn to snow and ice if we didn't hurry. As if everyone felt the pressure enter on the strong wind currents that battered our caravans, we pressed forward, heads down as we plowed into the gale. Even the law would think twice about traversin' this area of the territory under these conditions with so little to gain by pursuin' us.

We struggled to put miles between us and the high country as our horses pushed into the wind, their manes flying in the tempest of this late October afternoon. I blew on my hands as Isla shook the reins, urging our horses to go faster, but they had only one speed. Slow. At this rate, we would spend the winter in the high country, a daring deed at that. I brushed my hand over my growing belly. Though my time was far off, I already imagined what lay ahead for the baby. Poverty. Hunger. Forced escape into the wilderness, just one step ahead o' the law. This was no life for a child. Me and my baby stood a better chance alone at my old homestead. I wondered if my friends still cared for it, or if it had fallen to wrack and ruin. Whatever its condition, I needed to speak with Jamie soon.

I watched him on his horse as he spurred his clan on, guiding their every move. When Jamie had announced to the Travellers that I was with child, I noticed the rise of his chin and the puffing of his breast with pride like a Great Bustard in mating season. And I loved him for it. For the thrill it gave him to know he would soon be a *faither*. But what sort of life could he give his daughter, if indeed that's what our baby would be?

"Oh, Jamie," I whispered. "Why did it ha' to be this way?" *Why could ye no' give up the stealin'?*

But I knew why. Life and circumstance had given him no choice. When he couldn't save his *faither*, he had put on the mantle of leadership as a means of saving his people. Sadness crept in like a thief in the night, robbing me of my joy. A gladness that should have seen me dancing in the meadows to know I was with child. Jamie's child.

Isla seemed to sense my shifting mood and placed a hand on mine, even as she navigated the rough terrain ahead. I held a parasol above our heads to keep the rain from dripping down on us in a torrent, but it did little to protect us from the cold and damp. We would dry when we found a resting site, not a moment before.

"I know ye want things to be perfect for ye and yer wee one, Esme," Isla said. "But tha's not how life works, ye ken? Life is messy and raw, and the sooner ye understand it, the better off ye'll be. Ye want to protect those around ye—Jamie...yer bairn."

I nodded, tears marching like rain down my cheeks and mingling with the real rain pouring down on my parade. I sniffed, whether from the emotions coursing through my veins now that I was pregnant or simply because of all that had happened in the past several months.

"Well, ye cannot protect anyone if ye don't acknowledge Jamie is doin' his darndest to protect us all. Yes, his head is on the chopping block."

I winced at her choice of words and turned away, loathing to face that fact, but she grabbed my chin and pulled it toward her.

"Life is tough, Esme Stalwart. Tougher for some than for others."

I felt the sting of her words as if she'd slapped me, because it was true. My life had been easier than hers until now. Despite living in the dangerous Borderlands, I hadn't the stigma of being born a Traveller, hated and despised because of my race, my skin color, my eyes. Everything about her and her people had been outlawed, her very existence a stain on the "true" citizens of Scotland. The Travellers had no choice but to steal. My head knew it, but my heart still cradled the training I'd received growing up, those commandments I held dear. But the commandments had been a lie. Thou shalt not kill had all been a ruse. What about war? Thou shalt not commit adultery, but what about Jamie's *faither*? As long as those in positions of power were the ones doing it, then none of the commandments applied.

With the back of my arm, I swiped at the tears staining my cheeks. I knew what Isla would think of me if I returned to the

Borderland. She would never forgive me, but God save me, I had to think of my baby.

"I need to talk to you, Isla," I said.

"No need. I already know what ye're going to say."

Though her face was stoic, I saw the hurt and resignation.

"Ha' ye told Jamie ye're leavin' yet?"

I swallowed hard, the truth laid bare before me. "Not yet."

"How do ya think he'll take it, hmm?" She pierced me with a look.

My shoulders slumped. "Poorly, I imagine."

"Poorly, ye think?" Her words stung hot with fire behind them. "Poorly!" She shook her head, any hope of her understanding gone. "Just like the laird, ye are. Can't keep yer hands off us, then take what's not yours to have."

I heard the growl underlining how she felt about me. Shame burned in my chest, because she was right. I was doing to Jamie what the laird had done to her.

"I'm sorry," I whispered. "Ye're right."

For a moment, she paused, the horses following a course without direction. Her eyes locked with mine, a shared understanding between us now. Though anger still burnished her cheeks, she took my hand in hers.

"Promise me then. Ye'll ne'er tell Jamie about this discussion, aye? It would break his heart." Hot tears welled in her eyes.

"I promise," I said.

She picked up the reins and continued on.

"For what it's worth, Isla, I love your son. And I would ne'er do anything to hurt him. I'm just—"

"Afraid?"

I nodded.

"I know ye are. We all are. It's the life of a Traveller. Ye ne'er know where the next kick will come from that will knock ye off yer feet." Her jaw worked in anger at the unfairness of it all, but as she had told me just moments ago, life was unfair. "But if we stand together, Esme, it's a darn sight easier. Remember that next time ye think of takin' my grandchild away from me."

She let out a "ha", and I fell back in my seat. Of course! If I left, not only would Jamie lose a daughter, but Isla would lose a granddaughter. Then and there, I decided to live the rest of my days making it up to her...to Jamie. They deserved better. My fear for him, for any of us, held no place here. We were all in the same boat, and we needed each other. I knew that now.

Can ye ever forgive me, Jamie? Isla?

Chapter 48
Destiny Jacqueline Kismet

We arrived at a small cottage tucked in an alleyway. For hours now, we'd travelled back roads that were little more than goat trails. How had Benjamin known about them? My skin pricked at the realization that Benjamin was a master of escape and disguise. Who was he really? He seemed way too worldly and knowledgeable for a simple librarian, but then again, what did I know about librarians? Most people assigned them the stereotype of brainy sorts. And I suppose Benjamin did appear the stereotype, what with his vest underneath a dark suede jacket and jeans topped off with loafers.

Before he got out of the car, he leaned over and kissed Cassidy, her eyes closed. When she opened them, they shimmered with happiness, despite the fact we were now on the run, but from whom, and why?

Michael must have been observing me watch Cassidy, because he squeezed my hand in reassurance, as if to let me know everything would be alright, but would it?

I exited the car. The sky blossomed into a carpet of blue, much like the bluebells I'd seen along the sides of the road. Huge, billowing clouds offset the vast expanse. If not for the circumstances, I would have relished this day, the weather, the spring flowers cropping up overnight. But today was different.

Michael came around and held out his palm to me, the gesture a question. *Come with me, yes? Help me, I need you.*

But need me for what? I hesitated for no more than seconds before taking his hand. Whatever lay ahead, we were in this together. All of us. And though I might not understand what Michael had planned, I trusted him, God help me.

I steeled myself as we pressed forward toward a stone house with a thatched roof and white limestone exterior. As I stepped inside the cottage with the lovely red door, I spied a living room with a huge stone fireplace and a kitchen to the left done in soft creamy green tones, a house not unlike one I would have loved and cherished if it had been mine.

"This belongs to my sister and her husband," Benjamin said. "It's their summer cottage."

Cassidy let out a cry of delight and flung herself from one room to the next, clearly in love with the house. Benjamin regarded her with a hint of mirth dancing in his green eyes, as if picturing the two of them together, playing house, married with children.

My heart plunged, along with my stomach, since first learning of the connection between Esme and Jamie, Cassidy and Benjamin. And now Isla and me. Again I wondered if Michael was a laird in his previous life, if indeed he had one. In answer, I heard a whisper. *Isla.*

Ye can see why I fell in love with him, ye ken, Destiny? But he had other plans.

Her voice faded away. So Michael *was* the laird in the previous life. Did that mean he loved Isla then, as he loves me now? That he was righting a wrong in some way by marrying me in this lifetime?

I plopped down onto one of the oversized couches, not waiting to be asked. The whole room had a lovely shabby-chic sort of floral cottage feel. It gave me the peace I had been hoping for. But then I heard a whir in the other room and saw Benjamin and Michael's eyes connect—read the fear in them. I rushed to my feet to see what had made the noise before either of them could stop me. To my horror, as I entered the room issuing the mechanical sounds, I saw not one or two computers, but dozens of them. They lined every inch of the room. They were sorting data. Reams of it. Facts and figures rose and fell from the screens, one after another.

I turned to the pair. "What is this?" I demanded.

Cassidy, who had been inspecting the kitchen, came over and pushed the two men apart to view what I had.

"Benjamin? Dad?"

I read the uncertainty in her voice and saw the horror written into both men's expressions. No one spoke. Finally, I broke the impasse.

"I think it's time the two of you tell us what's going on here," I said. "How are there this many computers in the middle of nowhere?"

Their mouths fell open, fear settling in the whites of their eyes. Benjamin scratched his neck to buy some time, while Michael shuffled his feet as though wondering if he should flee.

"Dad?" Cassidy's voice trembled, and I walked over and stood beside her to form a united front.

Benjamin cut the tension by saying, "Why don't we go in the kitchen. Get something to eat. Then we can talk."

Michael seconded that idea, but not before I'd heard the breath of air he'd been holding whoosh through his dry lips. "C'mon."

He put an arm around me, while Benjamin tugged at Cassidy's hand. Reluctantly, she let him take it.

Once we were around the table and nibbling on some cheese and crackers Benjamin had drummed up from the cupboards, he began. "You know those statistics we went over with the two of you the other day?" He rubbed his head, as though trying to ward off the tension.

Cassidy and I nodded our heads warily.

"Well, there's a method to our madness. You see..."

But before he could get out the words, a knock sounded at the door.

"Get down!" Michael hissed. He reached over and pushed Cassidy's head down, and then mine, so we were kneeling under the table.

"This isn't funny, Michael," I hissed as I grabbed onto Cassidy's hand. "You're scaring us."

"Shh!" Benjamin whispered.

The pair pulled out guns from beneath their coats, and my heart plummeted. I bit my lips to keep from screaming. Overnight, my life had turned into a nightmare with no end. I knelt there, trembling, Cassidy hunkered beside me.

"I'll check it out," Benjamin said.

He went to the front door that I had pronounced lovely when I entered. Now there was nothing lovely about this place. Instead, what had seemed a sanctuary only moments ago had turned to peril.

I listened to Benjamin as he spoke to a man at the front door. Minutes later, the fellow entered, a rather tall, burly man with a gun at his side.

"Who are these people?" Cassidy mouthed.

I shrugged, but my heart hammered in my chest. Warily, we stood.

"Now do you want to tell us what's going on?" I said, my voice still shaking.

"Cassidy, Destiny, I want you to meet my colleague and friend, Callum. He will be our bodyguard for the foreseeable future. And one other thing," he added.

"Oh?" How many more surprises did he plan to spring on us? I wondered with just a touch of anger.

"The FBI knows about us...well, not us specifically, but about the Resistance."

"And?"

"And a man with the code name Cobra has assigned a team to investigate."

"So we're being hunted," I huffed.

Michael's shoulders sagged. "We're being hunted."

Chapter 49
Cobra

In forty-eight hours, Frank would head to the UK aboard a Gulfstream G550, his mission more urgent now that counterterrorism was involved. Though the FBI still couldn't pinpoint what was about to take place, the amount of chatter had increased recently, and they'd managed to decode a few of the messages warning of something big in the works, but what? That could mean anything. He quickly packed his bags as he had in times past, then massaged his temples.

The headaches had returned the closer he got to leaving, so he gulped down some aspirin and water as he ran through his briefs. He also needed to see to Mia's protection while he was away. He quickly dialed a private number.

"Sid, I need you to put a detail on my wife while I'm gone."

He explained his fears. Fortunately, Sid had been with the department for years and knew Frank's wife well. Once that was sorted, he finished packing, then called downstairs to Mia, who had taken the day off to be with him.

But before she could answer, the doorbell rang, and he heard his daughter talking to Mia. That was followed by a male voice, no doubt her boyfriend. The guy was nice enough, but he hadn't grown into his body yet, and he reminded Frank of a puppy with too-big feet and large ears. He decided not to hold it against the kid. Hell, he'd been young once. Had stood awkwardly at the door of some young lady's family home, feeling like a dweeb.

For some reason, a memory surfaced—or at least it felt like one—of him standing at the door of a well-heeled lady's house. He remembered the way her father had made him feel—small, unimportant. Afterwards, he had vowed he'd never allow any man to treat him like an underling again. Since that time, he'd been the one to make others tread lightly around him. He'd been the one in control. Only the memory hadn't been his, had it? He shook his head as though trying to dislodge the memory. To give it clarity. Once again, he worried he was losing it. As though he was inhabiting somebody else's brain, not his own.

"Frank!" Mia called up the stairway. "Come down, Jen's here with Liam."

Frank groused. Why couldn't it be like the old times, with just the four of them? But then again, his kids had to grow up some-time, and the truth is, she'd chosen well. He had to give her that.

He placed his gun inside his bag, having clearance to carry one overseas due to his job. Then he zipped it shut and headed down-stairs. Before long, he was out on the patio grilling hamburgers and laughing at Liam's jokes. He pictured growing old here, having barbecues with Jen and Liam and their passel of kids. Seconds later,

Jacob walked through the open sliding glass patio door dressed in shorts and a sweatshirt. Kids. They'd rather look cool or rad, or whatever they were calling it these days, than be smart and dress for the cold. It seemed his son had grown a foot since the last time he'd seen him, and he was built like his old man. Sturdy, with only a bit of a paunch, probably from drinking too much beer with his friends at the dorms. Frank wished they could eat out on the patio, but the weather was still too chilly, so they would be forced to eat indoors. Frank liked the camaraderie of a patio barbecue.

Before long, the smell of hamburgers flooded the air, and everyone moved indoors, grateful for the warmth when they shut the sliding glass doors. Everybody spoke at once. He'd come from a home that prized formality and conformity above all else, but he'd bucked the tradition by letting everyone talk at once. It felt more natural, somehow.

Frank watched as Jen skulked around the edge of the table, grabbing bites of food off of his and Mia's plates to gentle backhands. It had always been like this. She could never sit still and always needed to be moving, like him. That's why he liked his job. One day, he'd be at his desk, the next he'd be who-knew-where on one investigation or another. But he couldn't help thinking it hadn't always been like this. That once upon a time, he'd been very staid.

Jen was in the middle of telling him about her upcoming test in art history, when the phone rang. Normally, he wouldn't have answered, but it was official business. For one brief moment he considered ignoring it. But then duty got the better of him, and he took it.

"Frank here," he said.

"Frank?" He heard the worry in Shannon's voice. "I think you should come now. They're cutting another couple of positions, and Frank?"

"Yeah?"

Mia mouthed, "Who is it?"

But Frank merely shook his head and turned away.

"One of those people is me."

He stood there, stunned, unmoving.

"Did you hear me, Frank?"

He read the hysteria in her voice. What would he do without his secretary? She knew him better than almost anyone there. She'd helped grease the wheels for meetings with countless people. Without her by his side, he might not have solved half of his cases. So often the people he was investigating would clam up, turn off the tap, but then she would come in with cookies and a kind word that calmed even the most troubled waters. How many times had she promised the persons in question they were dealing with the best, a real class act? Promised them, too, that Frank would do everything he could to make things easier on them. By the time she was done with them, he'd had them eating out of his hand, and he'd never abused that privilege.

He looked at his wife, his kids and sighed. Yet another meal left unfinished, another chance to connect with his wife and adult children gone. But he couldn't leave Shannon to the wolves alone. He had to at least try to help. Mia would understand, especially after what happened to Juanita.

"Hang in there," Frank said. "I'll be right there. And Shannon?"

"Yes?"

He'd never heard her cry before, but he detected a sob from his normally stoic secretary. His heart broke for her.

"Don't let them remove you from the premises until I get there, okay? Once you leave, they'll never let you back in. Understood?"

She didn't answer. She was too busy crying.

Chapter 50
Esme Stalwart

That night, as I lay tucked into our warm bed, the firelight casting shadows on the inside wall of our caravan, I caressed the swell of the baby within me. What would she be like, this child o' mine? Would she be staid and steady like me, or as wild as the moors that scented the hills with heather come springtime?

"A halfpenny for your thoughts," Jamie said, as he turned on his side to face me.

"Only a halfpenny?" I teased. "I'll ha' ye ken, Jamie, my thoughts are worth far more than that."

He laughed, then leaned in to kiss me, his warm scent a blend of thyme and meadowsweet. Our lips lingered, as though neither one of us wanted to part for fear of our future...what there was of it.

How had I ever thought of leaving, of returning to the Borderlands on my own? It wasn't as if the Borderlands was any safer. If anything, it carried a weight all its own, what with the changing loyalties every time a new clan fought for territory. Throughout history, the borders had shifted, like the sands on the shore after many a tide. One day you might be on one side of the divide, and the next wake up to a new border and a new government. The Reivers had helped those along the Borderlands…and hurt them too, depending on which way the wind blew. But I didn't want to think about that now.

I scooted in closer to nestle my head in the crook of Jamie's arm. It was nice…this. Goin' to bed with my man. Wakin' up with 'im, too. I could get used to it. But I knew time was fleeting, a mere mirage—appearing one moment, disappearing the next.

"Jamie?"

"Hmm?'

"What shall we call the bairn?"

He wrinkled his nose, which he often did when thinking. It gave him a comical expression that endeared him to me.

"I was thinkin' perhaps we could call her Fiadhaich."

My shoulders slumped at the meaning. *Wild and untamed freedom.* With a name like that, she was sure to be the spittin' image of her *faither.*

"Why? What were *ye* thinkin'?" he asked.

He eyed me with suspicion, but I refused to look away. "I was thinkin' of perhaps something sweeter like Kaileigh. It has a beautiful ring, aye?"

He shrugged, and yet I saw just a hint of agreement in the sparkle that tinted his eyes. For a time, we lay in silence. Isla had left us on our own of late, preferring to stay elsewhere to give us our privacy. Though she never said where, someone as lovely as she had only to hint at desire, and her bed would unfurl, I felt certain.

"Here, woman." Jamie pulled me into a tight embrace, my face nearly buried in his chest. "We'll no' talk of names just yet. There'll be time for names. Now is the time for action."

He laid his chin on my head, the subtle growl shifting in his throat. There would come a time when I would pray for these moments, I knew. When he would return from a raid, bloodied and beaten. I longed to stay in the cocoon of his warmth, the security it provided, if only an illusory one.

"Jamie?"

"Hmm?"

"When will you go?" I said in a small voice, as if by speaking softly it would forego the future.

"Soon," he answered on a sigh. "But if ye're worried I'll forget ye, Esme Stalwart, fat chance of that."

I smacked his chest, hearing the humor in his words. If he could list all the things about me he would change, I feared the list might unfurl out the door, as I was so unlike him. And yet our shared fear had pulled us together in ways that nothing else could. We clung to each other, our fingernails needling into the other's skin, but neither of us cried out at our one bit of security in a world gone mad. But perhaps it had always been so.

"Jamie?"

"What, woman?"

"Don't let them catch you."

For several moments, he didn't speak, but I felt his head shift as if peering down at me. Because he knew what I was asking of him. *Don't let them send you to the gallows.*

"I won't," he promised, but his voice was husky with emotion.

I had asked him to ensure something he had no control over. His life. His safety. But somehow by asking, it made me feel like I could prevent the wheel of fate from turning, prevent the future from takin' its pound of flesh.

Stay safe, Jamie. Stay with me, my mind breathed. As if the owl just outside of the firelight had heard me, it let out a screech of warning. For once I wished Isla had stayed and used her magic to alter the outcome. But I knew it couldn't be altered when I saw the bird's shadow as it flew past our open doorway, alerting us of the upcoming changes. Warning us of death.

Chapter 51
Destiny Jacqueline Kismet

The news that we were being hunted left me angrier than I'd been in a long time as I stood quaking in the small cottage "snug", the Scots' version of a cozy living room.

"So this is why we need a bodyguard?" I demanded. "Benjamin? Michael? Anyone?"

My voice rose to a shrill pitch, but I was past caring. I deserved an answer, and I deserved it now. Cassidy stood shoulder to shoulder with me in the middle of the cottage, her eyes flashing with fire and ice.

"Okay, Des, it's like this," Michael said.

Benjamin threw a hand out to stop him. "First, let me give you a bit of background about the history of the Borderlands. Sit!"

"Now?" I shot back, my fury settling on him.

"Trust me," he said, "this will explain a lot about me, about why we're doin' what we're doin'."

"And what *are* the two of you doing, Benjamin, Michael?" I countered.

Benjamin motioned for me to sit and for Cassidy to follow. The two of us shared a look of frustration, but in the end, we had no choice. If we were ever to get to the bottom of this…this… whatever it was, we must first wait it out.

When we were all seated on the couches and on overstuffed chairs, Benjamin began. "For centuries, the Borderlands was an area of lawlessness. They were called the 'Debatable Lands' because the English and the Scots fought over territory, and the clans in the territory took turns exerting considerable control over the area. Jamie's family members were Reivers, or in a word, outlaws. They had to be…to survive. The area was too dangerous to grow crops, and cattle and horse rustling ran rampant. Without it, people like my family might never have survived because we were Travellers. The lowest of the low, in terms of the caste system. Did you know that?"

I shook my head. "But what does this have to do with us?"

Benjamin sighed and looked to Michael for support. My husband nodded for Benjamin to continue.

"See, throughout history, powerful men have determined other men's fate. Some leaders are benevolent, while some are not. When the latter ascends to power, it creates chaos for the rest of us. It affects our ability to live, to work, and to feed our families."

The room grew stiflingly hot, and the bodyguard stood to open the window. An invigorating breeze blew in as if to clear out the cobwebs, releasing the tension in the room with a breath of fresh air.

"During these times, it's up to us to help our families survive and try to reverse course before the world is thrown into turmoil. My ancestors stole from the rich to give to the poor. We were considered heroes to many but evil to others, primarily the rich. We were sometimes ruthless, though my specific ancestor did much to deter such ruthlessness. Still, it existed."

"And your ancestor is..." I held my breath, knowing before he said it, what the answer would be.

"My ancestor was Jamie MacPherson."

My stomach pivoted, and when I spoke, my voice was tight with emotion. "*The* Jamie MacPherson?"

He nodded. "One and the same."

"So that's why *you* called us here?" It came out like an accusation.

He shrugged. "Well, not just me, but that's for another time."

I bet.

Once again, Cassidy grasped my hand, and we held onto each other, a lifeline to the world we'd once known. One that had imploded the minute we'd opened the geocache. I closed my eyes against the hot sting of tears. If only we'd just kept going, walked past it and never looked back. But would it have changed anything? Would the present be the same, where Benjamin and Michael knew each other...worked together?

I turned to Michael, whose face had blanched, now that the truth was out, at least part of it. "And what's your role in all this? Are you a...Reiver?"

For a split second, I saw the lie forming on his lips, but in the end, he couldn't go through with it. He nodded his head. "In a way. We're protecting families...lots of them. Families who are seeing their life savings flushed down the drain, while those in power high-five each other for snapping up all the cheap stocks and bonds now that the middle class has lost everything. The entire tariff negotiations were a ruse to put money back in the hands of the rich and powerful. To get rid of anyone who's not a loyalist. To ensure the rich get richer while the poor get poorer. Did you know you and I will pay for the tariffs, not the companies, meaning it will create inflation?"

I nodded.

"And do you know where the money from the tariffs goes?"

This time I shook my head.

"It goes into the US Department of Treasury. From there, it can be used for anything. The only oversight is from Congress, which, as we all know, is a rubber stamp for the President. By 2035, they will have raised over one trillion dollars in tariff money that you and I, the middle class and the poor, are paying."

"But couldn't that help pay down the national debt?" I asked, hopeful.

Michael folded his hands together. "What it's used for is up to the sole discretion of the President. The same president who has bankrupted nearly every business he has ever owned. Plus, he's left contractors to pick up the cost."

"Oh."

Michael gazed at me as though imploring me to understand, and the rub of it is, I *did* understand. I understood all too well. And while the world was exploding into haves and have-nots—which a generation of young men fought to prevent—we were returning to the past with a vengeance. One where women no longer had a place in the military, where their voting rights were being diminished daily, and where a woman would once again die in a back alley abortion because the thought of giving her child away in a country where she had no purchase, and no hope of a job to support her child, left her with few options.

I gritted my teeth and let out a howl of fury and anguish. Michael came to kneel down before me. Slowly, calmly, he forced my chin up so I was facing him.

"That's why we had to do something about this, Des."

"We who?"

"Generals, military, politicians, and concerned citizens. Many people are joining the Resistance because we can't let one man, one group of people, undo all the good out there. Do there need to be changes in the government? Sure! But not like this. Not by taking away everything that has helped deliver a nation...and Europe...out of poverty. We were working to bring the rest of the world up to speed, but we were derailed before we could accomplish it."

I stared at the hearth as though it could provide answers. Over the fireplace hung a pair of intertwined hearts, a confirmation that

I was not alone in all of this. We all had each other, but for how long? In a world like ours, anything could happen at any minute. Families could be torn apart. Immigrant and otherwise. This was not the world I wanted to live in.

"What can we do? How can we change it?"

A hint of a smile played across Michael's lips, whereas Benjamin breathed a huge sigh of relief to think I might finally be on board.

"Cassidy?" Benjamin said, holding a hand out to her.

She paused for a moment, her gaze switching to mine to see how I felt about things. I nodded. Though I wanted to pretend none of this was happening, to hide my head in the sand, I couldn't. Not now. Not anymore.

She gave me a tentative smile. Then she reached out for Benjamin's hand. Whatever course of action we took from this point on, we were in it together. For our nation. For our people. For the future.

Chapter 52
Esme Stalwart

With our daily movements came a change of weather. The cold had set in with a vengeance, tugging at our clothing, seeping into our skin. We huddled each day on the bench seat of our caravan, our bodies cravin' warmth. For the past few months, my baby had grown inside me. Now I felt her kicking to be free of her confinement. We needed shelter and a permanent encampment soon, but first we had to find a laird who would allow us to stay the winter on his land. But who?

I had begun to think we would never find a place to land when, on a rare sunny day in winter, Jamie returned from a foray into town with an announcement.

"Everybody, gather 'round," he called.

We did so with relish. Like always, the caravan came together in a circle, Jamie the clan's axis point. Men and women from every angle appeared haggard and worn from a month or more on the road, each day crowded with the routine of a Traveller's life, but even a Traveller could become weary.

"We've been given permission to stay on the Armstrong land."

"In exchange fer what?" one of the more enterprising young men shouted.

Jamie chuckled. Nervous laughter followed among the others. "We can't expect to live here for free, can we?"

Somehow Jamie managed to make any chore seem like a holiday, any punishment an opportunity. It was why people loved him so, me included.

"Well, now, some of the king's men are pushin' fer more land along the Borderlands, they are. They're spoilin' for a fight. And it's high time we did a little pushin' back, aye?" He winked for good measure, the laughter that followed real this time. "So, what do ya say? In exchange fer our help fightin' the border war, we can stay on Armstrong land for a while and collect any cattle and horses we rustle in between skirmishes. The laird may even buy a few of 'em off of us."

A murmur arose like a thousand bees, erupting into a nearly unanimous cry of agreement. Only I sat silent, frightened. What would become of these men if the king's army was stronger, more resilient than our little ragtag troupe? And yet, stranger things had happened. We definitely had more at stake. I decided to trust him.

For the next two days, we settled in, happy to stay put for a while as we set about quietly arranging our camp. But on the third day, the air tensed with excitement, and the men around us began to prepare for battle. Jamie brandished his sword, and the men practiced sparring in the center of the camp. Soon, the clang of metal upon metal rang out sharp and true, and the tang of sweat and the grunts and groans of the wounded filled the air, though in truth, they were minor cuts, unintended for sure.

Isla led the charge, setting up our caravan and several others as sites for any wounded men. We gathered blankets and lint to absorb any fluids. Then we stocked up on honey, animal grease, and cloths as well as animal skins with which to wrap the wounds, should it be needed, and it *would* be needed. Afterwards, she sent the women on scouting expeditions for herbs and roots, "fairy herbs," as she called them due to their so-called magical properties. Yarrow, vervain, foxglove and mugwort. Peppermint and wormwood, too.

Soon the shelves were lined with all sorts of salves and liniments. The inside of the caravan took on a musky odor that reminded me of earth and something tangy, indescribable. I could taste it on my tongue, as though it had entered my very pores and taken possession of me. But I learned to live with it, as I lived with the ever-growing mound inside my stomach, my precious girl. When no one was looking, I would speak to her, tell her how much her *mam* loved her, wished her only the best. Despite my daily worry about what was to come for my man and the others, this one portion of my life kept me grounded. Kept me sane. She was the part of Jamie no one could take from me...I hoped. I began to pray...to the Christian God, to the pagan gods, to any god who would listen. *Please keep her safe*, I prayed. The petition became a daily mantra.

On the fifth day, the men mounted their steeds. Tension settled around their eyes and in the heavy hearts of the women to be left behind—I, one of them. The night before, Jamie and I made love slowly and with such great passion that I recalled it now and experienced the responding ache to know it may be weeks or months before I would see him again. He leaned down from his horse and kissed me one last time. As he did, I felt him pull away, as though emotionally distancing himself from me, already out on the Borderlands fighting his foe in his mind.

"Oh, Jamie," I pleaded. "Stay safe. Come home to me in one piece."

He quirked a smile, his lips tilting so that one side of his mouth was higher than the other. "Of course!" He tipped his hat to me, which made me laugh. Then he winked one last time and spurred his horse forward. As he headed out of the camp, leading his men to battle, he lifted his sword into the air and let out a war cry.

"Creag Dhubh Clann Chatain!"

Black Rock of Clan Chattain. A reference to the MacPherson's historical ties to the Chattan Confederation.

I watched him go off to war, my heart heavy. "There goes your *faither*," I whispered to my bairn. For several moments, I stood there, my hands cocooning my unborn child. Then, when the last of the men disappeared on the winding road south, I turned back to the caravan where soon we would be administering poultices and plasters, and attending to our dead. I just prayed Jamie wasn't one of them.

CHAPTER 53
Cobra

"Ah, there's the old Cobra now," Ron said, his hair now gray at the temples as he held the door of the elevator open.

It had been a long time since anyone had used Frank's code name, the one given him when they'd prepared an elaborate sting on a drug cartel some years back. He was to lead the strike team. The operation had gone off without a hitch until he learned one of his men had been caught in the crossfire and fatally wounded. Whenever anyone used his former code name, it took him back to that moment, the smell of gunpowder, the shouts, the relief when the criminals were handcuffed and hauled away. But then he'd heard the news, and his feelings of relief changed instantly.

He entered the elevator, his throat as raw as if he'd just heard the pronouncement. *Dead.* He'd been the one to speak to the guy's wife, to tell her what a hero her husband was, and he was, no doubt about it. But even heroes lived complex lives...had personal flaws. No one knew that better than Frank.

"Sorry to hear about Shannon," Ron said. "She was one of the good ones."

"What do you mean *was* one of the good ones?" Frank asked, panic rising in his chest. "She didn't leave the premises, did she? I told her to stay put until I got here."

"Yeah, I saw her with a box of things heading to the elevator not ten minutes ago. Said they canned her and told her if she didn't leave now, they'd arrest her. They escorted her out by armed guard."

"They *what*?" Frank fumed, fire burning him from the inside out. "Is she still here?"

"I don't know. She was heading for her car. The women in the office are—"

But Frank didn't hear anymore. He punched the button for the next stop and leapt off the elevator. He looked for the stairs and took each step two by two, nearly sliding down the railing as he leapt from floor to floor.

"Please still be there," he muttered, out of breath by the time he reached the ground floor.

He bumped into one of the clerks on his way out, almost knocking her down, but he had to find Shannon. She'd been a secretary, mother, and friend, all rolled into one. He and Mia had been there for her daughter's christening and again at her graduation. He wasn't about to let her down now.

As he ran outside of the building, he saw her car press into gear across the parking lot. He shouted and waved, all the while sprinting and sidestepping cars and people in an effort to get her attention. Finally, she saw him and squealed to a stop.

"They wouldn't let me wait for you," she sobbed, her eyes red. "I tried. I really did."

Now Frank understood how Mia felt when they'd removed Juanita and sent her packing—like he'd lost his right arm. Shannon wasn't just an employee. She kept his life operating smoothly. Kept him from tearing his hair out at all the tedious paperwork and meetings. She'd always known just how to cheer him up when life gave him lemons, and he seemed to be getting more and more these days. What would he do without her? Worse, she was a single mom. What would she do without an income? She couldn't even count on unemployment. The administration had seen to that. And after so many years of dedicated service.

"I'm going to try to get you back," Frank promised. "And if you need money to tide you over, just name it. I could sell some stocks."

Those, too, had tanked because of the tariffs, but he couldn't worry about that now. Maybe Mia was right. Maybe he'd had his blinders on for too long, hadn't seen the changes coming, hadn't prepared. The party had changed. Big time. He almost didn't recognize it, and yet he'd been with them for so long, he couldn't imagine a different way of life. A different political persuasion.

Shannon was still too choked up to speak.

"Come by the house tomorrow," Frank urged. "Mia would love to see you, and then you can tell us all about it, okay?"

"Okay," she managed to say. "And Frank?"

"Yeah?"

"Thanks."

He simply nodded, then moved away as she put her car in gear and headed out of the lot. For several moments, he stood there, watching her go, this day etched into his memory forever. Because it was the day everything changed. He just didn't know how or where it would lead. More than ever, he wanted to go somewhere far away and put all this behind him until he could figure out what he wanted for his future. But for now, he would pick up the pieces of his life and go on.

Chapter 54
Destiny Jacqueline Kismet

The men told us as much as they could about their plans, which was little indeed. Instead they kept up the mantra "trust us," as though women were too weak to be a part of the plans. I fussed over that ridiculous notion in the walled garden out back of the cottage as I paced the grounds. The cottage had become a prison of sorts, though a lovely one that tugged at my senses with its rich aromas and creamy textures. I had always wanted a garden such as this, but we'd never settled anywhere long enough to have one. Now that I was here, I yearned to be free, to explore the outdoors, which I could just make out through the locked gate with the spoked wheel set into it that allowed me a glimpse into the outer world. From what I could gather, we were near a forested area. And yet we had taken such a circuitous route to get here, I had no idea where we'd landed. When I'd asked, Michael simply said, "The less you know, the better."

Cassidy, who'd been in a heated discussion with Benjamin as I'd headed outdoors, trailed me now. When she caught up with me, she put her arm through mine and laid her head on my shoulder.

"What are we going to do?" she moaned.

"I don't know," I said, truthfully.

Like me, this had come as a huge shock to her, and the shared revelation had thrust us together in a way nothing had before. Every day, news filtered in on the television, our cell phones, the computers hooked up in the room that buzzed with activity. Benjamin and Michael monitored them at all hours of the day. Today, on Michael's laptop, I had caught a glimpse of an offshore bank account, but when Michael noticed me looking, he quickly shut down the monitor so I couldn't see. Now, as I thought back on our lives together, I began to see things I hadn't then. Small events that didn't add up. Harried looks, unexplained angst, relief when nothing appeared amiss. Worse, he had suffered depression at times that arose out of nowhere. Or so I had thought. What did I truly know of my husband?

That I loved him. That I always wanted to be with him.

At least there was that. I swiped at a tear that fell unheeded.

"Oh, Ma, don't worry. Everything will be okay," Cassidy said.

"Will it?" I gave her a side glance.

She'd worn a cheerful dress with spring flowers, a sweater over it to fight off the chill, and boots to keep her warm. Though it matched the garden, it did little to lift our moods, which had plummeted to know we lived in a world of turmoil, a world of too many secrets, few of which we were privy to.

"Do you mind me asking what you and Benjamin were fighting about?"

I knew I'd tempted fate by delving into her private life. She had always been secretive, like Michael. It's as if the two had shared a world completely apart from me. A world only they understood. It had given them both a sense of peace to have each other, but it left me feeling like an outsider. Had Cassidy known, in some small way, about Michael's life, his work? Had she understood him in a way I never could?

Because you were clueless, Des.

"Still am," I muttered.

"What?" Cassidy asked.

"Nothing." I shook my head, waiting for her to tell me—or not—about her and Benjamin.

Cassidy peered at the cottage, her eyes narrowing slightly as if by staring hard enough she might see through the walls, see what the two men were doing. Finally, she turned back to me, and as if viewing me for the first time, she smiled, but her mouth was pinched, like she'd sucked on a sour lemon.

"Benjamin asked me to marry him."

I pulled in a breath before I could rein in my emotions, one that revealed my feelings all too well. She'd just met Benjamin. What did she really know about him, about his work?

You're one to talk, Des.

"And?" I said, determined to let her do the talking.

"And, I think I love him. But I also know that whatever he and Dad are doing, there will be repercussions."

I blew out the breath I'd been holding. At least she was thinking clearly.

"What did you tell him?"

"That I want a year to decide. To figure out where this all leads before I commit." She fingered the key-shaped necklace at her throat, which she did whenever she was anxious, I noticed.

Good girl! Though I liked Benjamin, too, if he *was* the reincarnation of Jamie, a huge mountain of trials awaited Cassidy. Awaited *them*. Better to take it slow. To get to know each other. Besides, a marriage founded on lies was never a good way to start—I should know. And yet, my marriage had turned out well, because despite everything, I loved Michael with all my heart. Even knowing we were in possible danger hadn't deterred that.

It was my turn to cast my eyes on the cottage, to envision Michael, his strong arms and warm heart. His smile. I ached when he was away. Now, perhaps we could be together for good, but for how long? If he was mixed up in something nefarious, no matter how important the reason, our time together might be cut short. How is it that two generations of men and women, worlds apart, could share such a difficult past and present when all any of us wanted was to live a good life? To raise a family. In peace.

"You know, Ma," Cassidy began. "Benjamin told me something today…something that made sense."

"Oh?" I pressed a loose strand of blonde hair behind her ears.

"He said that throughout history, no one had it easy. That there *is* no perfect time. There were benevolent rulers who made life better for a while, but eventually, someone ruthless always pushed them aside."

Though I knew she was right...that *Benjamin* was right, I couldn't help wishing things could be different. Why, in all these centuries, couldn't human beings evolve, become better? Come to care for each other, the environment, the world they lived in? One day they would blow the whole damned thing up, killing every man, woman, child, and beast.

I turned to the keyhole of the gate and stooped to view the world beyond. Its beauty. Its grace. Someday, all of this might be gone because of some megalomaniac who thought only of himself, *his* happiness, *his* greed. The rest of us were all subject to his whims. Why couldn't it be different? Why shouldn't we throw men like him and his sycophants to the wind?

As if God had heard my prayer, the wind whipped up, tugging at my sweater and refusing to let go. Now, if only we could manage to make it come true, so the rest of us could live in peace. But how would stealing from the rich to give to the poor help accomplish any of that? I reached for Cassidy's hand.

"Better get inside," I said, peering up at the clouds rolling in. "It looks like a storm is headed this way."

It took no further encouragement. We barely made it inside before the rain started, then the hail. Until, finally, the clouds unleashed their fury, wiping away the dust and the dirt left behind.

Chapter 55
Esme Stalwart

I fought down the bile in my throat as the first casualties appeared on litters. Head wounds wrapped in linen, arms at odd angles, missing legs. The last casualty hadn't long for the world, I felt certain. I shuddered, despite the glare Isla shot my way to keep my emotions in check.

And still, no Jamie.

My hands moved of their own accord, as if by keeping busy, I might forestall the inevitable—pretend that no harm would come to him. *Where are you, housband?* But the only answer was the cries and moans that rang out across the glade.

Any woman within hearing distance ran to help, all hands rushing to the task of keeping the men alive. Isla ripped open the shirt of one young man, Lachlan, if memory served. He was a bonny lad with fair red hair and eyes the color of the sky. His *mathair* heard his cries and came running, her screams heard throughout the encampment. The color drained from the poor boy's face, making him look like a porcelain doll I'd once seen in a shop window meant for rich folks, not the likes of us. A wound to the lad's chest assured us he had not long for the world, and still we tried to save him, to somehow chase away fate, commit it to the abyss forever, but it wasn't to be. Instead, we moved on to the next patient whilst the few men left behind—older ones—picked up their shovels. One slung him over his shoulder and carried him to a location far from camp. They would need to dig deep to keep wild animals from excavating the boy's carcass and shredding it to pieces, gnawin' even on the bones in their feeding frenzy. Once again, I shuddered.

I set my sights on the next young man, whose face I couldn't place because of the blood flowing from his nose and the swelling of his eyes. At least this one would live.

"Here!" Isla ordered. "Ha' the boy drink some comfrey tea to settle him whilst I set his arm."

"What are ye' talkin' about, woman?" One of the old-timers groused. "Gi' the poor boy a shot o' the whiskey. He'll be naught worth a fig, if you sew him up with only comfrey to whet his whistle."

The old man's bushy white eyebrows settled over his beak, his handlebar mustache quivering at the unjustness of it all. By the set of his jaw and his rheumy gray-blue eyes, I knew he relived the past trauma of his own youth. And as if to confirm it, I noticed a jagged scar that ran the length of his jaw up to his ear, where part of it had been severed.

My stomach plummeted to see such misery, but having lived my life on the Borderlands, I'd seen much over my short time on earth. Too much, some might say.

Before I had the chance to take it all in, I saw Isla place her hand deep inside a man's chest, blood oozing out of the gaping wound.

"Esme! Be quick about it," she ordered, motioning to the man's chest. "Put your hand inside and clamp the artery with your fingers while I get some thread and a needle."

I paused for only a moment, but long enough to earn a shout of "Hurry" from Isla. Steeling myself, I placed my hand inside the man's chest as promised and felt the warm surge of blood, grateful for the warmth on such a cold day as this. Steam rose from the open wound, the metallic smell of death riding the wind currents. My stomach twitched, and I thought I might be sick, but to my relief, my stomach held its contents, nausea rolling over me in waves. And still I held tight.

"Okay," Isla said, returning with thread and needle that had been dipped in boiling water and sanitized with the cheapest whiskey possible. "Whatever you do, don't move until I say so."

She guided my fingers as, one by one, she inserted the needle and made stitch after stitch. Where had she learned such a technique, I wondered? But I had no time to ask as more and more of the wounded came forward. Fortunately, not all were men from our clan. Many were from other clans, either conscripted into the fight or Reivers, like my *housband* and his band of men.

And still no Jamie.

I could only hope it meant he was safe, still alive, and not one of the fallen who had yet to be collected and brought to bury without even a modicum of a funeral.

For the next several hours, we worked, Isla and I, along with many other women, some coming from far and wide to help tend the wounded. One such enterprising woman crept up beside me. She seemed too timid for this type of work, with her pale skin and freckles and bright red braid that ran down the length of her tunic. Though shy, I sensed her underlying resilience.

"What's your name?" I asked as I poured antiseptic into the wound of a man who let out a loud groan. His body tensed, as though struck, then he fell back against the litter, his eyes fluttering mercifully closed so as not to experience any more pain.

"The name's Hannah."

I rolled the name around on my tongue as I hurriedly moved to the next man, a big burly Scot from another tribe. He glared at me, as though daring me to treat him, but I glared right back and whispered, "Not to worry. Isla knows what she's doin', aye?"

For one brief moment, he simply stared at me. Then finally, he gave a short nod, and I offered him a drink for the pain.

"Okay, Hannah," I said. "Pour this on the next man's wound."

The poor young soldier was still in his teens, a lad barely off his *maither's* teat. Why send children such as this into battle? And yet we had no choice. Fight or die. Food for the likes of us was a luxury. A home, other than a caravan, an impossible dream. If not for the laird taking Jamie in as his own, he, too, would ha' ne'er seen a home other than a caravan, at least not until he had met me.

"Where are ye from, Hannah?"

"Aberdeen, Miss," she said, leaning in and doing as asked. "My *housband* is fightin' in the war."

"But you can't be more than—"

"Fourteen?" Her pale face flushed a deep pink, her expression stoic.

"Did ye want to marry at such a young age?" Days ago, I wouldn't have thought to ask such a personal question, but if the skirmishes had taught me nothing, it had taught me to make friends fast. Before some were buried.

Hannah paused, looking around for any ears that might be attuned to her answer, but everyone was too busy attending to the wounded and dead. Then, the stoic expression returned, and she shook her head.

"My *faither* insisted. Too many mouths to feed, he said. There were eight of us in all."

I whistled. In a place where poverty ran rampant, eight children to feed and clothe must have felt like an impossibility. Often girls were sent off to wealthier families where they became cooks or maids, or if they were boys, stable hands or grifters. Or worse, warriors, conscripted at an early age, cannon fodder for powerful men—rich men, who either hoped to become richer or wanted to keep what they had from others who would take it if they could.

"Well, Hannah, ye are welcome here as long as ye like, hear?" I pierced her with a look.

I caught the briefest of sighs. "Thank ye, ma'am."

"Now, back to work." I placed a hand on her shoulder as we set out for the next man to be looked after, a man who knew Jamie and had seen him in battle.

Chapter 56
Destiny Jacqueline Kismet

I rose before dawn. Normally, someone monitored the computers at all times, but as I got up to use the bathroom, I peered out the window and saw the end of a cigarette glowing in the darkness. The guard! If I hurried, I had just enough time to get into Michael's laptop before anyone noticed.

I tiptoed downstairs, wincing each time the step creaked or the cottage groaned. Finally, I arrived at the landing and went straight to work in the cozy snug. I opened my husband's laptop and typed in the code.

Last night, after dinner, the television played the latest news from home. It seemed to be broadcast on nearly every channel. I watched as the stocks plummeted, hundreds of IRA accounts flushed down the drain in a matter of moments. Though I'd been afraid to look at our accounts, I couldn't avoid it forever. I held my breath as I entered my PIN and waited. When the screen finally came up, I gasped, then covered my mouth, my fears coming to life in a single snapshot. We had lost—

"Thirty-six thousand dollars," Michael said from behind me.

I jerked back in surprise. "Don't scare me like that," I whispered, shooting a hand up to still my racing heart.

Michael sat down on the sofa arm beside me. "Have you ever wondered why the tariffs were placed on all these countries?"

"To make the stock market plummet?" I queried a guess.

Michael quirked a brow. "Very good. You're a quick study. And why do you think anyone would want the stock market to plummet?"

I *knew* why. Most of the middle class would lose their retirement savings, and then billionaires could sweep in and buy up stocks for a pittance. I told Michael so.

"Wow! I'm impressed."

"I'm not as dumb as I look," I said with a smile.

He chuckled, then squeezed in beside me. "It's one of the biggest heists in history. Years have been spent getting the middle class to where they are now as a direct result of Roosevelt's New Deal and the rise of the unions. Together, they brought us out of the Great Depression. In a matter of a month, most of that has been reversed. Think about it."

I closed my eyes, wishing I could unsee what I'd just witnessed with my own two eyes. At this rate, we would be broke by Christmas.

"How will the middle class and poor survive?" An edge of hysteria crept into my voice.

"I don't know. As for us, I read the fortune cookie ahead of time. I pulled most of our money from our accounts and brought it with me. But I didn't have time to pull the stocks out."

My shoulders slumped in relief that we had at least part of our savings. We were the lucky ones. We still had a safety net, albeit a somewhat smaller one than before.

"Now what do we do?" I asked, concerned about our next steps.

"We fight."

Never before had my husband spoken with such force or conviction. Just then, I heard a rustle and turned. Benjamin entered the room in his bathrobe, yawning. Somewhere, he'd managed to find a cup of coffee. He placed it onto the coffee table, then sat opposite us.

"Now do you understand why Jamie fought for his people? Stole to survive?" Benjamin said as he rubbed his eyes.

Moments later, Cassidy entered the room, her eyes widening in surprise to see all of us seated around the laptop.

"What? A party, and I haven't been invited?"

"Some party," I said. "Look."

She took a seat next to me and leaned in. "What am I looking at?"

"Our stocks have dropped by $36,000 since the tariffs took place."

"The rub of it is," Benjamin said, lifting his mug, "is that as soon as the transfer of wealth is complete, the tariffs will come off, and no one will be the wiser that they've just been conned. Welcome to the new world order." He sipped of the complex aroma of

Colombian beans that now cost a small fortune. "I bought this before the tariffs," he added with a touch of irony.

"Then let's all have a cup," I declared, handing the laptop to Cassidy. "Nothing like fiddling as Rome burns." But even as I spoke, I tasted the bitterness at the back of my throat. The America I knew and loved had been trashed and burned in mere months. Every day, I read of new freedoms being taken away. Freedom of speech on campus. Even people within the party in power feared to speak out, at risk of putting themselves or their loved ones in danger.

With heavy hearts, we set about making breakfast. I had just finished scrambling the eggs and setting the bacon onto the table, or rashers as they were known here, when the guard entered.

"Where have you been?" Michael growled.

"Checking the perimeter," the guard said.

Though introduced as Angus, his real identity was strictly guarded so none of us could finger him if caught.

"And?"

"And I found this." He dug a hand into his pocket and pulled out a cross.

"Where did you get that?" I said, the hackles on my neck standing on end.

"Found it lying in the dirt." Angus, a burly man who looked like a dock worker with thick black eyebrows, frowned. "Why? Have you seen it before?"

I nodded, my throat suddenly dry. "Not that one, exactly, but one like it." I turned to Cassidy, whose lips had all but disappeared as she stared at the object, so similar to the one in the geocache. Surely, it couldn't be a coincidence.

Benjamin jumped to his feet and grabbed it from the other man's hand. He turned it this way and that to get a better look at it in the light. In a matter of seconds, he'd gone from a healthy shade of pink to a pale white, and his hands trembled as he held it.

"I know this cross. I've seen it before... Oh, good God!"

He dropped it as if burned and watched as it clattered to the floor.

"How? How could such a thing reappear after all these years?"

He fell into his seat and placed his head in his hands. As he did, I saw him there, but it wasn't him. It was Jamie, moaning and rocking, while speaking in Gaelic, something incomprehensible. And then I saw the blood dripping down the side of his face.

So, the war had begun. *Their* war, three hundred years ago, and our war now—only with ours, I didn't know how it had begun, nor how it would end. I just knew if we weren't careful, history would repeat itself and we might end up like Jamie MacPherson. Dead.

Chapter 57
Cobra

Frank peered up at the tall edifice that had been his work home for much of his adult life. Always before, he'd been eager to face each challenge, but today, everything was different. He didn't go straight home when he left the parking lot after consoling Shannon. Instead, he stopped at a bar, something he hadn't done in years. He just needed time to think, to lose the feeling of utter despair. It's as if a mania had swept the nation, one that he had helped usher in, but it wasn't what he'd expected, and for the first time in his life, he doubted his decision.

"What will you have?" the bartender asked.

Frank decided on a beer, which the bartender poured. Then he slid it to him without spilling a drop. Frank took a sip.

"Care to share?" the bartender asked.

Frank shook his head. He just needed a minute to dull the pain of losing someone as valuable as Shannon, both on a professional level and on a personal one. It was hard to find someone who fit him like a glove. She understood his moods and was top-notch at her job. Where would he ever find someone to replace her, even if the current administration would allow it?

He glanced up at the TV set that hung suspended over the bar. Yet again, he watched the headlines. It seemed like every day something new popped up. This time it was the Scots out protesting the US president's arrival in Aberdeen for the announcement of the opening of a new mall. Frank had read somewhere that the president's mother was born in Scotland. Many had been forced out of the Highlands in the Highland Clearances, including her maternal ancestors. She'd come to America as a domestic servant, so how had she risen in the ranks to marry a wealthy businessman? And how had she raised a child with such little empathy for the poor and underclass? Who despised immigrants from the southern US border, calling them all sorts of despicable names.

Frank didn't want to think about it. He just wanted to numb himself, to forget this horrible day. He polished off the glass of beer, then grabbed his jacket and headed for home. By the time he arrived, Jen and her boyfriend were already gone. He winced when Mia told him between sips of her latte.

"She needed to get back to her dorm to study up for her exams, but she told me to tell you she loves you."

That hurt even worse than if she'd called it like it was—he'd missed spending time with his daughter. Again.

"Tell you what. Why don't we put together a family vacation this summer?"

"Really?" Mia said, setting her cup of coffee down on the island countertop.

"Really. Now where's Jacob?"

"He's upstairs playing video games on your computer."

Frank sighed. If he'd told him once, he'd told him a thousand times not to touch his computer. You never knew when a private business email might come over in his email folder.

"I'll deal with it."

Before he could leave, Mia placed a hand on his arm, the concern evident in her expression. "How'd it go with Shannon? Were you able to save her job?"

Her question was a punch to the gut. He bit his lips to keep from saying something he might regret, from railing against those who had decided to can such a kind person, not to mention a fantastic worker.

All he could do was shake his head over the pain lodged in his throat.

"I'm so sorry, Frank."

"She'll be by for dinner tomorrow—before I go—"

"To Scotland, I know."

Her words felt like an accusation.

He nodded, then he ran upstairs to talk to his son. As he opened the door, his stomach dropped when he heard a whirring noise and saw a map scrolling through with dot after dot, all color-coded.

Jacob turned to him, his eyes wide and his voice thin.

"Dad, what is this?"

Chapter 58
Esme Stalwart

Hannah and I had been busy for days now, tending the wounded, the sick, the disabled. And still they came. We hadn't seen a skirmish like this in a long time. I had slept little in days, workin' in a catnap whenever possible, but it wasn't enough. The crow's feet around Isla's eyes had begun to take shape with each passing day, the fatigue evident in the set of her shoulders. As if the very earth itself had witnessed the tragedy, the skies wept a steady stream of tears that dripped down on the inhabitants of such a cruel world. And still we kept on, even as our spirits flagged.

"Still no sign of Jamie?" Isla asked, a mother's worry evident in her words.

"Nae," I said, feeling just as deflated as her. If he didn't come home soon, he may not come home at all, and I couldna bear the thought of it.

Hannah squeezed my arm. "He'll return. Ye must ha' faith."

Faith, a word bandied about in excess despite the chaos surroundin' us. Though I tried to summon a smile, my lips had no will for it, but my traitorous eyes gave me away as tears welled up inside them, spilling over like the skies above. They washed away dirt. Fatigue. Hope. And still the wounded arrived on one litter after another.

Finally, on the fourth day, when I could stomach it no more, the rains stopped, and with it the constant influx of injured. The earth stilled, and a few birds chirped a tentative peace. I'd had no time to ask questions, too busy tending to the sick and dying. But on this day, I sought one man who appeared heartier than the rest and was one of the last to arrive.

"How is the battle goin'?" I ventured to ask.

"Aye, we got 'em on the run now. We rousted the *Southrons*, we did."

I gripped his arm at talk of rousting the British. Part of me wanted to believe the man. The other part knew it may only be a wounded man's boast.

"Did ye see Jamie?" I demanded. "Jamie MacPherson."

The man peered at me long and hard, one eye partially closed. "Ye're his wife?"

I nodded, the set of my shoulders betraying my desperation, the silent plea resting on my lips.

"Ah! A sly one, that. Ye'll see him alive, I would bet. If anyone coulda survived the onslaught, it woulda been him."

"Then why isn't he here?" I demanded, my tone pitched and frantic.

"He'll be the last to return, if I don't mind sayin' so. He's hard for a fight. Doesn't give up easily, that one. If not for him, half of these men woulda been dead already, they would. But your Jamie kept them goin'. Gave them all a speech, he did, about what it means to be a Reiver, to protect the Borderland, to care for our people. That Jamie is one in a million, but he's no' loved by the rich; I can tell ye that. Takes to thievin' he does."

"To keep us alive," I reminded him. "All of us." I lifted my chin to encompass the entire band of men, women, and children."

"Ye're right about that. He takes care of more than just his people. A true gent, if ye ask me."

His words offered unexpected comfort in this time of difficulty, and I thanked him for it. Now that the wounded were all cared for, Isla came by and pointed toward the caravan.

"Get some rest, Esme. Ye've been up fer days."

"As have ye," I reminded her.

"Yes, but I just finished a two-hour nap, so off with ye. I'll take watch and wake ye if ye're needed."

I thanked her profusely, more exhausted than I'd ever been in my life. My entire body ached with fatigue as I made my way into the caravan that now smelled of herbs and disinfectants. But I cared not a wit. Instead, I crawled up onto the raised bed in back and barely managed to cover myself with Isla's colorful spread before nodding off into a fitful sleep.

It ended sometime later with the sound of hoofbeats racing into the clearing. Disoriented from the deep slumber that had engulfed me, I sat up, uncertain if I had heard the sound or if it was merely a dream, or perhaps a nightmare.

I tried to crawl out of my bed linen but became entangled in the bedding and fell unceremoniously on my rump. There I sat, crying like a wee child and cursing the fool that had brought me to this moment, when I saw a face pop up through the open doorway.

"Jamie!" I screeched.

"Dear god, woman. What are ye doin' on yer backside?"

He laughed, as did I, the laughter muddled with tears. I sat like that for some moments, when at last I saw what I hadn't before. Blood. On the side of his head and dripping into his shirt.

I clambered to my feet to go to him, but Isla arrived before me. "Put him on the bed," she ordered.

She reached in her bag for a Celtic cross and gave it a kiss for good luck. Then she shouted for Hannah to bring her bag of medicines. And it dawned on me what she meant for me to do. We were to sew up Jamie, Isla and I. Together.

Chapter 59
Destiny Jacqueline Kismet

One day bled into the next, each more harrowing than the last, the television set a constant drone in the background. "Turn that off!" I finally said, the stress of it giving me a stomach ache. But just as Michael walked over to turn off the set, breaking news came through.

"The Pope is dead."

All the air whooshed out of my chest. Though I wasn't Catholic, I liked the Pope and what he represented. He, of all the men in the Vatican, had cared about the poor, the sick, the hungry. The outsider. Like Jamie. Like us.

What next? I thought of all the storms in the Bible and prayed we could somehow steer a course away from the shoals of our greed and heartlessness. I wondered if God would even recognize his creation, should his son return to earth. We had learned nothing since the day Jesus had been hung on the cross. Nothing at all.

Michael must have seen my rising panic, because he stood and crossed the room, where he tossed his arms around me and held me tight. Benjamin and Cassidy entered the room, and seeing us, paused before the television set. Their shared look of concern said it all.

"We can't wait much longer," Benjamin said to Michael.

"Wait for what?" I balled my fists, frustrated by the lack of information.

"Ladies, sit." Michael ushered Cassidy and I to take a seat on the sofa while he stood, Benjamin coming to stand beside him.

"I know we haven't been very forthcoming."

"Very forthcoming?" I growled, tired of being left out of the loop. "This involves our lives, too, Cassidy's and mine." I pointed at my chest. "We should have a say about whether we want to be involved in this...this whatever you're up to." I threw up my hands in defeat.

Michael steepled his fingers beneath his chin. "What we're about to do is dangerous. It could land us in prison...or worse."

The bottom fell out of my stomach and a squeal of fear rose inside me, spilling onto my tongue in a bitter wash of anger. Hot tears stung my eyelids. I peered up at the ceiling, then closed my eyes in order to grab hold of my emotions. Once they were in check, I breathed deeply, then lowered my head to face him.

Calm now, I said, "Go on."

"Benjamin knows a way to rectify the wholesale theft taking place in the stock market. For the loss of jobs."

Benjamin broke in, his black hair falling across one eye. "You see, in the coming years, AI will replace workers worldwide...millions of them. When that happens, there will be a worker's revolt and much bloodshed. What we're trying to do is to forestall that. Without jobs, people will have no homes, no food."

"Like in the Great Depression," I murmured.

"Maybe worse," Benjamin conceded.

The room suddenly felt stuffy, and I jumped to my feet to open a window to allow some fresh air into the room. To my surprise, a wren entered. According to a birding book I'd once read, wrens represented hope and freedom. I prayed it was an omen...a sign. Wrens abhorred captivity, much as I did since being sequestered in this tiny cottage. Over time, the walls seemed to close in on me, and though I'd never suffered from claustrophobia before, I began to feel it now. The wren's happy chirp offered a respite of hope and purpose.

"How can we stop it...this Depression, or whatever you want to call it?"

Cassidy leaned into me, as though seeking comfort in my presence. I threw an arm around her as we closed ranks.

Benjamin answered me in a roundabout way. "The irony of all this is, without money, no one will be able to purchase anything from these companies, which means many will go out of business, so in effect, they're killing the goose that laid the golden egg—the buyer. Us. You'd never have this many wealthy people if we hadn't first had a middle class...a middle class that the unions fought to create and uphold."

"Because it's a symbiotic relationship," I added.

"Exactly."

"So fewer purchasers will mean fewer—"

"—-wealthy people, yes. So the titans of industry will have to fight each other over the remaining spoils, which means far fewer rich people." He bit his lip. "Imagine it this way. Take an insect, like an aphid (the owner of a business). It feeds off plants, but if it kills off the host plant (us), then it will no longer have a food supply, and they will soon die out."

I shooed the wren out the window and lowered the sash slightly. "So, in effect, by getting rid of the worker, they're cutting their own throats. No more workers, no more people to purchase their supplies."

"The sword cuts both ways. That's why industry needs workers, and workers need industry."

Back to my earlier question. "So how do you plan to stop the bleeding?"

Benjamin broke into a wide smile as he glanced over at Michael, who still appeared pensive.

"This is where it gets interesting...and where we can either become heroes or wind up swinging by a rope."

I pictured the fiddle I'd seen at the museum, purposefully crushed when no one would sing the rant Jamie had written for his time on the gallows. Then and there, my stomach lurched. I ran to the open window and unceremoniously heaved my breakfast onto the ground outside. When I was done, I wiped my mouth.

"Now I can think clearly," I said. "Go on."

Chapter 60
60 Esme Stalwart

Jamie's scalp reminded me of a scar I'd once seen on an elderly man, a single line with intersecting tracks. I checked it daily until at last, he grabbed me with one arm and swung me onto his lap.

"Will ye ne'er let me be, woman? Like a mother hen, ye are, always checkin' me o'er for damage. Well, I can tell ye I'm as right as rain, I am, and ye best get used to these wounds."

For the next half hour, he reminded me of the many scars he'd accumulated over the years, one where some fencing had unraveled and left a gash curling up his arm. Another war wound bisected his chin, and still another had nearly taken off a finger. I had to laugh, because he seemed to enjoy the recollections of his many injuries, as though they were a great source of pride. And I suppose the reason for the wounds *was* a source of pride for many reasons, not the least of which was that he'd protected both his homeland and his people and had living proof written up and down his body.

"Is it over?" I asked. "The fighting?"

He pierced me with a look. "Is it ever over? It's the way of the world. Men have been fightin' for any number o' reasons for centuries and no doubt will for centuries to come."

Call me naive, but I had always imagined we'd become more civilized one day. Jamie had burst my bubble for any hope of that. For a while, we sat in silence beneath the shade tree as he stroked my arm with his fingertips. It sent a shiver of delight runnin' through me. Just then I felt the baby kick and placed his hand on my stomach so he could feel it. And just as suddenly, an echoing kick seared my conscience. What if Jamie never lived to see the baby? What then?

As if he read my mind, he cupped my hand inside his and looked me in the eyes, as though seeing me for the first time and finding me worthy. "Ye musn't worry about the future, Esme. Ye canna change the past nor anythin' to come, so you might as well live for the here and now. It's all we have, in the end."

His words were tinged with melancholy that filled me with tears. I had to admit, I'd been a lot more emotional lately. Isla said it was natural and to expect it, but still the sorrow came out of nowhere, shocking me into silence.

As I sat there, wallowing in self-pity, I saw Jamie lift his chin to one of his men, and moments later, a little slip of a pup came bounding up on paws too big for the wee dog, a rough collie, if memory served.

"Who are ye, little man?" I said, scooping him up in my arms. And like that, I had all but forgotten the world and its many vagaries.

The dog lapped at my chin, its puppy breath and energy fueling my laughter.

"He's yours," Jamie said, and held his paw as though making introductions. "What will ye name him?"

I paused, thinking. The wee beast tilted his head, and I couldn't help but think of Jamie, a braw young lad, so that's what I named him.

"Braw?" Jamie said, as though disappointed. "I was thinking more along the lines of Whisky, since he's the color 'o whisky, 'cept for the white. Besides, I traded it for him."

"Traded whisky...for a dog?"

"Aye. It 'twas William Duff's very own dog, it 'twas."

The skin on my neck prickled, and for one brief moment, I thought I might scream. What was he thinkin', stealin' William Duff's dog? Fire warmed my cheeks, and I stood so suddenly the puppy rolled off my lap and landed in a heap.

"Ye've got to be jokin'," I hissed. "William Duff already has half the county out lookin' for ye. Why on earth would you risk it?"

Jamie shrugged and reached over to pick up the dog, which he sat in his lap and began petting. "I thought it only fitting, aye? While he and his men were out searchin' for the likes of me, I doubled back to his manor and talked one of the groomsmen into sellin' me the dog. He was only too happy to comply, considerin' how the old coot treats 'im."

Angry tears stung my eyes. It was bad enough the Travellers were outlawed and their lives worth nary a halfpenny, or as many around these parts called it, a *bawbee*. But did Jamie have to rub it in by stealin' from the man?

"He's a *wurm*, Es, a maggot. Runs the county like it's his own fiefdom, never caring about the likes of us, whether or not we live or die. A stolen pup is the least of his worries."

"Is that why ye took so long to return home?"

"Aye." But then his expression softened. "And because I knew ye were lonely without me. I thought it might help if ye had a companion when I was gone, a protector. And the baby, too."

How did he always know the right thing to say? I sat down beside him. As much as I appreciated the dog, I wanted *him*, but I knew he had obligations to the clan...and to himself. As if Braw knew we were discussin' him, he came up and lapped at my face, wigglin' like a regular *saithe*, the cod so common around the coastline.

"Okay, okay! I surrender," I said. "You boys outnumber me, like always."

"That's my girl," Jamie said, happy to see I'd finally warmed to his gift of a puppy. "Now!" He patted me on the rump. "I could use some of yer fine cookin'." He winked at me, the charmer. If only I didn't sense something was wrong, that even now William Duff was scourin' the land for Jamie and his men. But it was Jamie he wanted. Jamie, who had once been the son of a laird and a rival. It would be the crowning glory to the jewel of Duff's legacy to free the county of my beloved Jamie. And I could do nothing to stop him.

Chapter 61
Cobra

The computer kept ticking away numbers, figures, maps, all in a colorful array. When the numbers finally clicked off, all that was left were the words, "We're watching you."

"Dad?" Jacob repeated. "What is this? What's happening?"

Jacob's hair was cut tight at the sides, curly at the top. For just an instant, Frank saw him as the child instead of the man, his expression the same as when he'd found a scary bug in the backyard.

"I don't know, son, but you shouldn't be playing on the computer."

"But this isn't normal, right?" His pale blue eyes stared up at Frank, his smattering of light freckles again reminding him of the child he'd once been.

"No, it's not normal, son."

Nor did the computer warning seem in keeping with anything he'd seen or heard about the ring he was investigating. By all accounts, these weren't the type you'd find writing hate speeches in their basements with no accountability. Joe had thought they were insiders.

So if not them, who?

Suddenly, it was as if the room temperature had dropped because a chill whipped through him. No. *Could it be?* His secretary had just been canned along with the top administration. Could the new administration be firing a warning shot over the bow? Making certain they all remained in check. *And checkmate.*

He'd read that authoritarian regimes installed fear in their people, and especially the people inside the government, but would they go this far to scare him? The answer surprised him.

Yes.

"Son, why don't you go downstairs and help your mom prepare dinner? I'll take care of this."

"But, Dad—"

"No buts. Just do as I say, son."

He hadn't meant to sound gruff, but he needed to get to the bottom of this. Things were happening too fast—faster than he could keep up. And he didn't like the looks of it. Now, more than ever, he was glad he'd asked for a detail for his wife.

He spent the next hour logging through his browser history, but like before, everything had been wiped clean. Finally, he stood and stretched. He needed to get back to his family before Jacob jumped ship too. But before he could, the phone rang. He picked it up.

"Hi, Frank?"

For years he'd been taught to read people. It's what he did for a living: watched body language, listened for tells, and here was a big one. His head of security's voice sounded hesitant, as if afraid—

"Oh no!"

"I'm afraid so, Frank. Your wife's detail was pulled."

"By whom?" Frank demanded.

"By our newly installed leadership. I'm sorry to say, your wife's on her own."

"Thanks for letting me know," Frank said. "And Harve—"

"Yeah?"

"Keep in touch."

"I will," Harve said. Then he hung up the phone.

Frank stood for a moment staring out the window. When had everything gone so wrong? He'd faced challenges before—numerous challenges—but this was by far the worst.

He released a slow sigh. Fortunately, he knew private contractors he could call upon. One of them would protect Mia while he was gone. He'd see to it. Now, to make the calls. Then, to apologize to Mia for once again ruining a family get-together.

He was just about to leave his office when a shadow formed against the wall. Probably just the tree giving off shade where once there had been light, but then again, it was still too early for that. And the shadow took on a...*human* form.

"Come," the shadow said. "To Scotland. We ha' work to do."

Frank swallowed down the bile in his throat. That's when he heard Mia call from below.

"Are you coming, Frank? Jacob needs to get going."

He paused for only a moment, his heart sinking and his stomach sour. Then he turned, only too eager to leave the shadow behind.

"On my way!" he called.

Once again, he'd need to make up for his poor performance as a father. When he returned...from Scotland.

Chapter 62
Destiny Jacqueline Kismet

Cassidy held my hair back as I leaned over the toilet, heaving again and again until finally nothing was left to expel. Afterwards, she washed my face with a warm cloth and handed me a toothbrush. To think, just one month ago I had been home, hoping against hope that all would turn out well, that we wouldn't jump off this cliff we were on, but I was sadly mistaken. I shook my head, climbed to my feet, and peered in the mirror. My eyes were bloodshot and my skin sallow. Furthermore, I had yet to learn what Benjamin and Michael had planned and how it involved Cassidy and me. Downstairs, I heard the door screech open and men talking in low voices. But then I heard the door shut and the men's voices ebb.

"Okay, Ma, spit!" Cassidy ordered, then handed me a glass with fresh water to rinse my mouth out. Then she began brushing my hair, which seemed especially dry and lifeless today.

Once I was relatively cleaned up, she took me by the hand and walked me to the upstairs bedroom, then plunked me down on her bed. From where I sat, the wind whistled in the trees. She opened up the window wider to birds chirping, unaware of the changing world around them and the havoc that seemed to flow at a steady pace, like water over a falls. Its roar was deafening to those like me, who were wound just a little too tight. All across the airwaves, newscasters offered ways for people to overcome the stress of everyday living.

When has that ever happened?

Not since the 60s, when the collective lives of those affected by Vietnam had witnessed the daily battles on the six o'clock news, storing it inside them like ticking time bombs.

"Did your father or Benjamin tell you any more about their plans?"

Cassidy tensed. "They thought it better to hold off talking about things, seeing you didn't take it well."

"Great!" I groused. Just another reason to keep the whole scheme a secret. If my life was going to change in unexpected ways, I needed to understand how and why.

"Mom," Cassidy said, her expression pensive. "I've been thinking."

"Oh?" Did I *want* to hear what she had to say? Cassidy had always been my rock. I cherished her opinion above all others. But what if she wanted me to go along with their plans, sight unseen? I winced because it wasn't in my nature to go along to get along. It's not the way I was built. The way I operated.

"I think Dad and Benjamin have something really huge planned."

"How huge?" My spine tingled with an unnamed fear. "What are we talking about here?"

Cassidy pursed her lips, her bright blue eyes hooded. "I overheard the two of them talking…in the computer room. They said there's no going back afterward, that once they set their plans into motion, we all have to go into hiding."

For once, I heard the trepidation in her voice. My strong, beautiful daughter, who never let things bother her until she was in the privacy of her own room, now lived in fear. If *she* was afraid…

I allowed the thought to trail off, not wanting to comprehend the ramifications of that statement. I licked my lips. "When? How?"

She shook her head. "I don't know. That's all I heard. Ma," she said, her voice quivering now. "I'm scared."

"So am I, honey, but we have to be patient. Your dad is a cautious man." Or at least he had been until he'd left to go overseas. What changed? But then I thought of all the amazing, competent people who had lost their jobs simply because they weren't loyalists to the new president.

A shot of adrenaline rushed through me in a cascade of emotions. Had he really left his job as he had said, or had he lost it and just didn't want to tell me? I'd never thought to ask. In these highly partisan times, anybody could lose their job, even career government workers who had devoted their entire lives to our country. Veterans, bureaucrats, the people who kept the mail running. On the news, the commentator reported the government was talking about privatizing USPS, an institution that had seen our country through nearly 250 years, Benjamin Franklin himself appointed the first Postmaster General by the Constitutional Congress. The same man who had experimented with a kite, a key, and lightning to prove that lightning held an electrical current. How many times had I been taught that as a child?

I have to stay positive.

"So what do we do?" Cassidy asked.

Somewhere, deep inside me, my spine stiffened with a new resolve, and I stood. "What we do now is march in there and demand to know what's happening. This is our life, too, Cassidy...yours and mine."

For the first time in a long time, she smiled. "Phew! I'm glad you said that. You may look like a cream puff on the outside, Ma, but I know there's a backbone of steel in there somewhere."

"Gee, thanks," I said. It felt good to laugh.

We packed up our emotions and tucked them away for now as we headed downstairs to the living room where the two men sat waiting, their expressions pensive. I opened my mouth to speak when the front door burst open and three men entered, one the guard, along with two other men I didn't recognize. The third man stood between the two, head lowered and his hands zip-tied behind his back, both men taking one of his arms. A red welt blossomed on his right cheek as if he'd been...

Punched.

"We found this guy snooping around. We think he's one of Duff's men."

"Wait!" I said, throwing my hands up. "William Duff of Braco? The one who set Jamie up to die?"

Benjamin came to stand beside me and placed a hand on my shoulder. "No, Destiny. A distant relation to William. He works on the police force here in Aberdeen."

A chill shattered the warmth I'd felt earlier. So, were we all acting out some ancient play, only in a different lifetime, the stakes much larger this time around? Except that now, Esme Stalwart wanted the end to change, for Benjamin to survive, and for the pair of them, Cassidy and Benjamin, to live on. And I was to be the person to facilitate this, only the man who wanted Benjamin dead... My limbs trembled and my skin paled.

"Don't you dare get sick, Ma," Cassidy warned. "We need you...Dad and me...and Benjamin."

Reluctantly, I nodded, heeding her warning. If I meant to save the lot of them, I would need that steel backbone, now more than ever.

"Okay, what can we do to help?"

Chapter 63
Esme Stalwart

The border wars with the English bought us the time we needed to disappear into the countryside, as we'd done so many times before. We packed up our caravan and battened down the hatches. Soon, we were back on the road. The Travellers, known for a nomadic lifestyle, had itchy feet, and as soon as we set sail, the excitement filtered through the train as Jamie's horse trotted past us at a crisp pace, its hooves clopping against the hard-packed earth. And I had to admit as we drove deeper into the woodlands, the air smelled fresher, more raw, as though I'd become untethered by the roving landscape owned by no man. I lifted my face to the sun, exhilarating in its warmth, a rare treat these days. For once I understood the desire to be on the move, for the countryside to ride past us in a rolling wave of vegetation. Hunkered in the middle of birch and oak, creeping lady's tresses thrived alongside twinflowers, both bearing white, bell-shaped flowers with just a hint of sweetness.

The sick and dying had been left behind with other, more settled clans, if one dared to call a Reiver Clan settled, for they were the very epitome of wild, often vicious, and most definitely cunning, much like our own people.

Isla snapped the reins. No longer the healer, she'd faded into the background as before, yet her beauty radiated strength and resolve as our caravan swayed to the rhythm of flight.

"Where will we go now?" I asked Isla.

Last night, the men had settled around the fire talking into the wee hours of the mornin', planning, as they always did, as a clan. Occasionally, one of the men would become riled, but Jamie, with his usual charm, soon settled him with a dram of whiskey and a round of song.

"We're headed north again. Seems young Jamie has heard of a festival up in Aberdeen."

I turned a sharp eye to face Isla on the wooden bench. "Aberdeen? But that's near Banff...and Laird Braco!" My stomach dropped, and my knees felt weak. As a son of a laird and a child of the Travellers, Jamie kowtowed to no one. I feared his audacity might well be his undoing someday.

"Not to worry. We'll winter over in a dale Jamie knows well toward the East Coast. We'll wait until spring to go to the fair. By then ye'll have that bairn of yours."

Isla winked, then clucked at the Gypsy Vanner, horses known for their large white bodies and big black spots with an all-black mane, their forelocks feathered and white. Their breed was specific to the Gypsies who travelled the continent, and they suited me fine, for they were beautiful and strong, like Isla herself, and I attempted to model their likeness, however unsuccessfully.

I rubbed my belly as if to divine what sort of child Jamie and I would have. Would she be bold and proud like Jamie, or more circumspect, like me? I peered down at my growing belly. I'd come from a family who lived in that no man's land, where borders shifted yearly. When things got particularly rough, my *faither* shipped me off to live with an aunt up north. At the time, I'd thought that the way of things, how people always lived. The constant movement back and forth made me a Traveller by birth, if not by blood. Only later, when my *da'* was killed in a particularly bloody skirmish between two rival clans and my *mam* packed me up and moved me and my sisters northward, did I learn the truth—that not everyone lived a life of war and strife.

I pulled my shawl more tightly around me, my mind a rush of memories. It wasn't until I'd become an adult that she told me the truth. "The house still stands, and as the eldest daughter, it's yer birthright, since there are no men to look after it."

She'd said it in such a cavalier manner that I'm certain she believed I would want nothin' to do with it. But for me, in some strange way I cannot fathom to this day, it represented security, though a less secure place I could not imagine because neither time nor allegiance had changed anything. The Borderlands were still in flux.

"Did Jamie ever tell ye how we met?" I asked Isla.

"I figured he and his men were probably fighting for some laird or the other. Or for the Englanders, whoever paid them best."

"Aye," I concurred. "When he found out I was livin' alone in that vast wasteland, he'd a wondered I hadn't been killed or…" I let the words die out.

"How long were ye livin' out there before Jamie found ye?"

"Only a few months. I hid when anyone came to call, but Jamie discovered me out in the cowshed, underneath some hay." I smiled at the memory. Me with a head of hay and him with that sardonic grin. "He pulled the hay from my hair and then and there promised me his undying protection."

Isla chuckled, her golden brown eyes even more riveting than Jamie's. When the light shone through them, it gave them an otherworldly glow that made it hard to look away.

"That's my boy." She said it with an almost shy quality, proud of the son she'd raised, but a stranger too, half laird, half Traveller.

"He made certain the men looked after me when he was away."

She paused, her head slightly cocked as though inspecting me. "Ye're a lucky woman, Esme."

"Oh?" I said, not understanding her meaning.

"Had Jamie not come along when he had and offered his protection, ye'd not be here now. The Borderland is a dangerous place for a woman alone. Very dangerous."

As if the earth itself had registered her meaning, the sun hid behind a cloud and the air cooled. I shivered because I was indeed lucky but too young and stupid to have known it…until now.

Chapter 64
Destiny Jacqueline Kismet

"Here's your go-bag."

Michael passed out four bags, one for each of us. I peered inside at the sundry belongings he'd placed there. "What are these?" I asked, pulling goggles from the backpack.

"They're thermal imaging goggles. They detect heat...in case."

In case what? I wondered, my stomach doing flips.

Benjamin appeared from the kitchen with a large screwdriver.

"What are you doing with that?" Cassidy asked, fear written in the whites of her eyes.

Benjamin stared down at it, as if he'd forgotten it was even in his hand. "I'm destroying the hard drives of our computers. All except the laptops. We'll take those with us."

"The hard drives?" *What next?* I turned to Michael for an explanation.

He threw up his hands to ward off any more questions. "Des, Cassidy, we're bugging out. We can't leave any trace behind."

"Excuse me?" I growled, my frustration setting my molars grinding. "What exactly are we running from, and why?"

"Stop, Des! Just stop," he shouted, then stormed out of the room alongside Benjamin.

Cassidy and I glanced at each other, her face as pale as mine, no doubt. We decided to follow them, where, true to their word, they rushed through the computer room, metal grating against metal as they dismantled computers two at a time. Dusk had settled in, and with it an uneasiness that made the air thick with an undercurrent of panic. Sweat tinged their brows as they finished destroying the last of the hard drives on the computers before burning the machines in a pile out back, then burying them in a deep well.

Michael turned to Benjamin. "Where'd you put Duff's man?"

"The guards are keeping him in the cellar for now. They're going to stay behind, blindfold him, wait a week, and then release him far from here. Give him something to disorient him for a while until we've had a chance to flee."

I breathed a sigh of relief that they didn't plan to kill him. If they had, there'd be no turning back.

"If anyone else comes snooping around, our men will keep them busy, give us time to flee. Our army will protect us—"

"Army?" The hackles on my neck rose at the mention of an army.

"Des, we have to get these laptops out if we're going to have time to launch."

Hot tears of anger welled in my eyes, and a fire burned in my chest. I pictured Isla and her plea to save Jamie. Now, I was beginning to wonder if I could save any of us, let alone her reincarnated son.

"Please don't tell me—" My knees began to buckle, and Michael caught me.

"Not that kind of launch, and I have no time to explain. We have to get out of here...now. Get your backpacks on and let's go. Those are your orders!"

He barked it with such grit and determination that it dawned on me he was used to commanding men. Was he part of a SEAL Team, or some other elite force that went into foreign countries either to get people out or target terrorists?

Cassidy helped me with my backpack, then put on hers. She marched beside me as we headed out into the night.

"Goggles down," Michael whispered.

We did as ordered. Immediately, those closest to us put off an eerie green light, while anything static, like trees and buildings, showed up as darker images inside the round lenses. We were ordered to hunker down as Michael and Benjamin led from the front, their pistols raised while scanning for any movement. Michael cocked a finger, pointing north. With a heavy heart, I realized that any hope of returning to our life before was now gone. Cassidy and I were in, whether we liked it or not.

We'd been walking for nearly an hour when we caught sight of a patrol. To avoid being captured, Michael handed each of us a reflective suit. We quickly suited up and kept moving. Benjamin pointed toward a gap in the hills that would ostensibly put a mountain between us and them. Michael nodded, and the pair scampered up the hillside, Michael leading, while Benjamin circled back to make sure we made it safely up the incline.

We didn't stop until well into the wee hours of the morning, when Benjamin led us inside a cave in the hillside.

Cassidy entered ahead of me and spun around as Benjamin lit up the cavern with his flashlight. "How did you know about this place?" she breathed.

As soon as I crossed the threshold, I gripped the rock with my hand to steady myself and gasped. Inside were the remains of an ancient wayfarer. The simple wooden coffin had been opened, and loose bits of sheeting blew in the wind. I rushed in to kneel beside it, but Benjamin stopped me with a hand.

"Be careful. The Travellers wouldna take kindly to someone messin' with their dead. They're superstitious, they are, and they believe the spirits will haunt you if you interfere in any way."

He eyed me with such seriousness that I knew he believed it and, furthermore, didn't want to see me hurt. I stepped back and nodded as he closed the lid.

"My people ha' used this cave for centuries to hide away from the world when we were not wanted. It allowed us to live under harsh conditions. There are many such caves throughout the continent."

I imagined what it must have been like, huddled against the cold, foraging and hunting for food in winter, depending only on each other for survival. Births and deaths took place in areas like these, no doubt.

"We best stay in this half o' the cave," he suggested.

In the time we'd been on the road, Benjamin had grown the beginnings of a beard and appeared more rugged than when I'd first met him and believed him to be a librarian. Now, I envisioned him not only as my son, Jamie, in my previous life, but as the headstrong yet charming man who could make even the hardest heart smile. All except for William Duff. He'd become a burr, chafing at the man's skin.

I patted my hands together for warmth.

"I'll start a fire," Benjamin announced.

"I'll help you collect the firewood," Michael agreed.

The two disappeared through the wide gap in the hillside, hidden only by some brambles. Once they were gone, I turned to Cassidy, who had taken a seat around a stone firepit in the center of the cave and was inspecting something in her hands.

"What is it?" I asked, bending down to see what she had discovered. "Oh my gosh. Is that a—?"

"It sure is," she murmured, her breath rising amid the damp and musty smell of the cavern.

I plopped down on my rear for a better look. "Well, what do you know?"

Chapter 65
Cobra

The closer the plane got to Heathrow Airport, the more Frank wished the days before he'd left had been different. He'd missed spending time with his kids, his wife, and he'd even failed at saving Shannon's job. Worse yet, he'd canceled dinner with her before he left, with everything so up in the air. What *had* he done right? he wondered with a sigh as he leaned back into his seat, his eyes drifting to the white clouds. Well, at least if Mia really needed him, she could contact him. They'd developed a code, years ago, to signify if the call was urgent, and one to signify if it was life or death. Fortunately, they'd never had to use it, and he hoped they never would. At least that gave him a measure of comfort.

He leaned back against the headrest, eager for a bit of shut-eye. But then, out of the corner of his eye, he saw flashes, like miniature lightning bolts. He blinked rapidly and was relieved when they disappeared. His relief was short-lived, however, as snippets of memory began to pour in. But memories of what?

A large Georgian manor house. *Click.* A black-and-white herding dog at his side. *Click.* A courthouse scene where Frank seemed to be battling it out with his architect, a man named William Adams. *Click.* The woman with the soulful eyes. *Click.* Him yelling for the sheriff to hang the man at all costs. *Click.*

Was *he* the man yelling, and if so, who did he want hanged? Frank pressed on his forehead to quell the random thoughts. Then he stared out at the landscape below as the aircraft descended through the clouds and toward the outskirts of the vast city of London. The Thames wound its way through the middle, ironically named the River Isis in certain locations.

Flash!

When he stared out at the landscape below, he scarcely dared to breathe as the window morphed into an ornate mirror where he caught a glimpse of the man whose mind he inhabited. Staring back at him was a square-jawed aristocrat with a strong chin and long narrow nose, eyebrows arched perfectly over cynical eyes. His hand rested inside his jacket like Napoleon, as if immolating the despotic leader of France. In the distance, he heard a man calling his image's name: "William Duff."

Frank must have begun mumbling to himself because the woman next to him scooted as far away as possible in the airplane cabin's tight quarters. He forced himself to remain calm. Maybe he *was* going crazy. He'd hoped that coming here would lessen the headaches and the flashes of memory, but instead, they'd only intensified.

He gripped the armrests, his knuckles white. Not until the plane landed with a thump did the images halt and his breathing become less labored. He grabbed his luggage from the overhead compartment, then rushed to exit the plane. Ten minutes later, he hailed a taxi that would take him the 16 miles to New Scotland Yard, which was originally housed on Great Scotland Yard Street in Whitehall. The police headquarters had taken its name from its location and stood on the site of a medieval palace that had housed Scottish royalty back in the day.

Once there, he paid his driver, then entered the neoclassical-style building through the sleek, curved glass front. At the lobby, he showed his credentials and was escorted inside to a bank of elevators and up to the fifth floor with windows that offered a wide command of the city. He was met by the man he had corresponded with over the past few months, Commander Philips, a tall chap with graying hair and skin the color of walnuts.

Philips ushered him into a room, introduced himself, then shut the door. "So what do you have?" he asked, eyeing Frank's briefcase.

Frank laid the briefcase on the table and clicked it open, handing him a bulleted list that his secretary had printed out so they could go over the finer points of his investigation.

Before she had been fired.

His throat burned at the memory.

The man scanned them briefly, his eyebrows lifting as he came to the end.

"Now, your turn," Frank said. *Quid pro quo.* "What has Scotland Yard found?"

Chapter 66
Esme Stalwart

The time passed more quickly than expected. We'd reached the dale by late summer, where we wintered over before movin' on to Aberdeen. Parts of the dale lay like a windswept ocean before us, the hillside devoid of all vegetation. Whereas Scots pine and Douglas fir anchored the northwestern portion of the valley—part of the early Caledonian forest—this section was more open. And as Isla promised, the first pains of motherhood came early on a cold December morning. Snow dotted the hillsides, where I had just enough time to prepare breakfast and ready myself for the coming day, when a sharp twinge jabbed me in the middle. I let out a short gasp and doubled over. Isla, who was tending the fire, ran over to me, her skirts smelling of ash and smoke.

Soon, the caravan was abuzz with activity as Isla and Jamie helped me to the vardo to give birth. I no sooner stepped inside, than my water burst, leaving me drenched and shivering from the waist down.

"Quick, son, help her onto the bed," Isla ordered as she ran to gather supplies. "And you," she said to one of the many people staring inside the caravan. "Get Baillie! Es is given' birth."

I recognized the midwife's name and saw a young girl go scurrying off in pursuit of her. While Isla prepared, Jamie somehow managed to lift me onto the bed with its red satin downy duvet. I quelled at the idea of getting it wet, but I was in too much pain to do anything about it. Once he had me on the bed, Jamie lifted my chin, a smile lighting the corners of his face, yet his eyes reflected his fear. My Jamie, a Reiver who had seen countless brawls, worried about my safety and that of our child's. Unable to speak just yet, I ran a hand across his cheek, encouraging him to be resilient. He took my hand and kissed it.

"Ye'll be fine, Es. Ye're strong as an ox, ye are."

I stifled a laugh, which set off another wave of contractions, and I cried out in pain. Thankfully, at that moment, Baillie arrived with a bag of supplies while Isla kept the water boiling. Carefully, she dipped in fresh rags to wipe me and the baby down when I was done given' birth.

"You best leave, Jamie," Baillie ordered. "Birth is no place for a man."

And indeed, Jamie had gone a shade of white that set off alarm bells, while the men standing at the opening of the caravan joked, "He's goin' all peely wally on us, he is."

"Tim-berrr!" another one shouted to a chorus of laughter.

"Off with ye...all of ye!" Isla growled. She helped Jamie out where he was swept away by the crowd of gawkers, barely landing on his feet before he disappeared among the maelstrom of well-wishers.

Once they'd left, she slammed the door shut and locked it, lest someone with a bit too much rum in his veins decide to crash the party, be it as it may. The room quickly filled with the smell of citrus and lavender. Then Isla made a cup of cramp bark tea to reduce my pain. Over the months, I had witnessed her give it to other expectant mothers, and now it was my turn. Between contractions, she lifted my head and had me drink small sips to prevent me from vomiting. The taste, though revolting, did help in time, and I eased my head back onto the bed, sweat dotting my brow.

For the next several hours, fresh waves of pain rolled over me until my legs shook with fatigue and my hair dampened from the effort of birthing our child.

"How much longer?" The question came out more as a plea than a simple quandary.

"The babe's in position now, so she should come soon, aye?" Baillie wiped the sweat off my forehead, but I tossed and turned, the slightest touch scorching my insides and making me want to retch.

"I know it's not easy." Isla's words gentled me. "But soon, ye'll have a bonnie wee daughter to call ye're own, and then the pain will ha' been worth it, ye ken?"

I tried to nod, but even that seemed too much of an effort. I shut my eyes tight against the bright light of the caravan, but it shone through my eyelids. Then a searing pain shot through me as a new contraction hit. I bit down hard and grimaced as I pushed down.

"She's comin', Es! I can see the crown. The baby has Jamie's hair. Keep pushing!" Isla encouraged.

"Red...hair?" I said between airy gasps.

"Aye, gonna be a spitfire, she will," Baillie assured me with a wink.

I pushed down harder. After several moments of gritting my teeth and groaning, I both heard and felt a whoosh, all at once. Soon, a bairn's cry followed as my baby entered the world of the caravan, a difficult world at that.

"Let me see her!" I cried, leaning forward with the help of Baillie.

Isla lifted her up and laid her on my stomach. The infant was covered in a creamy white coating, a stranger in a strange land. How would I ever explain it all to her when I understood so little of it myself?

"Ah, my little Fiadhaich or Kaileigh." Jamie and I had yet to agree on a name. "If yer *faither* ha' any say on it, ye'll be as wild and free as that red hair on yer head."

Isla eyed me. "Don't go given' her any ideas, now, Es. She'll ha' enough to worry about in a world of Travellers. No use fillin' her head with useless notions. She'll be just as free...or trapped...as the rest o' us."

That sobered me in an instant, and without warning, I began crying, softly at first, then great big sobs of sorrow and loss. Tears for all the turmoil she would face, the simple meanness of those who considered us others. I hadn't been born into it as the rest had, and the shock of it had never worn off. Or the stares, the whispers, the abject cruelty from those townspeople who thought of us as less than human. It had awakened me to a world I'd never known. One I wish I'd never had to face. I'd always thought of people as inherently good. Now I knew the truth. Even people I would have considered upstanding in the past could be cruel in the right circumstances. It taught me a lesson I would never forget.

Not used to emotional outbursts, Isla clucked and called to Baillie. "Go get Jamie. He'll know what to do!"

He returned five minutes later, his face flushed and the smell of drink on his skin, a gift from the men, no doubt, who had helped him celebrate his new offspring. Rather clumsily, he rushed to my side and stood beside me, his head even with mine where I lay on the raised bed. My tears had subsided only slightly, and I tasted their saltiness on my lips.

"What is it, Esme? What has you so troubled?" he asked, but then his eyes fell to our newborn. They filled with an unnamed tenderness at the sight of her.

"What do ye think o' her?" I hiccupped, peering down at my sweet girl, who peered up at me with huge blue eyes.

"She's a beauty, that one. We'll name her Kaileigh."

A smile graced my lips at the sound of it. "Kaileigh Fiadhaich McPherson."

He ran a finger tenderly over her forehead, and then I gave her a kiss for good measure, her smell sweet, like honey. Until now, he kept one hand behind his back. But then he showed me what he had been hiding.

"I brought our wee one a gift," he said.

Where he'd "found" the gift, I could only imagine. Still, I accepted it for what it was—a gift that a Traveller would never be able to afford in a lifetime. It was a porcelain doll, with hair as golden as the sunshine and with beautiful blue eyes, like hers. And she wore a blue silk dress with dainty little shoes. Although it was much too posh for a bairn, I would never tell Jamie that. Instead, I bent forward and kissed him, then we pressed our foreheads together, ready for anything that came our way.

Chapter 67
Destiny Jacqueline Kismet

"Is that a doll?" I asked.

The shock of seeing something so refined inside a cave left me reeling. I looked at the doll, then at Cassidy. The doll had long wavy blonde hair and beautiful blue eyes. But more than that, it was wearing a dress that closely resembled one of Cassidy's dresses as a child. It took my breath away.

"What's wrong, Ma?" Cassidy demanded, seeing my look of distress.

"It's...it's just that...the doll. She looks so much like you, and the dress—"

"Didn't I have one almost identical to it as a kid?"

For a moment, I thought my legs might give way, so I promptly sat down next to her at the makeshift firepit.

"Where did you find the doll?"

Cassidy's face grew ashen as her eyes drifted over to the wood coffin. "I found it near the back wall of the cave. It must have fallen out of the coffin."

It was now that I saw what I hadn't before. The rectangular box was much too small for a full-grown adult. Whoever was in it couldn't have been more than a year or two at best, if even that. A child had died here...a Traveller's child. I couldn't say why, but I was suddenly so short of breath I felt as though I might pass out. Yet I could see I wasn't the only one affected because Cassidy's hands began trembling, and soon tears streamed down her face as she made the connection I had. And yet, our angst seemed out of proportion to merely finding an ancient relic. It felt personal. It *was* personal.

By the time Benjamin and Michael returned, Cassidy was trembling so hard that Benjamin threw down the logs he was carrying and ran to kneel beside her. His eyes caught sight of the doll and widened. Soon, his face matched hers.

"I'm so sorry," he whispered. "I should ha' been there for ye."

What did he mean he should have been there for her? A shiver of fear trickled down my spine. I couldn't help but think it was Jamie talking to Esme some time in the past. Had it been *their* baby who died? Some latent memory worked on my conscience, trying to force me to remember, but try as I might, nothing would come.

Michael scowled as he inspected us all. "What's going on here, Des, Cassidy? Why is everyone so upset?"

Then his eyes drifted to the doll, to the familiarity of it all. I felt as if a shard of glass had pierced my heart, because I could see by the tremor in his shoulders that he recognized the doll, and he saw the resemblance between it and Cassidy.

For several seconds, we all stood staring at each other in an impasse, no one daring to speak. Finally, I shook my fist.

"For God's sake, somebody say something. Both of you recognize this doll. How?" I turned to Benjamin. "You first."

He ran his hands through his hair and closed his eyes as though wishing away the memory. On a sigh, he opened them. "Jamie gave Esme this doll for the baby...when it was born."

"Christ!" Michael swore, his face paling a shade.

"And you?" I asked Michael.

"The laird gave this doll to his other child before he died—a daughter. The girl was grown—"

"So, she didn't need it anymore," I finished for him.

"Right."

The frigid cavern felt claustrophobic suddenly. "And you know this because...?

He worked his jaws as though fighting back emotions he'd had yet to shed. "Don't make me say it, Des. We all know why we're here, don't we? To right the wrongs of the past."

My stomach gave way, and I spilled the contents of my breakfast onto the stone floor of the cave. A bitterness flooded my mouth. Michael's shoulders slumped. He quickly set the logs in the fireplace, then bent down beside me and cradled my head.

"I was wrong to take Jamie from his mother, Des. But I spared him ten years o' misery, and I would have spared him ten years more had I lived."

I began to hyperventilate. So it was true. Michael was the laird…and Jamie's father.

"Help me get Des outside," Michael ordered.

Benjamin grabbed my legs, and Michael my head, then together they carried me out into the dim sunshine. I immediately curled up into the fetal position, my body wracked with tremors.

"It's okay, Des."

And although I heard Michael speak, it was as if from a great distance. Instead, all I could hear was a thrumming in my ears as though a thousand bees were buzzing at once.

"What's happening to her?" Cassidy demanded, her voice strained.

"I don't know," Michael said.

But I knew. My body was taking in what my mind could not accept. We were all reliving some ancient drama, only this time it was meant to end differently, where a child didn't die, and a man didn't end up swinging from the gallows.

Chapter 68
Cobra

New Scotland Yard

For once, Frank's code name seemed appropriate, because he felt like a coiled snake ready to strike. What he'd read and learned from Commander Phillips left him winded.

"You've found the cybercriminals then?"

He pounded a fist on the commander's table, his face hot, but it was as if another person were the one doing it. Since coming to the UK, the two worlds seemed to bleed in and out of each other so that Frank wasn't sure which world he was in, the present or the past.

"No, we've found traces of them on the continent, but no physical contact. We had a man in the field who thought he'd spotted them at a cottage in the Scottish countryside, but I'm afraid we've received no word from him since then, and that was three days ago."

"Three days?"

"We've sent a team to inspect the place, and though we've found a few things that were suspicious—"

"Like?"

"A bank of computer hookups, for one. And the place looked lived in, but we found no one, so whoever was there had fled by the time we arrived. I've had men scouting the area, but as yet, we have little to go on. We've traced the owner of the cottage, but it turns out to be a fictitious name, probably purchased under an alias and false ID."

Frank leaned back in his chair and splayed his fingers to give him time to pull himself together. For such a highly decorated man, the Commander had few belongings to show for his years of service. Just a small series of law books and a state-of-the-art desk and computer.

"As I've said, we have a search party looking for our officer. But I have to tell you, this operation is probably one of the largest ones we've seen, which is why we've contacted Interpol."

Frank whistled at the news.

"It could be they're able to send out messages from all over the world but are located locally. Or, the most likely scenario, they have cells worldwide."

"What's their agenda?" Frank asked, knee bouncing to slow the nervous flutter in his belly.

"We're not sure." The commander shuffled some papers on his desk and fastened a clip on one corner, then set them aside. "But so far, there's been no evidence of violence, nor have we received wind of it in the few communiques we've been able to obtain. Most of it seems to be in code, but one thing's clear."

"Yeah?"

"They're not happy with changes being made in America to circumvent the constitution, nor the worldwide lean right and the violence in Gaza. And they're especially unhappy with the budding Fascism in America and abroad. But what seems to have caused the biggest outrage is the growing destruction of the middle class and the rise of the billionaire class."

Always before, Frank had been pretty militant about America for Americans. He railed against the constant regulations that stifled industry and entrepreneurship. You worked hard to get ahead. He had no empathy for slackers, people who didn't pull themselves up by their bootstraps. In fact, he'd had a fight on that very topic with his wife before he'd left for overseas.

"Frank, how can you stand by while people like Juanita are pulled from their homes and sent abroad without a trial?" she'd demanded as she laced up her running shoes. "Juanita moved here when she was three. She doesn't even *know* anyone in Guatemala."

He'd thrown up his palms. "Look, my hands are tied. Her family came here illegally. What do you want me to do?"

"But *she's* legal. Since when did you stop caring about the constitution...about the *law*?"

She'd purposely thrown that in his face. Knew exactly which target to hit. "Look, you may not be happy with all of this, and I may not be happy about losing Juanita and Shannon, but we're both going to have to deal with it. And you may not like our president, but I like his policies."

"What policy? Name a policy!"

He couldn't very well mention the border, not with Juanita gone, so he used the only leverage he had—state's rights.

"Yeah, when it suits him," Mia shot back.

That was the last time they'd spoken except to see Frank off, and even then she'd turned her face when he tried to kiss her on the lips.

Now, as he sat across the desk from the commander, he came upon a plan.

"Why don't I do a little investigation of my own? Would you mind if I took a look at the cottage where your agent disappeared?"

The officer leaned back and weaved his hands behind his head. "Tell you what. I'll get one of my men to go with you, but be careful. I don't need all three of you disappearing, understand?"

Frank got to his feet. "Understood." He grabbed his briefcase, then threw his dress jacket over his shoulder. "I'll check in at one of the local hotels. Then we can start first thing in the morning."

The officer stood and shook Frank's hand. "And Frank..."

"Yeah?"

"Don't go being a hero, okay? We have enough of those already."

Frank laughed. "No heroes here!"

Chapter 69
Esme Stalwart

For the rest of that winter, we stayed put. I almost believed our travelin' days were done, that we'd made this place our home, where despite the harshness of the climate, we were happy. We thrived. And yet I knew it couldn't last forever. We were runnin' outta supplies. There came a day when I opened the cupboard and pulled out the last of the grains for boilin', and the clabber—the soured milk I'd grown so fond of for our morning oats. Isla and I exchanged a look of concern.

"I'll go tell Jamie," she said, wrapping her shawl around her for warmth.

"No, let me." I handed her Kaileigh, whose presence filled our caravan with joy. She was named after the Scottish dance, a festivity that lit up our winters and brought happiness to all those present.

Isla quickly complied, only too eager to dote on her dear wee grandchild. I covered my head with my red, green, and gold tartan shawl, vaguely aware they were the clan colors of Jamie's ancestors on his *faither's* side.

Touch not a cat bot the glove—the family motto, according to Jamie. I had laughed the first time I heard it, only to realize he was quite serious, but I suppose it made sense, being the Scottish wildcat wore a perpetual scowl that might unnerve even the toughest of men.

I threw open the door to a steady rain that needled me with its insistent downpour and ducked my head as though that might somehow protect me from the dreary skies above.

"Have you seen Jamie?" I yelled to one of the men who rushed around to feed the livestock.

"O'er yonder!" He pointed to the makeshift barn that the men had erected with which to house the horses and the many cattle they'd managed to procure on the last raid.

True to the man's word, Jamie was inside, mucking out the stalls and whistling a tune as if he hadn't a care in the world. His face lit up when he saw me, and he threw down his pitchfork as he came toward me. He wrapped me in a tight embrace, kissing me resoundingly on the lips. I tasted the sweetness on his breath as we tumbled in the hay. And though I would have liked nothing better than to while away an afternoon, free of cares, we had a village to feed.

"We're out of grains and bread," I said as my eyes feasted on him, my lips searching out his.

"Ah! You romantic." He tweaked me on the nose. "Is this what I get if I bring you back porridge and flour?"

"Cheese, too, if ye can find it."

"I can find it," Jamie boasted.

We were far from any village, and although there was safety in that, it meant weeks of travel and raids, dangerous in the best of times.

"Surely, you'd not deny a man sent into the wilderness for the likes of his clan a tumble wit' his wife, now would you?"

"Surely not!" I agreed.

The incessant pounding of rain on the metal rooftop played a melody that spoke of love and protection, of time that stood still. For the next half hour, we soaked in the warmth of the stable, with its sweet smell of hay and all things four-hooved. But more than that, we revelled in the feel of each other's touch, the intimacy as we rolled around in the hayloft to giggles and tender mercies as he fingered the skin at the base of my neck, his touch sending chills racing through me. I wanted it to last, like our love, for us to stay like this forever. When we were through rediscovering each other's bodies, we lay in silence, listening to the rain, more gentle now.

"When will ye leave?" I asked, the words coming out almost a whisper.

"We'll saddle up this afternoon. In the meantime, ye'll ha' to make do with the jerky and dried fruit, aye?"

I nodded, unable to speak against the lump in my throat. "I'll miss ye, Jamie."

"And I you," he admitted. "I love ye, Esme Stalwart."

"That's Esme MacPherson to you." I nudged him, and he laughed softly against the rain. We paused, each unwilling to speak. I was the first to break the silence. "Ye'll not forget me, Jamie?"

He turned to me with a ferocity I had yet to see and with a growl said, "Never, Esme MacPherson." Then he kissed me with such intensity it set my blood boiling, and soon, we were again entwined as one. Forever together in our hearts.

Chapter 70
Destiny Jacqueline Kismet

"It's time you knew about the coffin." Benjamin held a hand out to me as we stood on the shelf outside of the cave, but I merely stared at it as though it belonged to someone other than the reincarnation of Jamie MacPherson.

"It is," Michael agreed.

I peered up at Cassidy, who looked as if her entire world had come crashing down, all because the past had caught up with us. For a moment, I sat there, unmoving, but finally I took his proffered hand.

"Phew!" Cassidy said. "For a moment I thought we'd have to get out a crane."

"Very funny!" I replied, but she'd done what no one else could. She'd relieved the tension and made me forget all the buried emotions of my past life as Isla.

Cassidy swiped at her runny nose from her earlier tears. Benjamin brandished a lace handkerchief, an ode to the past. Somehow it seemed normal, now that the past and the present had collided.

"Here, M'lady," he said, bowing.

Cassidy giggled. Then Benjamin held out two elbows for each of us to link arms with him.

"I can see I've been outnumbered," Michael said wryly. "This way."

He led us back inside the cave where the child's wooden coffin lay. The pain of it struck me anew, but Benjamin released us and held up a hand.

"Before you get any ideas, read the top of the casket."

On it were written two lines, one in English, one in Gaelic. It warned of a curse should anyone disturb it.

"The Scottish are a superstitious lot." He raised a brow and quirked his mouth. "The spirits can be quite...shall I say, vindictive."

I reached out and touched the writing. To my surprise, the pen mark looked like a simple magic marker. *Surely...* I peered up at him with a quizzical expression.

To my surprise, he said, "Stand back." Then he promptly opened the lid.

I gasped, and Cassidy let out a shriek in response, but as we leaned in, we saw not the skeleton of a dead child beneath the sheeting but— "What is that?"

Michael laughed and sat down on one of the boulders. "Yes, Benjamin, why don't you tell the ladies what that is, exactly?"

Benjamin pulled first one piece of equipment out and placed it on top of the casket, then another. He blew dust off of the lid, sending a spray of it into the air that caused me to sneeze.

When the smell of dirt and grime subsided, I asked in a rather nasally voice, "Is that a—"

"Laptop?" Benjamin opened it. "Yes, it is. And this is a satellite communicator, so we can get reception, even outside the cave. It has been encrypted, so we can work out of here when we need to, though we have multiple sites worldwide."

"Worldwide?" Cassidy breathed, taking the words right out of my mouth.

"That's right," Michael explained. "We have a network of men and women who have decided the status quo no longer works. Our government is falling into tyranny, and we plan to stop it."

"How?" Cassidy and I said in unison.

"First off, we're goin' to disrupt the old world order," Benjamin said, his voice suddenly serious. "The rich have decided it's time they kill off the golden goose—the middle class. They get stinkin' rich quick, and the rest of us get the shaft. They don't care what happens in the long run, because they will never have to work again if they dinna want to. And if they do, they can name their price because every one of us will be grateful for the pittance we're given when so little work is to be had."

Michael stood and began pacing. "In third-world countries, governments have purposely kept the hourly wage low. Large companies swoop in and get cheap labor, and in return, they pay graft. If anyone tries to upset the balance, they're called on the carpet—told they can't pay staff more than a local doctor. It's a win-win for the government, which holds power with an iron grip, and for companies that make huge profits off the suffering of the working class. It has been going on for centuries."

I sniffed, the smell of must still thick in the air between us. My thoughts returned to Jamie and what the Travellers had endured. Death, the final outcome if they were found...alive. A weight settled on my chest to know someone could be killed simply for trying to live, to eat, to survive. My hands felt cold and clammy.

But then I remembered what I had read in a newspaper right before we had gone into hiding. One billionaire planned to release billions of dollars to help the poor and underclass. It gave me a glimmer of hope that not everyone was greedy. Not everyone turned a blind eye to suffering.

I walked to the opening of the cave, marveling at the beauty that cascaded before me. I had read somewhere that The Domesday Book, written in 1086, claimed the British Isles was 15% forested at the time. And before 1086, the land had even more trees, mostly oak, elm, and pine with a smattering of hazel. Now it was 5% forested. Then I recalled a vacation I'd taken up the Oregon Coast years earlier. My mouth had gone dry to witness the destruction of habitat. Mile upon mile of forest gone. Vanished.

"So," I turned to the men. "How can Cassidy and I help?"

Chapter 71
Cobra

It came at Frank in waves as he and his driver headed northward. Until they had crossed the imaginary line into Scotland, he'd had no sensation of homecoming, but the moment his feet hit Scottish soil, it was as if an avalanche of memories came flooding in on him. Horses pouring out of the hillside with Reivers on their backs, guns aimed. Even with all of the power and protection the man in the mirror had wielded in 1700s Scotland, the sight of them had sent a quiver of fear jittering down his spine then as it did now. If he was indeed the reincarnation of this William Duff, he'd bought the Reivers off to keep the peace—promised them money in exchange for their help in the border wars. It had kept them silent...for a while. Until the money dried up. He shook away the memories.

Today was a gloriously sunny day that promised summer and warmth. To the right were the beginnings of a forested area, but to their left...

"Stop!" Frank yelled. "There! Take me there."

Hugh Davies, who'd only been with the department for three years, seemed as pleased as Frank to get away from the hustle and bustle of city life. To take a trip through the countryside. But the tall, gangly thirty-something officer with glasses, a pale complexion, and wide-set eyes seemed puzzled by Frank's outburst. Still, he slammed on the brakes of the green Volvo.

"Sorry." Frank shook his head. "I know that place. I've been there before."

Hugh shrugged, then turned the car up the winding drive that hadn't seen wear in years. They bounced over the underbrush, well-worn crevices causing the car to lurch forward only to drop precipitously when the tire hit a hidden pothole. After several minutes, they arrived at the shack, and the pair got out. The white-washed stone had long since lost most of its color so that the original sandstone quarried locally from the hillsides showed through. The front door hung by a single hinge. To Frank's surprise, the hinge was made of iron, a luxury for those times, wood being the cheaper and more affordable option.

Hugh peered inside the cottage through an open window and frowned before turning to Frank. "I was under the impression you'd never been to Scotland before."

"I have been, but it was a very long time ago." At least he wasn't lying, not completely anyway. Whether it was a hallucination or real, he remembered this place, remembered *her*. What was her name? Emma, Eleanor...no...He snapped his fingers and whistled. *Esme.* She was the wife of someone he should remember, but who? His mind went blank.

He pushed open the door with a squeal from the hinge. Inside was just as he'd remembered it. Out here, in the middle of nowhere, he doubted few had taken the time to investigate the crumbling homestead. A musty aroma of dust and age hung in the damp air. What was left of an old bed stood rotting off to one side, the wool inside the mattress old and matted. A table stood off to the other side of the room. The few remaining dishes, too old and ugly to pinch, stood aging on simple wooden shelves.

"I hate to tell you this, but I think you have the wrong place, sir," Hugh said with an air of disdain. "This cottage hasn't been lived in for a century or more. You sure this is the one?"

Frank ran his fingers over the dusty table before answering. "I think I got my wires crossed. Must have been a house that looked like it."

Hugh chuckled, then stuck a pipe in his mouth and lit it. He blew out a puff of blue-gray smoke. "No worries. Frankly, if ya ask me, most of these cottages look alike."

"Yeah." Frank forced a laugh. Still...he'd been here before, maybe not in this century or the one before it, but he'd been here. That knowledge settled in his stomach like a lead bullet. He was about to leave when he caught a glimpse of a button on the floor. It was a woman's button. *Her* button. He pocketed it before Hugh was any the wiser. Then they headed to the Volvo and began the long trek back to the main road. When he felt the button's curves, he saw her eyes flash before him. Saw the defiance. The anger. The fear.

But then he pictured the button in his mind's eye. It was of three Celtic horses inside a Celtic knot. Frank pulled on his lip. Now where did a woman in the middle of nowhere get such a fine button as that?

Chapter 72
Esme Stalwart

The weeks dragged on, and we had taken to foragin' for food, but it was the wrong time of year to glean much. The ground was covered in permafrost that bit at my fingers and sent chilblains racing up my hands and arms. Isla watched over the baby in the caravan, where she kept a warm fire burning, while the women and I went out to search for tubers and such. We tossed them into the tartan sling at our side, the warmth from the wool a blessed comfort against the cold. Then we turned to the wild nuts and fruit—acorns and chestnuts mostly, whatever the squirrels hadn't nested away for winter. And there was the odd blackberry to be had, but my belly stung with hunger as I'd watched the pounds peel away and my skin hang loose.

Where are ye, Jamie?

The only answer was that of the Crested Tit with its shrill trill as it bounced around the upper canopy of the forest.

I returned to foraging, my sack only partially filled. And yet if we were to survive, what we gathered must feed an entire community. I peered at the faces of the other women, their stoic expressions revealing just how worn down from hunger we'd all become. Now, more than ever, I understood what it was to be a Traveller. An outsider. An outlaw. If anyone had asked me months ago if I believed in theft, I would have laughed. I would have thought them mad. But cold and hunger, accompanied by derision of the worst kind, had changed my tune. At last, I understood Jamie's actions. We'd been given no alternative. If we weren't allowed to work for a wage that would keep us alive, the only choice was theft...and this. My legs shook as I stood up to allow blood back into them. The sensation of ants marched up my feet and into my ankles, the feeling slowly fading the longer I stood.

I peered up at the sky. Storm clouds were taking shape. Some would bring fresh snow, no doubt. I wondered how Jamie was faring. Wondered if he'd found food and was even now on his way back. But then a darker side of me imagined him swilling his hours away at a local pub, singin' songs and playin' his fiddle in the warmth of a fire while those back at home starved. No, I was being unkind. I bit my lip, tears forming in the hollow of my eyes. Never before had I felt so hopeless. To keep from wallowing in utter despair, I stamped my feet and pressed on. At times, I imagined lying down in the snow, going to sleep. Leaving my daughter for Isla to raise. But then I imagined her precious little face, the way she looked at me with such love it took my breath away, and I couldn't do it. Couldn't leave her alone to face such a cruel and bitter world as this.

You are a Stalwart, I reminded myself. *Staunch, faithful, committed.* They were the heirlooms passed to me through a rite of blood. A rite of passage. *Then why do I feel so alone?*

As if she could sense my torment, Baillie, the woman who had helped to deliver my child, came to me and placed an arm around my shoulder.

"We'll get through this, Es," I promise. "We've seen worse than this."

"You have?" I turned to her in surprise. "This is not the first time you've nearly—"

"Starved?" she finished for me, her black braids tied at the back. "No." She shook her head, but I could read the weariness in her voice. "This is worse than most years, yes." She gave a short bitter laugh. "But there ha' been other times too. We do what we can. We toil our fingers to the bone for them." She nodded toward the camp, miles away.

It was then I noticed her fingers were bleeding from the cold and the many prickly things we'd had to dig through to get to what sustenance was available.

"Ye know what makes it easier?" she said with a sly smile, a glint forming in her eerily golden-brown eyes.

"No, what?"

"To sing, like yer Jamie does. How do ye think he's made it all these years? He'd a' gone mad if it hadn't been for that—and the fiddle." She began to sway, then swept me up in her tune and together we sang the "Wild Mountain Thyme", so fitting for the work we'd set out to do. Soon, we were all singing. A few even managed to dance.

Oh, the summer time is coming,
And the trees are sweetly blooming,
And the wild mountain thyme
Grows around the blooming heather.

Will you go, lassie, will you go?
And we'll all go together
To pull wild mountain thyme
All around the blooming heather,
Will you go, lassie, go?

I will build my love a bower
By yon clear and crystal fountain,
And all around the bower,
I'll pile flowers from the mountain.

I will roam the country o'er
Through that dark land so dreary;
And all the spoils I find,
I'll bring to my darling dearie.

If my true love, she won't have me,
I will surely find another
To pull wild mountain thyme
All around the blooming heather.

Oh, the summertime is coming
And the trees are a'blooming
And the wild mountain thyme
Grows around the blooming heather.

Will you go, lassie, will you go?
And we'll all go together
To pull wild mountain thyme
All around the blooming heather,
Will you go, lassie, go?

Just then I heard the crunch of hooves on snow, and out of the forest came an all-too familiar face. "So this is what happens when I'm bustin' me balls tryin' to find ye food?"

With a shriek of delight, I launched myself at Jamie who whisked me onto the back of his horse. For my troubles, he gave me a resounding kiss, one that had ne'er tasted so sweet. Then together, we made our way back to camp, where we no longer risked starvation.

CHAPTER 73
Destiny Jacqueline Kismet

We set to work right away, Benjamin at the laptop typing in encrypted messages that were unreadable even to us. While he toiled over the computer, Michael pointed to the stone circle where he'd set a fire going to keep us warm inside the cavernous interior. The shivering that had consumed me earlier gradually died, and soon I removed my coat and gloves, the warmth creeping into my bones.

"We have to be ready," Michael said. "As soon as we're given the word, we're to release the program."

"What will it do?"

Michael's face paled. Silence.

"So, you still can't tell us." I peered over at Cassidy, who was twisting her hair in tiny circles, something she had done as a child when nervous.

"I don't want you implicated if anything goes wrong."

The cave felt claustrophobic suddenly, and I gulped down air like a fish struggling to fill its gills. "Just tell me one thing... Will what we're doing help or hurt people?"

"Look, Des. What we're about to do will make a huge difference in so many people's lives. You've got to believe that." He took my hands in his and rubbed the back of them with his thumbs.

I gritted my teeth. "But will anyone get hurt?"

"Only us, if we're caught."

I released the breath I'd been holding. It wasn't the answer I'd wanted, but at least no one else would be injured in the process. My mind reeled over the possibilities. What could he and Benjamin possibly be planning? I tried to wrap my mind around it but failed. One way or the other I *would* learn the truth. If both Cassidy's and my lives were at stake, then we had a right to know.

"I *will* get to the bottom of this," I told him.

Benjamin stopped what he was doing, his eyes wide in alarm, but he said nothing, instead waiting for Michael to speak—to make the final decision. *So, Michael has seniority over Benjamin.* If I learned nothing else, I learned that.

"Let me ask you this—are you working for the government?"

Again, neither man said anything, but I thought I had detected just the slightest hint of a head shake. So not the government, at least not in an official capacity. Then what? Surely not a terrorist organization. I could never fathom Michael doing that. He loved his country 100%, which is why it galled him to see it come to this. A resistance organization then? That I could see, especially after all that had happened. Even people in the party were calling for that.

I held my hands over the fire, eager for what little warmth was available. As if that was the release valve, everyone breathed a sigh of relief, and Benjamin turned back to his typing. That's when I noticed Cassidy sitting close enough to the computer to view the contents of Benjamin's screen. Discreetly, I nodded my head toward it. When Michael wasn't looking, she returned the nod, and her head swiveled almost imperceptibly toward the face of the laptop. Her eyes widened, and I don't know if it was fanciful thinking on my part, but I could have sworn she paled.

We sat like that for some time. Finally, Benjamin closed the laptop and said, "What's to eat?"

Michael pulled out the backpack filled with supplies. To my surprise, he had purchased packaged dried meals ahead of time. He ripped open the top of a pouch with the words Thai Curry on the front and poured water into it and stirred. He then put it in a titanium pot, which was lightweight for easy lifting. The space soon filled with an aroma that bore the hint of coconut. My stomach responded with a growl.

While we were waiting for it to cook, he handed us each a stick of dried mango, which we bit off greedily, the sweet taste slowly dissolving in my mouth and helping me to forget our predicament for the moment. The lunch seemed to drag on. It took everything I had to keep from bolting for the ledge outside the cave entrance so Cassidy could divulge what she had witnessed on the screen. Finally, Michael handed us each a granola bar. When we finished gulping that down, I reached over for the pan and the cups of water we'd used to wash it down.

"How about Cassidy and I do the cleanup since you two prepped the fire and the meal?"

The men were only too happy to comply, so we made our way outside and to the stream below, careful to keep eyes out for anyone who may have followed us.

When we got to the stream, we knelt down and rinsed the dishes in the water, then dried them.

"So?" I said as I wiped my towel over the last of the dishes. "What did you see?"

"They're calling themselves The Reivers after the men who fought in the Borderlands of Scotland."

"Let me guess...in the 1700s?"

She nodded, her lips pursed.

"The Reivers could be violent." That thought gave me pause.

"But some of them—"

"Like Jamie?" I asked.

She swished her hand in the cold water as if to remind herself that all of this was real...too real. "Yes. Like Jamie. Some of them helped their people, using violence only when absolutely necessary."

Or when they needed money by acting as mercenaries for men in power, I added, but I kept my thoughts to myself.

"They sometimes righted wrongs," she said hopefully.

I had to admit, many wrongs needed righting, but knowing which ones to right and how to go about doing it—that was the question. Suddenly, my mind flew to something Benjamin had said back at the cottage. Something about the inequity between poor and rich. Soon, a kernel of an idea formed. We really *could* help people, by the hundreds of thousands if not millions, but how would we go about doing it? And would the men go along with what I set out to do?

I was about to tell Cassidy of my plan when I heard rustling among the underbrush and the words, "You ladies going somewhere?"

My breath froze inside my chest, because the voice was neither Michael's nor Benjamin's. Instead, it was the voice of someone far more sinister. I looked up to see a lordly man dressed in a black overcoat and boots the color of coal, his dark eyes trained on me with a malevolence that left me disoriented. Once again, past and present bled together, and there before me stood none other than—

"Lord Braco of Duff, at your service. Perhaps you've heard of me?"

My throat tightened, and I tried to swallow, but it was useless because standing before me was none other than the man who, on November 16, 1700, killed Jamie MacPherson.

Chapter 74
Cobra

Frank's mind felt as if it had splintered like a broken mirror, shards of glass everywhere, each image a picture of the past. A past he had yet to understand.

Who am I? he wondered as the scenery slid by in a kaleidoscope of color. A name kept playing over and over in his head. William Duff. His title, Lord Braco.

"Do you know much about Scottish history?" Frank asked Hugh, who was humming softly as he drove.

"Some, why?"

"Have you ever heard of a William Duff?"

Apparently, Hugh hadn't heard it was gauche these days to smoke a pipe, and especially inside a car, though the cherry-flavored tobacco wasn't unpleasant. Fortunately, Hugh rolled down his window and blew the smoke out of the Volvo before speaking.

"William Duff. Hmm." He stabbed the air with the stem of his pipe. "If I'm not mistaken, there was a William Duff from Banff. Didn't he sit in the House of Commons? I think it was in the early 1700s." For a moment he appeared reflective, then said, "Right!

He commissioned the building of a manor house in Banff, if I remember correctly. I think it's now a museum. We're headed that way, but first we need to locate the cottage. Did you want to stop there when we're done in Aberdeen? We're going to meet with the Aberdeen police to see if they have any information on our investigation. Commander Phillips has phoned ahead and clued them in on what we're looking for."

Frank turned the louvers of the vents his way for fresher air. "Why Aberdeen?"

Hugh peered out his mirror at a truck heading their way. "Odd. Wouldn't think we'd get many trucks in the back of beyond." Then he focused on Frank's question. "We've had a few hits from that direction. We don't know if they're false leads or if there's something to them, but since we're going to be so close, the commander wanted us to look into it. I guess I should have said something before we left. You don't mind the detour, do you?"

Frank shrugged. "Not in the least." Especially if it meant he got to stop by the Duff manor.

"Ah! There's the road to the cottage. We were getting pings from further up north, but nothing definitive, so the commander wanted us to backtrack to our investigator's last location before his move north. As you know, we've done an aerial search that suggests he may have been at a cottage in the woods. Best be careful, in case it's a trap."

Frank rolled down his window, needing air suddenly.

For the next ten minutes, they drove down a path so narrow that the shrubbery brushed the sides of their vehicle. Finally, the road widened onto a graveled area that surrounded a cottage.

The stillness of the place felt suffocating. Frank peered over at Hugh, whose eyes went wide, no doubt thinking what Frank was thinking. This was the perfect place for a person to go missing. It would be days before anyone located them.

Hugh opened the glove compartment and pulled out a gun. "I'm assuming you know how to use one of these in case you're not wearing one?" Hugh handed him the Glock 17 pistol, then retrieved a 9mm carbine from the back seat.

Frank always carried a gun as part of his FBI protocol, but he was thankful for a spare today as they exited the Volvo. When they neared the cottage, it fell eerily quiet, as if someone had closed up shop and left in a hurry. He walked over and peered in the front window that opened onto a snug.

"I'll take the front," Hugh whispered. "You go around back and knock. If no one answers, kick the door in."

Frank wanted to say, "Gee thanks," but thought better of it.

Quietly, he tiptoed around the back, looking in windows as he did. Nothing. In the kitchen, a kettle sat waiting for occupants that might never return. He knocked on the door and waited. One, two, three. Then he gave it a kick. The door swung open on the first kick.

Again, the house was eerily quiet, nothing but the breeze to indicate any sign of life. "Hello! Anyone home?"

When no one answered, he rushed through the cottage's interior to the front door and opened it. Hugh came bounding in. They each took a room, guns at the ready.

"Look at this!" Hugh called when they were through inspecting the place.

Frank followed Hugh's voice to a downstairs den. When he entered the room, he whistled. It had clearly been set up for a bank of computers, just as Commander Phillips suggested. Now, why would anyone need that many computers in the middle of nowhere?

Chapter 75
Esme Stalwart

I loved Jamie like sunshine in spring and all things good. While he was away, I had lain in bed, going over the contours of his face in my mind, the ridges along his brow, the way his eyes squinted tight when he was dreaming or when he wrestled with something, as he was doing now. I ran my hands across the stubble of his beard and made quiet shushing noises. Whatever haunted him in his dreams eluded him at daybreak, because he always arose with a cheerful, "Good day to ye, Es," as though convinced of the day's goodness before he set foot on the floor of the caravan. I laughed as he did so again.

"Why do ye laugh at me, woman?" he said, pulling me to him for a hearty morning kiss, his smell manly—making me want him.

But then I heard the baby cry, her mewls so pitiful that we both locked foreheads, our eyes closed, wishing for a moment of peace. But peace was not to be had—not on the Borderlands, nor here, amidst my fellow Travellers, the days hectic with chores. I sighed as we parted, our eyes sharing one brief, hope-filled moment.

"Best be at it then," he said with a wink.

I gave him a small nod, then hobbled down the wooden steps in front of the raised platform bed. Like everything else inside the caravan, it was painted a bright color, this one red, with rich golden accents. Isla had long since moved into one of the other caravans to give us privacy, but she'd left her herbs, so the tight space gave off odors so diverse that they all merged into a single fragrance. Thankfully, the sweet smell of clove won out, emitting a rich aroma that scented the room.

By now, Kaileigh was able to sit up in the crib Jamie had made for her. Like most of the Travellers, he was a skilled carpenter, which showed in every inch of the caravan, from the copper hammered door handles fashioned to look like dragons on the exterior of the vardo, down to the simple hooks he'd hammered in a similar shape to hang up our outerwear. He had spared nothing in the elegant detail, as though every swing of the hammer measured his love for us.

So how can a man like Jamie be outlawed?

I clucked as I picked Kaileigh up and bounced her up and down to a tune I hummed as I prepared to feed her. Already, she was beginning to look like her *da,* with his narrow nose and high cheekbones. Yet her eyes reminded me most of her *faither.* For even with lashes laced in tears, they held a glint of his humor in them, as though she'd just finished tellin' a joke that made the whole room fill with laughter, as it so often did any time he was around. It made me love her that much more.

Always fearful of a future that might not come, I gave her a quick kiss, tasting the honey of her skin, so new still, unlike mine that aged with every foray into new territory.

"So, what are yer plans for the day?" I asked.

Jamie poured himself a cup of tea in one of the bright mugs with the moon and stars on it. Then he held it to his lips for courage.

"There's a fair in Aberdeen. I thought I would take my prettiest two girls to see it." He stared at me over the rim of the mug, waiting.

My heart hammered in my chest. We so rarely got to do anything fun these days, what with our status as outlaws and the sheriff of Banff on our tails due to that no-good Braco. Oh, how I longed to say yes, to go with my husband as any normal wife might. To hold hands as he swung for the milk bottles to win me a stuffed toy for the bairn.

"I want to go—"

"But..."

"Is it safe?"

Jamie slammed his mug onto the countertop, its contents sloshing onto the wood and dribbling onto the floor. I moved to grab a towel and sop it up, but he beat me to it. Within minutes, he had it all cleaned up.

At last he studied me with eyes that could see inside a person, could sum them up with a quick glance, and know just what to say for them to see the error of their ways.

"Es," he said, taking me by the hand. "Ye can't spend yer lifetime afraid. There'll always be some scoundrel out there wantin' to ruin our happiness. It's the nature of the beast. Ye just have to know how to handle it."

I knew how *he* handled it...with his fists or his sword. Either way, it would end in disaster. I bent my head. He lifted my chin with a single finger and stared into my eyes, love filling them with starlight.

"I know ye're afraid, especially now that we have Kaileigh—"

I released a sob because he'd gone right to the heart of my greatest fears. I loved my child with all my heart and soul. To lose her would be to lose a piece of me. The same for Jamie. Each of them carried a slice of my heart.

"Ah, Esme, dinna cry, *mo chridhe*. I'll not let anythin' happen to ye, aye?"

When I wouldn't respond, he looked me in the eye and repeated the word "aye"?

"I know," I said. "It's just that I *feel* it."

"Feel what?"

My time with Jamie and the Travellers had dampened my ability to see the future as though a curtain had been placed over my eyes, my gift of sight gone. But it had returned of late, fillin' my dreams with unnamed shadows, the sound of swords and shouts, and of men brawlin'. I heard them now, in the distance, and knew that something dire was about to happen.

"Tell you what. The fair's not for a few more days. As soon as ye're done feedin' the wee one, we'll pack up and head toward Aberdeen. Our men will keep watch. Then, when the day comes, ye can decide if ye want to come with me or not, aye? Until then, dinna fash. Agreed?"

Reluctantly, I nodded my head, more to keep the peace than because I felt any better than before. If anythin', I worried more. Because, although the Scots were a superstitious lot, and the Travellers much the same, I worried that if I released my fears into the world it would somehow taint his future, as though I'd had a hand in it in some way, and I could never let that happen. So, I kept my silence. But deep inside, I saw it coming and shivered, fate wielding a mighty sword. And on that sword was Jamie's name. My only chance now was to save him in his next life. For, as in this one, I saw the future. Knew who he would become, who he would marry, and what life they would lead. And if my second sight was right, he would again be in harm's way. Only one person could save Jamie, or Benjamin, as he would be named. And that was Isla, or as she was aptly called in the future, Destiny. Destiny Kismet.

Chapter 76
Destiny Jacqueline Kismet

"**W**here are we headed?" I asked as we packed up what few belongings we possessed. My hands had already gone numb with cold now that the fire hissed from the water Benjamin had poured on it.

I shrugged off the memory, if indeed it was one, of the meeting with Lord Braco and his men out in the forest moments earlier. Had I really seen it, seen *him*, or was it a premonition of the future, something yet to come? Whatever it was, I shivered, fear clinging to me like a dense fog.

"To Keith, in Banffshire, Des," Michael said. "There's a fair there each year at this time."

I paused. Why did that name sound familiar? Something niggled at the back of my brain.

"Does anyone have a working phone?" I asked.

All three spoke up at once.

"You all have a working phone?" I frowned. "How?"

Michael produced a battery from his pack. I stood there, hands on hips. "How come no one told me you had a battery pack? You've been charging up your phones...all of you?"

They nodded sheepishly.

Michael handed me his. I scrolled through until I found an agricultural expo in Keith, my eyes pausing to read what was written. My heart hummed at the words Summereve's Fair. I scoured the page further until I found what I was looking for—Jamie was captured at the St. Maelrubha Fair after a brawl with Braco's men in 1700s Banffshire. If I wasn't mistaken, the St. Maelrubha Fair was held in Keith, where the current fair was held.

Alarmed, I lifted my head. Was that the premonition I'd had in the forest? Had Lord Braco come to gloat over what had happened? "Surely, you don't plan on going to the place where—"

"Jamie was captured and eventually executed?" Benjamin finished. A fire burned in his wide brown eyes, and his words all but went up in flames, as they were spoken with such fierce determination.

"But why?" I demanded, looking first at Benjamin, then Michael.

"I have unfinished business," Benjamin said. "And besides, that's the perfect place for retribution, aye?"

"Retribution? What kind of retribution?"

"To implement my plan." His eyes met Michael's. "*Our* plan."

"Michael, what's he talking about?" But then my mind connected what my eyes had seen on Michael's phone when scrolling through it. I quickly opened it back up to the word Oligarch. I tapped on it but saw only a list of encrypted words, none of them explaining what Michael meant by it.

"Dad?" Cassidy's voice quavered. Eager to escape the dark interior of the cavern, she slung her backpack over her shoulder, her goggles hanging from a clip, ready to go.

"Look," Michael said, holding his hands up, palms out. "Before you go getting any ideas, this *isn't* about retribution," he said to Benjamin. "It's about justice. It's about fairness. About not letting the oligarchy take everything the middle class has worked so hard to create."

"What did those codes mean?"

He paused, then held up a finger. "Everyone, hand me your cell phones. Your laptop, too, Ben."

We all glanced at each other, then did as asked. He picked everything up and headed out of the cave. "All of you, stay here. I'll be right back."

Once he had the electronic equipment at a safe distance, he returned and urged us to huddle together. "Those codes were encrypted because they're bank codes. Accounts."

A wave of heat flushed through me. "Whose accounts?"

The two men stood there, the silence palpable, like a living, breathing beast that could at any moment reach out and grab us. Finally, Michael spoke.

"Those of every billionaire in the United States and some abroad. And their company accounts."

I backpedaled and let out a gasp. My back scraped the cave wall, the moisture dampening my already damp blouse. When I was finally able to breathe again, I said, "Why? Why would you need their bank accounts? And even if you have them, you won't be able to get into them, will you?"

Suddenly, my breathing stalled in my chest. I needed air. For the first time in my life, I felt claustrophobic. I brushed past the pair of them, with Cassidy in hot pursuit. Once outside, I snatched up my phone—for all the good it would do me, since it still had no signal—and headed north. I wasn't sure where I was going. I just needed to keep moving. To try to wrap my head around what Michael had just said. Cassidy yelled to her father and Benjamin to come quickly, then followed me.

When the pair finally caught up to me, Michael grabbed my arm and twisted me around. I came to a halt with a jerk.

"What the hell, Michael? When were you going to spring this on me, huh? Would you have told me if I hadn't found it on your phone?"

I was yelling now as I moved deeper into the woods to avoid detection.

"Keep it down!" Michael hissed. "We're still figuring out what to do with the information. Nothing's set in stone yet."

Just then, the woodland floor rustled, and Michael pulled me down into the gorse. Benjamin followed suit, taking Cassidy by the hand and yanking her to the ground. We stayed like that for some time as footsteps approached, coming closer and closer until the sound was nearly on top of us. When the steps halted, Michael sprang to his feet, gun cocked. I heard another click as Benjamin pulled back the hammer on his gun. For one brief moment, no one said a word. Then the entire woodlands burst into a tidal wave of sound, and we were surrounded.

Chapter 77
Cobra

Why did the people staying at the cottage need so many computers?

Before Frank could come up with an answer, he heard a noise at the back of the house and grabbed his gun, Hugh right behind him. The back door slammed open, allowing a cool breeze to blow through. His heart beat double time. Had he left the door ajar?

He made a quick inspection of the outside perimeter of the cottage. Nothing. As he and Hugh reentered the house, he stepped on something that moved and heard a screech in response.

"What the—"

He peered down at his feet, where a black cat went skittering past and out the door.

"You stay here and guard the place, Hugh. I'll go see if I can find the cat. It looked well fed, which means someone is feeding it."

Hugh nodded. "Let me know if you need me."

Frank said he would, then he perused the outer wall of the cottage, where he'd seen the cat disappear into a recessed area hidden from view by a large shrub. Frank pulled the plant aside, an arborvitae if he wasn't mistaken. It concealed a stairwell that led down to what looked like a cellar of some sort, probably used to store root vegetables and canned goods back before electricity was a thing. He started down it, then thought better of going in alone. He retraced his footsteps to the cottage and called Hugh to provide backup. No use having another officer disappear.

"Follow me. I've found something."

The pair made their way outside. When Frank pulled back the shrubbery, Hugh whistled in response. Hugh trained his gun on the door, then nodded for Frank to go in. Frank eyed the steps as he descended. They'd clearly seen use recently, muddy footprints rubbing out the dust in places. And the lock was newer, definitely not the age of the cottage. Not even close. Whoever was coming here probably had the key on them. Or... Frank felt above the lintel. Bingo! He inserted the key into the lock, pistol drawn.

It took a moment for his eyes to adjust to the dim interior, but he heard a muffled sound from the dark rear corner of the cellar. He flicked on his phone light. Sure enough, a man was gagged, his hands zip-tied behind his back. Frank could only assume he was the missing officer. He rushed over, bent down, and lifted the man's gag.

"Hurry, get me out of here before they return."

"Who?"

"I think I found our cybercriminals, but they took off days ago."

"They did this?" Frank nodded toward the man's hands.

"They left a couple of guards behind, but they should be back any time now."

Frank grabbed the man by the elbow and lifted him to his feet. No time to waste. They would set a trap, then relock the door so when the men went searching for the missing detective, Frank and Hugh would rush them and make sure they were the ones inside the dark, dank cellar this time. But first they needed to remove the zip-ties from the officer.

"C'mon. Let's get you freed. We'll need all three of us if we're going to catch these guys."

"Right. Then let's get going."

Chapter 78
Esme Stalwart

For days now, we'd roamed the countryside, our movements taking us ever northward toward Aberdeen. Normally, I loved the open road, the feel of the wind on my back, to watch the meadows shift in color and texture as they greened in spring and reached full height come fall. Today, the heads of grass swayed in the breeze and moved like a wave toward some distant unseen shore. My heart felt heavy as the tide pulled us toward our destiny. But as my feet flew forward beside the oxen and horses in the caravan, I saw a white flash out of the corner of my eye, and when I peered into it, I saw the future—saw *them*, Benjamin, Destiny, and Cassidy. Only they were us, Jamie, Isla and me.

Then who is the man with them?

I had never seen him before, but by the looks of him, he was a laird. Though their images wavered as mere wraiths, I made out the red, blue, black, and white of his tartan and gasped, for I instantly recognized it. It was the tartan of the MacPherson clan. Could it be?

"Jamie's *faither*," I whispered, every nerve in my body tingling with anticipation.

Oh, if Isla could see him now. He was a big strapping man, who reminded me of the Sessile and English Oaks that inhabited the Borderlands. Like my people, the copses were made up of neither one nor the other, but a mixture of the two, the Borderlands constantly changing sides and with it a man's identity. A woman's too.

And the man was handsome. Right off, I understood why Isla was so taken with him. He had long wavy black hair one moment, short the next. And the tartan changed as well to some type of dark blue breeches and a matching blue *lèine*, though it looked like no *lèine* I had ever seen. It's then I realized his form flickered in and out of the present and the future, back and forth until I felt dizzy from it. I lifted my hand to my brow while putting my other hand on the solid form of the oxen in hopes of steadying myself.

"You okay there, miss?" One of the Travellers came up behind me, his bushy brows pulled together in concern.

"I...I'm just...catching my...breath."

I forced a smile as I turned my focus to the old man...Thom, it 'twas. If I told him that wraiths lived in the meadow, he'd have believed me, but I didn't want to put him to the test. Not today. Not with so much at stake.

"If ye fancy a ride, I'm certain my Molly'd take you. Our caravan's just there." He nodded to a green one with two thin oxen and a rounded hood that sheltered his wife's face from the sun. "She'd love the company, she would."

"And I, as well." I circled back, the old man at my side.

"Molly, Esme's feelin' a bit poorly. Can she ride with ye for a bit?"

"Aye, up then." Molly yelled, "Whoa," and held her rein in the air as my foot sought purchase. "Where's yer bairn?"

"Isla has her," I confessed. I hadn't slept well last night, or any other night since we'd been on the road.

"Well, ye look the worse for wear, so back you go!"

She nodded toward the rear of the caravan, where a raised bed awaited. I dutifully followed her directions. For all their poverty, a Traveller's bed was meant for comfort, a comfort I'd found nowhere else. The goose down layered me in an envelope of soft bedding that cushioned the jolting movement of the caravan. My eyes felt heavy even before my head hit the pillow, and I would have drifted into a deep slumber except for the hushed conversation I couldn't help but overhear.

"Aye, poor lass, and her with a new bairn."

"Has a weight on her shoulders, that's for sure," the old man agreed.

Molly tsked as she clicked the reins, and the oxen began a steady move forward. "It's no way to raise a child, what with Jamie off on adventures."

"Watch your tongue, woman," Thom said to his wife. "That boy has kept us alive, he has. Fed each and every one of us."

"Aye, true, but he tempts fate, he does, what with stealin' from Lord Braco. The man has a vendetta out for him. Posters plastered all over town, according to Seamus."

"Ach! Seamus is always tellin' tales."

"Not this time. He says he'd seen it with his own eyes. Others, too."

I heard the fear in her whispered voice, and all thoughts of sleep flew out the open caravan door.

"I tell ye, it t'were a poster, it was. A wanted poster. Her Jamie's a marked man, and she best know it."

"Hush now, wife. Ye'll scare her with yer words. Ye leave her be, see?"

His words left no room for barterin'. I lay my head back on the pillow as I heard Thom's voice fade into the distance. But his words still haunted me, as did Molly's. Our only hope was to leave the country, but I knew my Jamie. He would never leave the land he loved. Nor his *maither*. These people...this *life* meant the world to him.

For some time, I lay on the soft bedding, feeling only the lumps and the constant hum and lurch of the wagon. Finally, my eyes sank lower, and I was able to sleep. Then came the nightmares.

Chapter 79
Destiny Jacqueline Kismet

"**J**amie!" one of the men yelled, slapping a hand on Benjamin's back, only Benjamin was wearing clothes from the...

"1700's," I whispered.

Soon an entire contingent of men swarmed Jamie, Cassidy and I, as we were relegated to the periphery of the clearing. They looked askance at Michael, though I daresay Michael was Jamie's father, the laird, because he no longer wore jeans and a blue shirt. Now he had on breeches and what I had come to learn was a sporran, a leather pouch with the laird's crest emblazoned on it. The crest reminded me of a circular belt, with the Scottish cat inside it and the words "Touch not a cat but a glove." If the claws on the cat were any indicator, I understood the suggestion of using a glove.

"Do you see them?" I asked Cassidy as I questioned my sanity.

Her face drained of color, and she nodded. "Ma?" Her voice quivered. "Is that Jamie...and Laird MacPherson?" Tears laced her words, but she choked them back.

"I think so," I said, taking her hand in mine and curling my fingers around hers.

"Who are those people with him?"

The men were a scruffy bunch with scars to prove their lot in life. Their clothing had been mended, then mended again, with stains on the legs of their breeches and dirt on their *léines*. And their use of language sent a blush to my cheeks. For once, it was Cassidy and I fading in and out, whereas Jamie and the laird appeared solid, as did the rest of the group.

Jamie lifted a hand to call us over. Our forms shifted, becoming more solid the closer we got to the group.

"This is my band of Reivers," Jamie explained. "We fight on the Borderlands when we're not stealin' and givin' to the poor." He winked at us.

The young man—no, *my son*—had a charisma that charmed those around him—reeled people in. From the adoration on his men's faces, it was clear they would follow him anywhere, even into battle.

The men donned their hats and mumbled something incomprehensible, a welcoming of sorts.

Then a fair-haired young lad with bright blue eyes stepped forward and said, "The fair's about to start in Aberdeen. 'Tis a good time to pinch a few feathers, no?"

Cassidy and I exchanged sideways glances because Benjamin had schooled us in the history of Jamie and the fair, where a brawl had taken place, and he and another man were captured and taken to the gaol.

And hanged.

A shudder raced through me as I witnessed the hours and days before Jamie's death. Cassidy must have sensed it, too, because her grip tightened on my hand until it felt like claws biting into my skin.

"It's okay, Cassidy," I whispered. "It's not real."

"Then why does it feel so real?" she hissed, tears spilling onto her cheeks.

My daughter, who normally kept her emotions in check, especially in front of me, leaned into my shoulder, head down, the hot tears soaking my shirt. We stood there, locked in a melodrama with no way out. But then my maternal instincts kicked in, and I yanked her chin up.

"You listen to me, Cassidy Leeann Kismet. Jamie may die on the gallows, but Benjamin won't, do you hear me? I'll make sure of it."

Cassidy sniffed. "But how...how will you save him?"

"I don't know, but I will."

And as if that was what Esme had been waiting for all along, for me to commit to saving Benjamin, and Jamie once again became Benjamin, and the laird bled back into Michael. The Reivers, however, stayed as they were, only now they wore modern clothing and looked like any other twenty-something males.

"Who are these people?" I asked Michael, who seemed to know all of them every bit as much as Benjamin.

"They're part of the Resistance. They're helping us with our plan."

"Speaking of plan," I said, tugging at his sleeve to find a spot alone where I could speak to him in private.

Cassidy seemed torn. Stay with Benjamin, or come with us? In the end, she stayed with Benjamin.

Once I had Michael alone beneath a large oak tree, I urged him to sit, the bark rough against our backs. "Michael, I don't know what you plan to do with the bank accounts, but I have an idea."

He quirked a brow in surprise. "*You* have a plan?"

His eyes drifted to the group of men. No longer did they look like grifters. Instead, I would have taken them for IT guys...or librarians. None of the men had the hard edge of a Reiver. And yet they were the same men, only three hundred years later.

"I do. You say you've been able to find a back door into bank accounts?"

"We have," he agreed, his eyes a question.

"If you could get into those accounts, could you get into others?"

The wind rustled from off of the hillside, bringing with it the hint of barley, meaning we must be close to Aberdeen. Michael stretched his legs and flexed his fingers as though trying to loosen the tension he'd been carrying.

"I suppose we could, but what's all this about?"

"You said you want to make a difference in people's lives, right?"

He shrugged but nodded.

"Well, I want to make a difference in people's lives, too, but I need your help."

I lifted my chin to where the men stood, engaged in idle chatter with the occasional sound of laughter wafting across the glade. Behind us a small stream burbled as if in accordance with what I wanted to do.

"But first, I need to know—so those guys, the Reivers, are now in IT?"

Michael hesitated, then finally said, "Yes. They work for Jamie...I mean Benjamin, why?"

"Because we're going to need them...all of them, if we're going to make this happen."

A low growl rumbled in Michael's chest. "I'm not sure I like it when you get ideas."

"I know," I said, slinging his arm over my shoulder. "But you love me, right?"

He growled again and sucked in a deep breath. "God help me, Des, but I do. Now, are you going to tell me, or what?"

I giggled, relieved to finally be getting things off my chest. "Okay, Michael. It's like this..."

Chapter 80
Cobra

Though they'd lain in wait for two days, no one returned. Finally, Hugh called Commander Phillips and let him know the situation. It was decided that Frank and Hugh would take the missing police officer, Johnny Lafferty, with them to Aberdeen, then he would return to Scotland Yard, where he would be debriefed. In the meantime, they'd send a team to scope out the cottage to conduct a forensics search on the place for any clues left behind.

By the time they reached Aberdeen, Frank's headaches had returned. He rubbed Tiger Balm onto his forehead and temples, but despite the heat from the balm, it only grew worse. Then Mia called to tell Frank she wasn't feeling well.

"Probably just the flu," she assured him.

"Take the day off and stay in bed," he urged.

She promised to do just that. Then she said goodbye and hung up. But as they drove down the narrow streets of Aberdeen, worry plagued Frank. Something about the hesitant way Mia spoke made him wonder if she'd wanted to say more. He knew they'd left on shaky terms, but they'd always made up, usually before the end of the day. Frank pressed his fingers to his forehead, willing away the pain.

Up ahead, the Northeast Divisional Headquarters for Police in Aberdeen came into view. Originally a concrete and glass facade, it was now housed inside Marischal College, a large granite Neo-Gothic-style building on Broad Street, its many small spires reaching skyward. It was the second-largest granite structure in the world, according to Hugh, in a district that was dubbed Granite City because of the amount of granite that surrounded it.

Inside, they met with Detective Langston, a short, beefy fellow with a gruff voice and an even gruffer demeanor. He showed them into a spartan room and shut the door, then got right down to business.

"So, we've had an APB out for Johnny here," he said, folding his hands on the table once everyone had taken a seat. "Where'd ya find him?"

Hugh spoke first. "We found 'im in the cellar. Hidin' in plain sight, as it were."

"He had been zip-tied and gagged," Frank added. "The cellar entrance was hidden behind shrubbery, which is why no one located him before."

"We had someone down there, but they couldn't find 'im. Good work, men." Then he faced Johnny. "Can you identify the men?"

"There were two," Johnny said, "but they wore masks and stocking caps. One was tall and thin, the other shorter and stockier.

Other than that, nothing. They came by twice a day, at dawn and dusk." He held up a finger. "Wait...!"

Detective Langston lifted a brow.

"I feel like these guys were not your ordinary *neds*. Or hoodlums, as they call them in your country. They seemed...educated. Men you'd find in an office rather than street thugs."

"How so?" Frank asked.

"Their fingers."

"Fingers?" Hugh said, eying Frank.

"They were long and lean. Clean. Like they never saw a lick of work. Their clothes, too. Jeans, sure, but nice ones." He shrugged.

"So, what do you make of it?" Frank asked the detective.

The detective chewed on his lip for a moment, then narrowed his eyes and leaned forward. He swiveled around in his chair to a table behind him that held stacks of paperwork in an inbox and outbox.

"See here," he said, stabbing a page with his finger as he laid a stack of papers out in front of them. "News is coming in from all over the planet, it seems. There's a group that calls themselves the Resistance. They've planned huge rallies to fight the oligarchy and the right-wing sweeping through much of the world just as fascism and nazism swept through the world starting with Mussolini in 1919 and ending with Hitler in the 40s. But I think there's a splinter group among the Resistance. One that operates separately from them, that's more hardcore." He scratched his forehead, fatigue written into his expression. "So far, they've done nothing we can point to, but we're getting chatter about them. Nothing definitive.

But someone knows something. We've just got to tap into it." He struck the page again with his index finger.

"So you're comparing the right-wing to fascism and nazism?" Frank bristled.

The detective shrugged. "It has all the hallmarks: nationalism, an authoritarian leadership, militarism. That includes suppression of all forms of dissent, including in the media and courts, even if that means imprisoning or assassinating the opposition. In both fascism and nazism, they scapegoat entire groups of people. Loyalists are placed in positions of power, so there are no checks and balances. Don't forget the destruction of human rights and refusing to follow the constitution. It's creating chaos worldwide. What would you call it?"

Frank heard Mia's words in the man's assertion, but somehow it didn't sting quite so much coming from another man.

Mia. He couldn't put his finger on it, yet he knew she was keeping something from him, but what?

Hugh placed a hand on the table. "So, do you have any information for us?"

"Only this. An operative has gone missing. His plane schedule was rerouted from the US to Scotland. We're looking to see if he's booked a hotel nearby, but we've come up with nothing so far. Of course he could be using an alias. We don't know if his disappearance is connected to the Resistance, but he was working on the case and hunting down leads. It could be he's been abducted, but we just don't know yet."

Frank gripped the arms of his chair. "What's his name?"

The man paused, as if deciding how much to divulge. Then, as though coming to a decision, he steepled his fingers and leaned forward.

"The name's Michael. Michael Kismet."

Chapter 81
Esme Stalwart

I had to tell Jamie what I had overheard in the caravan between Molly and her husband. I had been waiting all day for him to finish with the chores so we could have a moment to ourselves, but before I knew what was happening, a horse and rider rushed into camp, the man out of breath. The women yanked their children back to give the rider room as he slid off the back of his horse before it even came to a complete halt.

"Jamie!" the man cried. "You've got to get packin', man. You and everyone with you."

Jamie sauntered over in that easy way he had that was somethin' of a swagger, his presence filling up the space, so I stood in awe, mouth open, watching him work. Even in the direst of situations, he kept calm. Only I knew his tell, a simple flexing of the jaw before that wide smile lit his features.

"What's the hurry?"

He wiped the sword he had been honing until it gleamed in the light of the sun. It sent sharp rays cascading across the glade. I saw more than a few people turn their heads at its brightness.

"Braco's scouring the fair for any signs of ye and yer men. He wants yer head, he does. Says he'll have it on the post before morn."

Jamie laughed, dipping his chin so all might see the foolishness of Braco's claims. "My head, you say?"

"Aye?" The man appeared puzzled and looked around to see if anyone else understood Jamie's lack of concern.

I wanted to run to Jamie, to tell him to turn around because the man's words confirmed my suspicions, the ones laid out by none other than Molly, who side-eyed her husband with a nod.

"Well, fine sir, I appreciate yer concern, really I do. Now, I think it's high time my boys and I paid a visit to this fair, dinna ye think, men?"

A hearty round of cheers rang out, followed by words flying back and forth between husbands and wives in their determination to see their men safe. Within minutes, the flasks were brought out for "liquid courage," as the case may be, and someone ran to get Jamie his fiddle so he could play a tune. Soon the men seemed in fine fettle, while all around me I saw women chewing on their lips or hissing a sharp word to their children who danced around to the music, never knowin' that their da's were about to head off to a war of their own makin'.

Though I tried to get Jamie's attention, he avoided my eyes, no doubt fearin' if he looked me in the eye, I might talk him out of goin'. Because there's one thing I knew about Jamie. His even temperament made him a great leader. But to be a great leader, he must be a great man first, and as such, he never let me forget it.

My eyes stung with tears as I ran in search of Isla. Perhaps she could talk some sense into him, but when I found her back at the caravan, I saw her resigned expression as she fetched the aromatic herbs and potions she would need once the men returned. *If* they returned.

"How?" I said to her, hands splayed. "How can ye be so...so...?

"Accepting?" she said in a hush, pointing to the sleeping bairn.

I fought the ache in my throat, the raw fear that rested there and in my chest. In the cradle Jamie had built with his own two hands, our baby slept. Had he no thought of her, of us?

"Esme, ye have to understand, it's our way. It's how we ha' survived. If it were up to the likes of the Bracos of this world, we would not exist except as slaves to men who have no other use for us." She pointed to the oxen tied to the vardo. "We're of no more value than the oxen or the plow. We are objects to them, don't ye see? They care nothin' for us except for the cheap or free labor we offer them. They dinna see us as human."

Bitterness laced her words, and she spat afterwards, as though clearing a bad taste from her mouth. All the things I had planned to say to try to win her to my side flew out the colorful window sashes flapping in the breeze. Never had I seen a group of people who cared so deeply for each other, who lived and died for each other. Her words humbled me, and I said no more, only watched as the men got drunker and the evening wore on. Come morning, they would be gone, and so too my hopes to change fate. Jamie's fate.

When he came to me that night, we made fierce love, as if we both knew this would be the last time—that he wouldn't be returning. I drank in the smell of him—cinnamon and cloves, and some other scent I couldn't quite name. Our fingers intertwined in a dance, our bodies warming to the tender touch that heated me to the core. By the time our bodies melted into each other, my breaths came in short gasps, and his name laced my lips as we called out to each other. I wanted it to last forever. For daylight to never come. But in the wee hours of the morning, before dawn made its first appearance on the horizon, he snuck quietly out of bed so as not to wake the bairn.

"Jamie," I whispered. "Ne'er forget I love ye."

He paused, as if I'd struck him in the chest. Then he turned back for one last kiss. "I won't. And you remember, too, Esme. I will always love ye, until my final breath, do ye understand?"

Tears of sadness filled my eyes. For one brief moment, he took my hand and studied me as if memorizing the details of my face. Then he was gone.

Chapter 82
Destiny Jacqueline Kismet

"**T**his just might work," Michael said, then called Benjamin over to discuss my plans.

For the next half hour, we sat beneath the shade tree, Cassidy coming to join us, while Benjamin's men took a lunch break, their cars in the underbrush on the ridge above us.

"Do you think your men can find a back door into all of these accounts?" Michael asked, their heads bent over Benjamin's laptop. "Their entry will need to be untraceable."

"Of course," Benjamin said, as though it were a foregone conclusion. "We can use the government's records to trace them."

I swiped at a bee buzzing in my ear as I watched the pair work. For years, I'd known Michael was in IT, but I'd had no knowledge of the extent of his abilities until now. The two spoke a language foreign to me about interfaces and codes. Fortunately, the same AI that would someday make it so businesses required fewer and fewer workers, and therefore more unemployed people as a result, would also help us locate the accounts we needed.

Benjamin ran his hands through his dark black hair. "It's goin' to take time, and we may be runnin' out of it."

"What do you mean?" I asked, a kernel of anxiety settling in my stomach.

"The men... We've been talkin'. The FBI has Scotland Yard involved now. Interpol, too. They know someone has been into the government files, but they don't know it's us just yet."

A tsunami of fear washed over me. Cassidy and I spared a glance at each other, neither wanting to be the first to speak.

"How do you know that?" I finally said.

"I can't reveal my sources. Just know we have people everywhere."

His words landed in utter silence. How big *was* the Resistance? Were only Americans involved, or people all over the world?

Michael pressed his hand into my back to bolster me up. "Be assured, Des, that just because this is happening in our country, doesn't mean it's only occurring there. Evil people worldwide are lining up to see how far they can circumvent the laws. Our legal system has been breached. For all intents and purposes, justice no longer exists, at least not for the poor. The wealthy, the privileged, and the powerful have wielded a different kind of authority, one that allows them the freedom to do *whatever* they want, *whenever* they want, with no one to stand in their way. In a word, they are above the law."

"But how does our going outside the law change things, Michael?" I splayed my hands to make my point.

"When the law no longer has teeth, then we need to change things until we're once again governed by the rule of law, Des. These are not normal times."

A breeze rushed in off the snow-covered mountains that reminded me of powdered sugar on a cupcake. With it came the smell of winter wheat and churned soil. How I longed for the ease of these woods or something like it. Is this how Isla had felt—at home in the countryside...on the road? Always before, I'd lived a sheltered life. But now I wanted more. More of this, of the world. To have my family at my side, always. No more of Michael skipping off to parts unknown. I wrapped my arms around my chest. For the first time in my life, I could admit how lonely I had been all those years with Michael gone, traveling, while I held up the fort at home. For years I'd felt like a single mom, raising Cassidy by myself for months on end. Whenever Michael was home, he'd been attentive, loving, but our work schedules conflicted, and I rarely saw him. As a result, I'd always felt like an outsider. While other wives had their husbands at their sides for Little League games and science fairs, I'd stood alone, a fifth wheel, never knowing quite where I fit in. I didn't want that anymore. I wanted us together, a family unit, even if it meant running from the law.

Michael must have guessed at my sudden melancholy, because he pulled me into a tight squeeze, his expression tender and loving.

"I know you think we haven't thought of the consequences, Des, but we have. This isn't for us. It's for our country—for the people who have been lied to, who have no way of making a living. We're about to see poverty on a scale never seen before if we don't do something quick."

I rubbed my arms, goosebumps rising on my bare flesh. The truth is, I understood him too well. And I understood the risk he was taking—that all of us were taking, Cassidy included. Tears filled my eyes uninvited.

"You don't have to do this, Des. I could send you and Cassidy home on a plane, and you could claim ignorance or say we kidnapped you."

Cassidy and I both let out a gasp.

"But then you would be gone forever, right?"

He refused to look at me.

"Right?" I said more fiercely, the pain of his silence a raw wound.

"Right," he admitted.

Slowly, he lifted his head to face me and, in that moment, I saw the sacrifice he'd be making—to lose everything and everyone he loved for a cause that might help millions of people survive. I reached my hand to cup his face. He leaned into it like a drowning man seeking salvation.

"Then I'm coming with you," I said with resolve.

"And I'm coming, too," Cassidy echoed.

Benjamin reached over and grasped Cassidy's hand. She leaned into him, their foreheads touching. Even if I'd left, Cassidy would have stayed. Just as with Jamie and Esme, Benjamin's charisma had worked its magic on our daughter, and I loved him for it, for caring for her the way he did.

"So," Benjamin inserted, "we're in this together."

I looked at Cassidy, then Michael, and with a wan smile said, "Yes, together."

"Where one goes, we all go," Benjamin chimed in.

I offered up a well-needed laugh. "Indeed."

And with that, we headed up the embankment to begin the final stage of our journey.

Chapter 83
Cobra

Ahead of them lay the manor house Frank had been determined to see. Tomorrow, they would meet back with the detective to learn if he had located Michael Kismet in the hope that he could offer more information. Until then, they had a free day to do as they wished. Johnny, still traumatized by his capture, was being questioned and planned to return to the cottage with investigators. Then he would be put on a train and sent home to recover.

"There it is!" Hugh cried, leaning down inside his Volvo to get a better view of the entire edifice.

Frank whistled at the sight of the monstrosity.

"The house was supposed to be the chief seat for the 1st Earl Fife, but the old boy got into some trouble," Hugh explained.

"Oh?" A memory just outside of Frank's reach nagged at him.

"See the stonework?" Hugh pointed to the elaborate details of the baroque mansion. "An architect named William Adam designed this. Used the stone from his own quarry. Worked on the manor for six years, but Duff wouldn't pay up. Adam took him to court and won, but he died before he ever saw a penny. Duff was a typical businessman and politician of his time, seekin' to soak every bit 'o labor out of his workers while never given' the poor architect his due. Because of that, the interior was never finished, and Duff never got to show off his wealth. Instead, relatives inherited it and eventually married into royalty. They gave it to the towns of Banff and MacDuff."

"Which royalty?" Frank asked, his interest piqued.

"The 6th Earl of Fife married King Edward VII's daughter, Louise."

"Edward, son of Queen Victoria?"

"The very one," Hugh assured him, stabbing the air with the end of his pipe. "The old bugger woulda shite his pants to know his people made it into royalty."

Hugh laughed at his own joke, but Frank felt only a heavy weight on his chest to know the upwardly mobile Duff was so reviled by first his architect and now Hugh. How many other people felt this way about him?

Frank needed fresh air. He stumbled out of the car, a series of flashing lights blinding him. Was he coming down with a migraine? He'd heard they sometimes started with flashing lights, but then his mind whirred back in time. Suddenly, he found himself standing next to the architect with his plans scrolled out on a table set on the lawn, a tent placed over it to protect them from the sun.

"What are you playing' at, Duff?" the man was saying.

Before Frank knew what was happening, his body had merged with Duff's, and he heard a bellow from somewhere deep inside his chest. "See here, Adam. I'm not payin' ye a single sterling for yer work."

"But I've spent a fortune on stonemasons. I ha' labour to pay, debts I owe for the materials, and ye've been demandin' more and more."

"Yer work is shoddy, it is."

The architect's ruddy complexion grew redder still. "Shoddy?" he shouted, then lowered his voice. "I'll ha' ye know my work is some of the finest around." He rolled up his plans and tucked them into a tube. "As far as I'm concerned, I'll see ye in court." And with that, he took his leave.

Hugh shook Frank's arm. "You okay, man? You looked rather pale there for a minute. I thought I might have to pick you up off the lawn."

"Sorry," Frank said, shaking his head. "I've been fighting a headache."

"Might want to get that looked at." Hugh's eyes narrowed slightly. Then he tilted his head. "C'mon. You'll want to see what they've done with the place." Again, he laughed.

But Frank already knew what they'd done with the place. Because he'd been here before. Only three hundred years ago.

Still, when he entered, he couldn't get over the decadence of the manor with its four-poster bed, chandeliers, and paintings worth a small fortune. Tapestries, too, some that took up an entire wall. Even a bust and full-sized statue graced the hall that led to the staircase.

"This guy...this William Duff... He was responsible for the death of Jamie Macpherson, was he not?"

"Did your homework, eh?" Hugh said, puffing on the end of his pipe. "Caught the bugger at the St. Maelrubha fair in Keith, not far from here."

"Does the fair still exist?"

"Now it's called the Keith Show. It's an agricultural fair that takes place in August."

"Can you take me there?" Frank said on a whim. For some reason it seemed important, as though his fate was intertwined with that of the fair. He had a feeling the migraines would never cease until he faced his past, owned up to it.

"I can take you there, but there's not much to see this time of year."

Then why were his hands shaking and sweat forming on his brow? "Still, it would be nice to see the place..." He couldn't bring himself to say it. That's where he'd captured Jamie McPherson and made sure he ended him, once and for all.

Chapter 84
Esme Stalwart

I was good for nothin' when Jamie left. Most days found me starin' out the window of the vardo, my thoughts elsewhere. On a mornin' when I shoulda been clearin' away the dishes and gettin' my dear sweet Kaileigh around fer the day, Isla knocked on the lintel and bade herself enter. But when she took one look at me, she rushed over and wrapped her arms around me.

"Ah, Es, dinna fash yerself about what ye canna change, ye ken?"

I nodded, head lowered, tears rolling down my cheeks. I'd awakened to a dream...no, a nightmare, where Jamie was being hauled off to the gaol, and I swear I could see it...see his head loll against the hangman's noose, his feet bare. How I'd wanted to grab my horse and gallop off to fight that *skellum* who'd caused it. To cut him down to size once and for all, but I couldna leave my bairn, and I knew Isla would stop me should I ask her to care for our daughter.

"What can I do, Isla? I canna leave him to the likes of Duff. He'll ha' his head, he will."

Isla sighed deeply, and when I peered up, I saw that she, too, had tears in her eyes, a woman who rarely showed emotion other than stoicism—the same stoicism required to deal with the vagaries of caravan life.

"I'm sorry," I said. "I didn't mean to upset ye."

She shook her head, but she couldn't speak, such was her misery at knowing her son was in danger. Now, it was I hugging her, the pair of us cryin' like wee babes. Kaileigh must have given into our melancholy, because soon, the three of us were wailin' like a bunch of banshees, until finally we began to laugh at how we must look, our eyes red and puffy, our faces wet with the dew of fresh tears.

"Come. Let's ha' ourselves some tea," Isla encouraged.

That was her answer to everything—tea, as if it had some magical power to cure even the worst of conditions, a broken heart. She chose peppermint tea with just a dash of chamomile for fear we might tire too soon in the day should we drink too much. Both provided a calming effect that each of us needed.

As we drank, I got Kaileigh around for the day ahead. She was an amazingly cheerful child, much like her *faither*, who managed to rally even the most churlish disposition. Soon, she had us laughing at her antics, my worry now tucked into a neat little corner of my mind. But I knew it wouldn't last forever. Therefore, I was already makin' plans to invite Isla to stay the night in the caravan. Then, in the wee hours of the mornin', I planned to sneak out with my horse and go in search of Jamie, because my second sight was almost never wrong. Once the deed was done, I knew Isla would look after my bairn, and our current wet nurse would take care of the rest.

I waited until the first blush of dawn to pull back the downy bedcover, the coolness enveloping me in a hug. On one of the dragon pegs by the door hung the supplies I had readied should Jamie need me, and whether he or Isla knew it, he *did* need me. More than he would ever know.

I tiptoed down the stairs, cringing as the last step creaked as it always did. I had just placed my foot on the bare ground, congratulating myself that I'd managed to avoid detection, when I heard words from behind me.

"Where do ye think yer goin', young lady?"

Isla!

I moaned softly so as not to awaken the others, but I needn't have worried because moments later, a horse and rider came barreling into the encampment, the horse glistening with sweat.

My heart fell to my knees, and I nearly crumpled because I knew who he was and why he was here.

Chapter 85
Destiny Jacqueline Kismet

"Why are we going to Keith?" I demanded when Benjamin told me the plan.

Michael seemed to be in agreement that it was a bad idea, but still we went with Benjamin's men, who drove us north, while the others departed in opposite directions so if anyone was watching, the observer wouldn't know who to follow. We'd been tucked into the back of the van along two bench seats that ran the length of the van's interior. Benjamin and Cassidy sat on one side, Michael and I on the other.

"I have unfinished business," Benjamin said, keeping his voice steady despite the lurching vehicle.

"With who?" Michael growled.

Benjamin's jaws locked and his eyes narrowed.

"Why would you want to go there?" I persisted.

He turned his head. For a moment, I thought he wouldn't answer me, but finally he said, "Because Cobra is going to be there."

"Cobra? The FBI agent who has been investigating the case?" My heart hammered in my chest at the mention of his name.

"The very person," Benjamin admitted.

"But why? Why would you want to go there if he's looking for you?"

Michael balled his fist. "Des is right. That's suicide, man. We need to put as much distance between him and us as possible."

Benjamin licked his lips. "Like I said, I have unfinished business with Cobra."

It was Cassidy's turn to intercede. "What do you mean, Benjamin? Why would you purposely bait the man who could ruin all of our lives?"

As she asked it, I'd been rolling the name Cobra around in my head over and over. I pictured a large snake that could strike at any moment. But as I bandied the word around on my tongue, it finally came to me. Cobra unravelled spelled...

"Braco! Cobra is Braco spelled backward...well, sort of, at any rate."

Benjamin stared at me for what felt like minutes, then finally gave a single nod.

"Oh my God!" I fell back in my seat. "Cobra is the—"

"Reincarnation of Lord Braco, our very own William Duff," Benjamin finished for me.

Just then the van hit a rock, and the vehicle bounced, sending us all sprawling. Part of me wanted to meet the man who had killed Jamie and destroyed the happiness of my daughter's forebearer.

The other part wanted nothing to do with him and for us to put as much distance as possible between us.

I grabbed Michael's hand and saw Cassidy turn to Benjamin, her look uncertain. In the end, she clung to him, as I knew she would, because she loved him as much as I loved Michael.

"What will we do?" I asked, turning to Michael for guidance.

He chewed on his lip, mulling over our options. "Look, vengeance never works, Benjamin. And you can't change the past, only the future. We have a chance to make thousands of lives better, maybe more. You carry on with this grudge, and it will only lose what little opportunity we have to make a difference."

The two of them stared at each other in silence. But before Benjamin could come to a decision, the van pulled to a stop, and the driver's door opened. I heard footsteps heading our way, then the back door of the van opened.

"Everybody out," the driver said.

"Where are we?" I asked.

But even before the driver answered, I knew, because I had slipped back in time to 1700's Scotland, and all around me were the sounds of cattle lowing and horses neighing. Men dressed in costume walked past on stilts. On a stage off to the left was a puppeteer who held up a puppet of a farmer, the other a Highland cow who danced coquettishly, then stuck the farmer in the rear with his horns to the laughter of people far and wide.

Bagpipes played on another stage off to the right, dancers dressed in the kilts of their clans as they did the sword dance around two swords laid out in an X. The smell of mead filled the air, as men made merry and women eyed them with a smile and a soft word.

I found I enjoyed the fair very much, and when I turned to regard the others with me, I saw they had all taken their own personas as well. Esme, Jamie, Laird Michael, and me, Isla. Even the driver's clothes were those of a Reiver in his Sunday best. Maybe I was wrong to worry. But then I saw Jamie tense, and my eyes trailed his. There, across the field, was a man with fingernail moon eyebrows, a long thin nose, and tight lips. My heart stilled as if it had stopped beating altogether. Whether I liked it or not, Cobra...no, *Lord Braco*...spotted us, his hand in his jacket, as though fondling his flintlock even now.

Chapter 86
Cobra

Like the reptile for which he'd been given the code name Cobra, Frank licked his lips and tasted the air to orient him to his prey, but as he did, he morphed into the man he had seen in the mirror so long ago—Lord Braco. William Duff. His heart sped up as his eyes locked onto Jamie and his wife, Esme Stalwart McPherson. A man bumped into him on his return from the "pie-powder" court, a makeshift court set up as entertainment for the spectators, while at the same time dispensing justice and teaching the perils of crime to a rapt audience. Frank scowled at the man, then began to wend his way through the mass of bodies, not caring that he'd left Hugh behind or that he'd stepped on a few toes along the way. His wife said he was like a Scottish deerhound when he set someone in his sights, and she was right. He even had the tall, sturdy features of the hunting dog, so reminiscent of a greyhound, brought to the British Isles by the Norman invaders in the 11th century.

All around him, an array of aromas wafted in, from the clootie dumplings, a sweet pudding made with dried fruit and spices, to the black pudding, sausages made from animal blood, suet, and oatmeal. Had he not been so focused on his prey, he might have yearned for a bite, but this was his chance to finally be done with Jamie MacPherson once and for all.

To his surprise, when he peered over his shoulder, he saw his "broken men," catarans, men hired as professional muscle who had somehow become separated from their clans. He had taken them in to ensure his will was law. He saw that Jamie's men, the Reivers, had formed a posse around him for protection as well. Like William's men, Jamie's men came armed with dirks tucked inside their stockings or at their sides.

"If it's a fight he wants, it's a fight he'll get," Duff muttered beneath his breath. "Blair, go get the sheriff and his men," he ordered. Then to the others, he said, "C'mon boys. We've got work to do."

He let out a guttural cry, which was all that was needed for a dozen men to take off at a run, knocking people down as the two sides brawled with ham-sized fists, elbows, or simply by tearing a person off their feet with a sharp jerk to the backside of their leg. Soon, the men were either in a heap or throwing blows back and forth, the crowd inflamed, some joining in the melee, others screaming and seeking sanctuary at a safe distance.

A loud snap rang out as one of his catarans head-butted one of Jamie's men, landing him against one of the tents and knocking it down to the screams of all inside. Duff circled his way around the outer rim of the crowd, searching for Jamie, who he'd lost in the mayhem.

Duff had all but given up hope he would find him when, in the distance, he saw Jamie, dirk out, circling one of his men. As quickly as his large frame would allow, Duff pushed his way forward until he could almost smell the sweet breath of youth. Soon, Jamie would breathe no more, if he had any say about it.

"So, MacPherson, we meet at last," Duff said, pulling out his flintlock pistol and pointing it at him.

"Ye point that thing out here, with all these people present?" Jamie said, still out of breath as he and the other man squared off. "If you fire that thing, ye'll shoot not only me but a mother or child, ye will. And then ye'll ha' not a soul to stand fer ye."

Duff shook his head. "It's you I'm aimin' for, man, and it's you I'll get." But he could see by Jamie's expression he had his doubts, as flintlocks were notoriously unreliable. Still, he had the short distance to his advantage if he got off a clean shot.

Jamie peered between Duff's man and Duff himself, treading carefully as he stayed just far enough out of reach to prevent the cataran from taking a swipe at him. Both men were breathing heavily now as each took a turn with the dirk, the other leaping out of the way at the last second. Duff saw his chances dwindling. He lifted his gun and fired, the smell of sulfur filling the air as a flash flared, a puff of smoke curling into the sky. To his dismay, however, he heard no cry from Jamie. Rather a scream from a woman who had fallen at her husband's side. He cursed the gun's erratic aim. It would cost him.

Just then, Jamie rushed him, head down, barreling for Duff's midsection. He let out an "oof" as the boy's skull crashed into flesh covered in a thick woolen shirt. Duff fell to the ground, the two rolling in the grass as women screamed and people gave them room to brawl. Jamie had barely managed to get to his feet and was pulling Duff up by his shirt he had scrunched in his fist, the other fist cocked backward for a bone-crushing punch, when an officer grabbed him from behind. He turned him around and punched Jamie in the face, but before he could cuff him, Jamie pushed the officer to the ground, then took off running. Had he not tripped over a gravestone in the nearby cemetery, he might ha' gotten away, like he had countless times before.

"Get him!" Duff yelled to his men.

Within minutes, Jamie was surrounded, blood leaking from his lip and dribbling down his chin. He narrowed his eyes at Duff, who merely sneered as they led him away. It had all been too easy. Now to speak with the sheriff. To make sure Jamie MacPherson never again saw the light of day.

Chapter 87
Esme Stalwart

Esme screamed as they led Jamie away, but Duff merely picked up his hat that had fallen during the scuffle, slapped the dust off against his knee, then placed it on his head as the crowd of people reluctantly dispersed or returned to their day at the fair.

"I warned ye not to interfere, Miss Stalwart...or should I say, Mrs. MacPherson."

Duff's smile held such evil intent that I yearned to wipe it off of his smug face forever. I raised my hand to slap him but in the end decided it wasn't worth it to end up in the gaol, like Jamie, which is where I'm sure Duff wanted me. Then I wouldn't be able to rescue my husband...if I could. But it would not be for lack of trying. Never that.

I managed to stand tall, but as Duff prepared to leave, he paused, inspecting me. Instinctively, I tugged at my buttons, my hand trembling as I discovered one missing. From his pocket, Duff pulled out a match of the ones I was wearing. The air escaped my lungs in a whoosh, for it was my button, and on it were three Celtic horses, a gift from Jamie after one of his forays.

"Lose something, did ye?" He laughed as he took his thumb and flicked the button at me. It landed on the ground at my feet. Then, with a final laugh, he turned and left. I reached down to pick up the button, then stood. My whole body shook with rage at the very indecency of the man. When I felt a hand clap onto my shoulder, I turned, spoiling for a fight, but all that ended when I saw who had laid it there. *Isla.* I sagged into her waiting arms, grateful for her comfort, needing a mother figure to help me in my darkest hour.

I waited until we were at the periphery of the crowd to break down, my fists balled in anger and my teeth gritted. "How could he, Isla? That good fer nothin' Duff. He set Jamie up, he did. He and his men. We ha' to get to the courthouse. Where is Kaileigh?"

"The midwife has her. She'll make sure she's alright until you can get this mess sorted," Isla assured me.

I squeezed Isla's hand. "I can't thank you enough, Isla."

She, who had known me for such a short time, had taken me into her bosom, given me and Jamie the use of her caravan, and treated me and Kaileigh like family. I knew not all *gudemoders* valued their newly wedded daughters by marriage as she had.

"Now, before ye get all soppy on me, let's go find yer man, aye? Maybe we can get him out of the gaol before this turns ugly."

Again I thanked her. Then together, we mounted our horses and raced off toward Banff to free Jamie. But it wasn't to be. No sooner had we arrived at the precinct offices than we were turned away.

"Ye'll need a stay of execution, ma'am," the clerk said. At the word execution, my heart sank.

I pinched my nose to keep from crying. "What will we do?" I asked Isla.

But before she could answer, it came to me. Jamie had always said if I needed anything, to contact his uncle, Andrew. From what I could glean, Andrew was a distant relative of Jamie's *faither*. None of the closer relatives would sully their hands with a half-Romani relative, but in private, Andrew had acted as mentor and protector. Jamie had wisely called upon him only when necessary. Now it was my turn.

"Isla," I said, taking her hand. "I need ye to do somethin' for me, aye?"

"What is it?" Isla asked, her expression reminding me of Jamie's when he was perplexed.

"I need ye to wait for me at the Rose Tavern. I ha' some business to attend to. I'll be back within the hour. Can ye do that fer me?"

"Aye," Isla agreed, but she grasped my hand. "Ye're not thinkin' of doin' anythin' stupid are ye?"

Stupid? I couldn't think of a smarter thing to do, at the moment, but I didn't tell her that, as I doubt very much she would have agreed. I flashed her a wan smile, squeezed her hand, then retreated in haste before she could question my actions.

Though I wasn't well versed in the streets of Banff, I recalled Jamie's words. "Should ye ever find yerself in trouble, Es, I want you to contact my uncle. He'll know what to do. I may be only half a MacPherson, but we MacPherson's stick together in a pinch, or at least that's what my uncle tells me." He'd flashed me that silly grin that both warmed my heart and sent it crashing, now that

I was challenged with such an important task. "Just head in the direction of the Moray Firth, and ye'll find my uncle's house on the outskirts of town east of there," Jamie had told her. "Ask anyone for the MacPherson house, and they'll guide yer way."

I lifted my hand to block the sun as I hurriedly wound my way through the streets of Banff in the direction of the Craigievar Castle. According to Jamie, unlike the Dunnottar Castle, built as a means of defense against Viking raids, and which Robert the Bruce reclaimed during the Wars of Independence, the Craigievar Castle was actually a pink, whitewashed tower house currently owned by the Forbes family. I knew if I kept it within my line of sight and continued east, I would eventually find Andrew.

Ten minutes later, I made my way down a rose-lined street, their pleasant aroma offering relief from the odors of sheep and horses that travelled down the cobblestones on their way to market. I paused to ask one dear woman if she knew where Andrew lived. She pointed to a house on a street corner just north of us. I thanked her, then scurried off before I changed my mind and turned into a *shilpit* who tucked tail and ran.

From where I stood, I could almost smell the sea breeze from the Moray Firth and imagined the raucous vibrato of the gannets as they wheeled their way through currents, gulls echoing their cries. As I kept walking, I saw one cheeky bird dive at a young woman seated on a park bench. It snatched a portion of her Scotch pie to her shouts of anger. That's when I saw it. The house with the blue door.

I walked up the rose-lined path to the front door of the manor. Nowhere near as big as the Duff house, it nevertheless was an imposing structure, much larger than my tiny cottage on the Borderlands. For several seconds, I stood there, hand poised to knock, when suddenly the door flew open and a woman wheezed at me.

"Who are you?" she asked.

The woman was plump and matronly, not at all pleasant, but behind her came a man's voice that grew louder the closer he got to the partially opened door. The woman opened it wider to give him a better look at the interloper at his doorstep. When I saw him, I let out a gasp, for he reminded me of Jamie. Then I fainted dead away.

Chapter 88
Destiny Jacqueline Kismet

As soon as Esme left me in front of the tavern, my stint as Isla ended, and I was once again Destiny Kismet. I stood there wondering what on earth to do when I saw Cassidy and Michael round the corner.

"Where on earth have you been?" Michael protested. "We lost sight of both of you during the cattle auction. What happened to you?"

"Wait, what? Who else did you lose sight of?" I asked. "Benjamin?"

"He was there one moment, gone the next. And Des..." Michael's face blanched. "I swear I saw someone searching for Benjamin...and me."

"About that..." I nodded toward the tavern. If what Esme said was true, she'd return and be looking for me, so I might as well stay put. "Let's go inside and I'll explain everything." We walked in and found a seat, where we ordered drinks.

"So what was it you wanted to tell me?" Michael said, glancing toward the door. He'd taken the farthest seat in the back and faced outward so no one could sneak up on him. I'd always questioned this odd trait. Now, I wondered if perhaps it was more than just a quirk in his character—if in fact it was a survival skill he'd learned on the job.

"Remember Cobra, Lord Braco?"

"Yeah?"

"He has Jamie."

Cassidy let out a cry, and Michael paled, then set his mug down with an almost imperceptible shake of his head. "Hurry and drink up. We need to get out of here." Already, he was waving down the waitress to bring him their tab.

I grabbed onto his shirtsleeve. "We can't leave now. I promised Esme I would wait here until she returns."

"You what?" Michael appeared confused.

"You've seen her again, Mom?" Cassidy snatched up her purse, ready to leave.

"Yes, and...like I said, they have Jamie."

A look of utter panic marred Cassidy's normally tranquil face because she finally understood—Jamie *was* Benjamin. She rose from her seat so fast that she tipped over her mug, and some of the liquid spilled onto my dress. I jumped up, dabbing at the cold liquid with a napkin.

"If they have Jamie, then it means they have Benjamin, too!" Cassidy squealed. "And if he's being held captive—"

"He can't become Benjamin," I finished for her.

Cassidy turned to her father, who rushed to her side and wrapped her up in his arms.

"It'll be okay," he assured her. But it was clear by the look of horror on his face he thought the situation was nowhere near okay.

"We've got to go after him, Daddy!"

I hadn't heard Cassidy call Michael *daddy* in years. As soon as Michael finished paying for our nearly untouched drinks, I tugged on his arm to get him to pause for a minute, everything happening too fast for my taste.

"Look, I think Esme is trying to save Benjamin, I mean Jamie," I whispered. "Let's give her a chance."

Michael looked at me as if I'd grown two heads. "Des," he said patiently. "You *know* how the story ends."

I felt as though I'd been sucker punched. What was I thinking? Of course I knew how the story ended.

"And if we're not careful, we'll wind up the same way. We've got...to...get...out of here," he reiterated, "before Cobra or Braco, or whatever his name is, comes calling. Only this time it will be *all* our butts on the line, and we still haven't done what we set out to do."

"We need the laptop," I said.

"The laptop," he agreed.

"But we don't have the ability to pull off the heist yet, do we?"

To my surprise, Michael smiled. "Actually, we do. Benjamin worked on the problem all night, along with dozens of people here and abroad, and we're finally ready. We can implement our plan."

"And mine?" I asked hopefully.

"And yours," he agreed. A whoosh of air escaped my lips, something akin to relief...or terror. Once the buttons were pushed, there was no going back. I steadied myself, my thoughts going completely silent, my brain on overload.

"We need to find a place to unleash the app," Michael said, hailing a cab.

"What then?" I asked Michael.

"We have a whole team of people ready to help us flee the country."

"Wh-h-at?" I sputtered as I blinked rapidly in an attempt to process what he'd said. But before Michael could answer, a cab pulled up and we all got in. He gave the cabbie a number.

"Right-O," the cabbie said.

Something in that one word brought back a memory, but of whom and where? A chill crawled up my back, and then it came to me.

"Benjamin!"

"At your service," he said, donning his cap.

"But how?" I demanded as Cassidy let out a screech of delight and wrapped her arms around him from behind.

"Let's just say I had help." He winked at us through the rearview mirror.

I had to laugh at the audacity of the man. Here he was, dressed as a down-and-out cabbie who appeared far older than his real age.

"I'd say I had a pretty good makeup artist and costume designer," he added with a twinkle in his eyes.

"Michael?" I said, turning to him for an explanation.

"I told you this was a pretty sophisticated operation." I heard the smile in his voice.

"So what now?" I asked.

Michael looked at his watch. "It appears we have exactly one hour to accomplish our goal, get made up, and then board a plane. Afterward, we get the heck out of Dodge."

Like we had in days past, Cassidy and I clasped hands. Then I said a brief prayer as we headed into the unknown.

Chapter 89
Cobra

"What do you mean there's been a stay of execution?" Lord Braco of Duff demanded, pounding his fists on the courthouse counter.

Duff had it on good word that MacPherson had been taken under heavy guard to the Tollbooth prison in Banff on Low Street, where he was stashed away in one of the cells. Once there, he was charged with the "Act against Egyptians" law, an obscure law written in 1609 that allowed any person of Romani descent to be detained, condemned, and ultimately executed.

"But I heard the judge's reading, good man," he shouted, then lowered his voice at the attention it drew. "He called him a thief. I heard it with my own ears, I did. Said he was to be taken to the Cross of Banff, where a gibbet was to be erected, and he was to be hanged by the neck until dead. He vowed it would occur at the hand of the common executioner on the 16th day of November between the hours of two and three."

The tall man sputtered, the officious oaf. "I know what the order said, but the accused's wife is getting a stay of execution. We are merely waiting for it to be signed. It is to be here at exactly three o'clock, no later. That's the latest word."

Duff glanced at the longcase clock. "What if it doesn't arrive in time?" he asked, hungry for vengeance.

"Then we will be forced to go through with the execution." The man shuffled some papers and nodded to one of the officers passing through the large foyer.

Duff once again peered up at the clock. If he could turn the clock back fifteen minutes, he might finally be able to dispose of his rival once and for all. He tapped his chin. He'd need to create a ruse, then return to change the clock, but how? He saw his opportunity when the clerk was called away on business. Although a few people milled around or sat in chairs, most looked as though they were waiting to hear about a loved one. Few would take notice of a man pushing forward the hands of a clock.

His heart beat wildly in his chest as he peered to his left and right, then sidled over to the clock, where he opened the glass face and used his finger to spin the clock hands fifteen minutes to the right. He had barely swung the pendulum to get the clock moving and then closed the glass face when he heard the jailer coming down the hallway. He gave the man a wan smile, then raced outdoors in time to hear the last hammer of the nail from the gallows as the executioner made his final preparations for the convict. A well of satisfaction thrummed in his chest when, ten minutes later, he saw Jamie MacPherson brought out in handcuffs, his fiddle in hand, as they led him up to the rope that swung from the gallows.

As Jamie passed him, the young outlaw stared at him in defiance. For one brief moment, Duff fought back the urge to turn tail and run, superstition causing him to worry that MacPherson's ghost would follow him all of his days. But the urge passed, and he held up his chin, his eyes trailing Jamie as they led the lad up the steps. A crowd had begun to gather, the murmurs growing louder as the time neared. In moments now, the bane of his existence would be gone—the man who had made a laughingstock of him among his peers. If Duff was ever to be named Earl of Fife, as he'd aspired to much of his adult life, he must end Jamie's thieving once and for all.

Then why did he feel no satisfaction?

Chapter 90
Esme Stalwart

I thanked Andrew, who had gone with me to the constable to try to get the stay of execution signed. Just as Jamie had predicted, he helped me, using what leverage he had as a laird. Tears swept down my cheeks as I raced through the streets, tripping over sidewalks and stumbling on loose rocks, the hem of my dress caked in mud. But I would not stop. Not until I was certain Jamie would be spared.

As I scurried from one thoroughfare to the next, I looked in windows, hoping to find a clock that would tell the hour. Finally, as I neared the gaol, I saw a clock through the window of a shoe-maker's shop. Ten minutes left. If I hurried, I would just make it in time. But to my horror, as I rounded the final bend, I saw not the Tolbooth Prison but rather a gallows and Jamie's head being placed through the loop of a dangling rope, all the while shouting and holding out his fiddle as he pleaded with any number of people to play a rant he had written for his execution.

"Jamie!" I yelled, holding up the signed stay.

But the crowd was too loud, and try as I might, I couldn't push my way through fast enough to get to the prison to convince the guards he should not be hanged.

At one point, an impudent man knocked me to the ground so he could get the best view of the prisoner who would hang that day. I lay on my backside, tears streaking my face, dirt clinging to my hair and hands. I jumped to my feet, the stay in hand, and waved it, screaming. But for all my effort, the crowd pushed and pulled to get a closer look, ripping the paper in the process. By the time I could finally make someone understand what I had, it was too late. Angry and frustrated, Jamie smashed his fiddle against the wooden structure so that none but him would ever play it. Then they hoisted him up. His eyes caught mine at that exact instant, but despite the sheriff's agreement to allow the stay, the bloodlust of all those present took precedence, and all I could do was scream Jamie's name as I watched his final moments in horror while he was lifted to his death, his feet kicking wildly beneath him. The color drained from his face, turning it the sickly color of dried blood. I couldn't watch any longer. I fell to my knees, rocking back and forth, as the words "Jamie, Jamie, Jamie" died on my lips.

It was only afterwards I realized what it was Jamie had mouthed to me as the rope claimed his life, the people his spirit.

"I love ye, Es."

Crushed, I crumpled the reprieve against my chest, as though a lifeline to the past. "I love you, too, Jamie," I murmured. "Forever and ever."

Chapter 91
Destiny Jacqueline Kismet

I felt it like a shock to my spirit, and I know Cassidy felt it, too. Jamie was dead, and as if to confirm it, Benjamin ebbed in and out of focus, the taxi veering out of control. I screamed, and Michael grabbed the wheel while I scrambled over the seat and worked to remove his leaden leg from the gas pedal. Cars screeched and honked as their headlights barreled down on us, Michael managing to swerve only at the last minute.

"C'mon, move!" I coaxed, tugging on Benjamin's leg. Finally, I was able to pry it from the gas pedal as Michael steered us toward a dip in the road where we would be out of the way.

When the taxi finally rolled to a stop, I threw my head back in relief. No sooner had I done so than I heard a wail so piteous that tendrils of fear rippled through me. I turned in time to see Cassidy...no, Esme, bolt past the open car door and throw herself to the ground on bended knee, keening so loudly that I felt it in my very bones. Never had I witnessed such sorrow, such pain.

I leapt from the car to comfort Cassidy, tears blurring my vision, Michael close behind. "Esme! Tell me what to do," I whispered. I had saved us, but I had lost Benjamin...Jamie.

"Turn back the clock," she whispered in return, her wet eyes pleading with me for help.

I shook my head. It couldn't be that simple.

How long did Michael say we needed? One hour.

"That's it!" I shouted with a laugh. "Turn back the clocks."

"What?" Michael said, his head tilted, as though not comprehending and probably thinking I was ready for the loony bin.

"Turn back the clocks." I ran to the taxi and began fiddling with the clock while Michael reluctantly changed his wristwatch. When we were done, Benjamin still faded in and out of focus.

"There must be another clock. What are we missing?" Then it came to me. "Our phones! Michael, Cassidy, quick! Turn back your phones."

Together we raced against time, in this case literally, as we set our phones to an hour behind. As we did, I saw Benjamin's body come into clearer focus, but still he remained a tad fuzzy.

"There must be another clock, but where?" I said, through gritted teeth.

Michael threw up his hands, while Cassidy pleaded with me to save Benjamin.

"What? What have I missed?"

Then it hit me. "Where's Benjamin's phone?" I demanded.

"In his inside pocket," Cassidy said, her voice holding out hope.

"Help me, Michael."

Michael opened Benjamin's jacket, and I felt inside, first one pocket, then the next. Nothing. I turned my eyes to Cassidy, whose face had gone white with fear. I leaned forward, willing my heart to stop pounding so I could think. Then it came to me.

"The glove compartment!" Sure enough, I reached inside, and there it was—Benjamin's phone. My fingers were shaking so hard that Michael took it from me and fumbled with the settings. Done. He handed it back to me.

"Thank you, Michael."

I reached for his arm, and in that moment, I knew whatever happened, we were a unit. One.

"Let's go," I said while Benjamin sputtered to life, as if from a deep sleep.

Cassidy threw her arms around him, tears cascading down her face.

"What happened?" Benjamin asked, looking bewildered, his face pale and clammy.

"We almost lost you."

For some reason, though I'd held it together throughout the ordeal, saying the words out loud barreled in on me like a freight train, and I crumpled on the seat, spent. In another life, this had been Isla's son, *my* son. He'd been hung, not on *a* cross, but the irony wasn't lost on me that it had taken place on *the* Cross at Banff. Jesus had died on the cross to atone for the sins of humanity. What sins had Jamie died to atone for? The right to exist, to feed his people in a world that viewed Travellers as little more than pests to be exterminated? How many other times in history had people been "otherized," made to seem less than human, exterminated for the want of feeding their families and keeping them safe? The answers would come, but not now. *Now,* we needed to find a safe location to implement our plan. To make a difference. To change the world.

Chapter 92
Cobra

"What do you *mean* there's no body?" Lord Braco demanded when he'd asked to see the deceased. "I saw Jamie MacPherson die with my own two eyes." He slammed a fist onto the counter of the constable's workstation.

The constable turned beet red, highlighting the touch of red in his thinning hair. "The executioner went to remove him from the gallows, and he was...gone."

The man paled at that last word, then pinched his lips together, his eyes wide as though he'd just seen a ghost, and perhaps he had if the outlaw was able to escape the gallows, the hanging witnessed by over a hundred people. It had been a festival to most, a boxing match, nothing more. But he'd heard Esme's wails, saw her drop to her knees. For one brief moment he'd felt almost...what? Pity, perhaps?

He blinked rapidly, refusing to allow himself to go soft, even for the likes of her. Good riddance! He'd purged the county of the scourge who had stolen crops and cattle, horses and dogs. *His* dog. He ground his teeth together.

"Come back later," the constable suggested. "Maybe we'll have more news then."

Furious, Duff stumbled out of The Tolbooth Prison and stumbled onto the street with its many smells, most of them rank. He pushed his way through the waning crowd, eager to find out what happened to the body. But before he got very far, he began to transform, felt his body change in some strange way, along with the look of the street that was now clean of horse dung and body odor. He peered down at his clothes.

Again, Frank blinked; only this time he was in the present, and he was dressed in the clothing of the 21st century, his knee breeches, waistcoat, and linen shirt gone. For a moment, he paused in the middle of the street until a car honked to get him moving. If this *was* the 21st century, then he wasn't looking for Jamie, but rather...

"The man reincarnated as Jamie," he whispered.

But who was he? And Hugh... Where was Hugh? Then it all came rushing back to him. The fair. Finding Jamie and his friends. The pummeling his men had given him. And finally, the gallows.

But where is the body?

Just then, his phone vibrated and he peered down at it to see a message from the constable. He had a name for their suspect. Benjamin Campbell. And he had been seen with three other people. *We believe they are planning to leave the country.*

If so, he had a short window of opportunity. Frank's best bet would be the airport. He peered down at his cell phone, at the times listed. But where would Benjamin go? He growled and snapped his phone off. For several seconds, he stood on the street corner, wondering which way to go. No matter where Benjamin ended up, he would have to leave from the Aberdeen Airport, where he would catch a flight. It would take Frank almost a solid hour to get there, even if he sped. He went in search of a car rental. Although he knew it would cost him, he decided on a BMW M5 for its speed, especially on corners.

Fifteen minutes later, he donned sunglasses as he headed out on the road, pushing the speedometer as high as it would go without drawing attention. He trained his eyes on the side and rearview mirrors, looking out for any police cars that might be scanning the area. Then he jacked the sound up on the radio, fueling his need for speed.

Small towns whizzed by on his way to Dyce, the town closest to Aberdeen, which housed the Aberdeen International Airport. But first he passed through Turriff, with its red sandstone and harling buildings, the latter with a roughcast plaster coating. A bull sculpture defined the downtown, reminding Frank that this was a cattle town as he ticked off the minutes until he arrived at the airport. If he could just get there first to stop Benjamin and the others before they were allowed to flee, he felt certain Jamie would die, as intended, on the Cross of Banff.

And then the world will be spared the do-gooder's crusade. He tilted his sunglasses further down his nose as he read the sign leading out of town.

But what about the Juanitas of the world? His wife's admonition played in his head.

What about them? Those people broke the law, Mia.

But then he cringed when he remembered the other argument they'd had as he'd eaten his Sunday meal after church.

Who do you think plucked that chicken you're eating, dug those potatoes, and planted that lettuce, hmm? You and half of our nation would starve without people like Juanita. She has family who work the fields, Frank. They're humans, not the criminals you make them out to be.

He threw his head back, sweat drenching his body. He rolled down the window to let the breeze roll in and imagined the sweet smell of alfalfa come summertime, or lucerne, as they called it. Maybe, once he was through at the force, he and Mia could retire here. Forget about world politics, for a change. Just be two ordinary people doing ordinary things. The idea pleased him. For the first time that day, he smiled.

In an hour, if luck was with him, he'd have Benjamin in custody and return home. He'd finish out his years with the FBI. Then he would plan his retirement in a bucolic setting like Banff. Everything else would be in the past.

Chapter 93
Destiny Jacqueline Kismet

We had traveled little more than three miles when a flagger stopped our car. Each of us tensed. I turned to Michael, the panic in my chest leaving me breathless.

"Michael?" I said, hoping he had an answer.

"Just wait," Michael hissed, his response an order to be quiet.

I leaned back in my seat, gripping the armrest. I glanced over at Cassidy, who was licking her lips, a nervous gesture that revealed her true feelings. Benjamin rolled up beside the flagman, who bent down to speak with us through the window.

For a moment, I was blinded by both the sunshine pouring through the window and the fear that made me go still.

"Sir," the man said. "Ma'am," he added, tipping his cap.

"Is there a problem?" Benjamin asked.

"I'll have to ask you to pull over there, at the turnout. Please turn off your motor."

Benjamin's eyes widened, but Michael sat poised, as though used to this type of order. Yet in his eyes I saw the wheels spinning, his mind running through the various scenarios as we did as ordered.

Once we were on the shoulder of the road, several men opened the vehicle's doors. "Please get out."

It was as if all the birds had gone silent and the earth had hushed in preparation of what was to come. Where were all the cars we had seen earlier in our journey? Now, they were nowhere to be seen. I suspected they'd been barricaded from coming any further, around the bend perhaps, which unsettled me that much more. I rolled my fingers together to hide my growing anxiety.

The lead flagger ushered us to a work vehicle. "Please get in, sir, ma'am," he said, encouraging Michael and me to go first.

Then came Benjamin and Cassidy. I noticed Benjamin held tight to Cassidy's hand, bless him. To my surprise, as we entered, instead of the normal work items one would expect from a road crew, the huge van was fitted with any number of computer consoles and men with headphones manning the makeshift desks.

"What is this?" I whispered to Michael.

But he didn't answer me. Instead, he shook the hand of one young man and said, "Good to see you, men."

He *knew* them? For the dozenth time I wondered who Michael was when he left home multiple times a year. I had gone with him several times over the years, but only on a small fraction of his actual trips. Otherwise, he'd travelled on his own, or so I thought.

"Sir, we have exactly five minutes to set the plan in motion and get you and your wife inside the bird." He made a whirling motion with his finger and a whistling sound all in one. Then he turned to me. "Would you like to do the honors?"

For a hair's breadth, I paused as one of the TV screens pulled up the latest shocking new video of the president laughing at the idea that immigrants would need to outswim alligators and snakes in Florida's Alligator Alcatraz.

That's all it took.

"I would be happy to do the honors," I replied.

The young man looked to Michael for permission. Michael gave a single nod, and the man rose from his chair. "Please, sit," he encouraged. Then he leaned in, the air in the room electric with excitement. In the upper-hand corner of the screen, a countdown clock ticked off the minutes. I had one minute and fifty-seven seconds remaining.

"Hurry, Ma!" Cassidy urged, panic lacing her words.

Benjamin's jaw set, and even the normally unflappable Michael seemed to tense.

"Stay calm!" the young man advised. "Then I want you to press this button here. Once you do, $42,000 will be deposited into the banks of every poor person in America. Twenty-four percent of the money will come out of the banks of the top 1% of corporate America."

"Michael?" I peered up at him and saw him flinch at what we were about to do.

"Des, we're only taking the percentage due in taxes that every single American pays each year—no more, no less."

My hand hovered over the button.

"This isn't just to help the poor, Des. We're actually saving these corporations from their own greed. Without a middle class to keep them afloat, most of them will lose everything."

I could see the alarm in Cassidy's expression, but I had to be sure we were doing the right thing. "Won't they just raise their rates and still keep the lion's share?"

"Normally, yes," the young officer said. "But we have a team of computer experts who will shut them down the minute they do."

"And Destiny," Benjamin spoke up for the first time since this all began, "AI will soon replace hundreds of thousands of jobs, so many of those companies will no longer require workers. They won't have to pay out earnings, pensions, or medical benefits. Instead, they plan to rake in all the money for themselves. Don't you see what you'll be doing by changing the status quo? Now, they can lay people off, but if they do, they'll have to pay those laid-off workers. It could be a win-win."

"How so?" I said, despite the frustration of almost everyone there as I used up precious time with my questions, but they needed to be asked.

"Companies won't have to worry that a worker will get sick or injured. In the meantime, those people who no longer have jobs can spend more time with their families. They can work on their passion projects—art, woodwork, whatever they choose."

"It could be a golden age for Americans," Michael added. "Not to mention people could sign up for a list of volunteer jobs that we provide. We might even require a certain amount of volunteer time per year. We could get artists to paint murals, people to help out on farms, or whatever they choose that would bring them joy and help our planet thrive."

Would it really be a golden age for Americans? All I knew is, if we didn't do *something*, things would only get worse. What we had been doing up to now wasn't working.

"Okay!" I said, placing my hand once more above the button.

I heard a collective sigh as, one by one, the group began the countdown. In less than seven seconds, life in America would change. The elderly, the handicapped, the women and children who lived in poverty would be able to sleep knowing they had shelter, food, hope.

"Seven...six...five...four...three."

I punched the button to the screams and hugs of everyone in the van. Numbers began whirring as thousands upon thousands of bank accounts were activated. A map to the right lit up the screen all over America. Tomorrow, thirty-six million Americans would wake up to find a note in their inbox revealing that $42,000 had been placed into their bank accounts. To access it, they must take a month-long course in financial planning, the trainers AI generated to hide identities. The program would employ innovative techniques in saving and preserving incomes. The course would include ways to beautify a home on a limited budget. It would suggest places to find food at reduced cost, clothing, furniture—even tiny houses, for those who couldn't afford a traditional house.

Cassidy snapped me up in a hug, but my mind still reeled at all the possibilities...and implications. We were now officially on the run. Though we'd given hope to hundreds of thousands of people, we were now a family without a home.

"Okay, ma'am," the officer said, the van roaring to life. "We need to get you all on the whirlybird. We have a private jet set to leave from the Aberdeen International Airport in forty-five minutes. Are you up for it?"

More than he ever knew. "Let's go!"

Chapter 94
Destiny Jacqueline Kismet

Michael's watch counted the hour. We had little time to make it to the Aberdeen International Airport, where a jet would be waiting to take us to destinations unknown. The next sixty minutes would be critical. If we didn't make it safely out of Scottish airspace now, we risked detection. The money wouldn't show up until midnight, United States Eastern Time, later for the Mountain Region and the West Coast. By then, everyone would know what we'd done.

"Remind me why the banks won't simply shut the operation down and refund the money?" I asked.

We sat inside an enormous hangar, each of us stationed on a chair in front of a mirror as makeup artists remade us into different people, followed by hairstylists. Then we would be given clothing meant to hide our identity.

"Because the corporations will give them the go-ahead," Michael explained as he was converted into an elderly lady so convincing that even I had a hard time believing he was a man.

I shook my head to the dismay of the woman fitting me for a man's wig as yet another woman wrapped my breasts tight so I would appear to be a young man in a business suit.

"Sit still!" she ordered, holding her hairbrush up in threat.

"Fine!" I said, my eyes flicking to Michael's in the mirror. "Again, why will the corporations allow it?"

"Oh, they may try to stop us, but we'll shut them down again and again and again if they do. We'll give them a brief example ahead of time so they know we mean business. Every day they are shut down will cost them money and their reputation. We're not asking for more than is due, and we'll make it clear it's the only way they can survive. And Des...?"

"Yeah?" I turned slightly, to the consternation of my hairdresser.

"Whether they realize it or not, this is for their benefit, too. Without a middle class, none of those corporations would be alive today. *We made them.*"

I read the passion in his voice, but more than that, I heard the truth, because before the rise of the middle class, wealth had been held by a small minority. By comparison to the early 1900s, the 21st century had been a boon for millionaires and billionaires alike.

"Did you know that in 1900, there were only 4000 millionaires in the US?" Benjamin chimed in. "In 2024 there were 22 *million* millionaires, with an expected increase of 7,500 millionaires in

2025. Agreed, a million dollars isn't what it used to be, but still, that's a lot of millionaires. And nearly a thousand billionaires."

Cassidy whistled. "Hear that, Ma? Where's your million?"

I had to laugh. Leave it to Cassidy to cut the tension. I peered over at her to see who she would be and saw an Arab businessman, while Benjamin was to be Cassidy's "female" assistant, complete with a hijab. Fortunately, Cassidy was tall and, with risers, could pull it off in her white robe and headdress. Did that mean we were headed for an Arab country? The thought made me hesitate, and I turned to Michael, who took my hand.

"Don't worry," he said, "once we're in the air, we could end up anywhere. We have to trust the system."

After all the subterfuge of the past few days, trust might take me some time. A *lot* of time, actually.

Once the hairstylists finished with our hair, the wardrobe person escorted us to private makeshift rooms to change. When we all came out, we looked at each other and laughed at our transformations, Cassidy especially, who now sported a full black beard and bushy eyebrows, while Michael looked surprisingly good for a woman.

"Are we ready?" I asked.

"Ready as we'll ever be, Ma," Cassidy said, tugging at her beard, which stuck fast.

A soldier came for us. I don't know what I was expecting, but what I saw as we neared the thump-thump-thump of the rotors was a giant US military Black Hawk helicopter.

"Michael? I don't understand."

He donned his aviator sunglasses. "You will. Get in."

We had no sooner lifted off and were in the air than Michael spoke to me through the headphones, the sound coming at me as if from inside a tin can.

"Not everyone is happy with the dismantling of our democracy," Michael explained. "Many in the military are prepared to put their lives on the line to protect it. Those are the true patriots."

I watched the young pilot, his future so full of promise, and yet what would this do to his military career? Which authority figure should he follow? One who had intentionally tried to dismantle our democracy in favor of an authoritarian dictatorship, or this group of resisters who were risking not only their lives but his? In my entire life, I never thought I would have to ask myself that question, much less answer it. Until now, I had believed our constitution was indomitable.

I watched through my goggles as the huge chopper wended its way westward toward Dyce, my entire body absorbing the thump-thump of the blades above us. Soon, we would board a private airplane. My thoughts turned to Esme, kneeling on the ground, keening as Jamie's body was hoisted into the air. He had given his life in service of the Travellers, who owed their very existence to his largesse at the expense of the gentry. How would she survive without him?

My eyes drifted to Cassidy, her hands held tightly in Benjamin's. Tears brushed her cheeks, her world about to change forever, but I knew she wouldn't have it any other way, because whether she knew it or not, I had seen the love in her eyes for the man who would one day become our son-in-law, if all went well. But we still had to make it out of the airport undetected. That thought caused my breathing to slow as I prayed we would get out safely.

Chapter 95
Cobra

"Quick! You go left, I'll go right," Cobra said as he entered the airport.

On his way over to the Aberdeen International Airport, he'd called for backup. He'd promised to keep the search low-key so they didn't sound any alarm bells that might panic passengers. After all, Benjamin and the others may have taken another route, but then again, this was the most logical exit point. There were five officers altogether. Interpol had been contacted and would be watching for any sign of the fugitives. They could land nowhere safely, not without being recognized and caught. Benjamin's photo, and those of his suspected accomplices, had been plastered at all the logical places they might land.

Duff's heart quickened as he raced up to one gate after another, scanning each of the passengers. He thought of all the world leaders who had entered and exited this airspace: Queen Elizabeth, Princess Di, oil emirates, and of course the US president owned businesses locally. Frank's entire career rested on finding the needle in this one haystack.

"Where are you, Benjamin?" But as he continued his search, his mind scrolled back in time, and suddenly, he was standing at the gallows once again, his eyes staring up at the empty rope. "Where is the body?" he growled.

"Sir? Can I help you?" asked a woman at one of the counters.

He stumbled backwards, nearly tripping over a line of luggage waiting to be tagged and spirited away into the plane's belly.

"S-sorry, I-I'm looking for someone." He turned, but not before he'd seen her reach below her station to press a hidden button to call for help.

He took off running, slamming into people and spinning around them in an attempt to find his prey. This could finally make his career. He *had* to find them.

Frank heard a shout for him to halt and saw a security officer wearing the CAA uniform, the equivalent to the TSA in America, headed his way. He spotted a passenger pushing a rolling cart and slammed it into the officer, who bent down in pain before shoving it away and hobbling forward, all the while speaking into the lapel mic at his shoulder.

Cobra wasted no time. He raced through one area after another searching for anything amiss. Then he saw the one thing that seemed out of place. A chill ran through him as he peered through the huge windows of the airport. A US military helicopter was in the process of landing. A Black Hawk.

"Now what is that doing here?" he whispered to himself. His fear turned to glee to know he might be this close to catching his prey.

But as he planned his next move, his phone vibrated. He pulled it from his pocket to see who was calling him. His wife. Should he pick it up? Normally, he would have left it for later, especially now, but they'd long ago developed a number's code for those times when it was important. His hand trembled. Never before had she used the code that meant life or death. Until now.

His eyes drifted to the window. The career-making catch of a lifetime, or his wife? Which was it? He paused, uncertain. Finally, he answered. Out of the corner of his eye, he saw people begin to exit the chopper. For one second, disappointment haunted him. It was just a group of oil emirates. But then he saw the fatal flaw. The one thing that changed everything. The shoes. *Women's* shoes.

"Hello, Frank? Are you there?"

Frank heard the tremor in his wife's voice. "Mia, what's wrong?" he asked as he searched for the nearest exit to the tarmac.

"Babe?"

"Yeah?"

"I have cancer."

He felt as if he'd been plowed into with a battering ram, the wind knocked out of him. He halted what he was doing.

"How bad?"

"Really bad. Can you come home, Frank? Please?"

Frank's throat went dry, and he couldn't speak. "How bad?" he repeated.

She paused so long he thought he'd lost the connection. "Mia?"

"They're giving me six months." He heard the sob in her voice.

Just then, the security officer rounded the corner, still hobbling, only this time he had five officers in tow. The ones who Frank had called in for backup. He held his hand up in the air to suggest they give him a minute.

"Please come home," she begged. "I need you."

Frank rubbed his temples to keep from showing emotion in front of the six officers. His eyes drifted to the helicopter outside. The four of them were climbing aboard a small jet bound for who knew where. For two lifetimes, he'd been bent on this vendetta. In the previous lifetime, he had lost his home. Now he stood to lose his wife. Maybe it was time to finally put the vendetta aside.

He said, "I'm on my way, honey. I'll be home as soon as possible."

Then he hung up and turned to the waiting officers. "It was my mistake. We're barking up the wrong tree. I just got word—they're on a boat out of the harbor. Put your men on it."

The five men jumped into action as Frank apologized to the remaining man for injuring his leg.

"Considering the circumstances, call us even." He gave Frank a wan smile, then turned to leave.

With a twinge of sadness, Frank watched as the last of the four entered the airplane. Moments later, it was taxiing down the runway and lifting off to places unknown. But he had more important things to attend to. He had a wife who loved and needed him. In his book, that made him lucky. With a sigh, he headed to the nearest counter to make arrangements to return to the states.

"I'm coming home, Mia. I'm coming home."

Chapter 96
Destiny Jacqueline Kismet

As I entered the plane, I took one last look toward the airport where Cobra or Lord Braco or Duff, or whatever he was calling himself these days, stood watching through the window. He'd seen me, too. I was sure of it. And he had resigned himself to our departure. I'd read it in the way he'd slumped down and turned away, his shoulders hunched. But why? Why had he decided not to pursue us? I may never know. I just knew I was grateful that Benjamin was alive and that now I could fulfill my promise to Esme. To Isla. Because I felt in my bones that Duff had decided to let Benjamin live, to let Jamie live. I read it in his body language. We had turned back the clocks—had kept Benjamin safe. Had kept Jamie safe.

As if to verify the truth of those words, my mind slipped back two hundred years, and I saw the noose pulled away from Jamie's neck, watched him slump down. At first, I detected no movement of his chest, but then it lifted, and he took a deep breath, as though a diver coming up for air.

He's alive! Jamie's alive!

As if we were no longer one, now that we had achieved our goal, I stepped away from Esme's body and once again became just plain Destiny Kismet, Cassidy's mother and Michael's wife. I wanted to scream, to dance, to tell everyone we had done it. We'd kept Jamie alive. For several seconds, I heard nothing, then the wailing stopped and Esme climbed to her feet, her steps halting as she rushed toward him, her eyes widening in disbelief. She cradled his fallen body, love evident in the tears that rushed down her cheeks and onto his shirt.

"Thought I was a goner, did ya?"

Just like Jamie to make light of a horrifying situation.

"I love ye, ya *clout*," she said, kissing him on his cheeks, his forehead, his lips.

He picked up his broken fiddle as she helped him onto unsteady feet. Then together, they stumbled forward. But as they did, Esme turned one last time and mouthed the words, "Thank ye."

I nodded, the knot in my stomach made worse by the knowledge I would never see her again, that this was her goodbye. We had done what we set out to, she and I. Now it was up to me to keep us all alive. I took one final look at the sprawling airport, then I dipped my head as I entered the Learjet, the engine's turbines already spinning for takeoff. As we took our seats, I wondered where we would land or whether we would be shot out of the air by some unseen drone or missile. In this world, anything could happen. All

I knew was, in one month's time, hundreds of thousands of people would be able to pay their bills. They could afford food, electricity. Housing. They wouldn't have to live in fear of poverty. Instead, they could survive, and if lucky, thrive.

"You okay?" Michael asked, taking my hand.

"As okay as I'll ever be," I assured him.

And with that, the jet engines roared to life, throwing me back against the seat as it taxied, then climbed into an uncertain future.

Αbout the Αuthor

As a child, I was one of those political nerds, my scrapbook filled with Newsweek and National Geographic clippings. I'd read everything I could get my hands on. In my spare time, I would solve mysteries along with Nancy Drew, and later with Agatha Christy. Who knew my hobby would one day turn into a living where I would be writing my own mysteries and solving my own who-dunits, bringing in modern-day politics along the way? But it's no surprise, considering we moved into my grandparents' house when I was seven, after they retreated to a retirement community. They left behind a stash of beautiful old books that began my love of reading. At bedtime, I would sneak a flashlight out of the hallway drawer, throw the covers over me, and stay up late reading those old books until one day my father discovered me. He soon put an end to my late-night forays...at least for one night.

Then, the house itself came shrouded in mystery (I feel a story here somewhere). Two old spinsters had the house built, but they were superstitious, so every room had to have three exit doors. All of them did, except for two rooms. Mine and the one next to it. *Wrong.* We soon discovered that underneath the closet floors, someone had created a false bottom so that when you lifted it up, you could fit a full-grown man in there. Heck a few full-grown adults. Not only that, it connected with the room next to it, where another false-bottom closet had been built.

Because I read mysteries by night, I felt certain there must be a hidden door other than the two my sister and I found in our closets. So, I searched through all of the cupboards, knocking on doors, feeling for an opening like the one under our closet. This went on for months, until one day, *voila!* I found it. Like any imaginative kid, I imagined lost treasure or a secret note from the past. So what did I find, you ask? *Sigh!* I found a peach pit wrapped inside an old white shammy cloth, placed inside a hidden compartment in our library. It was tucked behind our hearth and left there for good luck. So, I'm hoping my good luck will rub off and that you will tell your friends and family about this book. And, if you are truly a good Samaritan, I hope you will write a review and leave it on Amazon or Goodreads...or wherever you've purchased my book. Thanks again, and if you want to leave me a message, you can find me at . (I'm an editor too!)

Acknowledgements

Many times I've questioned whether I should write **The Borderlands**, much less publish it. Unfortunately, in times like these, writing has become an act of courage. Also, it doesn't have the typical happy ending. The main characters' fates are left to the reader's imagination. Furthermore, in the vein of *Robin Hood*, they do something illegal, though for a good reason. How could I ask anyone to read, edit, or review such a book in a climate like ours, especially if their views don't align with the story's views? Fortunately, a few brave souls agreed to do just that, and I will be forever grateful for their caring and kindness in the face of adversity. First and foremost, I want to thank my editor (you know who you are!), whose eagle eye caught what my exhausted eyes could not. She is one of the most gracious people I know. I'm lucky to have found her. She's a wonderful author in her own right, and I can't wait to have a copy of her new book on my shelf when it's out.

Secondly, I want to thank Laine S. for agreeing to read my book and for giving me her honest feedback. Like my editor, she's an amazing writer whose book cover almost forces you to buy her next novel. It, too, will hold pride of place on my bookshelf. (Plus, she feeds me cookies at our writer's meetings!)

And I can't mention Laine without also acknowledging Elaine S., whose work in the morgue has come in handy more than once, as Laine can attest. She's been our partner in crime at the writer's circle, the woman whose writing puts mine to shame.

Lastly, I want to thank Anne Thompson for giving me the courage and the confidence to publish this book. Without her, I might have buried this book forever and left it to the dustbin of time.

I've been truly blessed to have a wonderful book designer, Darrin B., who makes me happy every time I look at one of her designs. Many thanks!

And of course, without the support of my amazing husband, Les Craig, my smart and wonderful daughter, Sara Baker, and lovely granddaughter, Kaylee Baker Flynn, I would have no compass. So, thanks for being my "true north."

www.ingramcontent.com/pod-product-compliance
Lightning Source LLC
Chambersburg PA
CBHW010337170726
48283CB00009B/2849